Praise for *Rosethorn*

'This book is SO funny. It has a classic British fantasy-comedy feel in the style of Monty Python and the Holy Grail (a film that I adore), yet it's still modern and easy to read. The writing style feels so refreshing.' - *Jae Waller, author of the Call of the Rift series*

'Overall this book was a whole lot of fun to read. There is a fantastic humorous undertone throughout the story and I love how it is capable of pointing out the absurdism of a situation in which our characters find themselves in while never detracting from the events themselves… The story is so well written, that you dive in and just want to keep going. There were many twists and turns throughout that kept things fresh and interesting.' – *Elizabeth Daly, author of Legacy Bound*

'In short, if you like fantasy, you'll enjoy this. If you like British humor, you'll love it.' – *Cat Bowser, author of The Second Star trilogy*

'If you like comedy, fantasy, and political intrigue, definitely pick up this book, it will be well worth your time.' – *jamsworldofbooks, Goodreads reviewer*

'There is no better combination than high fantasy and comedy. If you're a fan of Terry Pratchett or Douglas Adams, then I highly recommend giving it a read.' – *Rhelna, Goodreads reviewer*

'100% it was fun, thrilling, hilarious and emotional. I've never read a novel so quickly. I was so gripped I couldn't put it down, and read the bulk of it within a week. Infectious humor and storytelling.' – *David B, Goodreads reviewer*

'Monty Python vibes?? Here for it. This story made me literally laugh out loud so many times. I love how this author made you care about each character early on but my favorite HAS to be Qattren. Read it and trust me you'll know why!' – *Stephanie, Goodreads reviewer*

Book 2
The Raining Thorns Series

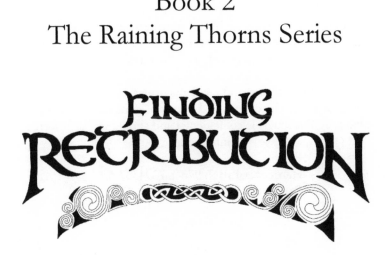

FINDING
RETRIBUTION

Donna Shannon

Hardcover ISBN: 978-1-7394337-5-8
Paperback ISBN: 978-1-7394337-4-1

1st Edition 2024

To my brother Tom, for making me put the pirates in.

avoid like the Herpes

Stoneguard

Stonekeep exploded now

shithole

The Shades

Nayport

Stoneguard

The Ary Islands

The Wastelands

avoid even more

N

Truphoria

hey, thats my house!

free clunge fo' dayz

The Forest

Waterside
Mausoleum

Crey's Keep

Sirpus

Adem

this place sucks

So does this one

X | o | X
o | X | o
X | | X

shit game anyway

7

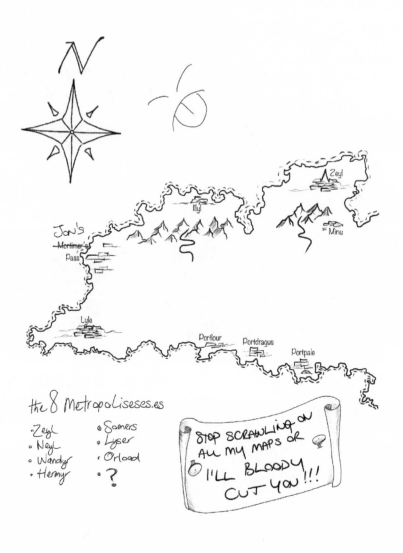

the 8 Metropoliseses.es

- Zeyl
- Neyl
- Wandy
- Hermy
- Somers
- Lyser
- Orload
- ?

STOP SCRAWLING ON ALL MY MAPS OR I'LL BLOODY CUT YOU!!!

Thdydlnds

(otherwise known as the Dead Lands)

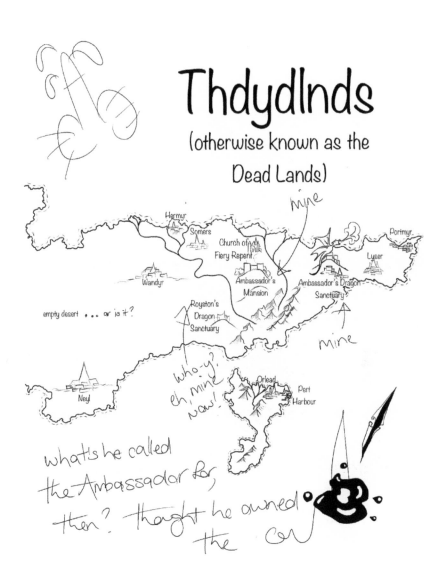

PROLOGUE

The Stonekeep, in the breakaway kingdom of Stoneguard on the third Tuesday of summer, 1345 YM.

aliyaa Horne nee Ckerzi glared at her youngest son through narrowed eyes. The toddler looked up from the block tower he was constructing and gave her a big four-toothed grin.

She had decided on the birthing bed that he was the Devil Incarnate.

His hair was like his father's – thick waves of pitch black, tumbling over wide brown eyes and a tiny button nose. His complexion was pale from his nocturnal inclinations, but he was an energetic and jolly child besides that. Time would tell whether he would have his father's square jaw and easy smile. Not that Aaliyaa was particularly taken with either.

A slam caused Aaliyaa to look up from the child.

Her husband Samuel entered, a bruised Vladimir following in his wake.

'What on earth happened to him?' snapped Queen Aaliyaa.

Vladimir, her eldest, was a wispy boy at twelve. Her heart nearly burst with pride all the same. He had the blood of the Far Isles. Where the Hornes had common features and a tendency towards alcohol, Vladimir held himself with pride, his narrow face upturned in spite of its heavy bruising. He was dainty but dignified, his face set in a display of inner strength. His face still bore the roundness of childhood and was often sulky and petulant, but that would fade with maturity.

Vladimir kicked a couple of Ronald's wooden blocks.

It would fade, she told herself.

Ronald yelped in indignation.

Vladimir flicked the boy a nasty hand gesture behind his father's back.

It would fade, she insisted again.

'The horse threw me off,' Vladimir said in reply to his mother, his thin voice breaking at points.

'Nonsense, you fell off,' Samuel said, harsh.

Samuel's broad shoulders bore a thick layer of muscle that was swiftly turning to fat. His plain brown garb was soaked with sweat and rainwater, and mud clung to the heels of his boots. He shook beads of sweat from his thinning hair and knelt before Ronald's creation.

'Excellent hand-eye coordination, this one,' he said, ruffling Ron's hair. 'Unlike his older brother.'

Vladimir scowled.

Ron giggled and said, 'Yap.' It was his only word as of yet.

'The boy's a heathen,' Aaliyaa spat.

Samuel slapped her across the face. Some people used corporal punishment to teach children a lesson, but King Samuel believed a child was only as good as his mother.

'Hold your tongue,' he said. 'Knowing you awake in the daytime, I'd be nocturnal as well.' He flung a fond glance at Ronald. 'The child progresses well. Surely that's a better sign from the gods than an irregular sleeping pattern?'

Aaliyaa didn't respond. She had a feeling she would receive more than a slap for calling Ronald a light-fearing demon. In fact, it wasn't just a feeling, it was a conviction.

'Shame as much couldn't be said for Vladdy,' continued King Sam.

'Vladimir,' corrected Aaliyaa. 'His name is Vladimir.'

'Mmm,' he grunted. 'How on earth did you talk me into giving him that name? Vladimir Horne. Makes him sound like a damn vampire.' He eyed his eldest in distaste. 'He even looks like a vampire, thanks to your excessive prayer regime.'

'I need the prayer regime,' Vladimir snapped. 'The gods alone will give me what I need: my rightful throne and my rightful queen.'

Samuel rolled his eyes.

'The Fleurelle girl, loath as I am to inform you, is getting married as we speak.'

'Seth—'

Vladimir inserted a raspberry to substitute his middle name.

'—Crey will be dead before he can soil my woman. I'll make sure of that.'

'From the other side of the necropolis? Good luck, boy,' Samuel snorted. 'And I doubt the gods have time to take a child merely to serve the fantasies of a Far Isle banshee.'

Aaliyaa held her tongue at that, her cheek still smarting.

Instead, she held Vladimir by the shoulder.

'My boy will get what he wants,' she said with conviction.

'He bloody well won't. He'll get what he's given: the Emmetts' youngest scion and the deeds he was born for. I won't have you causing wars for your own selfish needs. I brought him up better than that.' He glanced back at Ron and ruffled his hair again. 'And I won't have you badmouthing Ronald either. He's a fine boy and there's nothing wrong with him.'

'Except that he's a light-fearing demon,' Vladimir muttered.

Samuel glared at him.

In accordance with his upbringing values, he raised a hand and, without looking away from Vladimir, slapped Aaliyaa across the face again.

'Leave your brother alone,' he snarled. 'He'll outlive you by at least a decade, by my reckoning, so you'd better show him some respect. He's a fine boy,' he smiled down as Ron started a neighbour for his wooden tower, 'he'll make a fine man, and he'll make a fine husband for Lilly-Anna Crey.'

And he was right. Well... two out of three ain't bad for a drunkard.

Or so King Theo was thinking out of context, seven hundred and seventy-five leagues away in his keep just off Serpus, the capital of Adem.

He was currently observing the second most drunken leader in the world as Ambassador Krnk Bwl Xplsns (pronunciation undefined) slurred his way through a long congratulatory speech to the wrong Crey child.

Lilly, age three, snickered at him from her father's feet.

'No, Ambassador, it is Seth who is getting married, *Seth*,' Theo emphasised.

He gave Lilly a nudge to the shoulder in warning.

'Yuss, Seb, Seb, of course,' the Ambassador nodded.

'*Seth*,' he corrected, rolling his eyes.

'Yuss, yuss. Say, how is your father these days?'

'Smelly, I'd say, being dead for nearly a year and all,' Theo said in a dull voice.

Lilly giggled.

'Smelly,' she echoed, cracking up.

The king gave her shoulder another prod.

'Yes! He'll be down any minute, I imagine?'

Theo relented with a sigh. 'Yeah, why not?'

'Yes! Never seen a better swordsman in all my...'

'Yes, off you go, smelly,' Theo told his daughter.

He ushered his cackling daughter off and folded his arms, waiting for the Ambassador's reminiscing to cease.

Lilly wandered through the crowd listlessly, just one of a hundred little blond girls scurrying through the celebrations. She ignored the shrill exclamations of 'Aw! Look at the princess! How sweet!' and bolted for the front entrance. She had a hard time getting past her mother's doting ladies-in-waiting and punched a pair of nadgers belonging to a man trying to pull her in for a dance, but, stumbling on the hem of her dress, which she despised, she finally made it to the front of the keep...

And froze.

A dragon, a big, red one, rose above her imperiously, head tilted down to look at her.

'Ooh,' Lilly murmured.

The dragon lowered her head to Lilly's level and sniffed her. Upon establishing that the being before her did not smell at *all* edible, she opted to amuse it by throwing balls of fire into the air.

13

Red flame poured and burst high into the sky.

Lilly stared at the display, her mouth wide open.

A girl Lilly recognised as 'Seth's bed-warmer' – a term Theo had unwittingly passed on – hurried past with haste from the direction of the portcullis. Cienne skidded to a halt on the way to swiftly move the three-year-old away from the dragon, much to Lilly's irritation.

She was about to approach the dragon again when two big hands snatched her up by the ribs. A big reddish-brown beard came into view.

'Not for you, little one,' King Theo said sternly.

He hoisted her into his right elbow.

'Say, how much is that beast going for?'

'The Ambassador does not have this particular beast for sale,' said one of the Ambassador's attendants, 'but a similar breed and size could be acquired for a hundred thousand gold pieces, your majesty.'

'WHAT? That much for a dirty great lizard!'

Lilly gawked up at it. 'I want it.'

King Theo bellowed with laughter.

'I don't think so, little lady! Not after what you did to that cat!'

Lilly smiled sheepishly.

'If you tried that with a dragon, you'd be cooked alive! That would make you cry, wouldn't it?'

'It wouldn't!' Lilly exclaimed.

She never cried, not even once. She went through childbirth like it was a breeze, and when the want for night feeds came rumbling along, she climbed out of her swaddling blanket onto her mother and was already breastfed by the time Queen Eleanor knew what was happening. Nothing made Lilly-Anna Crey cry. Nothing in the world.

Her father cackled at her response and pinched her nose, placing her back on the ground.

'Back inside with you, little princess. There's a dirty great wedding cake inside with your name written all over it!'

'Cake!' exclaimed Lilly, running inside, all thoughts of the dragon forgotten.

King Theo watched his daughter go before turning back to the monster before him. Thinking of Seth, he swung back to the keep to drag his son out before the extortionist took the dragon away.

A minute later, all hell broke loose and palace gates were locked shut as the first rumours of the attempted assassination of Seth Crey made their fast descent to the city and beyond.

~

PART ONE: THE FUNERAL

I

orning broke over the border of the Wastelands as the sun's rays bounced from the spire of the Wasteside Mausoleum. Inside the ornate edifice, between gold-plated pillars and statues on the altar, lay King Theo's burned remains on a bed of stone, all wrapped up in silver cloth.

Two narrow queues of smallfolk traipsed through the mausoleum in single file. Yards of flagstone and navy carpet held King Theo's mourning public, divided by social class but united in reverence, and along the far walls stood the round entrances to the crypts of his predecessors. Running adjacent to two rows of benches filling with nobility, the dual rows sidled past the dais with a pause, a reverent bow, and a silent exit through the back door beside the vestry.

A quadrant of the king's personal guard stood to attention at each corner of the dais – with said attention, however, aimed at the high vaulted ceiling overhead. A half-helm tilted slightly back as the head below it released a wide yawn to the rafters.

On the flagstones just beyond the occupied mourners, two men straggled away from the queues to pay their own respects to the late king.

One carried a crowbar. The other a sack.

'What are you going to this door for?' hissed the taller of the men, the wielder of the crowbar. 'This one's the new king's crypt.'

It had been King Theo's wish that, upon his death, his son's tomb would be erected at the exact same time as his own. His prediction was that Seth would last roughly five minutes into his coronation before being assassinated again, more successfully this time.

It was also well-known that King Theo wished, upon this eventuality, for a tapestry to be hung inside with the words 'I told you so' written in *big* letters. That last one was scratched out once people realised that Prince Seth wasn't getting a coronation until he had saved back all the money he had given to his little sister to make sure it wasn't *her* that would be doing the assassinating.

17

'So? There'll be gold in 'ere too,' his companion argued. 'They'd put it in early, before it runs out.'

'With King Death in charge? Doubt it. First things first, eh?'

He clutched his crowbar in both hands, facing the entrance to King Theo's crypt.

You could tell which ones were the newest crypts by the distinct lack of deterioration. The entrance was a whole sphere, each half protruding from either side of the wall of the mausoleum – unlike their counterparts, all turned to rubble by time and neglect. A wide door stuck out of the front of it, facing the long strip of ultramarine carpet running down the aisle of the mausoleum.

The grave-robbers' eyes widened and they nudged each other.

The door hung ajar.

Inside, something smouldered quietly in the corner. Upon seeing the lighting of the tomb increase, it softly began to hiss.

The crowbar bearer froze. 'D'you hear that?'

'Probably King Theo deflating,' commented his friend. 'They always let off one last fart for the road. Come on, hurry up, before the nobs cop on to us.'

The crowbar wielder narrowed his eyes and entered, leaving a sliver of light from outside shine the way.

Exactly twenty wide, shallow steps down, the thieves' eyes adjusted to the shadows. They could see a ten-yard expanse of clear space ending with the king's final resting place, a stone slab in the centre of a round dais. Anything beyond that – no doubt where the valuables were on display – was shrouded in darkness.

The two men strolled on in the nonchalant manner of an expert at work and felt the walls. Gold was of primary interest, but big money came from war tapestries. The Creys were certainly known for their battles.

Upon his avid examination of the stonework, the sack holder's hand brushed metal. Thinking that the overwhelming smell of both the king and the incense would keep nosy onlookers away, he struck a light onto a small torch and lit the oil lamp.

Startled by the light, Lyseria shrieked and saw red.

Literally, because the crypt was now illuminated in dragon fire.

The thieves screamed and leapt back.

Crimson flames flew at the walls, lighting the remaining oil lamps and the tip of the crowbar in the robber's hands.

'Morning, gentlemen.'

They screamed again.

Behind the stone bed, lit in an ominous red glow, was the royal dragon, curled uncomfortably in the stone crypt. Sitting on the beast's back with his legs crossed beneath him, a fair-haired man in black gave his guests a friendly smile.

King Seb! was the first thing to come to mind. *King Seb's returned from the dead to avenge his son!*

Until the man's right eye wandered inwards, revealing him to be his marginally less evil grandson, Seth.

Giving his right temple a hefty smack, the new king blinked his eyes into focus.

'How nice of you to visit my beloved father on such a lovely morning,' he said, taking on a dry, sarcastic tone. 'Except I believe the usual custom is to honour the dead by looking at *them.*'

'We're just here to maintain the integrity of the building, sire,' the crowbar wielder said, thinking quick.

'And how does the crowbar figure into it?'

'We were testing the door,' he said.

The dragon growled.

The tip of the crowbar melted off.

'She can smell lies, you know,' Seth said. 'I believe it's a kind of seasoning to magical creatures, isn't it?'

Lyseria hissed in agreement.

The two whimpered.

'Have mercy, sire,' one of them whined. 'We only wanted a little bit of gold! We didn't think you'd mind!'

'Mind? Why would I? It's only my dead father you're robbing from.'

He planted a hand on each of Lyseria's ears, pointed her immense nostrils in their direction and *squeezed.*

The melted crowbar twanged on the ground.

The two ran screaming from the crypt, a small bolt of fire soaring in their wake.

Seth smirked, tilted Lyseria's nose towards him and blew smoke from across the top.

As irritating as the Duke of Osney was, the man had his uses – in particular his talents at gossip-mongering. No one planned a robbery without the Creys knowing about it. A pocket of gold went a long way in the darkest recesses of Serpus, and Osney knew that way like the back of his hand.

Though Seth had to admit, the 'robbery in plain sight' approach *was* a revolutionary one.

His face now black to match his funeral attire, Seth patted Lyseria's head and leaped from the beast to leave, wiping himself down with a handkerchief.

Something small and angry hissed in the back corner.

Lyseria swung her head around with a growl.

'Oi!'

She eyeballed Seth.

'Leave it,' he growled.

He stared her down and ascended the shallow slope to the surface.

Lyseria grumbled along in tow as, behind them, something smouldered very quietly in the corner.

~

The reverent silence of the mausoleum broke momentarily with a squeal.

Seth emerged from the wide crypt door, pausing to wave Lyseria ahead.

'Ladies first,' he said brightly.

Lyseria trotted out, her nose pressed to the flagstones, tracing an apparently interesting scent. The nose leered threateningly close to an ankle in one of the queues, which jerked away with a start.

'Out, go on!' Seth ordered. He flung the mourners a wave. 'Pay no notice, everyone, she's just nosy. Hey, hey, hey, hey, let him alone, go on!'

He waved at Lyseria.

Whose nose had travelled up a frozen mourner.

'Out, go on! Your purpose has been served! Out you go!'

Lyseria gave the man a lick – Seth assumed he had eaten lunch while waiting outside – and stalked out, indignant.

Seth handed the stricken man a handkerchief, embroidered with an 'S'.

'Sorry,' he said.

~

It was a nice day for a funeral.

You had to give credit to the weather of Adem: it knew how to be appropriate. The morning was sunny but overcast, the sunshine left behind by the summer still lingering behind a respectable amount of cloud. It wouldn't rain today, or so considered a stranger idly. That would be bad taste on an occasion to mark the extremely dry night that had allowed King Theo to be burned half to dust.

The stranger gazed from the throngs of respectful onlookers.

The royal family's emerald and gold coach rolled to the front gate. They got out to face the long path to the giant shard that was the mausoleum, a path already lined with hordes of raven-like worshippers. He watched the royal family trudge towards the spire and its surrounding circular tombs. Eleanor, Cienne and Lilly-Anna were barely distinguishable in black, followed by an entourage of ladies-in-waiting, miscellaneous children and the rotund blob that was the Duke of Osney.

Only Seth was missing – which was just as well, the stranger mused. A funeral was no place for his inimitable sense of humour, especially with the amusing shape of the place, which had just caught the eye of an attentive youth to his left.

'Fornication's a sin, isn't it?' the boy said, squinting uphill. 'So why's the royal mausoleum shaped like—'

'—two round objects and a stick? No idea,' finished the boy's father in one breath.

'Actually I was going to say it looked like a cock and—'

20

'A chicken? Don't see the resemblance,' the father cut in.

'No, as in, you know, the crown jewels?'

'Oh, it's specifically designed like that,' the stranger informed them.

The father dropped his head into his hand with a pained groan.

The boy's nose wrinkled. 'Are they really?'

'They're holy, you know. The crown jewels,' the stranger said. 'Amethysts and purple gems and that. Very holy.'

'And are they also shaped like a cock and—'

'Where has this… chicken fetish suddenly emerged from?' the boy's father snapped.

The stranger zoned out as Seth's family entered the mausoleum. Surreptitiously, he entered the throng.

Reaching into his hip pouch, he extracted a white mask and, slowly, slid it on.

It was just as well Seth wasn't around, he reflected.

He placed a broad, white hat on his head at a jaunty angle.

He was going to regret it once he met… the White Rook.

Cienne walked down the centre of a large chapel inside the front entrance. She released a tiny, tentative burp, her stomach roiling.

Queen Eleanor linked arms with her daughter-in-law, giving her hand a gentle pat.

Lyseria trotted past them to the front entrance.

'Uh!' Eleanor said.

Lyseria met her gaze and lowered her head in a sort of bow, striding past.

Eleanor, sensing the creature's inexplicable aura of human sentience, lowered her voice.

'What is *that* doing in here?'

'I imagine it's an explanation for Seth's absence somehow,' Cienne said wryly.

They strode to the front of the chapel, to where King Theo's wrapped remains lay in the centre of the altar, on his bed of stone.

'How are you, my love?' the queen asked in concern.

'Ill,' Cienne grunted. 'Though that may just be because I hate churches.'

Eleanor smiled sympathetically. 'It will be over soon. We'll tell Seth our big news after the service, that will cheer us all up.' She beamed. 'Good news at last!'

This doesn't feel like good news. And it smells like sick.

Cienne glanced around in search for her husband. She finally found him perched on the inner side of the top right bench, his gaze locked to his father.

She made her way over.

Many things were spoken of Seth's appearance, but he was mostly regarded as boyishly handsome-ish. His close-set eyes shone a sky blue between a long nose and a perpetually furrowed brow, marred by what Cienne had recently noticed to be a slight notch on the edge of his right eyebrow.

Which she suspected was only noticeable to *her* due to guilt for hitting him over the head with a shovel. That was before their passionate romance began... or at least before the point where Seth felt safe enough to hold hands with her.

To everyone else, his closely-cropped hair was his best feature – in that, at age thirty-four, he was one of the few men his age with a full head of hair that was still blond. Which was just as well. He didn't have the face for a King Theo-style beard to compensate. Besides, his hair was too busy growing on top to make a proper attempt anywhere else anyway.

Seth turned to face his wife and grinned, rising to his feet. A steady wave of choir-song swept across the mausoleum as the funeral began, and he took the opportunity to converse in the relative privacy it allowed.

'Hello, you.'

He took a lock of her silver-blond hair in each hand.

'Black becomes you, dear,' he commented, coiling the hair in his fingers.

Cienne wiped the tip of her forefinger on the bridge of his nose, making it wrinkle.

'The same to you, dear. But it's generally bad taste to wear it on your face.'

He leaned in to give her a kiss – and was promptly shoved backward by his mother to make room for a licked handkerchief. Most kings-in-waiting had servants for this kind of task, but Eleanor was nothing if not a contentious mother.

He grimaced as Queen Eleanor scrubbed.

'I can smell sick. Were you throwing up this morning?'

Cienne froze. 'You heard that?'

'Mmm. I don't blame you. Not after the sight he was in when you found him.'

She shuddered by way of reply.

He shivered also and wrestled his mother away from him.

Lilly wriggled past, wearing a dress, for a change.

'Hi, Lilly,' he said brightly, eyeing her gown. 'Got any trousers hidden under there today?'

'No,' she said in a dull voice.

'Oh.'

Cienne eyed her sister-in-law. Her face seemed pallid and slack, but it couldn't be helped. Grief and black mourning attire never went well with a fair complexion. The gown was quite lovely, though: the gold detailing embroidered along the modestly cut bodice brought out a similar shine in Lilly's mousy curls,

22

though the skirt lingered a shade too high on the ankle for Cienne's taste. Lilly never did have the patience for lifting petticoats to walk.

The archpriest of the Order of Salator Crey appeared at the altar from the vestry – Abraham Furlong, if Cienne remembered rightly. He stood in front of the late king as the procession filed into their seats and folded his hands behind his back, awaiting silence.

As the room settled, the man shuffled to a podium beside the king's body, ruffled some papers for a few minutes in the universal manner of opening a funeral, and began.

'We are here,' he said, his deep voice carrying over the rafters, 'to celebrate the life and legacy of King Theo Crey, and also our merciful lord, Salator Crey—'

'Hah!'

Seth earned a nudge from Cienne. He didn't like Salator Crey.

'We must pray,' the archpriest continued, irked at the interruption, 'to honour our late king, Theo Crey, and help his passing to the higher realms to serve our Lord.'

'Hah!'

'We must also…'

Seth nursed his ribs.

'… pray for his family, and his successor. *Who's going to need it,*' he added under his breath. 'And lastly, we must pray for ourselves, that God will deliver mercy on us in our time of need.'

He didn't deliver any mercy on my child in its time of need, Seth thought.

He dared not think any further on the matter. The wound still bled a little more with every passing thought he gave it.

The archpriest ruffled some more papers and began a reading from the Texts.

Seth zoned out at this point and stared at the monument of Salator Crey, the god who stuck his neck out to save his creation – or stuck his neck in a noose for it, according to the Texts.

To save a hoard of diseased followers from the wrath of a genocidal city council, Salator Crey had offered himself, a much-loved figure and national treasure, to die in their stead, telling the council leader it would ward off the pox-ridden peasants. As he dangled from the gallows of what would later be Serpus, the entire city wept – and was suddenly ambushed by Salator Crey's hoard. Legend had it that they had crept past the guard at the back gate, who failed to see them through a veil of tears.

The army never seemed to be celebrated, though, or so Seth noticed. They'd gone on and done great things in the name of Salator Crey, none more so than the kingdom they had forged for his fifteen-year-old son, but none of *them* got a statue.

Pox-scars must be too difficult to carve, Seth mused.

The hanging itself had been rendered in marble and hung on the back wall of every church in Adem – much to Seth's unease. Whoever had created this one had been worryingly specific. Every vein and tendon bulged from the monument's neck and head, and his eyes bulged even more, milk-white and vacant. It had terrified him at his grandfather's funeral and, twenty-two years later, it terrified him today.

Seth rose, disgruntled, along with the procession as a prayer progressed. A few seconds later they all sat down again. His knees were giving out already. They knew he still had another twenty prayers to go yet.

More throat clearing and paper shuffling ensued from the altar.

'... and now let us honour our king in the wake of his untimely demise, and ask for judgement for his unknown killer...'

Seth avidly examined the pews.

'... that he burn in the deepest hell for his sins, the sin of spilling the blood of Salator Crey himself, so King Theo may be at peace as His newly-appointed servant—'

'Who'd take over if he were really up there,' a voice whispered behind Seth's ear.

Seth shuddered at the thought.

Everyone rose for a hymn and he held his hand out, palm upwards.

A soft hand slid into it and squeezed.

He instantly relaxed.

The funeral droned on.

Seth and Cienne linked fingers tenderly for a moment, before getting bored and subsequently commencing Thumb of War. Queen Eleanor gazed sleepily into space, muttering along with the prayers, and Lilly stared at her father's remains, her lips pressed together.

The archpriest swung a metal canister around King Theo's remains.

The royal family's eyes watered.

'I think I might throw up again,' Cienne said.

'I think I'll join you,' Seth muttered. 'It really is disrespectful of them to bring their recreational drug use to a funeral.'

'It isn't recreational drugs, Seth,' his mother scolded in a whisper, 'it's incense.'

'The gnome swinging on the chandelier and I beg to differ,' he said dryly. 'I doubt he's as smelly as all that.'

Lilly felt a jab.

'Off you go, smelly,' he told her, ushering her along...

There was silence for a moment, broken only by the endless droning of the service.

A muffled sobbing made Seth grimace and strain his ears.

'Is someone actually upset?' he asked his mother and Cienne incredulously. 'They do know it's Theo Crey up there, don't they?'

He turned to Lilly.

Who was crying.

~

Father Toffer strode up and down the chapel fretfully, his crucifix once again in his hand. He glanced at the door again. She still hadn't arrived.

Surely Queen Aaliyaa would show up for her own son's funeral, wouldn't she?

Wouldn't she?

He clenched his crucifix tighter and paced more urgently.

It was hardly a worthy turnout for the former heir of Stoneguard. Fate had laughed at poor Prince Vladdy in the form of an unfortunate scheduling conflict. All of the major nobles had favoured King Theo Crey's funeral over the Horne boy and were currently tucked inside the Creys' Wasteside Mausoleum.

Probably the scenery, Toffer mused moodily.

The Wasteside Hills were renowned for their spectacular views of Adem's rivers, forests and surrounding cities – in the south and east of the hills, that is. On the other side lay blackened mountains, charred hills and cities so ruined even the foundations of the buildings could scarcely be discerned in the ashen ground.

A perfect spot to preach the power of Salator Crey, Toffer thought cynically. *Or the power of the Forest Queen, that is.*

He turned back to the miniscule procession. Most of the mourners were common folk come to gawk, but Ronald Horne sat at the front, looking ill alongside his new wife, Queen Qattren of the Forest.

Toffer shuddered.

He didn't like the look of her. Actually, the fact was, he quite *did* like the look of her, in spite of his vow of celibacy's opinions. It was the looks she was giving him he didn't like. Most people who knew of his recent part-time profession opted for the disdainful, guarded grimace, but this woman was laughing at him.

Toffer ground his teeth at the thought. He had expected a respectful distance from the nobility when the assassination contracts started coming in, but instead he had received *ridicule*. Fair enough, his first contract hadn't exactly gone to plan – or at all to plan, for that matter. But that had been weeks ago.

Since then, people had found out about his secondary, low-cost services – important people. *Wealthy* people. And so contracts had been drawn out, knives had been cleaned, bloodied and re-cleaned and kind recommendations had been passed around.

Only they hadn't been passed around far enough, as was evident by the pantomimes of assassinations taking place in the pews beside him.

Toffer ignored them and paced around some more as, at the front of the church, Ron wrung his hands, his gaze locked to his older brother's portrait.

25

A third hand joined his. Qattren.

'Are you alright, my love?'

'Yep,' he said, although he didn't feel it.

The portrait was scaring him. It didn't look a lot like Vladdy, but the artist had captured his slimy demeanour just right. And the excessive amounts of alcohol secretly circling his system didn't help.

The portrait stood on an easel on the altar, the portraits of the Seven lined up on the wall behind it. The painting was all that remained of Prince Vladimir. The explosion that had consumed the Stonekeep had consumed *him* along with it – by accident, Qattren insisted.

A communication error – 'Seth Crey not opening his bloody ears,' Qattren had elaborated at the time – caused Qattren's careful plan to frighten Vladimir into surrendering Stoneguard to fall apart in a cloud of dust. His last-minute rescue had been forgotten about. His remains had never been found. His portrait hadn't been finished either – there were still white splotches in the background.

Ron stared at it with ill ease. He wondered if he should be upset. He'd gone numb for a while after Qattren had told him, but he'd also felt a kind of guilty relief. Vladdy hadn't exactly been a model older brother. His childhood hobby was stoning Ron in the gardens for being a 'light-fearing devil-spawn', which was odd, seeing that if Ron was devil-spawn, surely his brother was also.

Then again, that had been his mother's fault.

He glanced back at the door, where rain poured in from outside. It nearly always rained in Stoneguard, something to do with land elevation or something. That or all the clouds over the Wastelands rained on both regions, just in case the rest of Stoneguard erupted. That's what the superstitious thought, anyway. It barely ever rained in Adem by comparison, he recalled. He wondered if it was raining now.

He also wondered where his mother was.

Where are you?

That was when the dog entered.

~

Aaliyaa stood in the rain, a cloak hanging loosely about her head and shoulders. A stretch of road led from the city walls to a crossroads. The keep lay north and the church slightly to the east of it, framing the hills in the distance. Aaliyaa headed for the church.

She had much to discuss with Vladimir.

She knuckled her way through a throng of people surrounding the church. Her son was inside, she knew, praying for guidance. She would join him. She'd spent too long in the Dead Lands, among the heathen worshippers of Arianna Lyseria. She longed to return to holy soil, despite the Seven's instructions.

26

Upon entering the chapel, she saw one of her sons — but it wasn't Vladimir. Aaliyaa glared at her little-loved youngest, then at the horrendous Father Toffer before her sights finally fell on Vladimir's portrait.

Her breath caught in her throat.

She examined everyone again, more carefully this time.

Everyone was wearing black.

Qattren touched Ron's arm.

'I know,' he said softly. 'We should leave.'

Aaliyaa howled.

~

II

The sobs came thick and fast now and, despite her efforts to contain them, the cries emerged loudly.

'Lilly,' Seth said in alarm.

A flash of copper light shone to his right. The procession rippled in panic.

Seth growled through his teeth. Now was not the time.

He slid his arms around Lilly's shoulders and pulled her head under his chin.

'Darling, you knew this was going to happen sometime.'

Lilly choked and spluttered. 'I didn't want it to.'

She buried her head in his shirt, hiding her face in shame.

Seth held her tightly and swung her slowly from side to side as that flash of orange caught his eye. Before he knew it, Qattren's gaze met his, her face impassive but her eyes burning.

His own shame, of a very different sort, crawled up his neck in a flush.

He hid his own face in Lilly's hastily tied mop of mousy curls.

'*And as for that girl, what was her name? Ah yes, Adrienne.*'

Qattren's eyes bored into his skull, latching on to the memory and pulling it out for him to see.

'*Puts you in your place, doesn't it?*' the phantom voice of his father sneered on. '*Knowing she doesn't want anything to do with you.*'

Seth inhaled deeply and broke eye contact.

The memory played on unheeded.

'*... I think I'll let him keep her as a little ornament. Her type aren't worth much else.*'

'*SHUT UP!*'

The spray of blood on his face felt warm in every visit to the memory.

27

Seth closed his eyes and shuddered as the echoes thankfully receded. The hasty forest fire still haunted him in the form of Qattren's unnaturally bright hair.

The service wrapped itself up with a final mumbled prayer.

The choir's lilt resumed from the sidelines as the guard surrounded King Theo's body.

'I don't want to see him get put in there,' Lilly murmured.

'That's alright, my love,' Eleanor soothed, leaning over Seth's lap to kiss the top of her head. 'We'll wait outside if you like.'

'I'll stay with you for a bit,' said Seth. 'It'll be ages till they get on with the rest of it. They like taking their sweet time with these things.'

Lilly nodded and wiped her eyes, her face burning with shame.

'I never cry!' she exclaimed, tears still flowing freely. 'I'm not a crying person! I've never, ever cried, not ever! Not even as a baby!'

'I remember, you thought night feeds were self-service,' said Seth with a grin.

Their mother made a face in remembrance, folding her arms over her chest.

Cienne made a similar expression.

'You okay, Cienne?'

She jerked her head up at Lilly's question.

'Yes, I'm fine, don't worry about me,' she said breezily. 'I just... feel a bit nauseous again.'

'Same here. Crying's harder than it looks.'

Lilly dropped her head on her brother's shoulder.

Seth gave her shoulder blades a squeeze.

'Seth,' Cienne added before she could change her mind. 'Can I speak to you outside? In private?'

'Private? That doesn't bode well,' he said jokingly.

He rubbed Lilly's shoulder and followed Cienne to the front entrance.

They arrived at the gravel path. Guards surrounded them in a ring running around the entire building: the hoards were getting restless at the lack of entertainment. Within the ring of guards however, it was serene.

Cienne rolled her shoulders and tried to relax. Blood-flow tingled up and down her arms, making her dizzy. She hoped she wasn't about to faint.

A light breeze blew in and ruffled Seth's hair. Cienne paused to admire this before taking a breath.

'Seth,' she exhaled, wringing her hands.

~

The dog flinched violently at Aaliyaa's screech and stumbled into a candle stand on the edge of the step beside him.

28

The five-foot-tall candelabra tilted like a felled tree and a few candles toppled off.

The flames licked the carpet.

Shit, the dog hissed internally.

~

'Mmm?' Seth asked brightly.

'Well,' she began with a short laugh. 'I don't know quite how you're going to feel about this, but... do you remember the day we, you know... on the dinner table, and Jimmy caught us...'

Seth giggled. 'That was a good day.'

~

The fire was quite noticeable now to all but the priest, who flapped his way to the door, and Queen Aaliyaa, who stood in the doorframe, her guttural shriek drowning everything out.

The small procession fled around her, the small Jack Russell at their heels, as the flames climbed first Vladimir's portrait, then the carved oak frames of the Seven's portraits, reaching for the oil lamps to either side.

~

'Well... you see...'

Seth lifted his eyebrows.

'What happened was,' she said, with a nervous grin, 'we're... we're going to have a baby.'

~

The Church of the Seven Gods exploded.

~

'A... a...' Seth stammered in shock.

'Baby.'

~

It started with the oil lamps. The first lamp on the top left ignited and erupted into an amber fireball. It hurled sparks across the hall to ignite the lamp opposite, which too detonated to repeat the process, over and over, from one side of the hall to the other. A plume of flames ate a line running into the ground – the oil store.

~

'I'm having a baby?'

Cienne grinned a bit more surely now and nodded eagerly.

Then they both fainted.

~

Toffer finally ran screaming from the building, tearing off his flame-consumed robes.

Aaliyaa stood where she was, still screaming.

The flames ate through the mahogany walls and took to the insulation in earnest. It reached the oil supply in the cellars and hurled the pews through the ceiling.

Aaliyaa didn't move an inch.

~

Cienne came to and found herself in the butler's arms.

'Are you alright, your highness?' Jimmy asked in concern. 'You both crumpled to the ground at the same time. You're lucky you didn't headbutt each other on the way down.'

She turned her gaze to Seth. He lay in his mother's arms, looking dazed.

'I'm going to be a mummy.'

'He means a daddy,' Eleanor clarified.

'I should hope so,' said Jimmy.

Seth grinned at everyone, Cienne in particular.

'I'm having a child!' he exclaimed, climbing towards his wife.

Who flaked out again, Jimmy catching her head with haste.

Seth frowned at her.

'It's a baby thing,' his mother said.

'Although characteristically exaggerated,' said Jimmy, rolling his eyes.

~

Once the royal couple had gotten their bearings, Seth and his mother strode on to King Theo's crypt at the end of the family mausoleum, leaving Cienne and Lilly outside. The procession parted in the centre of the hall to let them pass, and they caught up with the head of the crowd. They were just carrying the body through the crypt entrance.

Seth sucked in a breath, following close behind.

The entrance was dark, but he could just see the torches illuminating the chamber below. They proceeded down the shallow steps, built wide especially for this purpose, and Seth descended with them.

The incense caught in his sinuses. Seth made a mental note to ban the stuff as the priest waved his burner in a slow rhythm.

'We shall now commit his majesty to his sepulchral home,' droned the archpriest, 'where his soulless body shall rest for eternity until the realm's final day, the Day of Fiery Repent, whereupon he will rise with his ancestors and our Father, Salator Crey, to judge and save us all.'

The king was placed in the stone sarcophagus in the centre of the chamber. Seth took the time to look around as they fiddled with the king's position.

The entire crypt had been given a hasty re-furbish after the attempted robbery. Tapestries and filigreed metals disguised the soot marks left by Lyseria. A small antechamber to the right steadily filled with mourners as the procession filed in for the remainder of the service.

Seth blinked and swore silently. The gift-giving! He'd completely forgotten the gift-giving!

Well, in truth he hadn't. Three days earlier, he and Cienne had left an ornate sign at the foot of his crypt door bearing his nickname, 'the Grim Reaper of Adem'. They had left it anonymous. He didn't think the clergy would find it appropriate.

He rummaged in his pockets for a token, any token, and found, ironically, nothing but the dusty tinderbox he'd lit his torch with earlier.

'Your majesty,' a soft voice said from his right. 'My condolences for your loss.'

He hastily ducked the tinderbox back out of sight.

'Thank you for your condolences,' he said stiffly.

Qattren inclined her head, her gaze back on the late king.

'I've been looking forward to the gift-giving, truth be told,' she said. 'I've been intending to give this to your father for decades now.'

She pressed something into his hand.

Seth glanced into his palm curiously. It was a simple pewter bookmark adorned with a stainless-steel snake. A typical token from a dead man's son; to mark the dead man's place in their legacy and pass the mantle to his heir, to continue their path through the book of life, or some such shit, Seth recalled. He wondered at the significance of this in regards to Qattren and realised that Qattren hadn't been talking about the bookmark.

Qattren approached the corpse on her turn, a hastily bound scroll in her hands. She bowed at King Theo in reverence and placed the scroll at the foot of the sarcophagus.

Feeling foolish at being provided with his own father's funeral gift, Seth approached next.

Qattren leaned to his ear as they passed in opposite directions.

'The scroll is your grandfather's personal journal,' she whispered. 'He had asked for it many years ago, but I never got around to giving it to him.' Her tone was mournful.

Seth nodded slightly and knelt at his father's side.

Although the king's body was now covered in fine silk cloth, Seth could tell the body was not in its entirety. In fact, he knew for a fact it wasn't – he was the one who had burned it. He'd left the crown buried in a relatively easy-to-find spot – he wanted it back later – and he'd burned the remains of his murder victim. It had been a heinous, unplanned act, and for what? A delayed adolescent infatuation, nothing more.

Because he badmouthed Adrienne.

He wondered what kind of father that would make him – and swiftly realised he already knew what kind of father he was.

He placed the bookmark amongst the other gifts. The elation he had re-entered the mausoleum with had dissipated now, replaced with a heaviness.

'You deserved better from me,' he murmured, not entirely to his father.

He stood back as the procession filed past one by one, each bearing their own gifts. Eleanor left gifts on behalf of Cienne and Lilly as well, until finally the small pile grew level with the lip of the casket's opening. One last prayer was muttered by all but Seth, whose mind was elsewhere, and the small crowd proceeded back to the cathedral's main hall as the torches were extinguished one after the other.

The door finally closed, leaving the king in darkness.

~

In a realm un-chartable by human means, the Bastard stood shiftily before his bearded companion.

'HAVE YOU APPROACHED THE PROPHET, YES OR NO?' intoned the latter impatiently.

His voice held an otherworldly timbre the Bastard bitterly envied, a low monotonous drawl over the back of his own booming tones.

The Bastard swallowed. He really didn't want to answer this.

'Yes, sire,' he squeaked.

'AND HAVE YOU GATHERED THE NECESSARY INFORMATION?'

'Not exactly.'

The bearded man crossed his arms over his chest.

'WHAT DO YOU MEAN, NOT EXACTLY?'

'I... might have buggered it up.'

The man's eyes narrowed.

The Bastard wrung his hands.

'WHAT'S HAPPENED TO HIM?' the man asked dubiously.

The Bastard gathered his bearings and said in one explosive breath, 'I broke his brain.'

'WHAT?'

The Bastard winced.

'The operation went a little pear-shaped, I pulled out the wrong thing and he… he went insane.'

The bearded face looked like thunder.

'INSANE-ANGRY OR INSANE?' he asked to clarify.

The Bastard braced himself. 'Insane.'

The older man clenched his teeth.

'IT TOOK ME TWENTY YEARS TO BREAK THEIR DEFENCES AND TRACK HIM DOWN AND YOU DRIVE HIM INSANE?!'

A hysterical screechiness came over his voice at those last three words – shrieky and gravelly all at once, like three demons howling along with him.

'It was an accident!' the Bastard said shrilly.

'IT WAS A SIMPLE PROCEDURE!'

'It went awry! I…' The Bastard took a breath. 'I got into his head, right, and I figured out his memory system pretty fast, but… he had it hidden and I found, I dunno, a traumatic memory or something, and he saw it and went berserk and destroyed everything.' He wrung his hands again.

The bearded man's eyes narrowed. 'HE DESTROYED EVERYTHING? HE DESTROYED *INFORMATION*? HOW?'

'It was all painted out in illuminated lettering – except for the traumatic one, that was scrawled down and abandoned – and he started smashing all the cabinets they were in and ripping everything up—'

'HIS MIND IS RENDERED UNFATHOMABLE?'

'Yes.' The Bastard waited nervously.

The man unclenched his teeth and cleared his expression.

'THIS MEMORY,' he said. 'DID IT HAVE ANYTHING TO DO WITH THE PROPHECY?'

'No. Maybe. I dunno. I didn't really look at it, I was too busy looking at the pretty ones.'

He cowered from the man's fiery glare, sheepish.

'I just glanced at it and it didn't say prophecy so I bunged it somewhere towards the front, right where he would see *shit*,' he cut across himself in despair.

'NEVER MIND THE PROFANITY, TELL ME NOW,' the man ordered, 'IS HE TRYING TO MEND ANYTHING?'

The Bastard thought about it. 'Yes. He was piecing stuff back together when I left, but… I think he was putting it together wrong. He was muttering about how pretty Seth Crey was and how nice it would be to put his hands through his hair.' The Bastard wrinkled his nose. 'Which was strange, because his romantic fantasies before were more about how much he wanted one of the nuns to sit on his—'

'HE'S NOT GOING TO SETH CREY TO OFFER HIS SERVICES, IS HE?'

'Oh God, no,' the Bastard emphasised. 'He's terrified of him. He's far too shy to come up to him in person and talk to him.'

33

The man relaxed. 'GOOD. I RECKON SETH CREY HAS ENOUGH LOVE TOYS TO PLAY WITH WITHOUT HIM ADDING ANOTHER GENDER INTO THE MIX.'

He turned to admire the sunset, which was a quaint shade of lilac here.

'HE'LL BE STAYING PUT, THEN.'

'The archpriest isn't letting him out of his sight just yet,' the Bastard confirmed.

'HAVE HIMSELF KEEP AN EYE ON HIM, IN CASE HE LETS ANYTHING SLIP,' he ordered. 'EVERY MORSEL OF THAT INFORMATION IS CRUCIAL. IF HE STARTS TO PIECE IT BACK TOGETHER, I WANT TO BE THE FIRST TO GET IT.'

'Yes, sire,' the Bastard said with a bow. 'Shall I go after Aaliyaa?'

'OH, YES, DEFINITELY,' he agreed. 'SAVE US A JOB, WON'T IT, HAVING HER ON THE WARPATH. HAVE YOU LEFT THE SIGN AT THE CHURCH?'

The Bastard hesitated.

'I left... *a* sign,' he finished. 'They'll know I was there, put it that way.'

King Theo smiled.

~

Aaliyaa had finally wandered away from the wreckage in a trail of smoke, but Father Toffer remained. He stared dejectedly at the steaming debris in place of what had been his home, tears blinding him.

A monk approached in a daze and knelt before the priest, who sat cross-legged on the ground.

'What now, Father?'

The priest didn't reply. He just stared.

Not far away, trotting after Aaliyaa dutifully was a small white dog with a brown spot on his back. Father Toffer was gawking after it when the monk – Toffer couldn't recall the names, they all looked alike to them – prodded his arm.

'What? What is it?' he snapped.

'Shall we begin to rebuild the church?'

Toffer turned his gaze to the rubble. 'No.'

The monk frowned. 'But it's what we always do.'

'Not on this occasion.'

He swung towards the acolyte.

'Is our monastery in good keep?'

'Of course, Father. We send all new acolytes to the monastery. They tend it regularly.'

He smiled slightly. 'Good. Check the chapel basements and see if any weapons or money can be salvaged.'

The monk's brow furrowed.

Toffer smiled and explained in advance, 'We're going to complete an unfulfilled contract regarding King Seth Crey.'

~

III

The throngs had mostly dissipated by the time Seth emerged from the mausoleum. His mother was still inside, filing dutifully through the now-dwindling hoard of consolatory mourners, but Seth had gotten sick of that and wandered outside. What he needed was a drink – it appeared he was now due a celebratory one.

He could just about see Cienne in the distance, heading for a coach.

Seth smiled and made his way over.

A yard away, another man advanced on him, his weapon at the ready.

Seth halted behind his queen and tugged on a lock of her hair.

She pivoted to smile fondly at him. Her gaze flitted briefly to a white-clad stranger a few yards behind, her brow furrowing slightly in bemusement.

'Ready to go?' she asked, pulling her gaze from the oddly dressed man.

Seth nodded gratefully.

A flash of crimson caught his eye. He looked up to find Lyseria above the mausoleum, hurling plumes of fire into the sky. Seth rolled his eyes. A beautiful tribute any other day of the week, but entirely untasteful in the circumstances. On another note, it was scaring the procession.

'One moment,' he said to Cienne, signalling the guards to back off.

They obeyed eagerly. None wanted to be eaten on Seth Crey's account.

Seth stood a distance away from the mausoleum and whistled.

Lyseria landed before him.

'What did I tell you about the fire? Eh?'

He slapped her nose.

She grunted and head-butted him in the chest.

'Hey! None of that!' he snarled, slapping harder.

Lyseria backed off, huffing a sullen cloud of smoke.

'No fire during funerals! And don't think I won't have you put down for attacking the king, I'll mount your nuisance head on the wall myself!'

Lyseria burped a thick plume of black smoke into his face and took off.

Seth coughed, wiping a fresh layer of soot from his face.

'How can something non-verbal be so bloody gobby?'

He was about to turn back to the coach when something white and slimy collided with his face.

He heard a cackle and the pounding of running feet.

A white plate made of thick parchment slid from his face.

His guards surrounded him. One of them sheepishly handed him a handkerchief.

'A prankster, your highness,' he said by way of explanation, though it didn't explain to Seth why they hadn't stepped in earlier.

Seth wiped what appeared to be whisked eggs from his face and scowled. The man vanished into the throngs.

Unbeknownst to Seth, the plate at his feet bore an ellipse with 'The White Rook' written in swirling calligraphy within it.

~

The Hilltop Inn bustled with nobility by the time Marbrand entered, shutting the doors firmly behind him. The dining tables were packed with the black-robed elite as the guardsman manoeuvred himself around the guests.

A woman of ill repute brushed a hand along the front of his breastplate.

'Fancy retreating somewhere private, Sir Knight?' she purred.

'No thank you, I have a vow of celibacy,' he lied immediately, sidling past.

Even if he fancied bartering his wages for an hour with that overpriced disease-bag, he'd have probably fallen asleep midway. He despised the day shift.

He halted at the bar, leaning heavily on the mahogany as a broad man slid over.

'I am absolutely knackered.'

Marbrand nodded with feeling.

Elliot ordered two beers.

Marbrand drained his in one go and slammed the flagon down for more. It was surprisingly good.

'Captain says we're back on night shift tomorrow,' Elliot said.

'Good,' Marbrand grunted. 'I hate the day shift.'

He accepted his refill gratefully. He drank slowly this time, savouring it.

'Heard the bodyguards going on about the funeral,' Elliot said with a snort. 'Some prankster went and threw a plate of whisked eggs at the king.'

Marbrand blinked. 'The dead one?'

'No, the new one.'

Marbrand returned to his drink. 'Well, that's alright then. I reckon he deserves it.'

'If anything for making poor Silas cry,' Elliot agreed.

Silas, Marbrand remembered. The sole witness to King Theo's murder. He had seen the little snot Prince Seth kill his own father. *With an axe*, Marbrand added. And not even a sharp one – Marbrand himself had seen the murder weapon with his own eyes.

Best forgotten about, he told himself internally. Best if Silas forgot about it as well, if he knew what was good for him. He wondered how he was getting on. He'd seemed incredibly upset about the whole ordeal, which was unusual for a member of the Hornes' personal guard. Queen Aaliyaa had kitchen wenches crucified on a regular basis for fornication. You either had a thick skin in that job or you ran away screaming within the first week.

'Anyway,' he continued aloud, 'I doubt a prankster will do him much harm. Unless egg brings him out in a rash.'

Elliot laughed shortly.

They paused a moment to enjoy their drinks amidst the bustle of nobility. Elliot nudged Marbrand's arm. 'Here, Prince Ron's gone a funny colour.'

Marbrand jerked around and spotted him immediately. Then he ran over.

~

'They've already named him the Phantom Egg Flinger, though I doubt if he'll make a reappearance,' Sir Boris Necker said to Qattren casually. He brushed back his receding mane of grey hair offhandedly and continued, 'His majesty will no doubt want the man gelded for the affront, silly little twit the man is…'

Qattren listened politely, despite not having the slightest interest in the antics of Seth Crey's latest foe. She was only engaged in this one-sided discussion because it gave her an ideal view of the prince himself – or 'king', as he now called himself. Qattren would call him king when hell froze over. King-killer, on the other hand, now that was more accurate.

'Hello, Qat.'

She turned to the sound of her husband's voice and sighed heavily.

It occurred to her, not for the first time, that Ronald Horne was a complete imbecile.

She had only married him to gain a hostage. The new King of Stoneguard had been Aaliyaa Horne's thrall. Religious zealots were, in Qattren's experience, not ideal ruling material. Qattren's best hope was to convince Vladimir to relinquish Stoneguard to either her or the Creys or, should he make a nuisance of himself and get himself killed, place Ronald on the throne and advise him as his consort.

All that went belly-up after Vladdy's demise with the news that he had forced himself on Felicity Emmett and conceived a boy, leaving Stoneguard in the charge of the Emmetts – but at least the marriage had improved her social life.

Ronald was pleasant enough in himself for a young man of twenty-one. She tolerated him fine; even enjoyed his company. Except for on these particular occasions when he was drunk – which she thought she had stemmed for good.

'Love,' she drawled, 'do you feel ill at all?'

Ron froze. 'A bit, now that you mention it. Why? Do I look pale?'

'You've turned yellow, man,' Sir Necker said in astonishment.

Ron examined his hands with a frown. Sure enough, his skin had turned a sickly mustard colour.

'You've been drinking again, haven't you?' said Qattren dully.

'Consuming liquid *is* a necessity to live, dear,' he said dryly.

Then he collapsed.

37

Qattren heaved a sigh. 'Sir Necker, I would be much obliged if you could help me lift him up, please.'

'Of course, your highness.'

They raised him up by his armpits.

Marbrand emerged suddenly at their side. 'Allow me, your highness.'

Qattren relinquished her husband to him.

'Thank you, sir,' she said with a faint smile. 'Take him to this table, he can rest there until we can find him a healer.'

Marbrand obeyed without a word.

At the bar, Lilly had put her tears behind her for now.

She was currently rapt to Stanley Carrot's ramblings about his uncle Keith. Keith Large owned a knocking shop. Stan's waffling often inadvertently contained a multitude of hilarious anecdotes.

'... imagine sending me and the girls to a wake! It's horrible! It's borderline despicable – I mean, a king's funeral! It's awful! And I don't even want to dwell on what he's got planned at the Crook in a few weeks!'

'Well, don't then!' Lilly exclaimed, putting an arm around his shoulders. 'I have a plan. Remember I told you to stay put in case I needed you?'

Stan nodded.

Elliot eavesdropped from the bar behind them.

Lilly pulled a map from her sleeve and unrolled it.

Stanley's eyes widened. 'What on earth d'you want to go there for?'

'Dragon,' she said with a grin.

'A dragon?' he yelped. 'What d'you want my help for?'

'Company?' she said with a shrug. 'Heavy lifting, maybe? Cooking? I dunno, I'd just rather have you coming instead of a nagging palace guard calling me "your highness" and "milady". I plan to go in disguise.'

'Why?'

'For the adventure!' she cried out joyfully, spreading her arms. 'What fun is it being rich when you spend your life guarded by knights and frilly petticoats? I wanna go out and see places, feel excitement, smell fear, hit people, ride horses – I'm not gonna do that married to some rich mate of Seth's. I wanna do that now, while I still can!'

'And why do I have to go?' Stan wailed in despair.

'Because I bought you from your Uncle Keith and you belong to me now.'

'What?' he exploded. 'I'll kill him for this, the slimy old—'

'Yeah, yeah,' Lilly drawled, 'relax, the love of your life Prince Ron will be coming too.'

Stan's outrage turned to sheer euphoria.

'Prince Ronald?' he breathed in delight. 'Really?'

'Yeah, if we can keep him off the drink,' she said. 'I reckon it could be a laugh.'

'Who else are we bringing?'

38

'Nobody.'

'What? No guards? No armies? No—'

'Nobody,' she repeated. 'We want an adventure, remember? Not a state visit.'

Stan was silent. Lilly reckoned Ron's inclusion had probably convinced him.

'We are bringing weapons, though?' he said finally.

'Well, yeah, we don't want *that* much of an adventure,' she said, rolling her eyes. 'I'm fully trained in armed combat; my old man saw to that. You'll be perfectly safe.'

Stan cast a sceptical eye over her tiny form and privately doubted it.

He turned his gaze to the map before him.

The region nicknamed the Dead Lands was shaped like a skid-mark, seemingly featureless apart from the cities dotted around the coastline and a clump of mountain and hillside towards the east. Most of the cities were ports and harbours, he noticed.

To make it easier to leave, he thought critically.

A small marking on the right-hand edge informed him of the many leagues between there and Truphoria. The many, *many* leagues.

That's gonna be a problem, he thought, his brows meeting in distress.

He glanced at her hopeful features with a sigh. 'Oh, alright then.'

Lilly cheered.

'But I want nice weapons, mind you,' he added sharply. 'And feeding. And I won't do swimming either. I can't abide water.'

'Suits me, I can't swim,' she said with a shrug.

She glanced at Seth's table and sighed.

'He's got his speeching face on,' she observed, rolling her eyes.

Stan followed her gaze.

Sure enough, Seth stood behind his wife, banging an empty flagon on the table in front of her loudly.

'The king wishes to speak!' Queen Eleanor piped over the pub racket.

The crowd finally settled.

'Right, thank you for coming,' said Seth brightly. 'We all know my father liked attention, but alas he isn't here today to appreciate it…'

A treacherous voice in the back mumbled something along the lines of, 'Are you sure he's King Theo's get? He talks like a shit farmer!'

Lilly brayed a laugh.

Seth shot her a look and continued.

'However. They say the end of one legacy marks the beginning of another…'

He paused to throw Cienne a fond glance.

'… and my dad's case is no different. And that's why, despite the fact that he's sadly missed this day—'

Ron cut in by slamming his head onto the table.

39

Qattren and Marbrand jerked him upright.

'—I am very pleased to officially announce that I am going to be a father!' Seth grinned broadly.

There was a depressing silence littered with shrugs of indifference.

Seth frowned in bemusement.

'And Queen Cienne is going to be the mother!' Jimmy added in earnest.

The room erupted into cheers and applause.

Seth blinked around in utter bewilderment.

Jimmy dusted his hands off in demonstration of a job well done.

Cienne beamed at everyone.

Seth shook his head in annoyance and cleared his throat.

Jimmy signalled for quiet.

'So to celebrate the wonderful news, and the life of my old man, I would like to buy everyone a dri—'

'Errk!'

Jimmy intercepted this message with one of his own in Seth's ear.

'—a half-drink,' finished Seth with a sheepish smile. 'They're… very expensive, apparently.'

The crowd cheered unenthusiastically.

'Er, right, so let's raise half a drink to my father,' he said, lifting his flagon into the air. 'King The—'

'King Theo Crey!' echoed the guests before realising that he had been cut off.

The White Rook vaulted onto the bar in a racket of smashing glasses and leapt from table to table as guards chased him out of the inn.

Seth scowled through a filmy layer of whisked eggs.

Jimmy delicately dabbed at his face with a napkin.

'Somebody's eager to have you marinated in whisked eggs, sir.'

'Really?' said Seth, trembling. 'Well, when they bring him back, I'm going to take this fork and WHISK HIS BLOODY HEAD OFF!!' he howled, throwing a dinner fork across the table.

Lilly snickered. 'It's almost worth staying to see him become a father.'

'Not bloody likely if it means I'll be sold back to Uncle Keith,' Stan said darkly.

~

A red cloak swept across the sands, sending dust into Retribution Halle's eyes.

He rubbed them vigorously as his companion set to work. When he opened them, the vast desert had abruptly been replaced by the city of Copers.

Halle's jaw dropped open in awe.

To call the city a ruin would be inaccurate. This vast metropolis was the exact opposite of decrepit. It was clean, full, beautiful, fertile – and deserted. Its people fled in terror over a hundred years ago, or so Halle had read. Fifty thousand people, fleeing to escape a banshee or a giant serpent or something – but not without leaving seven virgins in the citadel, just in case they had to come back.

Halle snorted at the thought. He was glad of the Dead Lands' superstitious nature. It made it much easier to keep the city's location – and his plans for it – a secret.

He followed his companion downhill, towards the maze of buildings.

The two men each had fifty years on them, but Halle prided himself on his ability to hide the last five. His dark brown hair, cut to two inches long and as yet lacking the silver his companion bore, fluttered behind his receding hairline, collecting sand along with his rather large nostrils.

His own cloak, a fine navy silk, billowing behind him, he kept to the heels of the silver-bearded, red-clad Erstan Gould, fellow leader of the party that would rule the world.

A small sandstorm was building, blinding Halle, but soon the cluster of sandstone dwellings came into sharp relief. Erstan strode ahead with Halle three steps behind, watching the outer walls of Copers grow from a distant circle to a hundred-foot barrier over his head.

Erstan pushed open the doors with both hands, revealing the main thoroughfare to the citadel and the basilica beyond. Halle was admiring the red-orange walls of the citadel in the distance when Erstan spread himself across the entrance, blocking his path.

'Our acolytes are within,' he informed his friend, 'but you have a task to fulfil before you can enter.'

Halle lifted a brow. 'I thought we had approached all of the main rulers?'

'All but Crey. He could not be found when I approached his council. Dealing with a couple of grave robbers, or so I hear.' He extracted a purse from his belt.

'You're sending me?'

'Of course we're sending you. Who better to pitch our ideas than the head of operations himself?'

He tossed the bag into Halle's hands.

'Of course, you'll have to be convincing. They say the Creys are sceptical by nature.'

Halle tucked the purse into a pouch attached to his belt. 'So it shall be. I will return with his answer in haste, but the journey from here to Serpus is—'

'The journey will not be a problem.' Erstan clicked his fingers.

A whoosh caused Halle to jerk his head upwards.

A dragon the size of a pony flew overhead, his black exterior shining in the desert sun.

'He's fully trained for long distance,' Erstan informed Halle, 'as well as protective combat and cookery, provided you share the food. His highest speed recorded is five hundred miles an hour, so your voyage should not take too long.'

'Excellent,' Halle replied as the dragon landed behind him. 'I shall have him back here by the end of the week at the latest.'

'And we shall wait for you, Retribution Halle,' Erstan said grandly. 'Our gates are forever open to you.'

Retribution Halle grinned and turned to his steed.

Erstan gazed admiringly inside the doors before finally entering Copers, shutting the doors behind him.

He never came out again.

~

Marbrand jerked awake as the carriage bounced on a pothole. He stuck his head out, only to pull it back in quickly before it could hit the edge of the portcullis entrance on the way in.

The Creys' gold-embossed carriage rolled straight up to the inner ward, but the guardsmen swerved to the left, jolting to a halt outside one of the east turrets. Marbrand stretched as the guards were ushered out and took a quick look about himself.

A soft shower fell over them as the horses were fussed over by the stable. The day guards had retreated inside to wait out the rain while the rest of the escort wandered in and out of the armoury, returning weapons amid the captain yelling orders. Marbrand took the time to return to the barracks in the turret east of the outer portcullis, before Captain Necker could put him on day shift again.

He wound his way up the steps circling the tower and entered the narrow doorway. Everything about the tower was narrow: the bunks stacked one on another against every wall, the chests of possessions littering the narrow space in the centre of the room, the slim staircase winding up in a slender hallway behind his and Elliot's bunks. Two slits in the walls illuminated the tower in a dim glow, which suited Marbrand to the ground. He hopped up to his bunk above Elliot's, collapsed face-down into the pillow and fell asleep once more.

By the time he awoke, dusk was beginning to fall. The room was now full, the sleeping bodies of six guards plus Elliot heating the chamber to a dull mugginess. He was vaguely aware that he was still in his leathers, and was about to pry it from his sweaty torso when the turret door swung open.

'On your feet, lads, you're on watch!' exclaimed the voice of Captain Necker. 'Usual places, ladies! Maynard, Marbrand, the hunter's gate! Moat, front, Brunt, Selney, inner gate, the rest of ye on yer rounds, come on, toot sweet, while we're young!'

'Captain, a word?' called Marbrand.

'Unless it's work, I ain't interested! Hurry up, you lot, you can do your makeup on watch!' he yelled. 'You want a word, Marbrand, we'll talk at the hunter's gate. It's on the way to my bed in any case. Today, Moat, you can sleep when you're dead!'

The group stumbled around the room in haste, scrambling around for clothes. Still fully dressed from earlier, Marbrand exited to make his way up to the inner portcullis, Elliot at his heels.

The keep gleamed a warm auburn from the inside as the two jogged around it. Sounds of laughter and cutlery drifted out from the open entrance. A celebration feast, Marbrand guessed, in honour of the king and queen's impending arrival.

He wondered if Seth was getting worried yet. He'd heard a hilarious rumour that a cannibal popped up in the Crey line every fourth generation. The last one had been King Theo's grandfather – statistically, Seth's get was due to be the next Rubeous Crey. He hoped Seth didn't want many grandchildren. And considering his luck, he was bound to have twins.

His mind still on the new king, Marbrand circled the north gardens, the spiralling beds of hedgerows and flowers dulled to vague shadows in the failing light. A secluded notch in the wide back wall marked the location of the seldom-used hunter's gate. Barely anyone remembered this gate: Necker only posted guards here when he was overstaffed. The nobility preferred to traipse through the entire grounds on the way to a hunt – they had to make an impression. Marbrand pondered what impression Seth made as he traipsed through the entire grounds all those weeks ago, dragging a bloodied axe behind him.

It had been approximately eleven weeks since Seth Crey had killed his father. The murderous tendencies seemed to have stopped there for now, but Marbrand found he still couldn't stop fretting about it. A holiday was definitely in order. He supposed he could always leave to work somewhere else – but the pay was just too good here. And he actually got a *bed* here. The Stonekeep's sheer puniness meant all guardsmen had to sleep on the hearth like a pet cat, and he doubted anywhere else in the continent was much better.

Captain Necker's silhouette became apparent on the horizon. Marbrand ascended to the gatehouse and stood to attention. Elliot struggled up the stairs, lungs heaving.

'You want a chat?' Necker bellowed from the gravel below.

'Aye, sir,' said Marbrand, dragging Elliot up the final two steps. 'I'd like to request time off.'

'Time off? What on earth for? Nothing going on now the funeral's done, and the way this "Phantom Egg Flinger" is going, I doubt the king will be putting on any more public appearances for a while. Work'll be practically a holiday by itself.'

'Thought I'd go visit some family up in Stoneguard,' he said. 'Might take Elliot too since there's nothing happening here, see the sights.'

'Didn't know Stoneguard had any sights,' Necker said with a grunt. 'Can't see why not, we're plenty staffed for a while. How long you thinking?'

'Oh, a few weeks.'

'The boat alone will be that. Take what you want off, I'll see you when I see you.'

'Thank you, Sir,' Marbrand said with a salute.

Necker made for the keep, muttering something about a roster.

'What are we really going to Stoneguard for?' Elliot said, dubious.

Marbrand feigned confusion. 'To visit the family, of course.'

'The Emmett family, is it? Keeping an eye on them, sort of thing?'

Marbrand smiled. 'Getting sharper every day, you are. Pity really. You'd have made a great captain.'

Elliot barked a laugh.

'Yeah, I figure we could go home for a bit, see what's what. I have friends inside the palace, they can tell us whether our friend Mister Emmett has anything planned for the second heir to the throne.'

'Ron.'

'Precisely. I reckon we can stick around till the birth, see if Ron comes to visit his nephew. Then we'll know why the Emmetts are really here.'

They fell silent and stared out beyond the gate, Elliot facing the keep, Marbrand facing the forest.

Elliot frowned. 'Who's that?'

Marbrand turned his head.

A man in white was strolling nonchalantly across the grounds to the front entrance. He was carrying something white... and papery.

'He's heading for the keep,' Elliot observed. 'Is he the one from the funeral?'

Marbrand recognised the clothes immediately.

'Nah,' he said in disappointment. 'Missing the hat. Keep an eye out, though. I ain't missing it a third time.'

~

IV

The trout glistened at him from the centre of a platter lined with potatoes.

Seth swallowed a retch.

Its mouth was ajar in abject horror, one wide eye gaping up at him, milky and bulging.

'I hate fish,' he said dully.

'All they have left after the feast, sir,' Jimmy said, almost apologetic, 'until they get a delivery from the butcher house tomorrow.'

'You know I hate fish.'

Jimmy's face dissolved into the drooping glare of all long-suffering service staff.

'Well, you'll have to starve, then,' he barked before he could help himself.

Seth picked up the trout by its tail and slapped him in the face with it.

It clapped back onto the platter, gawking at Seth in accusation.

44

Jimmy grimaced through a layer of oily grease.

'Get me more of the starter, then,' Seth said moodily. 'I'm starving. You'd have thought *I* was the pregnant one here.'

'That or the child,' Jimmy muttered.

He sighed and took the trout to the kitchens, reaching inside his lapel for a handkerchief.

Seth watched it go with a feeling of relief and proceeded to throw fish cakes at the court jester.

'SETH!'

Seth leapt into the air in a shower of crumbs.

'COME HERE!!'

He made a face, rising to his feet. 'Are you alright, my dear?'

'NO!' snapped Cienne. 'You're wasting the fish cakes!'

'Some would say I'm utilising them for a better purpose,' said Seth, dropping his arms around her shoulders and his chin on top of her head. 'I find them much improved from very far away.'

'Well, I don't!' Cienne barked, shrugging out of his grasp. 'Don't throw them at him, you're like a child, you're wasting perfectly good food when you could be using it to feed our child. Give me the fish cakes, go on, get them!'

Seth stumbled his way back to his seat.

'Now, hurry up! I need them, no, don't drop them, GIVE THEM TO ME!!'

Seth flinched, juggling two cakes that were threatening to plummet to the floor. He plonked them in front of her. 'There you are, dear.'

Cienne pressed an entire fish cake into her mouth, *whole*. It was the size of her fist.

Seth suppressed another retch.

'Remind me,' he groused. 'When are we having the baby?'

Cienne scowled at him, the fish cake disintegrating in her mouth.

'No' shoon enuff,' she snarled, crumbs spraying.

Seth grimaced slightly. 'I'll say. I'll leave you to it, then.'

The second fish cake had already vanished. Seth legged it in case he was next.

He poked Jimmy in the ribs as his meal was being set down.

Jimmy made a 'zzz' noise by default, inadvertently jiggling the bowl.

'Heard anything about the weirdo in the hat?'

Jimmy rubbed his ribs, irritated.

'He's been nicknamed "The Phantom Egg Flinger", that's about all I've heard. A description's being put out. Captain Redneck's waiting for you to put a reward out.'

'Good for him.' He stuck his spoon in his mouth. 'Hurgh—!!'

The retch returned. With it dribbled a small waterfall of oil.

The spoon clattered to the table.

Seth leaned his palm on the table, an elbow in the air and a grimace across his face.

'Jimmy.'

'Yes, sir?'

'What kind of soup is this?'

'Mushroom, sir,' Jimmy said in reply.

'Why does it taste like fish, Jimmy?'

'Lot of omega-three in those mushrooms, sir. They call it brain food.'

Seth scowled at him. 'You've liquidised the trout, haven't you?'

Jimmy shrugged. 'Waste not, want not.'

'You're a slimy man, you know that?' Seth sneered, giving the bowl a shove.

'Wouldn't help the fish wastage if I wasn't, sir.'

Seth eyeballed him sourly.

'SETH!'

Seth's eyelids fluttered shut. 'Take her the bowl, Jimmy.'

Jimmy obeyed.

Seth slumped back in his seat. A flash of white caught his eye amongst the guests and he bolted upright, alert. He examined the bustle again and deflated. *Probably my imagination.*

He heard conversation from further down the table and casually eavesdropped, peeling open an orange lying idly in a platter on the table.

'When is it due, your highness?' her lady-in-waiting asked in excitement.

Cienne lifted one shoulder, too busy shovelling aquatic-based foods into her mouth to reply.

'Well, when did you last have your blood?' persisted the woman.

Cienne swallowed. 'Weeks and weeks ago. I thought it was early-onset menopause.'

Her eyes thinned.

'I was wrong,' she said in a low voice.

Seth shot her a sidelong glance and turned to his mother, the placid member of the household.

'So when's it due?'

'Late next spring,' his mother informed him.

He wrinkled his nose. 'You mean she'll be eating like that for the next year?'

Cienne nodded.

He shuddered. 'Looks like I'll be holding off on the kissing in the bedroom.'

Something in Seth's comment clicked and without warning Cienne turned to him in front of all the guests and said, 'Let's go to bed *now.*'

Seth looked uneasy. 'Maybe... later, my love. Oh, is that Lilly calling for me? Back in a minute.'

He hurried across the room under Cienne's icy glare.

After as avid a search indoors as he felt he could get away with, he finally found his sister in the courtyard with her friend Stan. 'Hello Lilly.'

'Evening,' she greeted.

They stood by the fountain in the centre of the yard, bathed in soft amber light. Several braziers hanging from the walls illuminated the square in the gaze of twilight, casting the flowing water into sharp focus between the shadows of guests around it in lazy circles.

A white-clad man flashed in and out of view briefly.

'Escaping from Cienne, I take it,' she continued in amusement.

Seth scowled at him. The man approached a group of women and Seth swiftly lost interest.

'Yeah. I figure if anyone can keep up a conversation until she drops, it's you.'

She punched his arm.

Following a pointed finger from the group, the white-clad man approached them.

'Message for the king.'

Seth cowered. 'It doesn't have anything to do with eggs, does it?'

The man frowned slightly. 'Er, no. It's just a letter.'

He produced a scroll of parchment with a slight bow.

Lilly reignited her conversation with Stan as Seth read, his eyebrows pressed together.

'... so basically, we can take the dragon and be there, I dunno, evening probably, and she can drop us off somewhere unseen where she'll fit in, they have dragons everywhere, and the disguise will mean we'll be unnoticed—'

'What are you talking about, Lilly?' Seth cut in.

'We're going to the Dead Lands dressed as merchants,' Lilly said cheerfully. 'Then we can have a proper adventure without waiting around for an entourage.'

'And what are you planning to sell?'

She paused for a long moment.

'I dunno,' she said dully.

'Maybe we can be ship hands,' Stan suggested. 'Pay our way with labour, then get off and be travellers or something.'

'Good idea!' Seth exclaimed. 'When are we going?'

'*You're* not going,' said Lilly.

'What?' he asked, appalled. 'Why not?'

'I want an adventure in the Dead Lands, not a pampering day with you and your maids.'

He scowled.

'Looks like I have business there,' he said in retort, waving his message under her nose. 'So we'll have to go together. And I'm not flying on that bloody dragon. I'll look a right tit.'

She sighed. 'Fine, if you say so. But no entourage,' she warned.

47

'Fine, fine,' he said mildly, his hands in the air. 'But don't disguise yourself too heavily. The Ambassador wants to meet us at the docks.'

'Ambassador?' she echoed. 'What does he want?'

'You'll be finding out in *intimate* detail very soon.'

He smiled at her bemusement, holding up the note.

'You'll be marrying him.'

~

Ron's eyes flitted open.

'Ronald Horne, I warned you.'

Oh, bloody hell.

Ron's bedroom –which Qattren rarely occupied unless there was bad news – glowed a blinding white courtesy of a chandelier illuminated in blue-white flame. Ron wilted within the pristine silk sheets of his colourfully-dressed four poster bed. Its monstrous size dwarfed him to a childlike stature, along with the empty space of his bed quarters. The room bore little more than a tall wardrobe and a small chamber pot under the bed – one of Qattren's magic ones that abruptly emptied anything that dropped into it, which Ron found out the hard way when his pet kitten climbed into it one day, never to be seen again.

What also dwarfed him to a childlike stature was Qattren's withering glance. She towered over him from the end of his bed, peacock feathers dangling from her skirts and her hands on her hips. Her handmaid Vhyn lingered at her side, a pale blue Faerie in an airy white gown.

He glanced guiltily at his wife. 'I only wanted to smell it.'

'With your mouth?'

'It was very watered down.'

Qattren rolled her eyes and swept from the room, her handmaid Vhyn scuttling at her heels.

'Stay here for the remainder of the day until the yellow hue fades,' she instructed. 'And stay away from alcohol or else. One more binge will kill you – which will be fortunate compared to what I'll do to you.'

She slammed the bedroom door behind her.

Ron closed his eyes and dropped onto the pillows, his forearms over his face. He hated her. He had liked her when he first met her, but looking back made him laugh. *Boy, were you ever stupid.*

He squirmed deeper into the red and blue patterned silk and let his mind drift over the last few weeks, which he spent cold turkey under the instruction of his 'loving' wife. He recalled the preliminary rehabilitation meeting, where she had suspended a liver in mid-air and fed it increasing amounts of alcohol until it withered. He shuddered. He should have listened to everyone else – she was a madwoman.

He replayed the wake in his mind

– 'Pint, please,' he said cheerfully.

'Sorry, no can do,' the barman said apologetically. 'Wife's orders.'

'What, yours?'

'No, yours.'

'Figured as much,' said Ron glumly.

He turned to slam his back on the bar sullenly.

King Theo's wake, as did all post-funeral celebrations, bustled with cheery jubilation in a bizarre attempt at rebalance. Bodies squirmed against the bar on either side of Ron, grappling for the barman's attention. He folded his arms and stood where he was in stubborn, spiteful silence.

A conversation erupted to his left and he opened an ear.

'Marbrand,' a Crey guardsman was saying. 'You know, the one from Stoneguard. 'Parently, he was trying to rescue Prince Ron from Howard Rosethorn, who was a fugitive of Vladdy's at the time.'

'Who wasn't a fugitive of Vladdy's?' his companion said.

'Heh, good point,' he said with a laugh. 'Well, we reckon he came along to lure Ron back on the throne, take the regency from his pregnant sister-in-law's lot.'

'Lure him? With what, booze, I expect.'

'Yeah, probably,' he laughed.

Ron pondered.

Booze, he thought, and the throne of Stoneguard, or no booze and no crown either.

Deciding to avert the less desirable part of the deal when it came, he went in search of Marbrand for his free pint of beer.

He approached a large guardsman leaning on the bar and poked his shoulder.

'I'm looking for Mister Marbrand, he owes me a bribe,' he said simply.

Elliot looked him up and down. 'For what?'

'In exchange for reclaiming my rightful throne on his request.'

He spotted Elliot's bemused expression and added, 'I'm Ronald Horne, by the way.'

Elliot thought about this for a moment. Then he bought him a beer.

'Cheers,' he said brightly, wandering off with the flagon pressed to his face. He paused. 'I may need more drink later on. To help me formulate my plan.'

'Sure,' Elliot said, unconcerned.

The next Ron remembered was splintered conversation and a lot of falling over as Qattren ferried him home as discreetly as possible.

He sighed his way back into the present as a wave of nausea washed over him. Any more drink would kill him. But he couldn't help it. Qattren was never home these days, leaving him with no one to talk to that could speak his language. Teaching Faeries how to play Ludo with sign language was about as easy as tying a shoelace was to a cat – and to Ron, but that was beside the point. He was just so bored.

49

A fraction of conversation from the wake sprung to mind. He recalled hearing Lilly-Anna Crey talking a short distance away from him. Or perhaps a long distance, he wasn't sure. She was a loud talker.

'For the adventure!' she exclaimed. 'I wanna go out and see places, feel excitement, smell fear, hit people…'

That sounded like fun. He sighed again. Qattren wouldn't let him.

But what did it have to do with her anyway? a rebellious inner aspect of himself said in the voice of Lilly. *You agreed to marry her! You're the King of the Forest! She's just a queen, you're above her!*

He was a king now, he realised. A king with no responsibilities, no borders, no limits. Except where alcohol was concerned, but the adventure would make him forget about that.

A king with no borders.

That thought made him feel a little better.

~

The Ambassador stared out of his conservatory in silence.

The Church of Fiery Repent stared back at him in all its glory. Its exterior gleamed in filigree decorations, every inch laced with silver curves over the red sandstone. A giant obelisk stood in front of the entrance, marking the underground tomb of Arianna Lyseria, the Creator of Dragons.

The Ambassador stared out at the obelisk, a two-hundred-foot-tall pillar of amber sandstone, carved all over in high relief with thousands of scales. No building was allowed to exceed this height in the Dead Lands – the obelisk's task was to demonstrate Lyseria's towering influence on the world in the form of her creations.

The colossal Cathedral of Fiery Repent was the highest edifice next to this obelisk, and the largest in the world, to accommodate the millions of worshippers from around the world to pay homage to Lyseria. Her tomb lay two hundred feet beneath the scaled obelisk, while between them lay a necropolis housing each dead warrior that fought in her honour, whether they fell in battle or died as champions.

The Ambassador stared out at the monument as his thoughts drifted to his fiancé-to-be. Lilly-Anna Crey.

The last time he had seen her, she was twelve years old. A fierce little thing, and King Theo's last hope for an heir after Prince Seth's 'demise'. He'd arrived at the Creys' Keep for a visit to find King Theo searching the grounds for his wayward youngest.

~

– 'Ambassador!' King Theo exclaimed, clapping a hand on his shoulder. 'You're early! I'm looking for my daughter, you haven't seen her, have you?'

'I think I recall a number of ladies congregating in the gardens—'

'Oh, she won't be there, then,' King Theo scoffed. 'She prefers a big sword in her hand rather than a cup of tea. You'd know her if you saw her.'

And he did, almost immediately. Their eyes met as the scruffy, mousy-haired little girl crept up behind her father. Her right hand wrapped around a very large sword hilt, the left tied with a shield, she signalled to the visitor to be quiet.

'What brings you here, then? You only come all this way when you want something,' King Theo said, forthright as always.

Lilly's eyes twitched sideways.

The Ambassador slid to the right.

'Yes, your majesty, I have come to propose a marriage alliance.'

Before Theo could ask who he wanted it with, Lilly launched her shield into King Theo's back and knocked him flat on his face. She leapt over his sprawled form and spun to face him.

King Theo snarled as he rose, pulled his own blade free and ran at her.

The Ambassador watched in amusement as the girl parried her father's blows with remarkable skill. She ducked and dodged deftly, darting in between her father's blows to butt him with her shield, to no avail. The man was built like a fortress wall, firm, unwavering. He would not be so easily beat.

They sparred like this for ten minutes before Lilly pulled an ankle up, knocking King Theo onto his back. She aimed her sword to his throat and kicked his own from his hand.

'Do you yield?' she taunted in a high-pitched, childlike tone.

King Theo anchored a foot on her shield and straightened his leg.

Lilly flew onto her back, legs flailing.

He stood and loomed over her.

Her chest heaved, dragging wheezing gasps through her lungs. The tip of her sword darted towards his face valiantly.

The Ambassador snatched King Theo's sword from the ground behind him and lightly touched the tip to the back of his neck.

'Do you yield now?' he taunted, one brow raised.

King Theo grumbled.

'Nrgh, I yield,' he muttered reluctantly. He flung a glance at his daughter. 'I would have beaten you, though, and you know it.'

'That is her advantage,' the Ambassador said, flicking the sword around to snatch it by the blade. 'Allies.'

He handed it hilt-first to Theo.

'I didn't need you, though,' Lilly objected, her voice tight.

She sheathed her sword to accept a hand up from her father.

'Aye, but they can be handy when you do,' King Theo told her, hoisting her upright. 'When you have the opportunity to use them, that is.'

His gaze flitted upwards.

Inside a third-floor veranda stood Prince Seth, glaring down at his father with his fair hair settled over his eyes. A young woman of an age with the prince

51

emerged from inside, fair-haired and beautiful, and guided him away from the edge. She caught sight of King Theo and lifted a hand in greeting.

'Your son?' the Ambassador asked.

King Theo gave Cienne a nod in return.

'And his wife,' he replied, his gaze locked to the veranda. 'Albeit awaiting a consummation.'

He tore his eyes away and waved a hand at Lilly.

'Back in the armoury with those, little lady. And be careful!'

Lilly made a face at the nickname, sheathing the swords with care.

King Theo walked the Ambassador through the grounds. A long stretch of green marked the archery field, the target boards on the walls abandoned. North of the green stood a large gazebo, in which the aforementioned ladies congregated in the late summer afternoon.

'Twenty-two years, he must be now?'

'Yes,' King Theo grunted. 'Still, I suppose there's hope for him yet. I was older than that myself before my damned father could be arsed to pick me a wife. And then look what I got.'

He jerked a thumb to their left.

Queen Eleanor sat despondently in the gazebo, hoping against hope that Lilly might decide to put a dress on and join the ladies for a cup of tea.

The Ambassador dragged his gaze away with difficulty. Eleanor had always captivated him, despite whatever King Theo had against her.

'Still,' he went on, 'there is a difference between poor parenting and a childhood trauma. At this rate your boy may never recover.'

King Theo simply scowled.

'There is hope yet in your daughter, however.'

Theo burst out laughing. 'Lilly? She'll be a knight, that one.'

'But marry her to the right man and your country will remain safe in her hands.'

He faced the Ambassador quizzically. 'You want me to marry her to you?'

'Why not? I have a fine enterprise at your disposal. It will be a fine trade for the girl – in addition to one of my pets, of course.' He lifted a sly eyebrow.

King Theo twitched an upper lip. 'Years I've spent training her what you've just witnessed there,' he told him, 'along with an liberal amount of scepticism for the palace council. And you would have me swap her for a pet? Your wild flame-mongers are the bane of the realm. And your "fine enterprise" brings in one ounce of profit a year after the gold spent to feed the country – gold spent for food originating from *my* country. You think I'd sell my only daughter for an ounce a year more than I already have? No chance! What do you need her for, anyway? You have a son, don't you?'

'Yes, but he is illegitimate...' he said feebly.

'Ha! I see what you're up to! You want my last functioning heir to let your line inherit my land!'

'You have to admit, your majesty, without a male heir, your line will end. It's thin enough as it is with the family penchant of sibling murder, and is scheduled to dwindle out completely. Your son is damaged, your wife is long past it at this stage—'

'PAST IT?! Well, maybe,' he conceded to that one, 'in fact, definitely, actually, but that is beside the point! Adem has always been ruled by the Creys, and always will be. I'll have a grandson out of the boy one way or another, and as for Lilly, she'll be wed to the younger prince of Stoneguard like myself and King Samuel have already agreed. He's much better suited and around the same age as her. I mean, you're older than me, man! What would you want with a twelve-year-old child? Nothing I want to think about! Ha! Marry her to you? Over my dead body!'

The Ambassador gave in. 'As you wish, your majesty. But you know King Samuel as well as I do. He's a flake of the highest order. It will be ten years before your girl sets her eyes on that boy, and there's no guarantee her prince will be up to the job to produce an heir.'

'Like you are, you mean?' snorted King Theo. 'You have heirs all over the country, I'm sure.'

'Well, yes,' he admitted, 'but paramours lose their charm beside a real princess—

~

The Ambassador's memory was interrupted by his ceiling caving in.

He swung around to find that a man had fallen through his conservatory, apparently from the back of a dragon.

'Can I help you?' the Ambassador asked curiously.

The man rose to his haunches with a wince, picking shards of glass from his palms. He had the pox-scarred face of the lower class and his complexion was fair, revealing him to hail from Truphoria.

'I come from Adem, your grace,' he said, tremulous. 'His majesty King Seth Crey sent me to inform you he would be delighted to accept your proposal for marriage.'

I thought I recognised you, the Ambassador thought fondly, gazing at Lyseria's silhouette as she flew overhead. *Although I remember you being less... unceremonious.*

'He also said he would be much obliged if you could return the dragon,' the messenger added, breathless.

He flopped face-forward into the broken glass.

'I take it he wasn't too bothered about you, though,' the Ambassador said amusedly. 'Still, I think we can put you somewhere until you recover. As for you—'

He turned to face Lyseria and took a step back.

'We'd better keep *you* away from the males,' he said thoughtfully.

53

~

Gomez Emmett was staring out from the camp when he heard sobbing.

Felicity sat in the litter parked alongside him. She had been in there all day, just weeping.

He leaned in and stroked her mousy curls.

'It's alright,' he murmured. 'He's gone now. He's gone forever.'

'It wasn't his fault,' she whimpered. 'He didn't want to. She made him.'

Emmett didn't doubt it. He left his little sister to weep, turning his gaze back to the countryside.

Stoneguard bored him. It had no distinguishing features apart from a river working inside the borders and a few mountains beyond that had escaped the demon flames of fifty years ago. A far cry from the magnificent architecture of Mellier's capital, though the heat was less stifling.

Some taller, bleaker mountains jutting from behind Stoneguard's living hallmarks brought a hint of the Wastelands into view. Technically the dead area of land was still a part of Stoneguard – making them Emmett's territory. He doubted if the new King Crey would put up a fight for it.

He scrutinised the peaks passively as the bustle of camp sounded around them. Emmett Sr had appointed his best men to accompany his offspring to the ruins of the Stonekeep as plans to rebuild the keep commenced. The removal of the rubble and scorched earth was still a work-in-progress, but the site proved an ideal spot for a militia camp. It provided a panoramic view of half of the entire country.

A tap on his shoulder diverted Emmett from his thoughts. He faced a stranger, dressed in plain clothes wet from the rain.

'You asked for me, my lord?' he said with a bow.

Emmett inclined his head in greeting, his eyes drifting back to the landscape. 'Any news on the Creys?'

'The Dead Land Ambassador sent a marriage proposal for Lilly-Anna Crey. From what I hear, Seth Crey has accepted.'

The corner of Emmett's mouth turned upwards.

'A foolish act from a foolish man.' He faced his servant. 'How is she travelling?'

'By dragon, apparently.'

His upturned eyes portrayed clearly what he thought of that notion.

'Have the crew ready, then. I want what we discussed completed within the year, before her idiot brother decides to stake a claim on us.'

Emmett shuddered. He and Felicity were currently unmarried. It would only be a matter of time before someone tried to butt in on his newly acquired inheritance.

As though by divine providence, a white-clad man jogged towards them, carrying a scroll.

Emmett snatched the parchment without a word and unravelled it slowly.

Ambassador Krnk Bwl Xplsns begs leave for his son, Rlnd, to join in matrimony with Lady Felicity, to form an alliance between the Dead Lands and Stoneguard.

'The Ambassador thought you might have a reply?'

Emmett regarded the letter impassively. With indifference, he ripped it in half.

'Give him this as my reply,' he said levelly, handing the two halves to the man.

Leaving the messenger to gaze at the torn parchment in bewilderment, he returned his attention to the litter.

Head bowed and her tears veiled by a sheet of mousy hair, Felicity paid the men no attention, nursing the beginnings of a bump in silence.

'Keep an eye out for Aaliyaa Horne on your travels,' he told the captain. 'And whatever you do, keep her away from Stoneguard... and especially from my sister.'

~

V

'Seth.'

Seth ignored her and strode across his study.

'Seth, look at me!'

He extracted a roll of parchment and a quill.

'Seth! I am not marrying that old fart!'

'Tough! It's either him, his son Roland or that alien across the Wastelands, your choice.'

Lilly gritted her teeth and shoved past him to knock the inkpot across the ornate oak desk in a temper.

Jimmy watched black ink spray across the once-immaculate white walls and heaved a sigh, already predicting the ranting lament of the chambermaid.

'I don't want to get married! Why do I need to get married anyway? You have a kid now, nearly! Make *it* do it!'

Seth propped himself against the desk with one hand to glare at his little sister.

'We *are* making *it* do it, for your information. We have plans for it already, well,' he amended, 'Cienne has plans. If it's a girl, we're marrying her to the Emmett girl's kid.' He shrugged. 'We'll turn a blind eye to any extra-marital activity. We know what the kid's relatives are like.'

Jimmy snorted in agreement, exiting to hunt down the aforementioned cleaner.

'And if it's a boy, we let him ride around the countryside on a massive horse and search for his own princess, as tradition decrees,' Seth concluded with a dramatic gesture.

'I didn't see you ride around on a massive horse when you were a prince,' Lilly said with an accusing glare.

'Their *gums* show when they *grin*,' Seth said, shivering. 'It will be a *desperate* time before I ride anything with a smile like that. Anyway, you'll be marrying what's-his-face in exchange for his dragons. You wanted one of your own in any case, now you can get it free of charge.'

Lilly ground her teeth. 'Being forced to ride a man older than my father isn't what I call *free of charge*!'

'It will be!' he said in earnest, ruffling Lilly's hair. 'He has a son already, you won't even have to so much as look at the man. You're only marrying him so that we can make friends. After the wedding you can bugger off around the world for all I care.'

'Our father would never have sold me to a wrinkled old dotard!'

'Our father isn't here,' he said simply. 'I am.'

Lilly's breath whistled through an increasingly compressed jaw.

Jimmy re-appeared to hand a scroll to Seth.

'Word back from the Ambassador, sir. He sent it back with Lyseria.'

'Thank God,' said Seth in relief. 'I half expected him to steal her.'

'The letter explains why he didn't.'

Seth opened the letter carefully. 'Oh, I see.'

'Jimmy, please talk him out of it,' Lilly begged. 'Please.'

'Not my authority, mate.' Jimmy could never bring himself to call Lilly Crey 'your highness'. She was just too common. 'The king's word is final, plus it's one less room to fumigate in the mornings.'

'Oh,' Seth cut in, pointing at the scroll, 'you won't be taking the dragon, either.'

'Oh, great!' Lilly snapped. 'Am I allowed to bring clothes or is that forbidden also?'

' "After an incident upon the messenger's arrival, we would prefer you to arrive by conventional means",' Seth read aloud. 'That basically means they want you on a ship.'

'I hate ships,' she said in a dull voice. 'Tell him Lyseria dropped the messenger on route. Since you want rid so badly, I'll head off today.'

'She isn't a bloody horse, Lilly,' Seth snapped, 'she's a monster. If she sees she's heading there again, she'll head for the nearest male and chuck all excess weight off, princess and all. And anyway, the Ambassador wants to pick you up at the nearest port, which is…' he consulted his map, '… Portmyr, and I doubt he has sufficient provisions there to cater to a sex-depraved dragon.'

'And she's renowned for her habit of smashing up ships when she's bored,' Jimmy pointed out. 'Not likely to make Portmyr very friendly.'

Lilly huffed and set her jaw.

'In any case,' said Jimmy, 'your excuse about losing the messenger wouldn't exactly work… unless you really wanted to make an enemy of them.'

'Why's that?' Seth asked curiously.

'His son was the one who brought back the dragon.'

~

For a man on holiday at a king's castle, Orlando Buwol Uxpolisin wasn't particularly happy. Not that happiness was a regular occurrence in the life of Orl: growing up with a surname commonly mistaken for 'Bowel Explosions' made a perpetually unhappy man of him. Not to mention the fun fact that his name, if said in certain accents, sounds remarkably like the word 'Oral'.

What was making Orl unhappy was the message he had just given the family butler a moment ago.

Lilly-Anna Crey, the most interesting woman he'd ever heard of, was getting married. To his seventy-year-old father.

Contrary to popular belief, Lilly-Anna was to be Karnak Buwol Uxpolisin's first wife. Orl's mother was a paramour, making Orl technically illegitimate – along with the other twenty half-brothers and -sisters of his that didn't make the upper class simply because their father grew bored with their mothers. But Orl's mother was special. So special in fact that Orl was officially legitimised, by the Dead Lands' ruling sovereign, no less. Before he fled the country screaming, that is, but that was a whole other story.

Karnak had been a simple ambassador back then – not the impromptu ruler he'd become in Prince Dom's absence. No one cared much who fathered his children back then. One womb was much the same as any other.

The one Orl had sprung from was long gone now, along with the rest of his mother. A fever took the former barmaid, mainly because she was too engrossed in Myths of the Eight Metropoli to fight it off. It was one of the thousands of rare books Karnak had wooed her with that Orl had yet to read.

Orl doubted he'd get a chance to read them for a while. It appeared he was going to be busy.

We're getting married. How do you feel about that, Mother? Because I feel awful.

His father was marrying a young woman, younger even than Orl. It seemed like an insult to Mother, even though she despised the idea of marriage. An eloquent word for slavery, she would say.

She'd also tell him to marry the woman. A business opportunity, he would tell her, and she would agree. She never took things too personally. *Still feels like treachery.*

Then there was his own marriage.

He'd been quite looking forward to husbandry, before he'd heard of Felicity Emmett. Now he wanted to curl up and die. He needed a life partner with something interesting about her, not an infamously vapid moron. *I should have known I'd never be happy with this*, he thought sourly. Happiness did not happen to Orl – Karnak was too busy stealing it.

Tears flooded his vision in a hideous wave. He hid his reddening face behind one hand, his shoulders trembling under the weight of a landslide of murmurings from his sub-terrain-level self-esteem. *I had to be a bookworm, didn't I? One of the eternally forgotten. Remember the time you were locked in the library when we were moving home? That wouldn't happen to a Crey, would it? Only you. Only Oral Bowel Explosions would let himself be left behind by his own family.*

The front doors of the keep creaked open.

Orl wiped his eyes to see a young woman and two men standing before him. The girl wore men's clothing, giving her the look of a stable boy rather than a princess, but Orl recognised her immediately.

And he sobbed some more.

~

Marbrand gave Orl a queer glance and exited the inner portcullis.

Elliot was still counting sheep when he left him to head for the stables, which suited Marbrand just fine. Elliot Maynard was considerably more docile when he was too sleepy to complain of hunger.

Marbrand was halfway towards a change of heart himself. The new Regent of Stoneguard gave him a bad feeling in his gut. It was the eyes, he decided. His eyes were too narrow, too black. His brand of evil made the Creys look like eccentric soiree hosts.

Hopefully Ankovich still worked in the household guard. Despite sharing a nationality to the Cientra-born Aaliyaa Horne, he bore a distinct hatred for the woman. Getting the low-down on the current affairs of Stoneguard without interference from its rulers would be a piece of cake.

Feeling optimistic, Marbrand gave the stable boy his instructions and made for the entrance to his barracks, where Elliot teetered on the edge of consciousness.

'You awake enough to ride?' he asked, poking a broad shoulder.

Elliot jerked his head up, blinking rapidly. 'Nghrnh.'

The stable boy led two mares over, one grey, one dappled brown. Marbrand handed him a gold pound for his trouble, impressed with the swift service.

'Necker left me our wages earlier,' he said to Elliot as they mounted up. 'Left a generous bonus as well, probably to make sure we come back. Thought we might pick up some supplies.'

'Nghrnh,' said Elliot.

'It'll be bread and water, mind,' he said. 'Can't cook.'

'Wife's job, that is,' Elliot said, his first coherent sentence of the day.

58

Marbrand grimaced as they made for the barbican, a long skinny bridge set a dizzying thirty feet above the castle moat. He tried to focus on the centre of the bridge rather than its blunt edges. He disliked heights.

His grimace was for something far more daunting, however.

'Speaking of wives, I ought to see my own wife while we're passing. She was pregnant last I saw her.'

Elliot brightened. 'Oh, lovely, how far gone is she?'

'Twenty years.'

Elliot winced. 'Ah.'

'Then again,' he said quickly, gratefully leaving the bridge behind him to enter the throngs of Castlefoot Market, 'p'raps I'll give her a miss. Maketon's a long way out for a flying visit.'

A small commotion round the side of the local inn caught his attention.

Marbrand peered over, scowling.

'Might not be passing that way, is it?' Elliot said with a smirk.

Marbrand was no longer looking at him.

There was a teenage girl in the centre of a small crowd.

The crowd were armed men.

~

Seth eyed the youth in front of him and faced Jimmy.

'Is he always like this?'

'I would be, with a name like that,' Jimmy said in reply.

Lilly hovered sheepishly between the keep and the inner portcullis, directly in front of her future stepson.

Orl shook and sobbed uncontrollably.

Lilly attempted to search out any kind of hint as to her fiancé's appearance. Orl had a warm olive complexion and thick waves as black as pitch, but that was as much as she could see past the delicate hands covering his face.

'Do you think they've met before?' Jimmy asked Seth behind her. 'You don't cry like that until meeting her for the *second* time.'

'You cried the first time you met Lilly,' Seth said in remembrance.

'She threw a shield at my face,' he recalled, indignant. 'I thought it was some sort of mating ritual.'

Lilly ignored them, giving the young man a prod.

'Oi,' she said gently. 'Don't cry, we're not that bad.'

'We're not the ones who named you Constipation,' said Seth jovially.

Jimmy blew a raspberry.

Seth giggled uncontrollably.

Lilly turned and kicked him in the crotch. She seldom needed an excuse, but forcing her to marry a stranger at short notice was, she felt, a valid one.

Seth fell to his knees.

'Uncalled for,' he squeaked.

Lilly tugged Orl's hands from his face.

'Are you alright?'

Orl sucked in a breath. 'I'm fine.'

'Are you sure?'

'Yes.'

He eyed Seth.

Who was banging his forehead against the gravel.

'I don't think he is, though,' he added.

'He'll live. Come on – let's get you a drink. The Crey idiom is that if anything fixes anything, it's booze.'

Seth stumbled to his feet, a hand over his vitals.

'Do you need me to get you a cold compress?' said Jimmy.

Lilly cackled.

Orl sniggered too, despite his tears.

Seth glared at him.

'You better not cry your way through the wedding service,' he drawled. 'She's going to be hostile enough as it is without you bringing the mood down.'

Orl dropped his gaze to the ground.

'D'you have to be a git to absolutely everyone you meet?' Lilly snarled.

She shoved Seth's shoulder.

'Ignore him,' she told Orl in a low voice. 'He's just getting arsy because his missus won't let him come.'

'In all senses of the word, now,' Jimmy added with undertones of mischief.

Lilly released a loud, involuntary snort.

'Shut up,' said Seth with a grimace.

He and Orl locked eyes again, Orl cowering slightly.

'I assume you want a ship?' Seth sneered.

'Yes, your majesty,' Orl said, his shoulders raised. 'My father thought I might accompany Lady Crey to the Dead Lands?'

'Lady Crey? Who's that, then?' said Lilly.

Orl smiled at her, the first genuine smile since he could remember.

It quickly tapered off at a sharp glance from Seth.

Oh God, Lilly thought, deflating. *So he's one of those brothers.*

She'd heard of men who took badly to their sisters being defiled. It seemed incredibly unhealthy. Lilly recalled the times before he'd 'returned from the dead', those wonderful teenage years spent sneaking Seth out of the castle and into the nearest brothel. He'd never had a problem with the whores defiling his little sister. Clearly a well-meaning young man of gentle humour was *far* more dangerous than three prostitutes with a possible disease of the nether regions.

Or an elderly foreign ruler, for that matter.

'Don't get too attached, my friend,' Seth snarled. 'Lady Crey is to be your stepmother; don't you forget that.'

Orl's bottom lip buckled.

60

Seth stepped back in alarm as the man threatened to cry again. He tried a change of tact.

'Well, have fun. Lilly has plenty of money for the pair of you. Off you go, Lilly!'

'Right you are,' she said, throwing Orl a wink. 'You don't mind dragons, do you?'

Orl was abruptly coated in a sheen of sweat. Clearly his trip hadn't been a pleasant one.

'You are *not bringing* the *bloody dragon*,' Seth growled.

Lilly gazed at Lyseria mournfully.

The beast curled up east of the keep, sunning herself. She seemed serene, which was more than could be said for Orl.

'Oh, she didn't toss you up into the air on the way over, did she?' Lilly said in sympathy.

Orl froze, interrupting his frightened trembling.

'She *does* things like that?'

'Yeah, it takes getting used to when she gets all silly. She doesn't mean anything by it, she's just playing—'

'I'll organise your route for you, since my baby sister can't be trusted,' said Seth, turning to Orl. 'Come in for a drink. You're going to need a thick concentration of alcohol in your blood stream if you're spending copious amounts of time with *her.*'

Lilly stuck her tongue out.

Seth pivoted on one heel, re-entering the keep with Jimmy in his wake.

Orl was about to follow when his arm was yanked sideways.

'Ow! Where are we going?'

'You haven't *lived*,' said Jimmy from behind Seth, oblivious, 'until you've tried the cook's hooch, it is to die—' He turned to face thin air. 'Sir?'

Seth swung around, blinking at his visitor's absence.

'Lilly!' he snarled, storming outside.

The two and Lyseria had vanished.

~

Marbrand leapt from his mare and sprinted to the inn. No one paid him or the group an ounce of attention. Muggings were commonplace in Castlefoot.

He slowed to a stroll to the alley between the inn and the bakery and pulled his sword free.

Three men pinned the youth to the ground while a fourth stashed her money in his cloak. By the look of them, her money wasn't all they were looking to steal. Marbrand crept up behind them as the girl kicked and screamed. They took no notice of him.

He tapped the thief on the shoulder with a leather gauntlet.

The man turned his head to find Marbrand's blade sliding across his jugular.

Marbrand threw the perpetrator aside and faced the other three.

They released the girl, each pulling a cutlass from behind their backs.

Marbrand swung at them, slashing two men across the face.

The middle one ducked to his knees.

The girl squirmed as the kneeler held her down. She bolted to the end of the alley, slipping from his grasp. He had bigger problems. Namely the broadsword sticking out of the middle of his face.

His cutlass clattered beneath him.

One man's nose hung by a thread as he launched himself at Marbrand, his blade raised. He lost more than his nose as he folded in a pool of entrails.

The last mugger took one look at the carnage and bolted, nursing a deep scratch on his forehead.

Marbrand tripped him up and slammed his sword into his back, stapling him to the gravel beneath him.

Once the writhing and squirting had more or less ceased, Marbrand shoved his weight from the hilt of his sword, stretching his back into an arch. His bones creaked a lot more than the last fight he remembered.

He cast a quick look around the market to ensure no more accomplices were on the way. Slowly, he toed around the bodies towards the girl.

She squirmed away from him and flinched violently away from his outstretched hand, as if it were aflame.

'It's alright, miss,' he said gently. 'You're safe now.'

'Who are you?' she rasped, holding her plain dress in her fists.

He realised it was torn across the bodice. Her dark hair stood up where her attackers had pulled her head back. She barely looked thirteen and her voice sounded younger still.

'I'm a guard of the Creys' palace, miss, you've naught to fear.'

The child eyeballed him.

Marbrand pointed at his breast, where the Crey crest was stitched roughly into his jerkin.

The girl lifted a trembling hand.

'Despina,' she whispered.

Marbrand grasped her hand firmly and pulled her to her feet. Her legs swayed dangerously and he steadied her under the armpits, half-lifting her to the market.

He found Elliot where he left him, minding the horses. He carried Despina to his mare and lifted her on top, perched sideways in the saddle.

'Who's this?' Elliot asked, curious.

'Her name's Despina,' Marbrand answered.

He leaned his left arm on the horse's neck beside the girl. He gazed up at her.

'My name's Marbrand, his name's Elliot. Elliot, the young lady's left her money behind in an alley, somewhere in the pocket of a man with no throat. Fetch it for her, would you?'

He nodded sharply.

'I dropped some bread and things too,' Despina said. 'You can have it. For helping me.'

Elliot snapped a salute and headed for the alley.

Marbrand regarded her.

She eyed him uneasily, brushing her hair behind her ears. It was too short to stay there and flopped back over her eyes again.

'How old are you, girl?'

'Fourteen,' she replied.

'You're awfully small for fourteen.'

'Comes from being poor, sir.'

He conceded with a nod and a smile. 'Can you cook?'

'I can cook soup.'

'What kind of soup?'

She frowned slightly. 'Only one kind of soup where I come from, sir.'

He smiled again. He was starting to like Despina. 'And can you clean?'

'Well enough.'

'Where are your parents?'

'Mum's in Stoneguard. We don't speak of my father.'

'Like most of the world, then.' He laughed once, then his face went serious. 'Why travel alone? Haven't you friends to go with? Family?'

'Mum's the only family I have, and we… don't get along. I have no friends.'

Marbrand shook his head. 'You've two now.'

She gave him a tiny smile.

Elliot returned with a rucksack full of foodstuffs on one shoulder, the men's weapons in one hand and Marbrand's sword in the other. 'Thought you might need these.'

Marbrand took his sword, eyeing the cutlasses in disgust.

'I'll leave those here, I think. We don't know where they've been.'

'I'll give you ten gold coins apiece for them, previous whereabouts notwithstanding,' a passer-by offered.

Marbrand accepted the money offered. Gold's gold, after all.

'How does a trip to Stoneguard push you?' he asked Despina.

Her eyes narrowed. 'With you two?'

'Oh, he's harmless,' Marbrand said, jerking a thumb at Elliot.

'Yeah, and he's too decrepit to do much harm to anyone,' Elliot retorted.

Marbrand flung a distasteful hand gesture behind him, his eyes still on Despina.

'Tell you what,' he said. 'There are sentry towers a mile from here in all directions. Let me take you to one and verify our identity. I assure you, abducting, luring or assaulting little girls is *far* from my cup of tea.'

'Or mine,' Elliot said quietly.

Despina hesitated.

'Do I have to go back to my mother?'

He shook his head. 'Wouldn't have a servant then, would I?'

'Can I be a boot boy or something?' she asked. She flapped her skirts. 'My pretty dress isn't quite working out for me.'

Marbrand smiled in approval. 'A very sound idea. Boot boy it is.'

She deflated in relief.

He shot her a half-smile, patting the mare's head.

'Budge up, then,' he said brightly, pulling himself into the saddle in front of her. 'Main road to the Wastelands is looking crowded. We'll take the scenic route.'

'The Wastelands?' Despina said. 'Isn't it illegal to pass the border?'

''S not illegal,' he informed her.

He pivoted their steed onto the west road out of the market, Elliot following suit.

'It's just against all laws of general mental health preservation, but that's more superstition than anything else.' He shrugged. 'Brought a hundred men there not long ago and brought 'em all back alive. From the border, anyway. A few got killed before we left Adem by some muggers, but those muggers got what they deserved for trying to reckon with the awesome power of the White Island ceremonial war hammer.'

'The one you nicked from 'em, you mean,' Elliot said.

'He couldn't use it properly,' Marbrand objected. 'For that he deserved to die.'

'He was trained in the arts of war in the Far Isles back in '34, so he says,' Elliot informed Despina. 'Bloody delighted when we made camp at the Wastelands and finally got a good look at the hammer. It was almost worth the countryside nearly burning to a crisp again. D'you remember her, that crazy bird with the strange fire?'

'How could I forget?' Marbrand muttered with a shiver.

'Flipped out and vanished into thin air when we were making camp,' said Elliot. 'Talking to ghosts or some shit. She went all odd as soon as she clapped eyes on the place.'

'That's what'll happen to you when you explode into dust on a periodic basis,' Marbrand said.

He craned his neck to peer back at Despina.

'Not afraid of ghosts, are you?'

'Ghosts are alright,' she said after a moment. 'Ghosts don't frighten me.'

He nodded. 'Me neither.'

He kicked the mare forward and they cantered for the border.

~

A farmer exited his barn after birthing a calf, wiping his hands on a cloth. He leapt back inside upon seeing the royal pet descending upon the farm from above.

Lyseria dropped her passengers into a cart full of hay.

Lilly's head popped out from the yellow straw, followed by Orl's.

'Come on,' she said quietly, climbing from the cart with Orl at her heels.

Lilly had directed them to the royal farming grounds north of the castle, where food supplies for the palace were produced – along with the occasional royal child. Or so Lilly surmised. It was common knowledge that the corn and wheat fields were Cienne's favourite 'hiding spots'. No one would expect Lilly Crey to be caught dead in there.

Feeling a bit ill at the thought herself, Lilly led the way into the infamous cornfield.

On the other side of the field was a stable, Lilly knew from a birds-eye view of the premises. She would take two horses, fast ones, hopefully – it was prerogative, she figured, to steal horses so long as you were a princess on the run. She'd even leave some money, out of respect.

Then they would flee for a port and hop on a ship. Maybe a pirate ship, she thought wistfully. That would be a real adventure. She'd even be willing to forgo her hatred of sailing if there were pirates involved.

They crept through the cornfield in silence.

'Will I get the blame if we get caught?' Orl asked tremulously.

'Nah, they know me,' said Lilly, wading through the stalks. 'I've got away with worse, even when my old man was around.' She proffered a hand. 'Lilly-Anna Crey, Lilly for short, current youngest scion of the kingdom of Adem.'

'Orlando Buwol Uxpolisin,' he said, taking her hand. '*Not* Bowel Explosions.' He cleared his throat, sheepish. 'Orl for short. My lady.'

Lilly snorted. 'I'm no lady. I'm hardly human. Seth likes to tell everyone I was birthed from the wrong hole. Speaking of which, d'you ever get called "oral" by mistake?'

'Yes,' he grumbled.

He softened this reply with a gentle smile. *He has a nice smile, albeit on a funny-shaped head,* Lilly thought.

'So, Orl,' she said, pronouncing his name – correctly – with a low twang. 'I see you can manage a dragon pretty well. How are you on a horse?'

Before he could reply, a disconcerting noise startled them. They froze, listening.

Clicking noises were coming up behind them.

'Is that what I think it is?' Orl asked in a high voice.

'Illegal? Highly,' said Lilly, stiffening. 'Our farmer has been a very naughty man.'

Slowly and with great trepidation, they turned their heads.

The corn stalks disguised the path, but the noise was unmistakeable. The scorpion scuttled erratically between the stalks. The noise accelerated. It had sensed them.

'We need to leave,' Lilly said airily, backing away. 'One sting means hallucinations, two means paralysis, three means—'

'—death,' Orl whispered.

A collection of crooked limbs pounced over the stalks, making the two flinch back. Lilly's pulse quickened. She didn't know they could leap that high. The thing was huge, its half-dozen limbs reaching to roughly the size of Orl's hand.

The two bolted through the cornfield. They split up as the clicking quickened, ringing deafeningly in Lilly's ears. She vaulted over broken stalks and sprinted towards the cottage west, and the scorpion followed, the clicking growing more and more excited...

And then Orl screamed.

~

VI

Nothing brings life into clearer perspective than acute abject terror.

Orl's heart thudded in echoes between his ears. His life was flashing before his eyes. Not the part that had already happened: most of that was too dull and miserable to relive. This was new material. The days sprinted past, kicking dust into Orl's eyes in too literal a manner for his comfort. Two scenes materialised simultaneously, one over the other in translucent layers. Both were wedding scenes.

One was his own, he saw, watching himself stare in horror at a bloated skin that was apparently a heavily pregnant Felicity Emmett.

The other was his father's. He looked terribly, terribly old. And a bit filthy, he saw with bemusement.

Lilly looked... Lilly looked...

His shriek pulled him back into the cornfield and into the present in time to see the scorpion sting him a second time.

~

Lilly rammed her shoulder into the front door, blowing it inwards.

'Oi!' she shouted.

The farmhand jumped, knocking his dinner upside down.

'Princess?' he squeaked. 'Oh God, you weren't in the cornfield, were you? The thing, it was just to keep the crows away, we meant no harm to anybody, we have an antidote in case—'

'Give me that antidote,' she said fiercely.

~

His legs were numb, much quicker than he figured they would.

They crumpled beneath him, sending his face skidding into the ground. He refused to realise the horror of the situation and instead focussed on his surroundings. He tasted dirt. He heard clicking and strategically ignored it. He saw a kaleidoscope with Lilly in the centre, smiling at him. He felt his pulse pound through his entire torso… but his legs felt nothing.

He heard another sound.

'… Orl…'

And it was gone, replaced by:

'Oi! Off! Go on, sod off! Bed!'

And then there were arms around his shoulders, wiry, skinny, strong arms, a smell of sweat, a shirt smelling of sweaty straw, but it wasn't bad, quite the opposite…

He was vaguely aware of being rolled over, until sunlight blinded him. Suddenly a face blocked the light and a vial slid between his lips, releasing a syrupy liquid.

That face…

'Lilly,' he whispered.

'It's alright,' she soothed, giving his shoulder a squeeze. 'That was the antidote, you'll be alright in a bit…'

'I love you,' he blurted. 'I love you, Lilly… Lilly…'

~

'Lilly? LILLY! I hate you!'

'She can't hear you, sir,' Jimmy said patiently.

Seth's brow wrinkled like a drying leaf. He scanned the skies, a hand over his eyes.

'What's she thinking of, taking my dragon? Mine! And with my visitor, too! I knew she'd be awkward, and now they're going to bugger off to God knows where and get her eaten.'

'Nobody will eat her, sir,' Jimmy said. His eyes widened slightly. 'They might eat Lilly, though.'

'Good. I hope they settle the bill afterwards.'

A slight blur in his peripheral vision brought his gaze upwards. 'Is that her?'

Lyseria dived, landing on top of the keep behind them with a shriek.

She released another, more frightened-sounding scream and bolted for the back of the palace. Jimmy frowned at her.

'She seems spooked, sir,' he said. 'You don't think she's seen something horrible, do you?'

'Oh, I'm not that bad,' a female voice said.

They both turned and screamed in unison.

There wasn't much in the realm more frightening to look upon than a semi-materialised woman. Qattren's upper torso hovered in mid-air as the rest of her gradually put up an appearance.

'Good God, don't do that!' Seth shrieked, clutching his elbows. 'Just travel in a coach like a normal person!'

'I'm afraid that was quite impossible,' she said, smoothing down her silver and ebony gown. 'Your sister has gone missing?'

'Where did you find her?'

'On her way to the Forest to pick up Ronald.'

'*Your* Ronald? Why?'

'She's been planning a vacation abroad with a mutual friend. I overheard her discussing that Ron would join them.'

'Getting to be a bit of a bunny boiler, aren't you?' said Seth. 'Listening in on conversations about your other half.'

'I listen in on everyone's conversations,' she said, 'and you were correct at the wake, that red head of mine is no lie, so remind me. Where are they planning to go and why?'

'She's due to marry the Ambassador of the Dead Cities, so she'll want to be heading there first,' Jimmy supplied. 'Men with a dragon farm don't take well to being messed about.'

'She was saying something about getting a dragon,' Seth said. 'Which is a bad idea for two reasons, most notably the one we already have. That animal tends to have a shag-or-slaughter attitude to almost everything. But why would she want to take your backward husband? He'd be more of a liability than anything.'

'He managed fine in the Forest by himself on his first visit while you were being fussed over by your paramour,' said Qattren testily. 'And liability or not, he has run away. I imagine to find your sister.'

'Run away?' Seth asked with a laugh. 'You let your delinquent *run away* and you couldn't find him with all your magic and things? I hate to say it, but I'm disappointed.'

Qattren lifted an eyebrow. 'Why would I hunt him down? He's a grown man, he can do as he wishes.'

'Why? I can't,' Seth said glumly.

'Ron doesn't have the responsibilities of impending fatherhood,' Qattren said. 'Congratulations, by the way.'

'I'll celebrate when she gets her figure back, if it's all the same to you,' he muttered. 'On another note, if you don't want him dragged home by one ear, why do you need to know where he's going? A man's holiday is his own business.'

'Not when he's married, as you've eloquently insinuated. It would just be nice to know. If trouble should befall him on his trip, it would be easier for me to help him.'

'Last time you tried to help me, you walked a few yards into the Wastelands and for no apparent reason decided to run away very fast,' Seth said.

'At least on this occasion I don't have to answer to a moron driven by pure carnal interest while his intelligence rides unconscious at the back of the coach.'

Jimmy gave a brief laugh. 'He tried it the other way around and Cienne brained him.'

'She'd have brained me anyway. There's no winning with that woman.' Seth heaved a sigh. 'Love's like scratching an itch in your bum-crack. It's satisfying in theory, but when it comes down to it, it's annoying and it makes you sore.'

'That would be thrush, I'm sure there's a cream for that,' Qattren said.

Jimmy clapped a hand over an involuntary grin and pivoted to hide it.

Seth shot him a scowl.

A man entered the inner portcullis in front of them at a limp, halting a yard away in a low bow.

Seth recognised him immediately. 'Where is my sister, Mister Bowel Explosions?'

'That *isn't* how you pronounce my *name*,' Orl seethed, straightening. 'Lilly has gone ahead in search of Ronald Horne, so that they can travel to the Dead Cities on an informal basis. She instructed me to return here and recover.'

Seth gave him a sidelong glance. 'What happened to you?'

'We stopped at some farming grounds north of the palace and I was attacked by a psychedelic scorpion,' he said, dreamily. 'Lilly gave me an antidote and left for the Forest. May I sit down, sir? My right leg is still numb.'

Jimmy hastily lent him an elbow. 'Those things are highly illegal, sir. They can poison a man to death in half an hour.'

'Is Lilly alright?' asked Seth sharply.

'Yes, Lilly's perfectly fine, perfect.' He smiled.

Seth made a face. 'You'd better get him his drink. Describing *Lilly* as perfect means whatever got him did serious damage to his sense of taste.'

Jimmy bowed and half-carried Orl into the keep.

'I will be leaving, then,' Qattren said after a moment.

'Alright,' Seth said eagerly, turning his gaze away from her. 'Tell Lilly she's dead when she gets home, will you? If you see her?'

'I will be sure to,' she said with a smile. 'I take it you don't want to accompany me and tell her in person?'

'Uh-uh,' he said, shaking his head. 'I have an illegal peddler to torture, it appears. More to the point, I don't much like it.'

69

'Yes, my methods of transport are a bit much to take in when you're not used to them. Oh, and Seth?'

He turned. 'Yes?'

Poof!

'AAH! Don't DO that!'

In the east antechamber of the keep, Jimmy let Orl drop into a chair.

'Unless being attacked by venomous creatures gives you a kick, you haven't by the sounds of it got a lot to be smiley about,' said Jimmy. 'What's got you so happy?'

Orl gazed at the ceiling with a beatific grin. 'Lilly.'

Seth made a beeline for the door, which hung ajar. Upon hearing this comment, he stopped himself from entering the antechamber and leaned on the doorframe.

'She makes people cry, usually,' Jimmy commented, echoing Seth's thoughts.

He took the opportunity to sit across from him and relax, legs crossed at the ankle.

Seth hovered outside, eavesdropping.

'Not me,' Orl said in a daze. His eyes bulged. 'He's going to kill me.'

'Who?'

'My father.' He shook his head in disbelief. 'What was I thinking? I'm to be married to Felicity Emmett! What have I done?'

'What have you done?' said Jimmy, leaning forward in intrigue.

'The bloody attack took my senses! I would never have let her kiss me if I was in my right mind.' He buried his head in his hands. 'I feel terrible. I've just coveted my own step-mother!'

Jimmy lifted his eyebrows. 'You had actual sexual contact with Lilly? I didn't know she actually *liked* blokes.'

A splutter and a loud curse outside drew Jimmy's attention to the left. He grimaced.

Seth was staring into the open door and was not looking impressed.

~

The sun beat green rays through the foliage into the mossy ground beneath, giving Ron the last of the summer's heat. Birds rustled and chattered overhead – less birds than usual. They were already migrating to the Far Isles on the other side of the planet before the sun could head off without them.

It looked like Lilly had headed off on her own trip without Stan, or so Ron observed as he approached the source of the screaming. That or he'd gotten his east and west mixed up and wandered into the Faerie Forest instead of their meeting point at Serpus – which would mean the end of an ordinary man's journey.

However, it seemed Stanley Carrot was more than the ordinary man.

70

Ron made his way to the coach idly.

'Go away! GO AWAY!' Stan shrieked, throwing shoes and bottles at them from the top of his coach. 'Get away from me, or I'll have you with my crossbow! GO AWAY!'

The Faeries leaped to reach him and started pulling on his ankles.

Ron sighed.

When King Theo was crowned, he became the first king with the good sense to legally declare the Faerie Forest unfit territory for human presence. He was also the last king to enforce the law: King Seth couldn't care less if Adem burst into flames so long as it didn't affect him personally.

Now that Theo Crey was dead, people seemed to have forgotten the true horror a Faerie can wreak when his/her blood is up, and they trespassed the Forest on a regular basis. None of them left again. If a man were to want to return, they would have to somehow break the Faeries' hypnotism, ward off the creature(s)'s limbs long enough to escape and leap from the tree without cracking their skull.

Because whenever the Faeries caught sight of a human, they instinctively, as Qattren put it, stole their free will and warped it to their desires – and didn't stop until they had had an orgasm at least thrice. She hadn't elaborated on what the desire of the average Faerie would be (or indeed to Ron on what an orgasm actually was), but Ron had seen an attack once and it had seemed a lot more two-sided than Qattren had made out, plus she hadn't done him any physical harm apart from ripping open his clothes, so he didn't understand what the problem was. The victim rather seemed to be enjoying the attack, or so Ron could make out between the cursing.

All the same, he strolled into sight of the Faeries and waved his arms in the universal 'shoo' motion.

They scattered immediately. They knew exactly who he was married to.

Ron squinted upwards. 'They've gone now.'

Stan peeked through the fingers covering his face. 'Thank God you showed up.'

'Thank my wife, she's the one who drove me out of the castle,' Ron grunted.

'Oh.'

There was a momentary silence in which Stan carefully pondered what to say. Ron always had the impression that Stan was mightily impressed with Ron for some reason and pondered something witty and clever to say to keep him that way.

This ponderous silence lingered a while longer.

'Got a pork pie here if you want it,' Stan said, sheepish.

'Yes, please,' Ron said pleasantly.

He clambered onto the roof of the coach.

The pale clouds littering the sky were opening, allowing the sun to finally pour down on top of them. They laid back on the roof side by side, each with an arm over his eyes.

'When's Lilly-Anna coming?'

Stan gave him a frown, insofar as he could with his arm in the way.

'How d'you know she was coming here?'

'Eavesdropping,' Ron said shortly.

'Oh. Cause I was supposed to be meeting her at the city, but I went too far northwest and ended up here. And the horse I had did a runner soon as I bumped into those Faeries, so I'll probably never get there now.' His gaze returned skyward. 'Though knowing Lilly, she'll have gotten bored of waiting after ten minutes and headed here without me. So she won't be long.'

They dozed together in silence.

The heat had died down a little by the time they awoke, and the sky was starting to darken. They glanced ahead of the coach to see a horse and rider approach at a steady gait. By the small frame of the rider, Ron guessed it to be Lilly.

'Oh, there you are,' she said to Stan, leading her stallion in a brisk trot around the coach. 'I was beginning to think you'd decided Uncle Keith's wasn't such a bad place after all.'

'Hah!' Stan climbed off the coach roof with Ron in tow.

'Where are the horses?'

'They ran off. We won't be able to carry these,' Stan moaned.

'Don't matter, I got supplies,' Lilly said, patting a large sack behind the saddle. 'Along with the best horse money can buy. I could only nick the one on very short notice, so we'll have to take turns. I suggest that on the turns I'm not on the horse, that I be carried,' she said, mock-haughtily. 'I *am* a princess, after all. There are standards to uphold.'

'You can keep the horse, I don't trust them,' Ron said darkly. 'It's the long faces.'

'Long faces?' said Lilly in amusement. 'You're as bad as my brother.'

She dismounted to help Stan and Ron sift through Stan's supplies.

'So what port are we heading for?' Stan asked.

'None of them,' Lilly said, beaming.

'Oh, so we're flying there, is it?' Stan said sardonically, flapping his arms.

'Don't be nasty,' Lilly scolded. 'My brother's on the warpath, so we're avoiding a paper trail. Luckily for us, Seth's been leaving the Forest ban fall to the wayside. Ships have been docking all around the Forest for weeks. We'll just hop on one and use our significant influence to steer them east.'

'For a twenty-week journey?' Ron said, sceptical. 'I'm Vladdy Horne's brother and you're a girl. Whose influence are you talking about, Stan's?'

'What, the brothel potboy has more of an influence than *me*? I'm a *Crey*!'

'You're a *girl* Crey,' Ron emphasised. 'Who's to say they won't haul us back to Seth for a reward?'

72

Lilly reached behind her back, 'Well...' and pulled a scimitar from a strap tucked against her spine, '... this fella, for a start.'

Stan and Ron exchanged glances and shrugged in unison. 'Fair point.'

The afternoon waned to evening. The three collected what they could carry from Stan's coach and followed the sun west, already making plans to set up camp in the Sleepless Meadow only a few hours' walk from them.

It would be here that the trio would meet Si Beult for the very first time.

~

'What is this?' Elliot asked in interest.

'Bubble and squeak,' Marbrand said, euphoric. 'Like my old lady used to make.'

'The trick is to burn it,' Despina said meekly. 'I'm good at burning food.'

The Wastelands stretched out in all directions. According to the old soldier, they were halfway across the short stretch of blackened land between the mausoleum and the border of Stoneguard, which wasn't bad going for a week's travel. They made camp, marking the end of their second day in the Wastelands. So far, no ghosts had bothered them.

Well, they had woken Despina up the first night, but not maliciously.

Marbrand shovelled his food in eagerly.

''S good,' he said, nodding.

'My mum used to do the proper cooking while I made up the leftovers,' she said. 'It was our little ritual.' Her expression turned stony. 'Till she threw me out.'

'What happened? Get yourself in the family way?'

'Nah,' Despina rolled her eyes, 'that was her speciality, which is why my poor father left.'

'What's his name?'

Despina shrugged. 'Forget. Summink weird, I think.'

Marbrand nodded and carried on eating.

'What was your old lady's name?' Elliot asked him curiously.

'Miriam,' he replied fondly.

Despina froze, a mouthful of fried potato sitting half-chewed inside her left cheek.

'She was a good girl, but having a small human growing in you can change a person, you know.' He turned to Despina. 'Mine would be older than you, about twenty now. Always wondered what became of him.'

'Or her,' Elliot said. 'Could be another Sadie Marbrand knocking around the place.'

'Sadie? I thought his wife's name was Miriam?' said Despina.

Marbrand made throat-cutting mimes on himself behind her back.

'Yeah, that was before he got his new name,' Elliot said with a goofy grin. 'Used to go by Sadie of a time.'

73

Despina stared at Marbrand in disbelief.

'We don't speak of that,' he said in a low voice. 'Ever.'

'Did your old lady have anything to say about it?' Elliot said jovially.

'Not often,' he admitted.

He glanced at Despina, who looked stricken. 'What's up?'

She tore herself out of her thoughts. 'Just seems like the name Sadie doesn't really suit you.'

'I should hope not!' he said hotly.

They laughed at this and ate contentedly.

As dusk fell, they slept under the stars on the dusty ground as Elliot and Marbrand took turns as watchmen. Despina fell into a dreamless sleep and awoke later in complete darkness.

She rose to her feet, rubbing her eyes.

Why is it so dark? Even the night had some speck of light somewhere. She strained to adjust her night vision, but there was nothing for her to see.

'Marbrand?' she said softly, in case he was asleep. 'Elliot?'

Why was it so bloody dark?

'Shh, not so loud,' a stranger purred.

Despina swung around.

A soft light ignited, revealing them to be in a small room, alone. The man who had spoken stood before her, his black clothes making him barely distinguishable in the gloom save for a head of close-cropped fair hair. He smiled cheerfully, waggling his fingers.

'Who are you?'

'DON'T WORRY ABOUT HIM, HE'S JUST THE HIRED HELP,' a different voice replied.

She pivoted again and gulped. The build. The jewellery. The beard. She knew who this was: everyone did.

'You're dead.'

'YES, THAT'S RIGHT,' King Theo said cheerfully. His voice seemed to have taken on an extra dimension in death. 'TURNED OUT TO BE HANDIER THAN BEING ALIVE, ALL THINGS CONSIDERED.'

'What do you want with me? Where are the others?'

'We've come to have a chat,' the Bastard said.

Despina couldn't have said why she knew he was called the Bastard. She felt the information had been thrust upon her.

'ABOUT OUR MUTUAL FRIEND, SIR MARBRAND,' finished the king.

Despina glanced behind her in search for him, but in the darkness, she couldn't tell if he was still around. 'What's he done?'

The two approached her.

'OH, NOTHING MUCH,' said King Theo's ghost.

'Yet,' the Bastard added. 'You see, we heard he was visiting a friend in the north. A friend of ours, as it happens.'

'AND WE DON'T WANT HIM PUTTING NASTY IDEAS INTO YOUNG MISTER EMMETT'S HEAD,' continued King Theo.

'Like abdicating from his regency?'

'EXACTLY!' Theo Crey exclaimed, halting behind her shoulder. 'QUITE THE GRASP OF POLITICS FOR A LITTLE GIRL, HAVEN'T YOU?'

Despina eyeballed him. 'What's Mister Emmett got to do with Marbrand?'

'You see,' the Bastard said from behind her other shoulder, 'we have plans for Mister Emmett. We think he could be a useful asset to our enterprises.'

'What enterprises?'

'OH, NOTHING YOU NEED CONCERN YOURSELF ABOUT,' King Theo said, flippant. 'WE JUST WANT YOU TO KEEP YOUR CHUMS OUT OF OUR WAY WHILE WE CONDUCT OUR... BUSINESS.'

'You know how it is,' the Bastard added. 'Innocent people getting caught up in other people's business tend to drift towards certain... unpleasant situations.' He screwed up his nose. 'None of us want that.'

'And what if I can't keep them out of your way?' she asked testily. 'I can't just tell them what to do. I've barely known them five minutes.'

'YOU COULD TRY, COULDN'T YOU?' King Theo coaxed. 'I GATHER YOU KNOW MISTER MARBRAND'S FAMILY. YOU WOULDN'T WANT THEM TO DRIFT TOWARDS CERTAIN... UNPLEASANT SITUATIONS JUST BEFORE THEIR REUNION, WOULD YOU?'

A chill ran up her spine. So it was that kind of conversation.

'I... I suppose not,' she said, with a slight stammer.

'I shouldn't think you'll have too much trouble,' the Bastard said softly, 'what with your abilities and everything.'

'AND THERE WILL BE ALL SORTS OF ADVANTAGES FOR YOU AFTER PERFORMING THIS LITTLE TASK FOR US,' King Theo added.

'Like what?'

'THE ABILITY TO BREATHE, FOR EXAMPLE.'

'And the ability to move your legs,' added the Bastard. 'You never realise how much you'd miss it until you're unable to do it anymore.'

'I can imagine,' she said.

'STILL,' King Theo said, 'A DEMONSTRATION MIGHT REINFORCE THE POINT A LITTLE.'

The Bastard nodded. He clicked his fingers.

Despina's legs buckled beneath her. She folded onto the floor.

She scrabbled at her shins, tried to slide them out, clawed at them. They were completely numb.

'Fix it, please!' she gasped, her arms trembling under her weight.

'Oh, alright, since you said please,' said the Bastard.

He paused, one hand poised in the air. 'Actually... nah.'

He dropped his hand to his side. With the motion came a spasm of agony that made Despina scream. She still couldn't move her legs, but in place of the

75

dead feeling was an agony in her bone marrow the like of which she'd never felt before.

'Now,' the Bastard said, lowering himself to her eye-level, 'you understand why this task is important?'

'Yes,' she squeaked, feeling faint.

'AND WE WON'T BE SEEING OR HEARING FROM YOU AGAIN?' added Theo.

'Yes! I mean no!'

'GOOD!' King Theo grinned. 'I THINK WE CAN DISPENSE WITH THE DEMONSTRATION, MY BOY.'

The Bastard's fingers clicked again.

Despina deflated, the pain ebbing. Feeling more herself from the waist down, she pulled herself to her knees, breathing in shallow gasps.

'Time to go?' the Bastard asked lightly.

'YES, I BELIEVE IT IS,' Theo Crey agreed. 'LOTS TO DO, YOU UNDERSTAND. BEST WE DON'T SPEAK OF OUR LITTLE CHAT, EITHER,' he added as an afterthought. 'WE'LL KEEP THIS BETWEEN OURSELVES, YES?'

Despina nodded and was left alone in the darkness.

~

Despina was being extremely quiet as the trio headed for the remains of the Stonekeep.

Marbrand glanced at her in concern. 'You've been quiet the past day or two. You alright?'

Despina squinted north, at the charred hill upon which the Emmetts' camp resided.

'Not really,' she muttered, rubbing her calf.

'Nightmares about those fools?'

'What fools?' she asked a little too quickly.

'The attackers. With the cutlasses.'

'Oh. Oh, yes, them,' she said in relief.

'They won't hurt anyone again. Old Lucky made sure of that.'

He patted the pommel at his side.

'You named your sword Lucky?' she asked in amusement.

'No, you don't name a sword,' he said in disdain. 'Doesn't make much difference to the blade. If it did, I'd name it Pointy. Here we are, not much further.'

Despina bit the inside of her lip. The dream from the Wastelands was still fresh in her mind, seeming less and less like a simple nightmare. The agony in her legs during her brief paralysis was too stark for a dream, not to mention the rest of it: she'd wandered in the pitch-black darkness for hours, unable to wake up or feel anything but the gravel beneath her feet until Marbrand shook her awake the next morning. She was half-convinced she wouldn't wake up ever, that she'd be trapped in the darkness forever.

And as for the two strangers...

She shuddered. She hoped she really wouldn't meet them again.

The horse halted with a snort, annoyed at the sudden stop.

'What is it?' she asked, craning her neck.

Marbrand didn't reply. He just stared to the right, where the church was, if she remembered rightly.

It wasn't there anymore. A burnt carcass of a building was all that remained of the church, and the smell lingering in the air told of an oil explosion.

They approached slowly, the horses kicking through pieces of debris.

'What happened here?' Elliot asked in horror.

'A fire must have hit the oil well in the cellars,' said Marbrand, gesturing towards the pit beneath the ruin. 'Blown the whole place to kingdom come.'

'Who did it?'

'Priest, probably,' he muttered. 'You know them and their candles. Not to mention their penchant for wine.'

Nah, it was me.

Despina flinched, the Bastard's voice echoing in her ear.

Total accident, I swear to you. But if he happens to make it up that hill, a few unpleasant situations might have to be less accidental.

Despina whimpered.

Marbrand swung to face her. 'What is it? You alright?'

'Um...'

He blinked repeatedly.

'No,' she blurted out. 'Emmett must have done this.'

Marbrand frowned. 'Emmett?'

'Well, yes,' she said in earnest. 'I mean, think about it, he's come from the other end of the world and been put in charge for the next twenty years. The clergy would want Prince Ronald back, being next in line, and what else would he do to make sure no one took away his only form of power?'

He blinked again. 'That may be so,' he said slowly. 'Quite the little politician, aren't you?'

The comment made her think of King Theo's similar observation. She shivered.

'We'd better get up to the camp and see if Ankovich knows anything about—'

'No!'

Marbrand turned again.

'He burned down a house of the gods,' she said rapidly, 'why would he stop at us? I don't want to be a black skid on the ground all because your friend wasn't as loyal as you thought.'

'She's got a point,' Elliot pointed out.

'And what about Ronald Horne?' he snapped. 'If he isn't safe with his strange wife anymore, then I want to know about it! I can't leave him to be killed, if that's Emmett's intention. I watched that boy grow up.'

'We'll take him away with us, then,' said Despina, desperate. 'Somewhere Emmett can't reach him.'

'No need for that.'

She turned, the two watchmen following her gaze.

A man stood by the stable a yard away, beside an old inn. An employee, by the looks of it – he had the usual attributes, grey hair, balding, flat cap. He brushed an old horse down slowly and deliberately as he spoke.

'I heard he was making for the Dead Lands, way off west. Off gallivanting with the Crey girl to get a dragon, according to the guests. Should be well out of reach by now.'

Marbrand and Elliot exchanged a doubtful glance.

'We can follow him,' Despina suggested. 'Make sure he isn't harmed. Then it won't matter who Emmett sends after him, because you and Pointy will be ahead of them.'

Marbrand pondered this, rolling a thumb over the top of Pointy's pommel.

'Sound's better than hanging around here,' he said finally, to Despina's relief. 'We'll need directions to the nearest port to the Dead Lands—'

'Maketon's the Dead Lands port,' she said quickly. 'I used to live there.'

'Hmm,' he said thoughtfully. 'So did I. Maketon it is. You'll have to refresh my memory on the directions, I haven't been there for twenty years.'

'Yes, alright,' she said, exhaling.

They headed northwest, around the hill bearing the camp of the infamous Mister Emmett. Despina looked behind her at the stableman to find King Theo dressed in his clothes instead, with a grin.

Somewhere in the back of her mind, she felt the Bastard smile amiably at her.

I can tell we're going to be the best of friends, he told her cheerfully.

PART TWO: WANDERLUST

I

Fifteen weeks later...

aptain Necker stood shivering outside the Creys' Keep in the wake of the slowest winter he'd ever met. The winters were getting lazier, he had decided. Spring was approaching fast, and the winter should have been retracting its icy grip and blunting its winds. Instead the winds were shaving Necker's face with a fury and the snow sucked at his boots as he paced the width of the keep entrance.

A messenger appeared with a visitor. Necker's eyes narrowed. It had been an eventful winter at the home of the Creys, all thanks to a great number of 'visitors' – all from the realm of the newly appointed King Regent, Gomez Emmett. It had all started with a letter.

Its contents were a mystery to all but the king's court – or at least the members Seth had blathered on to about it so many times they had it memorised. From Necker's recollection it went something like this:

Your Majesty, King Seth Crey of Adem,

I have received your letter stating your suggestion on the marriage of our kingdom's heirs. I am replying to the effect that we will be declining your offer for the following reasons.

Your forthcoming arrival has yet to make its gender apparent to the world. Betrothing our prince to a possible boy for the purpose of bearing future heirs to the throne would in my opinion prove... unwise.

Necker had laughed aloud when he learned Emmett had included the sarcastic pause in his letter. He laughed again now at the memory of Seth's reaction.

As for the option of betrothing it to my sister in the event of it being a boy, the notion is simply ridiculous. Felicity is not a dog. I will not whelp her as such.

Furthermore, your wife her highness Queen Cienne is a close relative of myself and Felicity. Our line is pure. We wish it to stay that way. On that note, the late Prince Vladimir was thought to have had relations with the mother of your child, and we simply cannot risk wedding the little prince to a possible bastard sister.

The look on Seth's face when he read that out! Necker had to stuff his fist in his mouth at the time. Everyone knew the dates were out on that possibility, slim as it may be, but it didn't stop Emmett sticking the boot in.

The last half of the letter was the cherry on the cake:

Another matter I wish to raise to you in this letter is the demise of our aforementioned friend, Prince Vladimir Horne. Information has come to light regarding unsettled debts between the houses Horne and Crey – amounting to the life of Vladimir Horne. It is in our best interests we have them settled before any... unpleasantness should arise.

Therefore, I wish to put to you a Peace Tax. This will be due quad-yearly in exchange for a dismissal of charges regarding your involvement with the prince's death. Failure to produce payment at any given time will result in a trial for regicide. Incidentally, your first payment of the Peace Tax is due right about... now-ish. We will inform you of your next bills as they are due.

Kind regards towards the health of you and your increasing family,
KR Gomez Emmett

The Peace Tax. It was the one pet hate of Seth Crey's that Necker could sympathise with. He wanted ten thousand pounds of silver four times a year to prevent him telling people Seth Crey had exploded the Stonekeep on purpose. If cash was particularly low at any time, a commodity of equivalent value would be cheerfully accepted.

So, Seth sent him ten thousand pounds of cow shit.

In apparent realisation that he had sent a patronising letter and got an equally shitty response back, Emmett reluctantly accepted this payment – and took out his exasperation on his small-folk by depriving them of the fertiliser.

Now Stoneguard's people had no winter supplies because of the inflated price Emmett had put on practically everything and the sudden, harsh winter quickly eradicated anything they had growing in any case.

And instead of taking the blame, Emmett pointed the finger at the Creys instead. The people of Stoneguard dutifully followed it... and had been arriving ever since.

Not that many of them survived the winter storms en-route, Necker mused. This one had barely averted the afterlife, he noticed as the latest unfortunate approached.

'Mister Halle, Captain, to see the king,' the runner announced.

'Got your forms?' said Necker idly.

'Forms?' the visitor repeated.

'You haven't got your forms, then?' Necker asked testily.

'Well, not exactly, no, but—'

'Welcome to Creys' palace, sir.'

'I thought I needed forms?' Mister Halle demanded.

'Forms from Gomez Emmett mean you're not welcome here, sir.'

'Oh, I see. Fair enough.'

Necker looked up to regard him properly. He stumbled backwards.

'You'll have to leave your dragon where he is, sir,' he stammered.

The dragon sniffled behind Mister Halle and glared at the clouds above them. It was a miniature, by the looks of it: the size of a horse, only with two wiry wings tucked behind its back and a hundred scales sticking out in the cold like the demonic equivalent of goose-bumps. The dragon cowered, shaking its shoulders from side to side. It clearly abhorred the cold.

'No problem there,' Halle said wearily.

His expensive clothes were burnt in places. A hole gaped out of the armpit of his jacket as he raised a hand to brush back his wind-tugged hair.

'If he wasn't flying in figure-of-eights throughout the journey, he was completely still and wouldn't move. Bloody thing. Went from a one-day journey to a fifteen-week death trip. Didn't have any spare clothes, either.'

'Shame,' Necker tutted. 'Still, so long as you've not come begging for anything, I suppose the king will see you. In you go.'

Halle inclined his head and headed into the castle.

Necker relaxed against one of the porch walls. He gazed at the dragon as the man's crunching footsteps receded. After a moment's consideration, he extracted a sausage he had just bought from the market and held it out to the dragon.

The beast surveyed it for a moment, and promptly sneezed on it.

Necker pulled apart the newly cooked meat in scrutiny.

'I need to get me one of these,' he muttered to himself.

~

Retribution Halle didn't have many talents, but making himself presentable to a king of the realm at short notice was a talent bordering on *sorcery*. In the time it took to be escorted into the throne room, he had transformed himself from a charred pauper into a freshly washed man of court – in appearances. He hoped the mingling smells of smoke and body odour didn't carry too far across a room.

Erstan Gould would be having a fit right about now. Halle was fifteen weeks behind schedule – *well*, thought Halle grouchily, *that will teach him for sending me on a faulty dragon.*

Suppose he thought he was clever, Halle went on detrimentally in his head, *being a big important member of Gomez Sr's council.* Before he was thrown out on his ear, that is. That was the main idea of the group: to 'give the bastard Emmett family what for'. Forget eradicating the corrupt small councils of the world and replacing them with a neater solution; let's bollocks everything up for everyone and start a war.

At least that was how their plan was coming together before Retribution Halle's magic tongue took power. That's what made Halle the perfect leader, in his own humble opinion – he had the right attitude. He could talk to people. *All* of the people, not just the bloodthirsty ones.

If he had a brain, Halle could talk a man into *anything*.

Keeping this in mind, he reached the front entrance of the keep as the doors were opened and entered the pleasantly heated throne room.

King Seth looked tired. Not for lack of effort: his fair hair, cut to an inch long in the current trend, shone like spun gold in the candlelight, and his emerald shirt was spotless beneath the regalia required of his title. It was his eyes – not only were they misty from a lack of sleep, they had aged. The litany of laments from Stoneguard's small-folk were taking their toll on him. Not to mention his troubles with his pregnant – and hugely volatile – wife.

Seth Crey's head jerked up at the sound of his arrival.

'For the last time,' he bellowed down the hall, 'I have *nothing to give you people!!*'

Behind him, beams of light from the weak winter sun rebounded from the gilded throne he sat upon. It gifted him the ethereal gleam of an angel, albeit a really annoyed one.

Halle quirked an eyebrow.

'Be that *as* it may,' he said, through thinly veiled sarcasm, 'I come only to ask for your ears.'

Seth Crey regarded Halle with a frown. 'Have you shown the captain your forms?'

'Oh, no, I didn't come with any,' he said brightly, raising his chin. 'I do not come with a problem, your majesty. I come with a solution.'

Seth's eyes narrowed. He scrutinised every inch of Halle from his carefully combed brown hair to his leather boots before swinging back up to his enlarged nostrils, probably to check if there was anything interesting inside.

Halle regarded Seth in turn calmly. Despite his clean-looking appearance, his shoulders drooped with fatigue. His close-set eyes were permanently narrowed at this stage. The iris of his right eye, once a clear cobalt blue like the left, was now turning to dark grey. Apparently, he'd lamed it with a smack to the head in battle. Halle's opinion leaned more towards the theory his wife had lamed it with a smack to the head during one of her 'episodes'.

'My name is Retribution Halle, esteemed member of the steadily expanding Democratic Republic,' he announced grandly. 'I come to you with a proposal to accept me as your Head of Council for the great kingdom of Adem.'

Seth blinked. 'Did you say your name was "Retribution"?'

'Yes, my liege. As an earnest advocate of the judicial system of the world, it has come to be a recognisable nickname.'

'And what's your real name?'

'Er… Huck, your majesty.'

Seth paused with a slight frown, mentally comparing each name in relation to the man standing before him.

'Yes,' he said, faltering, 'well, um, Retribution, I don't think we need a Head of Council—'

'Oh, I would recommend one, your majesty,' insisted Huck Halle. 'The current economic climate suggests that the monarchies of the world are struggling with the daunting task of fulfilling the needs of their countries. With distracting household feuds and inbreeding, royal leaders and noblemen are becoming more unsuitable for rule – not your fault, of course, not at all, merely human nature.'

Seth began to bristle from the word 'inbreeding'.

Halle failed to notice.

'What I suggest is that you appoint a number of able-bodied men to perform this task on your behalf, a governing body to rule the kingdom in your stead. Everyone's doing it these days, you know,' Halle said, speaking to the trendy haircut in particular. 'Yours is the only country not to avail of this offer as yet. The Democratic Party extends to across the globe. That means all countries will have their own governing body, all of us close friends, with each body led by trustworthy men guided by you and your counterparts. I happen to be given the task of tackling you, as it were.'

Along with all the other countries, he thought privately, but Seth wasn't going to know that.

'I suppose you'll be leading our "governing body", will you?' asked Seth in a dull voice.

'Only in the most technical sense,' he said. 'It will be a group effort at most, and all suggestions will be put to your majesty first.'

'And what will I be doing whilst you're governing my kingdom?'

'Spending valuable time with your growing family, my liege,' Halle said easily.

That'll soften the little git. It softened all the other little gits he'd gone to: it was his famous line. Even the King of Portabella had been convinced.

'Why, anyone can see you're tired of this gruelling predicament, and your wife must be missing you terribly.'

He waited patiently for Seth's response, his hands behind his back, smiling faintly.

A single deep crease formed in the middle of Seth's forehead, like a pen mark dividing his eyebrows. He nodded slowly, a muscle throbbing in his left cheek.

'So,' he said, 'you want me, the king, to put you and your friends in charge of my country while I what? Sit on my ass and watch my beautiful wife turn into my mother while my horrible children tear strips off each other to inherit the right to sit on *their* ass all day like a, like a—' His voice rose with every word until he stopped.

He sucked in a breath and calmly said, 'Right, er, Huck, listen to me. It might be true that this whole winter is wearing me down. Why wouldn't it? My wife's hormones are through the roof and I'm afraid of sleeping in the same bed as her – again. What's more, maybe the current affairs are hindering me from sleeping in any case, therefore making me, as you say, unfit for the job – not my fault, I know, only inbreeding—oh sorry, a misquote. Human nature, wasn't it?'

Halle reddened slightly.

'And maybe I would like to get, I dunno, five bloody seconds of sleep without someone pulling my back pocket off, yes. Maybe that is true.'

He glowered at the indifferent Mister Halle.

'But why on earth would I give my children's birth-right to a pompous vampire with women's clothing and a name that sounds like a tobacco spit? How stupid do you think I am? See, you came a generation too late, my friend. My father—in fact, no, not even him, my *grandfather* might possibly have accepted this offer, but I'm not interested. When I put this crown on my head, it was to do a job. If I want someone else to do it, I'll give it to my sister. Goodbye.'

Seth deflated, exhausted.

Halle's face did not change at all during Seth's speech and afterward he merely gave him a knowing smile. 'Ah, I see the strain on my liege's very heavy shoulders. May I present—'

'Do you have children?' Seth cut in.

'No, your majesty, in fact I do not—'

'Better make some then, before I have you neutered. Find a knocking shop somewhere and impregnate something. Preferably human.'

Halle blinked. 'I take it you're not interested in my proposal?'

Seth clapped sardonically.

'I see.' Halle spun on one heel, then spun back. 'If you should ever change your mind—'

'Jimmy, where's my scalpel?'

'Never mind, your majesty!' he squeaked, running away.

Seth sighed in relief.

Jimmy entered, scalpel in hand. 'You wanted to fix someone, sir?'

'No, I want to go to sleep. Is Cienne awake?'

'No idea, she's being largely avoided by the male population at present, sir.'

'Wise.' Seth rose from his throne.

'You're not going up there, are you?' Jimmy asked in alarm. 'I'm told it's certain death.'

'I only want to see her.' Seth swallowed. 'Preferably asleep.'

'Of course.'

Jimmy bowed to Seth, possibly for the first time in his career.

'It's been a pleasure working for you, sir.'

Seth shot him a look and headed for the spiral staircase.

His vision began to waver as his legs took him upstairs of their own accord. His head ached and he hadn't slept for days, but it had to be done, he supposed. He knew what she was like when she didn't get her way – he had a lazy eye to show for it already. Anyway, it might help him relax. Maybe.

He reached the top of the keep and entered his quarters. He crossed the peach-curtained drawing room and halted outside the bedroom, leaning a shoulder against the doorframe to gaze at his wife.

What he saw consisted of a huge mound of flesh covered in a sheet with a huge leather-bound book propped up on top. It was one of her distractions from the idea of her impending torture.

Seth had yet to distract himself from the ever-growing boulder of his own creation but nevertheless, he averted his mind from the thought and tried to concentrate on Cienne from the shoulders up.

Cienne gently placed her book aside.

'You finally managed to drag yourself away from the small-folk?' she asked in amusement. 'Better late than never.'

'Nngh.' *Thud.*

'Seth?'

Cienne sat up with difficulty, her arms wrapped around her belly.

He was face-down on the floor, snoring gently.

Cienne groaned aloud. She slumped back onto the pillows, arms folded, as Seth slept like a baby.

~

Meanwhile, approximately fifty-two hundred and fifty leagues away, two knights and their young squire hopped onto Portmyr under burning sunlight and sold their armour. They weren't going to need it anymore. The blacksmith who bought it noted briefly that their squire was a girl, but he didn't pay much attention to that. Any woman with half a brain travelled as a young boy or didn't travel at all and besides, armour was armour. So long as the stains inside it came from a stab wound and not a bleed of the nether regions, he was comfortable sticking to his own business.

Elliot sweated profusely beneath his light flannel shirt.

'My sunburn's giving me gyp again,' he complained, tugging the linen from his inflamed back with a wince. 'Can't we stop off at an apothecary and get something to put on it?'

'Nope,' Marbrand said brightly. 'The capital is at least two hundred and fifty leagues away, and we still need some form of transport. We need to save our pennies.'

'They only have camels over here,' Elliot said sulkily. 'I'll get stuck between the humps.'

'I'm pretty sure horses exist in this country as well,' Marbrand said in amusement.

'They have a breed that can survive two weeks at a time on a small cup of water,' Despina interjected. 'I read about them in a book. I also read some stuff about navigating in the desert.' She spotted Marbrand's searching gaze.

'My mother cleaned for a noble household. I got to read their books while she was working. Even nicked a few of them, when I could get away with it.'

'See? Got ourselves an expert,' Marbrand told Elliot. 'Nothing to worry about. And we're not even going anywhere near the desert yet.'

'Yet,' Elliot repeated.

They found a Truphorian man with a coach and hitched a lift on a cart of what turned out to be pickled turnips.

'The Ambassador likes turnips,' the coachman said, beaming with pride from the reins. 'Come up every week with his turnips and I always get a friendly hello. Likes 'em almost as much as our princess.'

'Lilly-Anna?' Marbrand asked, wrinkling his nose.

'Aye, he's had his eye on her since she hit puberty,' the man said, guiding the horses over the winding sandstone cobbles of Portmyr. 'Disgusting, I think personally, grooming a child that way. I'd be stoned in the street if I was marrying a girl a third my age. Just goes to show. You can get away with anything if you're a nob.'

'She's marrying him, is it?'

'So they've been saying at the ports. Be a few months before she arrives, what with going around the Wastelands and all.'

They nodded in agreement. You didn't have to come from Truphoria to know about avoiding Qattren's ghosts.

'Any idea when this wedding is set for?' Marbrand said.

'He's holding the arrangements until her highness gets here,' the man answered. His nose wrinkled. 'Has this funny idea that a wedding is for the bride to arrange. He clearly don't know much about our Lilly-Anna Crey.'

'It's going to be a disaster, then,' Elliot said.

'Most definitely,' the man confirmed.

Despina let her gaze wander as the men progressed to small talk. It was beginning to seem like the Dead Lands was living up to the nickname – there wasn't so much as a tree to be seen amongst the sandstone covering… well, everything.

Everywhere as far as the eye could see consisted of sandstone pavement or wall, with a scattering of scrawny people walking around them in the unrelenting heat. An optimistic housekeeper had placed flowers in hanging pots outside their front door – only for them to wilt into dried husks. She now saw why all the country's gold produce was spent on Truphorian foodstuffs. They couldn't grow anything here if they tried.

They're thralls to the heat, she thought.

Amongst the sparse crowd, someone's gaze met hers. She held it in horror.

The Bastard.

'Everyone in the shade today?' Marbrand said to the turnip man.

'If they have any sense,' he said with a weary nod. 'Not that many people hang around in these parts, anyway. They're usually in the Church of Fiery

Repent. It doesn't matter how hot the weather gets, the church still gets drafty and cold. D'you still get that back home?'

'Mostly in winter,' Marbrand said reproachfully.

She thought he'd looked pale for a local. The Bastard gave Despina a friendly smile and pointed down an alley, towards a person in a blue shawl.

Fetch, he mouthed.

Despina shook Marbrand's arm as the coachman waffled on.

'... say they have a wind machine in there, but I just think all churches attract an ominous cold wind—'

'What does Prince Ronald look like?' Despina cut in.

'Short black hair, brown eyes, fair complexion,' Marbrand said promptly. 'Though he's probably pinker in this heat, he always burned easily in the sun. Also favours the colour blue. Why?'

'Because I've just seen a figure with short black hair pull a blue scarf over their head and go that way,' she said, pointing down the alley in question.

'Are you sure?' Elliot said. 'I didn't see anything.'

She gave him a penetrating stare.

He paused, looking a bit dazed.

'Then again, I might have,' he backtracked with sudden conviction.

'He must have come by dragon, with Lilly,' said Marbrand. 'We'll have to postpone that lift, my man.'

'I come by every Sunday, don't hesitate to reschedule,' he said, tipping his cap.

They hopped off into the yellow-gold cobbles and sprinted after Ron.

Despina shot the Bastard a quick glance.

He gave her a thumbs-up before dematerialising.

Down the alley, a dishevelled Aaliyaa Horne held her shawl around her closely with her left hand. A small terrier hopped into the right and she vanished into a cloud of sand.

Marbrand, Elliot and Despina ran into a dead end in confusion.

'Where did he go?' Elliot wheezed, clutching his chest. 'Ron was right here!'

Marbrand took a step forward, kneeling.

'Not Ron,' he muttered, lifting a thimble-sized doll from the ground. 'Aaliyaa.'

~

II

Lilly gazed onto the horizon pensively.

There was still a good seven weeks or so to go on her voyage. According to her maps – however, she reckoned this particular ship would take at least twenty more than the average ship.

Despite the reason for this delay, she was bored.

A man on the main deck was performing sleight-of-hand tricks for some lady passengers from Maketon. The women were more impressed by the boyishly handsome performer's charisma rather than his rather bad tricks, but Lilly wasn't interested in either.

She was more interested in someone far less interesting some distance away – and she couldn't fathom why.

That moment in the cornfield returned in clarity: her administering the scorpion antidote, Orl shaking the paralysis from his legs, and then that other moment... Lilly's first one of those. That didn't require payment upfront, anyway.

She didn't know why she had kissed him. Ever since she had turned thirteen, all she had thought about was girls. Not the fluffy kind her mother tried to make her befriend in the palace, she never got along with any of them; except for Jimmy's cousin Katalina who had visited from the Far Isles to show off her extremely nimble 'needlework skills'. She figured at the age of twenty-four, she finally had her preferences figured out: it involved whores, the more of them the better.

Telling her that he was in love with her didn't suddenly turn Orl into a half a dozen whores. She never liked to break a boy's heart... although it hadn't been bad for a first try with a male. Yes, that's what it was: just a first try. It's not like it was true love or anything silly like that...

She overheard the magician behind her pronouncing that the vanishing coin...

'... has reappeared!' he exclaimed, flicking the coin from a lady's ear.

The girl twittered happily.

Silas Beult was quite good-looking for a commoner, she supposed. Lilly examined him with a critical eye. Nah. With his dirty blond hair and penetrating blue eyes, Lilly couldn't bring herself to fancy him. He was a shorter, older version of Seth – only Seth didn't have crippling charisma, just a crippled eyeball.

She watched Si lead one of his twits below decks – to show her some more tricks, she thought cynically. She descended to the bowels herself and made for the opposite direction, heading for the cabin reserved for her and her companions.

Ron and an anonymous crew-member sat around some kind of board game as Lilly entered.

'Where's Stan got to?'

Ron shrugged. 'Don't know. Haven't seen him since this morning.' He tore himself away from the game with a fretful frown. 'He's been acting funny since he got on the ship. I'm a bit worried about him.'

Lilly was a bit worried about him too.

The weather had gone from a blistering cold to boiling point as they caught up with the summer, yet every morning, without fail, Stan climbed to the crow's nest and *glared* at the sea behind him like it was his arch nemesis. After about noon-ish, he'd climb back down below decks and curl up in a corner, feverishly convincing himself that he was on land.

Lilly entertained the notion that he might have seasickness in the brain, but Captain Sot suspected something much worse.

'There's a legend,' he whispered one night, in the warped Truphorian accent of a man longer at sea than at land, 'about a pirate witch: a siren who haunts the ships going this route and sends the crew leaping overboard in a mad rage. She makes one crewman increasingly mad to spread her legend in warning... and then she kills them all!'

'That why we never heard of the pirate witch before?' asked the quartermaster, Si's brother Tully. 'Or are you just making it up like you always are?'

'Maybe,' the captain said mysteriously, handing around a bottle of port.

Lilly had interrupted him by slapping Ron's hand away from the bottle.

Sot swung his gaze at her, almost accusing. 'Or maybe she got your brother, tole him she were coming and scared the wits from him.'

Lilly reckoned Tully's theory was more correct, but there was no telling Captain Sot that. He was too superstitious for his own good.

Lilly left Ron to his game to search for Stan – and inadvertently entered the wrong cabin.

'OI!' Si yelled, yanking the covers over himself.

'Sorry!' Lilly said loudly, turning her head away. 'Seen Stan anywhere?'

'No! Funnily enough, I've been busy!'

'Sorry. I'll just leave.'

'Thank you!'

She shut the door firmly behind her. As an afterthought, she took a scrap of paper and a pencil stub from her pocket.

'I'll just make sure you aren't disturbed in future!' she called through the door.

'Fine, just bugger off!'

She tacked her notice to the cabin door. Thinking of the illiterate, she drew a diagram to accompany it.

A sharp wind blew from the east, making Lilly wince. Occasionally a winter gust would intrude on the hot ocean air. Any other time it would be a welcome relief, but they were a bit sharper this year. Lilly shook it off and scoured the upper decks for her merchant brother – per the story put to the pirates.

She hadn't expected to actually find a ship when she, Stan and Ron roamed the untouched terrain of the Forest, hoping to find a trading vessel passing the coast to the east. They hadn't even gotten halfway. A pirate ship had made port by a low cliff of the Forest and the crew were scattered around the Forest in the welcoming arms of its inhabitants – mostly.

'I prefer humans. Seems a shame to put my gift of seduction to waste,' Si had said – after he had relieved himself on Lilly's jerkin as she passed through the undergrowth.

After coughing up a 'stolen' bag of silver coins to the captain and crew, Lilly 'Crowe' was welcomed to join their exhibition down the import route to the Dead Lands, along with her brothers, Stanold and Ronley.

She expected the trip to be littered with keel-hauling and cat-o'-nine-tailing, but strangely, when a ship did come their way, they quietly snuck around it.

'Coming the wrong way, innit,' Captain Sot had explained. 'We want the ones coming up behind, from Truphoria. The one with all the goods.'

'So why come out this far?'

He didn't reply to that.

After a stroll around the decks, Stan was still nowhere to be seen. Lilly descended back downstairs to the sound of laughter from below.

'That's a pretty good likeness, for a sketch!'

One man laughed, waving Lilly's diagram in the air.

Lilly stifled a giggle.

Si emerged, fully dressed this time, and snatched the drawing from the disembodied hand.

'What the hell is this?'

Lilly laughed aloud.

'I'll have you for this, you little scrubber!' Si yelled over the heads of the crew.

'Oi, I scrub for no one!' Lilly called back as the crowd parted.

She strode up to him and admired the diagram a moment before shooting Si with what she called the Seth grin. 'Actually, it does look like you, doesn't it?'

She scampered upstairs as Si balled up the drawing and threw it at her.

Chuckling, she boarded the main deck as Captain Sot approached.

'What are the crew doing?'

'Admiring some artwork of mine,' Lilly answered with a grin. 'Why?'

'Two things, primarily,' he said, dripping with sarcasm. 'One, your brother just tried to keel-haul himself beneath the ship—'

Lilly's grin sloughed away.

'Oh God, he really is unwell, isn't he?' she said with dread, holding a hand to her temple.

'Two,' he cut in sharply, 'the three of you have led the Pirate Witch onto our ship!'

'Pirate Witch?' she asked wryly, thinking he'd finally lost his mind.

Then she followed his finger.

Qattren hovered outside the rail of the ship, Stan hanging limply in her arms.

~

Marbrand paced in front of Elliot and Despina.

'She's after someone,' he mused, his hands behind his back. 'There's no other reason she'd be caught dead over here.'

'Think she followed us?' Elliot asked.

'Without drawing attention to herself? Not her style.' He fiddled with the doll's skirt idly.

The town square bustled with activity – as far as a Dead Lands street did with eight people roaming the streets at a time. Marbrand was increasingly wary of any onlookers getting a good look at them, but there was no helping that. The entire country was practically empty.

'Did she use sorcery?' Despina asked. 'I didn't know she could actually do that.'

'A rumour, but a true one,' he informed her. 'Seen it happen all the time when I worked in the Stonekeep. She's no real sorceress, though. She uses spell books and the like, stuff that interferes with people's heads and moves objects around. Parlour tricks, mostly. Real magic can change time and space and even then, only the best can harness less than ten per cent of that power.'

And only in Sal'plae, she added, but didn't dare say it aloud.

She instead gazed at the inch-long rag doll between Marbrand's thumb and forefinger. It looked a bit like her mother.

'So who's she come to mess with?' Elliot wondered. 'That doll's obviously to do someone a mischief.'

Marbrand muttered his agreement, tickling a tiny nose with his little finger.

Despina scratched her own nose absentmindedly.

'She's religious, isn't she?' she said. 'What if she saw the church explode and wanted revenge?'

'She wouldn't come here if Emmett did it,' Elliot pointed out.

'Unless she came here for help,' Despina said. 'This place is known for sorcerers, maybe she has contacts.'

Marbrand nodded slowly. He pinched its nose pensively.

'OW!'

The men glanced at Despina.

She held her nose in one hand.

'Did this hurt?' Marbrand asked, pinching the nose again.

'Ow! Yes!'

The trio frowned at each other, then at the doll.

Despina gulped. Marbrand noticed.

'Did anything happen before you arrived at Castlefoot Market?'

'No,' she replied in a small voice.

'Anything at all?'

She looked him in the eye.

'No,' she said firmly.

His face went blank for a moment. He glanced at the doll, as if wondering how it had gotten into his hand in the first place.

'You best take this,' he said, handing it to her.

Elliot studied him. 'What you thinking?'

He paused a moment. 'I'm thinking she wants to scare us away,' he said. 'She saw us approach and knocked that up,' he jerked a thumb at the doll in Despina's hand, 'to hurt Despina and make us leave. Then she dropped it when she saw us coming for her.'

'You sure it was an accident?' Despina asked.

Marbrand frowned in thought for a moment.

'No,' he said finally. 'But you don't go to that much trouble to drop it at your enemy's feet.' He looked unsure.

Elliot studied him some more.

'Do you think she's sending us a warning? "Come near me and I'll hurt you for real" kind of thing?'

'I don't know,' said Marbrand. He blinked and looked at Despina. 'You said she might have contacts. Any idea where?'

'You got a map?'

He pulled a battered roll from their bag.

Dotted around the coast were the ports and cities, but seven dots were filled in completely in black.

'These are the ancient cities,' Despina explained. 'The Dead Cities. Or Metropolis, if you want to be fancy about it.'

'I thought there were eight of them?' Elliot asked.

'One of them was never found,' she said. 'It's in the desert somewhere, according to legend. There are records that show it definitely existed, but nobody can figure out where it is. They were deserted eons ago for superstitious reasons.'

'Ruins?'

'Not necessarily,' Marbrand piped up. 'Part of the reason this country is barely scraping by is because their good supplies came from and went into these cities. After the empire went to pot, they were too superstitious to live in them again – or even stick around long enough to tear them down. The places are deserted – even the Ambassador wouldn't dare enter them, and hasn't, ever since he came into power. Any group of looneys could survive for an age in them – prosper, even. All without the Ambassador knowing. He might look like an intelligent fellow by all accounts, but he's superstitious as all get out – won't even take the emperor's titles, he's so bad. They all are, here.'

'So we're going to all of them,' Elliot said in dread. 'We'll never make it in these conditions. They're all over the map.'

'We'll need proper transport, yes,' Marbrand agreed. 'Something fast.'

Despina read his mind. 'Dragon?'

'Dragon.'

'Dragon?' Elliot wailed. 'I'll never stay on one of them!'

'Why not?'

'I don't think I need to supply you with a verbal description,' he said cynically, gesturing down at his ample frame.

Marbrand snorted flippantly. 'They won't have time to worry about that, they cruise at a hundred miles an hour. We'll be there before it has time to sprain its back.'

'We still have approximately six hundred leagues to the sanctuary,' Despina reminded him.

'We'll order one,' he said cheerfully. 'Send a carrier bird, have one delivered by Friday. Be at the first city by evening.'

'Sounds too easy,' Elliot said. 'What if it cooks us?'

'Only dragons fit for riding are males,' he explained. 'They don't flame.'

Despina frowned. 'Are you sure?'

'Yeah, it's a menstruation thing. Females have it to protect their young, males just flap about like headless chickens. So we saddle 'em.'

Despina gave him a frown that indicated she had read otherwise, but he seemed insistent on ignoring it.

'What, they hire them out like horses?' asked Elliot.

'They'd have to. They can't ride camels everywhere, they're too slow. We just need to find a rookery or something: they're bound to have one somewhere. Leave it to me: we'll be witch hunting by the end of the week at the latest.'

He later hired a return pigeon at a very 'reasonable' two silvers a hundred leagues, which Marbrand reluctantly paid. As they slept in an airy hostel, in the one room that was all they could afford, Despina slept fitfully.

The Bastard was niggling at her again.

She awoke for the fifth time, rubbing sleep from her eyes.

A faint purple glow floated across the room.

She snapped her eyes wide open and watched as the glow descended on her two friends.

She stared as purple hands lifted a tuft of hair from each of their heads and cut it with the side of one palm, like a knife.

Then the hands and the hair disappeared.

Despina blinked in the darkness as a cold draft skimmed her face.

Aaliyaa was making dolls. She was sure of it.

So why did she leave behind hers?

~

III

95

Footsteps pounded through the bowels of the *Devourer* as the entire crew vacated to the upper decks. All except for Ron, who stayed exactly where he was.

Hovering inside his cabin door, which was open a crack, Ron peered out at the dissipating crowd. Keeping an ear on Sot's yelling to make sure it was nothing to do with him, Ron scanned once more for crew members before sliding out of his cabin.

Lilly and Stan had made great pains early in the voyage to point out that if Ronley Crowe swallowed so much as a mouthful of alcohol, he would die. They didn't specify that the death would be caused by his sorcerous wife, but with the ship's deficit of booze in any case, Captain Sot was happy to keep an eye on Ron's wellbeing.

However, Ron hadn't had a drink in fifteen weeks. And orange juice just didn't bloody cut it.

He made a beeline down the length of the ship, to a storage cupboard door. A portrait of Ron was tacked to the centre with a thick 'X' scrawled through it. It turned out that Lilly Crey was a spectacularly good caricaturist.

He glanced around once more before triumphantly swinging the door wide open.

Bottle upon bottle of amber liquid rolled out at his feet, followed shortly by barrels of wine and Ron's personal supply of the dreaded orange juice.

Ron grinned at the amber liquid. It was his favourite colour.

He lifted a bottle with a wide base and pulled the cork off with a pop. He was about to take a long gulp when something occurred to him.

Something about it was missing.

He stuck his nose in the rim.

'Bugger!'

It was apple juice. *Fresh* apple juice.

He rammed the cork back on and tasted a few more bottles. Juice. Juice. Juice. Ron nearly threw up after one bottle – cooking oil.

He tossed that bottle aside. That was when he noticed the barrels at the back were padlocked at the tap.

'Dammit!' he shrieked in fury.

～

Outside, two crewmen grabbed Stan under the armpits and hauled him on the deck.

Out of nowhere, Si appeared out of the nosy throng of crew-mates and grabbed Qattren by her hair as she stepped down from the rail.

'Who are you?' he demanded. 'Speak up!'

'Queen Qattren Meriangue, guardian of the Faerie Forest,' she promptly replied. 'I've come to speak to Ronley Crowe.'

'Bollocks,' he snarled. 'The Faerie Queen has blue hair. Everyone knows that.'

'No, red hair, blue fire,' Qattren corrected. 'Common mistake.'

'She's telling the truth,' Lilly clarified. 'We've met before.'

The captain glared at Qattren from the safety of a wide recoil.

'What were you doing with that man?'

'Rescuing him,' she said shortly. 'He leapt overboard in a fit of madness caused by a siren—'

'Bollocks,' Si cut in.

'I say you lured him overboard, witch,' the captain snarled in agreement.

'You would be wrong, then,' she said. 'If anything, I lured him back on board. And I'm no witch.'

'Aye, that's what a pirate witch would say!' he snapped. 'Pirate witches float on water, don't they? So what were you doing? Standing on a dolphin?'

The crew chuckled.

'Yes,' she said plainly.

The laughter tapered off.

'And I'm not a witch, I'm a sorceress,' she said. 'A witch would kill you immediately. Sorceresses can afford to be subtle.'

'Thought a sorceress was a witch?' someone muttered.

'It is! The pirate witch is a liar!' the captain roared. 'Take her to the brig and have her guarded day and night!'

Ron emerged from below decks, saw his wife and shuffled backwards out of sight without missing a heartbeat.

'I say burn her!' a man piped up.

'And quick, before she has us all!' another piped up.

'Good idea. Let's get on with it, shall we?' Qattren said with impatience.

'After you've just been swimming? You'd like that, wouldn't you?' snarled the captain. 'Pirate witches get power from water! We'll burn her tomorrow!'

Si pushed her ahead of him to the stairs.

'Captain, you're making a mistake,' Lilly said, following him to the helm as the crew and their prisoner descended to the bowels of the ship. 'I've met this woman before. She really is the queen.'

'Aye, and I'm the Creys' navy commander.'

'Please, captain, there's no point locking her in the brig, she'll just escape!'

'Oh no she won't,' he said. 'Our brigs a little more than iron bars, my love. Our *Devourer* is a cross-realmer.' He beamed proudly.

'A what?'

'Cross-realmer.' Sot frowned in annoyance. 'All witches and wizards and whatnot get their magic from Limbo. You know, Dreamworld, where you go after you die and that. This beauty is specially built to harness Limbo powers and travel between this world and that one at will. Using her magic to escape won't work because once she gets to Magicland, she's trapped there too in the same cell in the same boat, 'cept that we can't see her.'

97

Lilly acknowledged the final remark with a sceptical frown.

'Till she realises she's stuck and comes back, obviously,' he added.

The sceptical look remained.

'You mean this ship,' she said dully, 'this *very* ship beneath out feet, can travel to a realm that stops time and allows instantaneous travel and you *haven't done this earlier?*'

'Well, we dunno how,' he admitted sheepishly, 'you need a sorcerer to go to Limbo with. We just use the brig, 'cause she can't get out. It's still a state-of-the-art vessel for a pirate ship,' he insisted.

'So why've I never heard of you before if you're talented enough to steal such a state-of-the-art ship?'

He gulped. 'Couldn't tell you.'

Lilly gave him a dubious look.

Si emerged from below decks, flicking a key into the air and catching it.

'The witch is dealt with. She sends a last request, captain.'

'If it's a bath, tell her she can shag off. I ain't a complete twat.'

Si chose not to comment, but Lilly could see his opinion on that statement clearly in his eyes.

'Actually, she just wants a hairbrush, captain.'

Sot's heavy brow buckled into an impressive frown. 'A what?'

'Hairbrush. Bristly thing with a handle, you may have heard of it,' he added cynically. 'She established the brig was impenetrable and wants her hair pretty for her burning tomorrow.'

Sot looked at him blankly. 'Do I look like I have a hairbrush?'

'I have one.'

Si watched in amazement as Lilly-Anna 'Rats' Tails' Crey produced a hairbrush from her hip bag.

'Have you ever used this?' he asked in disbelief.

'No, but every woman owns a hairbrush on the principle that the day they lose it is the day they'll need one. Besides, it makes a handy throwing weapon and I keep the bristles nice and sharp.'

She thrust the brush at Si, who recoiled.

'Tell her I want it back.'

'So long as you don't start a mutiny with it,' Si said with a smile, accepting the weapon of mass destruction with an impressed expression.

Lilly left them to it and faced Stan.

He finally managed to sit up against the mast, she was pleased to see, and had been strategically placed facing away from the sea as he stared into space in a trance.

'You alright, you lug?' she asked jovially, crouching at his side.

He planted a hand across her face and shoved her onto her backside.

'Go away,' he slurred. 'I don't want to have sex with you now, or ever.'

Lilly lifted an eyebrow.

'Ha, ha,' she sneered, 'high-larious. The idea that the feeling might be mutual doesn't seem to occur to you, does it?'

She pushed herself upright with a sigh as he stared into space some more.

'Stan, can you tell me why you tried to keel-haul yourself?'

A glob of saliva soaring at Lilly's chin acted as a resounding 'no'.

Lilly sighed and retreated against the rail.

Below them, Ron stood in front of Qattren for the first time since he'd fled the Forest, thankfully with six safe bars between them.

'What took you, then?' he asked tiredly.

Qattren looked up innocently, her borrowed hairbrush making its rounds through her copper ringlets.

'Sorry, dear?'

'Come on,' he said. 'Does it really take a woman with the power of a sorcerous realm at her disposal fifteen weeks to find three people?'

'Ordinarily, no,' she said. 'This is no ordinary ship you've stumbled onto.'

'No, they've managed to lock you up. Can't you get out?'

'No,' she said. 'I also had difficulty finding it in Sal'plae. I had to scan the waters in this realm instead – frightening a lot of sea creatures in the process. It appears that these pirates have managed to acquire a fully functional Imperial.'

'A which?'

'A magic ship. From your family-in-law.'

Ron's eyes widened. 'People are after me, then?'

She nodded. 'Lots of people,' she confirmed, 'and none of them as friendly as little old me. As for this crew...'

Si lurked in the shadows some yards away as the two talked. Silently, he eavesdropped.

Once their conversation had tapered to a close, Ron nodded silently at an unspoken command from Qattren and made his leave.

Si caught him on the stairs, a firm hand on his shoulder.

'Now, Ronley,' he said with emphasis. 'That part about the crew? That won't be repeated. Understand?'

'Why?'

'If you don't understand,' he said in his ear, holding a small blade to his throat, 'there might have to be some... unpleasant situations. That's why.'

Ron gulped and nodded.

'Now, I suggest you head above decks and tell your friends about the people after you,' Si continued.

Ron nodded hastily.

'And the captain of this ship?' Si prompted.

'Didn't hear a thing about him.'

'Good man.' He relinquished Ron and patted his head.

Lilly saw Ron approach at a swift pace from below decks, his face pale and strained, clutching his throat with one hand.

'You alright?' she asked in concern.

He shook his head. 'I've just spoken to Qattren. Gomez Emmett's looking for me… and so's my mother.'

~

A man jogged across Portmyr at a brisk pace, panting heavily.

'Ah, you're the dragon handler, I take it?' Marbrand asked, leaning on the doorframe of the inn.

'Not for long, I'm resigning,' he gasped. 'The thing's gone out of control! He's your problem now!'

Marbrand bolted upright. 'Where is he?'

He nodded for him to follow.

Meanwhile, Elliot packed their belongings away as Despina sat in one corner, staring at her thumb-sized impression.

'Need a hand?' she asked distantly.

'Nearly done,' Elliot said cheerfully. 'Can you manage those ones?'

'Yeah, course,' she murmured, lifting two bags onto her shoulders.

'Best put that somewhere safe,' he added, nodding at the doll. 'Don't want anyone sitting on you, do you?'

Despina eyed it lying abandoned on the chair.

'You're right,' she said, putting it safely in her shirt pocket.

In the centre of the town, screams erupted as a giant black dragon roared deafeningly. The square was choked in thick smog.

'I thought males couldn't breathe fire?' Marbrand shouted, waving the smoke from his eyes.

'Who the hell told you that?' the handler yelled back. 'All dragons breathe fire!'

'But it's a menstruation thing, isn't it?'

'What? I've never heard that in my life! Everyone knows it's flammable stomach acids! What kind of male dragon doesn't flame? Males are famous for it!'

'So why'd you lend him to me?!' he screamed.

'Wanted rid of him, innit? Anyway, you said you wanted a big one!'

'Did you notice,' Despina asked slowly to Elliot on the other end of the street, 'anything unusual last night?'

'Like what?'

'GIVE ME THE REINS!' yelled Marbrand.

'Funny lights, strange noises,' Despina said with a feigned shrug of indifference. 'I might have been dreaming.'

'What?' the handler yelled.

'REINS! QUICKLY!'

'Nope,' said Elliot. 'Didn't notice a thing.'

'Oh. Because I thought I saw—'

A fireball interrupted them.

Marbrand swore and somersaulted into an alley as the square was consumed in a rolling plume of flame.

'Is that the dragon?' Despina asked in alarm.

'Marbrand had better hope not. He's just gone up there.'

They paused for a millisecond before sprinting towards the flames.

Marbrand sprinted to the blacksmith at the other end of the square. Swiping a shield from their stall on the way, he strapped it to his left forearm and shuffled to the dragon in a crouched position, reins in hand.

The dragon flattened his neck to the ground, searching for Marbrand.

Marbrand took his chance. He unsheathed his sword and sprinted for the massive snout at high speed.

Despina and Elliot were halfway to the square when the beast's head reared up, throwing a man into the sky by a set of reins.

Snout pointed vertically, still steaming, the dragon opened its jaws, waiting.

'Oh bollocks,' swore Elliot, skidding to a halt.

The jaws snapped shut, trapping Marbrand inside.

~

IV

The royal dragon feeder tugged a ton of feed across the grounds in disgruntlement.

When he found Lyseria's nest to be empty, he released the bag, cursing.

She'd gone hunting again.

He honestly didn't know why he had been hired. Whenever the thing needed feeding, he had to drag a ton of raw meat across the grounds to her nest at the back wall and by the time he got there, she'd either be sitting there chewing on a griffin or missing completely. It was the most pointless job in the world.

But it paid well, he convinced himself unconvincingly.

He dumped the bag in her nest and stalked off as, fifty feet above him, Retribution Halle sailed over the clouds on Lyseria's back, grinning.

It had been so easy. People often told of Lyseria's impatient temperament, but one look at the griffin had set the beast's mouth to watering so much that her only alternative to flying around the world for a complete stranger was to drown in her own dribble.

He lay on top of his folded arms and relaxed as Adem slid past beneath him. He hadn't gained control of Truphoria yet, but no matter; that was just one country. All he had to do was sit back as Lyseria outran the winter and reached his new home.

Assuming it was still where he had left it…

~

Ron's cabin door opened in the dead of night. Making sure that Stan and Lilly were fully unconscious, Ron's head slipped through the half-open door.

He screamed and clapped a hand over his face.

Lilly stood inches from the door, her hands on her hips.

'Qattren spoke to you, didn't she?' Ron said.

'I knew what you were doing,' Lilly growled. 'You left the broken lock-picking equipment by the door. Did you really think we were stupid enough to believe banning you from the cupboard would keep you away?'

'I'm getting very good with my alcoholism,' he argued.

'No, you're not! You've been trying to bust the locks on those wine barrels for the past week!'

Ron glowered.

Lilly exhaled, her arms folded. 'Go on, back to bed with you.'

Ron's gaze shifted from her to the cupboard.

He scarcely had a chance to bolt for it when Lilly's fist connected sharply with the otherwise untouched section of his lower anatomy.

'Go on,' she said firmly. 'Back to bed with you, I said.'

Ron exhaled with a squeak and limped back to his bunk, Lilly assisting via his armpits.

~

On the south edge of the desert, Royston Joyce, sub-leader of the Democratic Party, scanned the clear blue sky with his hands on his hips. His fine blue leotard gleamed in the sun, each gold-embroidered stitch glimmering.

'Don't tell me he's vanished as well!' he said sharply to a new recruit, who flinched in reply.

Sand dunes surrounded the mile-by-mile-wide farm as Royston stood in his office on a hill overlooking the entire complex. The room was made of bare ply board and decorated with a table and one single chair, but it also had a massive window out of which Royston glared at the horizon, his fair shoulder-length hair slightly singed at the ends.

The dragon farm was the Party's worst idea since Erstan Gould. (Because he was foreign, in Royston's opinion. Royston had a thing against Portabellans ever since his first and third wives each vanished with a member of King Fleurelle's court – not to mention the second one, who had run off with one of Fleurelle's nieces.) Sure, every bad idea has its pros: having swift transport at easy disposal was useful for travelling the world in search of land to conquer, and the farm's location was handy for getting to Copers.

Royston had never liked the city – Serpus was associated with bad luck merely due to its name meaning 'serpent', so why would it be a good idea to live in an anagram of the word 'corpse'? – but that aside, the farm was badly equipped. New acolytes with little to no experience with dragons had been placed in charge of the animals, and their already small number was dwindling by the day.

What dragons Erstan wasn't handing out left right and centre were escaping every week, and with no breeding plan set up, 'zero' was going to become an accurate description of the collection at large.

Royston had visited Ambassador Uxpolisin's sanctuary once. Their attempt was a midget copy – the pens were so tiny, the beasts curled miserably between the mesh walls, their confinements so tiny their rib cages had snapped from the pressure and punctured their internal organs. And they had been left like that, the acolytes too afraid for their own safety to assist in the welfare of their charges. Many of their finer beasts had died.

And to make matters worse, prominent members of the Party were disappearing. Most of them from under his very nose.

Royston slammed a hand on the windowsill, making the recruit jump again.

'I can't put up with this nonsense,' he growled. He grasped the boy's arm. 'If Retribution Halle returns, send him to Copers. I'll be there, looking for the rest of the Party.'

He clapped a hand on the lad's shoulder and turned his gaze to the desert stretching out in front of him.

∼

Captain Sot stared behind his ship worriedly.

Si was by his side, following his gaze.

'That's a good trading galley coming up behind,' he pointed out needlessly.

'Aye, I see it,' the captain said levelly.

Si waited patiently. 'We gonna turn and meet her?'

'Not yet, no.'

'You've chickened out again, haven't you?' Si said dully.

'Chickened out? What do you mean, chickened out?'

'We haven't attacked a single ship on this voyage!' Si pointed out hotly. 'Not a single one! We're supposed to be pirates, for Christs' sake!'

'I don't want to scratch the ship,' Sot said defiantly.

'Don't want to scratch—that's what it's bloody for!' Si exclaimed, throwing his hands into the air.

'It's a state of the art,' he said stiffly, 'one of a kind—'

'There's an imperial fleet's worth of them.'

'—high-tech ship—'

'Then it won't mind a bit of a bump, will it?' he said testily. 'If it's that state of the art, it can outrun her. Go on, ram her.'

'What? No!' he squeaked in horror.

'Chicken!' Si barked.

Above them, something red streaked through the clouds as Lyseria made a beeline for Copers. The two didn't notice.

'I ain't a chicken,' the captain said sharply.

'You are! If I'd known I'd pulled a chicken from the remains of that dragon attack, Sam Sot, I wouldn't have let you become captain!'

Sam's mouth twisted sulkily in reply.

Si sighed. 'We need to attack that ship sometime today,' he reminded the captain. 'We can't burn the witch on our ship, not if it's "state of the art".'

Sam pursed his lips. 'But you know we ain't no good at it!'

'They don't!' he pointed out. 'And the girl's beginning to suss something's up anyway, so if we don't make some kind of attempt—'

'But we ain't real pi—'

Si slapped a hand over Sot's mouth with an emphatic 'Shush!'.

Lilly approached from behind them, watching the incoming ship apprehensively.

'What d'you think of that ship?' Si asked her casually.

Lilly regarded it pensively. 'Should burn the witch up nicely,' she said finally. 'Are we gonna take it?'

Si waited for the captain to reply before realising his hand was still across Sam's face.

He removed it sheepishly under Lilly's questioning glare.

'Um... no,' Sot replied after a pause.

Si groaned.

'You've chickened out again, haven't you?' Lilly said dully.

'No I have not, stop saying that!' the captain snapped. 'I am merely...' He flapped his hands. 'Waiting for her to come to us so's we can attack from close quarters.'

'You said that the last twenty times,' Lilly said, rolling her eyes.

'Told you you were a chicken,' Si said.

'I am not a chicken! You know what, fine! You!' he snapped, pointing at an artillery man eating his lunch on the deck. 'Prepare the archers and the cannons to fire as soon as I give the word! And make them flaming arrows! Come on, sharply now, we have a prize waiting for us!'

The man, choking briefly on a bit of cheese, scrambled to his feet.

'You get your brothers and be ready to jump aboard,' he ordered Lilly. 'Si, give the girl some weapons. And find them other lazy sods! We're approaching that ship!'

Si cheered with one fist in the air, and the crew joined him.

Fifteen minutes later.

'Can we attack them now?' Tully drawled from the right-hand cannon.

'Not... yet,' Sam said cautiously.

The galley passed the *Devourer* on their right, close enough for them to destroy with an extended torch, let alone a loaded cannon. Lilly sat cross-legged by the rail and was saluted in greeting by the galley's captain.

'Captain,' Lilly pestered.

'Not yet!' he snapped.

'But they're practically shagging us!' she exclaimed, pointing.

'When I give the word!'

Lilly sighed and examined the galley intently. After a moment she leapt to her feet and bolted below decks.

Si was in his cabin, lounging on his bed with a female passenger. Thankfully they were both fully clothed on this occasion as Lilly barged in and slumped onto his table.

'Uh, d'you mind?' he snapped.

'I'm bored!' she complained. 'Look out there!'

She pointed out the porthole, where the horizon was obstructed by hull.

'I could reach out and touch that ship, and he's just gawking at it! You have one job as pirates, and he's letting that ship slide past! We haven't done a single interesting thing since I got on this ship! You are the most boring pirates in the world!'

'Oh, I don't know about that,' purred Si's friend, stroking his chest.

Lilly gagged. Somehow it was like watching Cienne carrying on with her brother.

'You didn't actually think he would attack that ship, did you?' Si said idly.

'Well, I think he ought to!' she said. 'If I were captain—'

'If you were captain, you'd be attacking shorelines, much less ships,' Si said with a half-smile. 'It's in your genes. Tell you what, why don't you go attack in his place? Be a laugh, if anything.'

His little friend tittered, though it was uncertain whether she understood the joke or not.

Lilly slid from the table and exited the cabin in a sulk.

It was only when she reached the top deck, where Stan and Ron sat cross-legged in boredom, that she realised what Si had actually said.

It's in your genes.

Lilly's hand lingered on the longbow strapped to her back. After a moment's careful planning, she bolted across the deck.

The captain had given up his pretence of gazing pensively at the galley and had just sat down to play draughts with Ron when Lilly sprinted past. His eyes widened when they caught the longbow.

'What are you doing with that?'

Lilly ignored him and strode to the edge of the deck, squinting up at the rope mesh stretching to the crow's nest. Sot watched incredulously as she scrambled over the rigging and lithely climbed the mesh.

'You're not going up there to—get down now!!' he roared, sprinting after her.

She pulled herself out of reach and hastily made for the crow's nest, her gaze set firmly through the mesh on the galley's captain.

Sot raced after her and leapt on the mesh line.

Stan and Ron watched in amazement.

'We need to hang out with her more often,' Ron said.

Stan nodded his agreement with a wide grin.

Sot's thin, gangly limbs slipped from the mesh in his haste.

'I am your captain and I order you to—AAH!'

Perspiration caused his hands to slip from the mesh. He fell back with one foot twisted in the ropes, leaving him writhing upside down in mid-air.

Lilly dragged herself onto the crow's nest and turned to face the galley, longbow in hand. She drew an arrow from behind her shoulder, steadied her feet, notched, drew and aimed.

On the trading galley, Orl leaned on the starboard rail in silent lament. He heaved a sigh as the Serpus-born captain prattled about his ship, his eyes on their stationary neighbour and his thoughts on Lilly-Anna Crey.

He was just watching a man wriggling from the edge of the mesh only a short distance away when the captain abruptly fell silent.

Orl shot him a glance and the blood rushed from his face.

An arrowhead protruded from the middle of the captain's throat, where scarcely a blemish had been only a few seconds before. With a little cough, the man crumpled to the deck floor in a heap.

Chilled to the bone, Orl spun on the spot, searched madly for the attacker and froze, his gaze locked to movement on one of the *Devourer*'s masts.

Lilly stood on the crow's nest, her longbow in one hand and the other giving a cheery wave.

Until a pair of hands snatched her throat from behind.

'You shouldn't have done that, Lilly,' Si barked from behind.

Lilly lifted her knee and brought her foot back, hard.

Leaving Si to stumble backward, nursing his injury, Lilly filled her lungs, clutching her throat.

'FIRE!!'

The *Devourer*'s two cannons exploded, followed by dozens of arrows. Lead crashed into the galley's starboard side in a shower of debris, sending its passengers flying backward. Specks of fletch arched into the air and speared the front sails.

Lilly grabbed a rope in both elbows and slid down it, followed by Si. Once she reached the main deck, Lilly clenched her longbow and, accepting a flaming arrow from a stunned Tully, she loosed fire onto the back sail.

It combusted immediately, turning from white to orange to black before crumbling away completely.

Everyone on the *Devourer* was alert now, fetching arrows and heading for a massive, wheeled brazier carrying a burning barrel of pitch, captained by Ron. Si had given up his attack on Lilly and had taken the helm, steering around to catch up with the galley in its feeble escape. Lilly took out the galley's helm with another lit arrow and was about to take out a nearby member of its crew when she suddenly recognised him.

'Orl!'

He spun to the sound of her voice and cowered at a passing arrow with a squeal.

Lilly loosed a short distance over his head and snatched a cutlass from a crewmate. The remains of the galley's sails exploded into flames as she leapt onto a rope and swung onto the galley's main deck.

Three men closed in on her as she landed aboard with a *thump*.

She swung at them on instinct, slitting one man's throat. Another cut her shoulder open, making her cry out.

Orl emerged out of nowhere and leapt onto his back, twisting his head sharply as Lilly's cutlass slammed into the third man's jugular.

'Hello,' he said, his tone nonchalant. Too nonchalant. He wasn't used to this, it seemed.

'Hello,' she said brightly. 'Fancy seeing you here.'

He grinned, albeit weakly.

The crew of the *Devourer* flooded aboard the galley as its crew began one by one to surrender. Once the commotion had died down, Lilly returned to the *Devourer* to find Captain Sot right where she left him – hanging by the mesh by one foot, looking increasingly angry.

'Before I take him down,' she said, turning to Orl, 'gather all the survivors and bring them here, would you?'

'Aye, captain,' Orl said with a grin, turning back where they came.

Captain, she mused as the crewmen surrounded her. *That's a title with a ring to it.*

Even if it did mean Seth might hang her for hijacking what turned out to be his ship. She winced, then decided to deal with that when the time came.

'Have all the survivors been recruited?' she asked as the crew settled. 'They have? Good. Now, before we loot the ship, I have a proposition to make to you. Considering that I was off claiming this lovely ship for us while Captain Sot has had his foot stuck in the mesh and has been hanging there for the entire battle... what say I take over his position for him?'

'Eh?' Sot squeaked, swaying in the wind. 'That's mutiny!'

'Pirate captain is decided by vote,' Si supplied. 'If the crew votes to replace you, it's within their rights, not mutiny. 'Course, you knew that already,' he said quickly. 'Just reminding you, is all.'

'It's mutiny if the previous captain is still alive!' he accused shrilly.

'That's true,' Lilly agreed. 'But we could always let a "fake" recruit kill you now and make it all legit. If you would prefer.'

Sot gulped, breathing heavily.

'Actually I reckon if the crew agrees—'

'We do,' Tully chimed unanimously.

'I thought she was captain already,' a recruit piped up.

'Just let me down,' Sot said, deflated. 'Please.'

Lilly nodded with a smile and gave Ron a signal.

Ron smiled broadly and scrambled up the mesh to Sot's aid.

'So,' said Lilly.

'No, you pillock,' Sot barked as Ron fiddled with the sole of Sot's boot, 'help me back on, don't just leave me fall on the—HELP!'

'What now, then?' she asked no one in particular.

Sot landed behind her with a thud.

'I think we'd better head to my father sometime soon,' Orl said with a nervous squint. 'You know, before he starts killing people.'

Lilly's face fell.

'Oh right, my future husband.' She sighed heavily. 'I wish I didn't have to do this, you know. No offence to your old man, but I generally have more of a thing for girls my own age.'

'Oh,' said Orl, trying to hide the dismay in his face.

The crew flocked towards the broken galley.

Lilly and Orl strode to the helm.

'I wonder how my father will react to being betrothed to a pirate captain,' said Orl.

Lilly froze. 'I think we should keep that part to ourselves,' she said finally. 'I don't think he's paying for a murderous pirate wife.'

'You'd be surprised. I doubt that would sway him. You are a Crey after all – usually that would be a turn-off alone. No offence.'

Lilly paused, reminded suddenly of an earlier remark about her family. *It's in your genes.*

Orl eyed Lilly fretfully. 'I didn't actually offend you just there, did I?'

'What? Oh, no, course not. Sorry,' she sidled past him, heading for the stairs, 'I'll be right back, I need to find someone.' She left him at the helm.

She hastened to Si's cabin and froze halfway there.

Tully was directing the removal of a dead body.

'What happened to him?' she asked in alarm, examining him. 'The galley didn't have a chance to blink, much less fire at us.'

'He weren't killed by the galley crew,' Tully said. 'There're no injuries. We reckon a panic attack or summat. There's been a few of 'em since the attack started.'

'A panic attack?' Lilly asked sceptically. 'Over what?'

'We all grew up in cargo ships, we ain't used to this type of bollocks,' Tully said, shaking his head. He scratched at his close cropped brown beard with a frown of frustration. 'We never planned to attack any ship, save for your—'

His mouth snapped shut.

Lilly frowned. 'Save for my what?'

He shook his head quickly and waved the others ahead.

'Nuffin. Mind my brother ain't with one of them tarts when you go in, he gets in a right mare when he's put off his stride.'

'What were you on about, though?' she asked, but he'd already shoved ahead of them and left.

Lilly made a face at him and, disregarding his warning completely, made for Si's cabin in double time.

~

On the main deck, Ron dropped down from the mesh after a job well done to find Stan clutching something minuscule in his hands.

Ron strolled over in interest.

'What have you got there, then?' he asked cheerfully.

'Never you mind!' Stan snapped, hiding the item of interest behind his back.

Ron scowled at him. 'So it's a secret, is it?'

'Might be,' Stan replied, looking shifty.

Ron stamped on Stan's foot and swiped the item as Stan hopped in agony.

'A tinderbox?'

Stan snatched it back hastily.

'What are you doing with that?'

'Gonna burn down the ship,' he muttered.

'That one?' Ron pointed at the galley.

'Not exactly, no.'

Ron's eyes widened. 'But we live on this ship.'

'I don't like ships,' he said by way of explanation. 'I don't like ships and I don't like water.'

Ron paused.

'Stan, remind me,' he said testily. 'What are we standing on?'

Stan frowned. 'The ship.'

'And… what is below the ship?'

'Water, of course,' he said, rolling his eyes.

'So what exactly are we going to be standing on when you burn the ship down?'

Stan started. 'Ah.'

'Ah,' Ron repeated dryly.

Stan looked sheepish. 'I just thought if I made it look like we were all dead, the siren would bugger off and find someone else to bother.'

Ron's expression was blank. 'What's a siren?'

'Bugger if I know. One's just been at me ever since I got on the ship. Trying to get me to do things to it.' He shuddered. 'I wouldn't mind if its persistence didn't distinctly remind me of Uncle Keith.'

'Hmm.' Ron lifted an eyebrow and pocketed the tinderbox, giving Stan's shoulder a pat. 'Don't worry, we'll be there in no time now that Lilly's taken over.'

His smile withered at the thought.

'Then we'll have to find my mother.'

'What's the matter with her, anyway?' Stan asked curiously. 'I thought mothers were supposed to love their children, not chase them across the world in vengeance.'

'She said I was an accident,' Ron said hatefully.

'So was I, but *my* mum's eyes never went red whenever I entered a room.'

'Oh, but I was royalty, you see,' Ron said bitterly. 'Royalty works differently from normal people. She called me an error. Not to my face, of course. She said it to Vladdy all the time, whenever my father had a go at him for being useless at archery or something. "You were planned, darling – unlike *that one*." She always loved Vladdy more than me. My father didn't, though, he despised them both. Dunno why.'

Stan listened without a sound.

'My father really liked me, though,' he said in a brighter tone. He gave a little laugh. 'I remember any time I missed a shot in archery practise, I got a pat on the head for trying. Vladdy just got glared at. I never knew why he disliked Vladdy so much, but *we* always got along really well. He said he'd rather have a successor who met the council in a treehouse than one who never saw the light of day.'

Stan half-smiled. 'Should have put you ahead of Vladdy in the succession, shouldn't he? That would have put your mum's back up.'

Ron's face fell and he shrugged.

'Nothing he can do about it now. We can only hope Felicity doesn't give birth to a miniature Vladdy.'

'Bet she hopes so, too. Sorry,' he corrected himself, 'that was insensitive, considering her ordeal and all.'

'Why?' he asked, nonplussed. 'Anyone could have a child by accident the way my mother left her birthing potions lying around.'

Stan paused thoughtfully.

'You think that's how they did it?' he asked in interest. 'Gave her a magic drink to make a baby appear, just like that?'

'Isn't that how everyone does it?' Ron asked with a frown.

Stan paused again.

'Yes, of course it is, how could I forget?' He gave a quick laugh.

Ron laughed also. 'You had me going for a minute.'

'Yeah,' he laughed nervously.

'Thought for a minute there was a *different* way of doing it.'

'No, no,' he said, forcing a grin.

'Would've looked silly if there was, me getting it wrong for so long.'

'Silly,' Stan echoed.

110

There was a brief silence.

Stan broke it with a question. 'And that Emmett bloke? What's his problem?'

'He's king regent,' Ron said. 'If I turn up and swipe his crown, he won't be king anymore. It's within my rights as second heir to the kingdom to take regency. If I want to. Which I don't.'

'Why not?'

'I wouldn't be a real king then, would I? Qattren would be telling me what to do,' he said sourly. 'Besides, I'd be rubbish at it. The only reason I know any of this "king regent" nonsense is because she blathers on about it so much.'

'Hardly,' Stan disagreed loyally. 'I reckon if your dad had put you over Vladdy, Vladdy would still be alive today. The power got to his head is what it is – you wouldn't have that problem because in your head, you're common as muck. Lilly's the same,' he added. 'She's running the ship now, because everyone here respects her. No one respects a twat. Your father knew it. It's like he said, better a king that organised court affairs from a treehouse than one who sits inside all day, trying to order around the gods.'

Ron gazed out on the ocean pensively.

~

Si's lady friend was ushered out on this occasion, and she gave Lilly a foul glance as Si shut the door behind her.

Lilly paid no mind to her. Si's back was turned just long enough for Lilly to grab him by the throat and press a knife under his jaw.

'Tell me how you found out who I am.'

'Dunno what you're talking about, princess,' he said patronisingly.

Lilly drew the knife closer, drawing blood.

'It's in your genes, you told me. What genes are they? And how did you find out?'

'I guessed,' he said with a snarl. 'Theo Crey was a maniac, just like you are. It was hardly difficult. And you're the spitting image of your brother.'

Lilly's nose wrinkled. 'First you try to kill me, and now you insult me?'

Si suppressed a grin.

'Why did you attack me in the crow's nest?'

'You were disobeying the captain's orders,' Si replied.

'You voted against him.'

'That was after.'

Lilly's eyes thinned. 'Swear fealty to me, then.'

'I swear fealty to Captain Crey of the *Devourer*.'

'Crowe,' she corrected. 'There are no Creys on this ship, understood?'

'Captain Crey-Crowe, then. Now let me go before I sacrifice my dignity and tell the crew I'm being attacked by a princess.'

Lilly released him.

111

He turned to face her, rubbing blood from under his chin.

'How d'you know what my brother looks like?' Lilly asked. 'His portrait's of a handsome man.'

Si gave her a half-smile. 'Seen him before in passing, just after the Stonekeep was blown up. He's not that bad looking.'

'From a distance, I suppose. What were you doing in Stoneguard?'

'Waiting for this ship to arrive. Back to your brother. He still depriving his poor wife these days?'

'No, she's expecting, why?'

'Damn it,' he swore, shaking his head. 'She was a bit of alright, you know. From a distance.'

'Oh, spare it,' she said with a grimace. 'I hear enough lecherous things said about her by my brother.'

'If it keeps her interested, then what harm? Take me to the palace with you on your way back. I'll show her a *real* man.'

'Yeah, if you behave. And that includes keeping my secret for me.'

She leaned closer until they were nose to nose.

'If anyone on this ship finds out who I am, I'll hold you personally responsible. And if they do, I'll cut that smarmy face of yours into three halves. Understand what I say?'

'Everything except for the three halves bit. You'll find there's a slight mathematical error there.'

'One half and two quarters, then. Oh, and mention of the queen being "a bit of alright" is treason, and disgusting. So don't do it again.'

'Oh, alright,' he grumbled. 'As you command, your serene highness.' He edged past her and moved towards a bureau by the window. 'So what's the plan now that you've nicked Sot's position?'

Lilly sighed. 'Better go get married, I suppose.'

'Aw, the curly-haired one proposed after the battle?'

She frowned. 'No. My brother sold me to his father, actually.'

Si raised an eyebrow. 'Ah, so you've the hots for the bastard son.'

'No!' she said hotly. She paused. 'At least I don't think I have. I always thought I mostly, you know… swung the other way, but…'

'Obviously not,' he finished.

She shrugged. 'Maybe I like both?'

Si scoffed. 'That's not a thing.'

'It is a thing! Your brother's into both, isn't he? There's a name for people who fancy men and women the same way, something beginning with "B"—'

'Yeah – Bloody Greedy.'

'Small-minded is all you are,' Lilly said, shoving his arm.

He shut the bureau as she sat on the table and turned to face her, toying with a decorative dagger he'd stashed inside.

'When's the wedding? I assume we're all invited?'

'That'll go down well, won't it? Apparently the wedding arrangements are on hold until I arrive – or if I arrive, anyway. I was thinking of leaving you lot to your own devices until I get back. Collect me some money while I leave for a bit to get *married*.'

She put a moronic inflection on the last two words.

'Don't you get money from your family?'

'Yeah, but this feels more like I earned it.'

Si smiled again and started cleaning under his fingernails. 'When are we burning the witch?'

'What day is today?'

'Friday. Witch-hunting day, according to Sot, but then, he never could pull a bird if his life depended on it.'

'Good a day as any, then. We'll put her on the galley at sunset.'

She half-turned to leave.

'Think your tart will let you out to watch?' she said with a grin, propping her right hand on the doorframe. 'Tully tells me you're a right nark when you're put off your stride.'

Si laughed wryly and flicked his knife at the doorframe.

It thudded to a halt in the frame – with Lilly's hand attached to it.

Si's hand flew to his mouth.

'My God, I'm so sorry! I didn't mean it to hit you! I meant to hit the doorframe!'

Lilly stared at him, then at her hand, trapped between the frame and the hilt of the blade. Her palm was on fire.

'You didn't have to nail me to the damn thing!' she shrieked.

'Look, don't worry, you're alright,' he soothed frantically.

Blood spilled down the doorframe.

'Oh shit, oh shit, what to do, what to—wait here, I've to get something!'

He bolted past her, leaving her pinned there.

'Wait! You can't leave me like this!' she squealed shrilly.

'I'll be back in a minute, I'll fix you up in no time! Do NOT pull that out!'

Lilly ceased trying to painlessly remove the dagger and instead tried not to sob.

~

V

Lilly leaned the small of her back on the rail and watched the celebration from afar.

Si's bedfellows weren't just pretty on the eye, it seemed – a girl with flowing red hair had hauled a hurdy-gurdy to the top deck and instigated a jig, leading the other two girls into a rousing backing track using a lute and a makeshift drum. They were quite good, Lilly had to concede. The redhead sang a catchy, if on the nose, tune about escaping to the sea, which was better than it had any right to be.

Twilight had fallen upon the top deck, casting a soft breeze through the sails. The gentle amber of candlelight flickered in its wake, the flames wavering on the tables lining the rail across from her.

Lilly raised her bottle to her lips – via her good hand. The bad one hung still in three layers of bandage and a sling, the throbbing abating with each sip of beer.

She eyed the culprit approaching the musicians.

Waiting first for the song to finish, Si whispered into the redhead's ear.

Her eyes widened with enthusiasm and she nodded quickly, flinging an instruction to the backing artists.

Si sang along under his breath to a lilting tune and sidled up to Lilly.

'I like this one,' Lilly said in greeting. 'It's pretty.'

'I knew the girl who wrote it,' said Si, leaning on the rail beside her.

'Slept with, I take it?'

'Eventually,' he said with a roguish grin.

Lilly lifted her upper lip. 'No taste, these women. Seriously.'

Si punched her hand. The good one.

The beat reached a higher tempo.

'Come dance with me,' Si said, offering her a hand.

Lilly grimaced at him. 'What d'you think I am, a *girl*?'

'You *are* one, aincha?'

'Just about,' Lilly conceded.

Si laughed and tugged her elbow. 'Come on!'

'Noooo,' Lilly groaned, stumbling along behind him. 'I don't like dancing, leave me alone!'

'Not a chance!'

He put an arm around her shoulders and swung her around to face him. Delicately avoiding the hurt arm bound to her front, he held the good hand out in his and placed the other on the side of her ribs, just under the sling.

'Just skip along, it'll be fun!'

'Skipping barefoot on nails sounds more fun than this,' Lilly whinged. 'I feel like a tit.'

'You're at a party, you're supposed to feel like a tit. Gotta practise being a tit for your wedding dance, innit?'

Lilly made a retching noise.

Si ignored this and spun her in circles, skipping on the balls of his feet.

Lilly finally wriggled away. 'I need more drink before doing any more of this. Bring me a beer – I'm a helpless cripple, remember?'

Si poked her sling playfully and she swatted him away, cackling.

She kept to the sidelines for the rest of the evening, cradling a bottle and watching the rest of the crew.

An odd melancholy overcame her as the party wound up. Lilly looked within herself for the reason, gazing at the stars, and it abruptly came to her. It was nostalgia, for her very first time on a ship. With her father.

Where were we going? she asked herself, baffled. It might have been Mellier, back when it merged with Portabella. Yeah, that was probably it.

She had fallen into the water, she remembered, picturing her small form flailing in the water before a crew-mate snatched her under the ribs and pulled her into the rowboat. She thought her father was going to scream at her when she came back aboard, but he hadn't. He had simply swept her up in massive bear hug and held her like that, pacing the deck and murmuring comforting words.

'But I'm fine,' she had said, baffled.

They hadn't just been for her, she realised in that moment, for the first time. They had been for himself, too.

Her vision swam. She couldn't let the others see her like this.

She fled below decks.

Lilly meandered around the vacant hammocks and sat on a beam sticking out of the floor, facing the corner of the room. Tears rolled from the corner of her eyelids. She brushed them off, releasing a sob before clutching her diaphragm in tightly, suppressing the rest that followed. With some mercy, she managed to stay in complete silence.

Footsteps fell on the floorboards outside.

'Lil, you in 'ere?' Si called in.

Lilly bent her head, holding her breath.

He stayed a moment, as though unsure of what to do. Hesitant, his slow footsteps quickened as he returned to the top deck.

The pain welled out, triple-fold.

Lilly buried her face in her good elbow.

~

Retribution Halle stood in the middle of the wilderness, Lyseria behind him.

A star-shaped medallion sat in the centre of his palm with one of the points facing north. He set his hand palm-up over a slight crevice in the sand and softly hummed three notes.

He felt the city coming before he heard it. A faint rumble spiralled into a roar. Copers rose from the sand before them, starting with the front gate beneath where Halle's hand had previously indicated.

Lyseria gazed into the east and launched herself skyward as Halle set his palms on the hardwood doors. He pressed on them firmly and they swung open.

He frowned.

There hadn't been a second gate before, had there?

He could distinctly remember peering into the front gate to see the city's main thoroughfare before Ernest blocked his path.

Instead a second pair of doors faced him, one of them open a smidge.

He made to enter the second gate.

A desert lizard scuttled ahead of him and slithered into the gap, opening the door a little more –

– and was flattened into a smear as the door dropped from its hinges without warning.

The hardwood rose of its own accord, returning to its previous position. Halle froze.

Had he just imagined one of the doors falling flat on top of the lizard?

He peered down at the two-dimensional lizard just outside the doors.

Apparently not.

He wondered if his fate would be similar upon contact with the door. The notion was extremely likely.

He searched his surroundings. He was in a small courtyard surrounded by sandstone walls and two sets of doors. There was a kind of motto in old letters above the falling door that, as soon as he gazed at it, seemed to morph into the familiar characters of the Truphorian language. It read:

The falling doors are tired of being opened.

Halle frowned. A riddle. Had Ernest mentioned any riddles before?

I doubt it somehow, he thought bitterly.

The falling doors are tired of being opened. So they fall down in exhaustion, he reasoned. But will they accept being closed? If it didn't, the riddle would logically have explained that they are tired of being *used*.

Worth a try, he thought glumly. *Better to be flattened than to slowly starve to death.*

He shoved the door shut.

It closed easily, paused for a moment, and opened widely away from him. Halle jogged inside before it could change its mind.

It swung back into its original position.

'That was easy,' he said cheerfully, turning to face the city.

A vast labyrinth stretched out in all directions. Halle suddenly found himself on top of a small hill, surrounded by winding alleys and walls. The immense maze circled him entirely, and the Falling Doors had vanished.

He tried vainly to find an end to the puzzle. The maze reached the horizon and beyond, leaving him trapped.

'Bugger,' he muttered.

A small dove cleared its throat from his shoulder. He jumped with a wail.

'That was easy,' it said in an amicable voice. 'This is not.'

~

Dusk fell on the *Devourer*, rendering its details unfathomable and leaving only the neighbouring ship's bonfire intact. Si had placed a wide bucket in the centre

116

of the broken galley to contain the fire. The crew were filling it with the remains of the masts as the graciously-appointed First Mate Sot spoke.

'As former captain of the *Devourer*, I commit this witch to the flames before us for crimes of witchcraft, attempted murder, and persistent lying.'

Qattren hung face-down from a wooden lever extended over the bonfire, her wrists bound behind her waist. The T-shaped lever bore a length of thick rope on each horizontal end: one holding Qattren around the waist, the other manned by Tully a couple feet away. Tully held her aloft with one hand and fanned himself with the other, barking at Sot an occasional obscenity supposedly translating to 'get on with it'.

Dangling over the growing flames with an air of indifference, Qattren stared directly at Sot, bringing him out in a cold sweat.

'As she witnesses her final moments, I ask this witch before us: do you have anything to say?'

'When are you going to get on with it?' she asked politely.

'Hear-bloody-hear,' Tully piped up from the lever, earning a foul glare from Sot.

Sot signalled towards the crewmen, who doused the flames in alcohol.

Qattren raised her legs into the air.

The flames roared, red tendrils reaching up to lick the skimpy shift the crew had allowed her to wear.

Stan and Ron's eyes locked onto her gently rotating form.

'How long will this take?' Ron asked tersely.

'Fifteen minutes for the fire to build up, the heat should kill her before she has time to explode into flames,' Stan said.

'Alright, give me that tinderbox, mister,' Ron said severely, holding out his right hand.

Lilly watched from a couple feet in front of them, sweating from the heat. She rubbed her newly bandaged hand, muttering 'bastard' with every twinge.

Si flanked her, looking a bit green.

'D'you think this will work?' he asked her.

'Course it won't,' said Lilly. 'I told you lot already, she's the one that set most of Stoneguard on fire. I was at the Wastelands last year watching her have a fit from the remorse, but no, you wouldn't listen.'

Si simply grimaced into the flames.

'I reckon it will kill her,' he said after a moment. 'Fire just speeds up decay. It's inevitable.'

Lilly made no reply.

They watched with narrowed eyes as the smoke clouds grey, blotting out the view at momentary intervals. The fire grew steadily to a dull roar and her knee-length scrap of dress blackened, but Qattren remained nonchalant. She didn't so much as break a sweat, Lilly noticed. The heat was building uncomfortably around the crew, much less around her.

Total silence fell on the bonfire, save for a sharp intake of breath from the occasional bang.

Ex-Captain Sot watched incredulously as the flames reached up to brush Qattren's stomach.

'The heat should have cooked her by now,' he muttered from Lilly's left. 'She's not even burning—'

The fire thrust upwards and finally caught Qattren's front.

Some recruits from the galley gasped.

Red fingers climbed over Qattren's body, transforming her pale garment into ash and red embers. The flames danced across her pale flesh, but left nothing in their wake – no burn marks, no reddening, nothing. Not even her hair burned in the inferno; rather it burned with it, the fiery locks camouflaged by the angry orange around them.

'She's not burning,' Sot said furiously.

He threw a frantic hand signal at Tully.

'Put her right in the fire! Put her right the damn way in!'

Tully released the lever, letting her drop into the inferno.

The crew recoiled as a shower of sparks flew out.

Qattren rose, shaking off the remains of her bonds and glaring at everyone, Sot in particular.

'You should have left me in my cell,' she said, her hair flying up like a halo.

The flames wrapped around her naked body like a robe, concealing everything beneath.

'Did you really think this would harm me? I *own* this fire, did you honestly think it would kill me?'

She stepped out of the bonfire and onto the deck, leaving a trail of flame in her wake.

The crew scrambled away from her.

Impassive as ever, Qattren strode through the parting crowd until she came face to face with Ron, standing five paces from the back of the ship.

'I'll be heading home now,' she said, her fiery robe crackling. 'You seem to have everything under control. Don't hesitate to call for me if you come under difficulties.'

'Right you are,' he said uneasily.

He glanced up and down at her body for the first time in their marriage. The fascination was less with the body itself and more with the tight-fitting yet opaque armour of flame.

'Give your mother my regards,' she said with a smile.

She evaporated instantly in a puff of smoke.

The fire began to spread. The crew raced for the *Devourer* as the galley started to illuminate.

Lilly pulled Ron across a plank leading to the main deck of the *Devourer*. Once safely aboard, Sot grabbed them from behind.

118

'You know her, do you?' he asked scathingly, spinning him around.

'Oh yes, she's my wife,' Ron said before clapping a hand over his mouth.

'Wife!' Sot shrieked. 'The witch is your *wife*?'

Ron gulped.

Lilly rubbed her eyes.

~

Jimmy poked his head between the double doors at four in the afternoon, precisely. The time was important. He'd missed the previous fifteen weeks' worth of four in the afternoons and was not about to miss this one.

The citizens of Stoneguard had flooded around the front portcullis to beg entrance, but Jimmy wasn't paying any attention to that. He was looking for a man in a white suit with a mask... and black boots.

Footsteps stumbled down the staircase.

Jimmy swung around with a grin to face Seth.

'Afternoon, your majesty,' he said brightly.

'Muh,' Seth grunted, slumping into his throne with a yawn. 'Have you lot made this horn yet?'

'Yes, sir,' Jimmy said.

He directed Seth's attention to the fireplace.

A large speaking horn protruded from the wall adjacent, its wide brass opening gleaming in the torchlight.

'It's set into the side of the fireplace, leading directly to the inside of your quarters. Anything she says into it will be perfectly audible down here.'

'Good, I'll sleep down here, then,' Seth said in relief, leaning back on the cushions. 'I'll end up with a twisted spine, but at least I won't be molested in the night. Any news today?'

'We've had word from Stoneguard, the council were just discussing it,' Jimmy said. 'You really ought to visit them sometime. They're thinking of revolting into a democratic republic.'

Seth blew a raspberry. 'Let them. What news was it?'

'Felicity Horne has given birth with no complications.'

'Oh great, Cienne will be pleased,' Seth groaned, dropping his head into his hands. 'Nothing wrong with him, then?'

'Only his name. Azrael.' Jimmy made a face.

'Ew. Speaking of names, do you know what Cienne's calling ours if it's a girl? *Virginia.*'

'That is a hideous name, sir,' he said dutifully.

'Isn't it?' He shuddered. 'Not the worst of my problems with her, either.'

'Indeed.' Jimmy paused. 'How is she, by the way?'

'Angry. Can't say I feel differently.'

'Well, the baby is taking an awful long time to arrive,' said Jimmy with sympathy.

119

'Oh, I'm not angry about that, he can take as long as he wants,' Seth said. 'I can avoid Cienne until then, she can't fit down the spiral staircase. What's bothering me is the moron with the white suit and the mask.'

'And black boots,' Jimmy added. He glanced out at the courtyard, to where a sundial resided beneath the setting sun. 'Well, it's four o'clock. Doesn't look as if he can make it today.'

'You always say that,' Seth said sourly. 'Then at the last second you go off to do something and he comes along and ruins my afternoon.'

'And your clothes,' he added. He paused momentarily. 'I'll just go and make some tea.'

'Do you have to? Can't you just stay here with me?'

Jimmy wrinkled his nose. 'I'd love to, sir, but I could really do with a cuppa and it's considered stealing if I'm not bringing any for you too.'

Seth made a pained expression and heaved a sigh.

Jimmy scurried behind the kitchen door and peered out from inside, completely unaware of the Phantom Egg Flinger's deliberate aims to wait until he was gone in case the butler might laugh out loud. Many people thought that the Devil laughed like King Theo, but he didn't, he laughed like Jimmy.

Seth tried grouchily to relax and groaned as the double doors opened.

'My liege, the crowds outside the main entrance are getting riotous,' said Corporal Moat, brushing a globule of snow from the tip of his nose. 'Are we really to dismiss all of them?'

'Yep,' said Seth. 'Every one of them.'

'Yes, my liege,' he said uncertainly. 'It's just that, erm, Lady Gertrude has arrived—'

'What!!' he yelped, bolting upright. 'Let her in, then, before she rams the gates! And hide my mother too! Tell her Granny's arrived!'

Moat jogged back outside.

Seth bolted for the speaking horn.

Jimmy winced.

If Seth thought Cienne was unstable, he had no idea what was about to charge through his front gate. King Theo Crey's parentage had half consisted of a rather feeble-willed king – that just left Lady Gertrude.

'That's Queen Dowager to you, Mister Moat!' bellowed the female equivalent of Theo Crey's voice. A bang marked her arrival through the double doors. 'Where is my grandson? Seth! Show me this wife of yours!'

Seth pivoted and collapsed against the speaking horn in mock horror. 'Father?! Is that you?'

Lady Gertrude Tillet roared her outrage at the joke. Nevertheless, she pulled him into a tight bear-hug.

Jimmy fetched a ready-made tea tray, making sure to add a generous helping of whiskey to his own cup.

'How have you been, dear? Where is this beautiful wife of yours?'

120

Seth squirmed out of her grasp with a wide yawn and reached for the speaking horn. He stuck his head inside as Jimmy returned with a tea set and a steaming pot.

'Darling?' Seth trilled. 'My grandmother's come to visit, shall I send her up?'

Lady Gertrude lumbered to Cienne's throne and sat on it. She and Jimmy eyed each other distrustfully.

She certainly doesn't look eighty-nine years old, he thought. *Or female.*

'Grandmother?' Cienne's voice floated down from above. 'Tell her to furghoff—'

'She's not very well today,' Jimmy said, apologetic.

'The child must take after its grandfather,' she said in reproach. 'Anyone would be unwell carrying a Theo Crey. Why has this butler served himself a cup of tea?' she suddenly bellowed.

Jimmy flinched, spilling a bit of his fortified tea on himself.

'Put it back! That's stealing! Honestly, Seth,' she said, shaking her head. 'You need to watch the servants of this day and age. You give them an inch and they'll take a mile. Send it to Cienne! She could do with it more than you in any case!'

Jimmy paused in the act of wiping his front dry and pivoted, irate.

'What happened to you, then? Last I heard, you were all but dead!' she boomed as Jimmy left. 'Your father claimed you had Walking Corpse Syndrome or some such and that you were incurable.'

'He would say that, wouldn't he?' Seth grumbled. 'No, I'm fine, and so is Cienne… physically, at least.'

'Oh, I do like her,' Gertrude said fondly. 'Nice quiet girl, unlike your mother.'

She frowned slightly at a new arrival in a white suit, but refrained from commenting.

The Phantom Egg Flinger loitered behind Seth, hands behind his back.

'I think you have it the wrong way around, Gran,' Seth said with a frown. 'My mother never hit anyone around the head with a shovel.'

'Oh, I imagine you deserved it. Portabellans don't turn to anger lightly. No, I couldn't live with your mother anymore when Seb died. She had her eye on that throne from day one, the scheming little pup.'

'She couldn't conquer her own sock drawer, much less the country,' Seth said, pouring the tea in Jimmy's absence. 'Do you take sugar?'

'No thank you, I'm sweet enough. She was a virgin when you married, wasn't she, little Cienne?' she went on with a fond smile. 'Sweet little lamb, all dressed up in those silly Portabellan skirts. Unlike your mother. Wasn't even pure when your father was betrothed, but Seb insisted.'

Seth dropped the spoon and knelt to retrieve it.

'Of course my mother was a virgin when they married. He would have known, otherwise.'

121

'Oh, Theo wouldn't have known one end of a woman from another,' she brushed off, 'the only sword he ever used was made of steel. But no, Seb had to befriend that silly Gertrude family – told me he chose her in my honour, as we shared a name, the silly fool – and poor Theo was left with the runt.'

Seth smiled and nodded, biting his tongue almost hard enough to draw blood.

It's only once a year, he reminded himself. *Just keep your mouth shut and your mother behind locked doors, and she'll be gone in a jiffy.*

'Never mind, you and Lilly turned out alright,' she went on, oblivious to Seth's annoyance. 'She's gone to get married in the Dead Lands, hasn't she? Surprised you found anyone at all, men these days are too feeble to manage women of Lilly's calibre…'

The Phantom Egg Flinger surreptitiously shifted forward, halting two paces behind the king.

Seth listened intently to his grandmother, totally oblivious.

'… so much like your father. They got on spectacularly, didn't they?'

'Did they?' said Seth, puzzled. 'I only remember him yelling at her for sneaking out in the early hours and kicking the shit out of the night staff.'

'Is that right? When you were ill, all he could ever talk about was Lilly and her combat training. He had her trained in everything he could think of, she flourished in all of it, apparently. He was extremely proud of her. Poor little mite was in pieces at the funeral, too.'

Seth nodded, staring at a point in the flagstones.

'Never mind, she'll be occupied soon enough. That Ambassador isn't known for slacking off in the bedroom depart—'

Flap.

A white smudge – with black boots – sprinted away.

Seth accepted a handkerchief from his grandmother.

'Still haven't caught the bugger yet?' she asked idly.

'No, he's a fast runner,' he said sourly, wiping his face.

Jimmy emerged from the staircase, observed the slimy paper plate on the floor in front of Seth and swore.

'I've bloody missed it again!'

Seth scowled.

~

'I still don't understand why I have to be locked up,' Ron said sourly. 'I didn't actually do anything.'

Lilly stood outside the sorcery-sealed imprisonment and glared at him from between the bars.

'You confessed to being married to an evil witch. I'm the captain, what else was I supposed to do? Besides, that will teach you for having a big gob.'

Ron huffed and slumped against the wall.

122

'You know, I thought we were getting to be quite good friends.'

'We are. The crew were voting for a keel-hauling.'

She left him to his sulking and returned to the main deck.

Si squinted out at the distance, where a smudge broke the blue void of the horizon.

'You ready?' he asked Lilly as she approached.

She walked past him without a word, her mind elsewhere.

She found her hiding place and climbed out towards it, longbow in hand. After twenty minutes, she finally made herself comfortable, settling her bow between her knees as the ship grew closer.

Aboard the *Red Sail*, the captain peered onto the ship a foot behind them.

Emmett, the flag on the mast declared, in the form of a spider, legs splayed.

He returned a wave from a member of the crew hovering on the crows' nest.

An arrow landed in the middle of his jugular, hampering his greeting but leaving his wave intact.

He dropped onto the deck floor. Crew members scrambled as arrows rained down upon them from the *Devourer*. The pirates sidled up beside the *Red Sail* and riddled it with arrows, all alight apart from the shots of a mystery archer who was nowhere to be seen.

The *Red Sail*'s twin masts were consumed with flames, its name now devastatingly accurate. Archers dropped like flies around the outside of the deck, all struck with the hidden archer's arrows.

Only one archer had caught a glimpse of Lilly, perched on the figurehead of the *Devourer*. He was rewarded with an arrow in the eye as she notched and drew again in double time.

The wooden figurehead of the *Devourer* – a shark with its jaws stretched open, revealing numerous rows of razor-sharp teeth – suddenly received a dagger in one eyeball.

Lilly jerked her head to the *Devourer*'s main deck and craned her neck upwards.

She spotted the knife-thrower, a bony little shit with a shiny bald head, standing two feet away from her. Lilly aimed as he disentangled another knife from about his person.

'Bollocks!' Lilly shouted aloud as the arrow sailed over his head.

Another knife spun past the left side of her head. His aim had been scuppered by Si, who had stumbled into him during a fist fight of his own.

Lilly seized her chance and notched again. She released it into the knife-thrower's jugular with an elated 'Yes!'

Five more minutes of fighting later, the *Red Sail* stopped and its remaining crew surrendered. Leaving her bow in the ornate figurehead's mouth, Lilly climbed back onto the *Devourer*'s top deck.

She found Sot by the helm, looking pale.

'He doesn't look well over there,' he said, his complexion pale.

'That will learn him for chucking knives at me,' said Lilly savagely, her back to the mast.

'Stan was throwing knives at you?' Si said.

Lilly frowned. 'Stan?' She pivoted. 'Oh shit.'

Stan slouched on the ground at the foot of the mast, the end of an arrow sticking out of his forearm and his face paling by the second.

'I must have got him when I missed my first shot,' Lilly said in a pained voice. 'Sorry, Stan! You alright?'

'My arm's falling off,' Stan said in a quiet whimper.

'Hang on, I'll get my kit,' Si said, jogging for the stairs.

'Your kit?' Lilly said. 'What, you some kind of doctor or something?'

'Yep,' he said brightly. He pivoted to waggle his eyebrows at Lilly. 'I'm the finest surgeon, chef and resident ladies' man you'll see on the seas – the whole package, me. Assuming you like your food tasteless.'

Lilly lifted her brows as Si skipped backwards down the stairs. 'You learn something new every day.'

'I thought he fixed the dirty great hole in your hand yesterday?' Sot asked.

'I passed out when I was still pinned to the doorframe,' she said, reddening. 'Embarrassing moment of weakness. Let's not speak of it again. Put Ron on this ship. We'll head for the Dead Lands on our own with some of the crew. You're in charge, until I find you.'

She eyed him up and down as Si returned. 'Can you manage that?'

Sot replied by throwing up overboard.

Si elbowed him and he bolted upright.

'Yes, captain,' he croaked before retching again.

'I'll help him,' Si offered.

'Alright,' she replied, turning to the crew assembled ahead. 'I'll be away for a bit if anyone asks. I'll just pick out a few men and put them on the ship before we lose any more time.'

'Shouldn't be too long a journey,' Si said, indicating ahead.

A grey lump materialised onto the horizon in the west – what could only be the harbour of Portmyr.

Lilly paused to admire it before her gaze lifted upward, to the sky above it.

'Damn it.'

A black beast brewed over the port ahead like a swarm. On closer inspection, it was a dense series of black clouds.

A storm was coming.

~

VI

Ron swallowed hard.

His cell on the *Red Sail* was lopsided, the floor tilting downward. Ron himself sat in the centre of a ring of excrement sprinkled over with mouldering hay. The cell had clearly been the home of some sort of animal in the past.

It also contained an inch of seawater and counting.

Ron stuck a hand into the hole in the wall beside him. The water outside lapped up and down in time with the increasing wind. A small stream dribbled past his elbow, his hand sinking below the surface. He let it dangle there, propping his head against the wall with a sigh.

His palm slid across something scaly.

Ron flinched violently and jerked his hand back.

'Ronald,' something whispered.

Ron scrambled backward, sending ripples through the pool around him. The whispering became a trill, a soft tune echoing into the cell.

Ron frowned. Tentatively, he lowered himself onto his elbows and peered out of the wall.

'Come to me, Ronald,' sang the siren.

'What for?'

It told him.

Ron's nose wrinkled.

'Don't be so disgusting!' he scolded it, turning his back to the hole. He shook his head in utter revulsion. 'Honestly…'

Rendering a mental image of the siren's words, Ron scrubbed his face with both hands with a loud shudder.

~

The Ambassador checked his calendar. It was definitely getting late.

The small-folk were getting sceptical about his newest proposal. He couldn't blame them as he reclined in a soft chair in his quarters of the Portmyr Inn. He'd waited a third of a year now for Lilly-Anna's arrival, and it was past time she and Orl had arrived.

Perhaps I should have let her take the dragon after all, he mused in retrospect. *Oh well.*

He'd give it another week, he decided, and then he'd start searching for bodies.

A knock came to his door and he bolted upright quite nimbly for a sixty-nine-year-old. However, it was not Lilly or Orl who stood outside, but a man roughly fifteen years his junior, covered in blood. Dragon's blood, by the vivid shade of red.

The Ambassador eyed him in interest.

'You're a knight, I take it,' he decided. 'Knights often like to demolish my livestock.'

'Ha, ha,' the visitor said dryly, handing him a tattered rein. 'I seem to have inadvertently slaughtered your dragon.'

The Ambassador raised an eyebrow.

'Taking into account that it was self-defence, I'd like my money back.'

'I imagine you would,' he said, in a tone like ice.

'You would imagine correctly,' the man retorted, irate. 'And I'd like three camels too.'

The Ambassador rolled his eyes, reaching behind him for some money.

'You haven't seen the Princess of Adem lately, have you?'

The man shook his head. 'I think she's stood you up.'

'She's not only stood me up, she's had me flown to Portmyr, no less,' he said with a sigh. 'Hopefully not for nothing.'

'Well, if she is coming, she'll want to hurry. There's a storm coming.'

The Ambassador peered out the window.

Sure enough, a monster of a storm cloud was brewing – and right over the port.

Marbrand clicked his tongue off the roof of his mouth.

'Rather you than me,' he said cheerfully on his way out.

~

Outside, Elliot and Despina stood idly by the wall as the door opened.

Marbrand re-emerged from inside, his bloody appearance alarming some passers-by.

'Everything sorted?' Elliot asked.

'All done,' he said, wiping his blood-spattered hair. 'Just have to collect the camels and we're off.'

They strolled to the stable house behind the inn.

'So what was it like, being eaten by a dragon?' Elliot asked.

'Not as bad as legend would have you believe. Course this one had a wide-set throat; I'd slid right past before the teeth could get a look-in. Anyway, you should know. He ate you too.'

'Doesn't count, really,' Despina said with a snigger. 'He did get stuck halfway down his throat.'

'I intended to get stuck, I'll have you know,' Elliot snapped. '*I* had the presence of mind to put my arms out on the way down. Lucky really. I blocked any chance of the dragon flaming.'

'Mmm, luck had nothing to do with it,' Marbrand grinned.

'Ha, ha, very funny,' Elliot said sulkily. 'Come on, we have a desert to cross.'

Marbrand stared out to the east, at the storm clouds staining the horizon a charcoal grey. 'Agreed. Let's go find a nice safe camel or two.'

They made off in the opposite direction, towards the dusty void where eight cities hid in the amber waste.

They passed the remains of a dragon with its entire torso split in half.

Marbrand admired it one last time, giving Pointy a proud pat on the hilt.

~

'Why am I still locked up? I demand that you let me out now!'

'Not until we make port!' Lilly snapped. 'I've told you a million times, the crew will mutiny if I tell them the witch-marrier is to be released, so you're staying here!'

'And why am I locked up?' Stan demanded.

'You tried to set fire to the ship again,' Ron said.

'Yes, but the siren told me to. She offered humbugs. You know how I am about humbugs.'

'Well, the siren offered *me* humbugs to break into the drink barrels, that doesn't mean I went and did it!'

'No, you just widened the rotting wall cavity in your cell for fun, didn't you?' Lilly sneered. 'You're staying put, deal with it.'

'I am a prince of the realm, I demand that you let me out!' Ron bellowed, pointing at her. 'If you don't release me this instant, I'll inform my wife of this and have you burned to a crisp—ooh, sweets!'

He dropped to the ground and trilled, his hands scrabbling across the floor.

'That won't work forever,' Stan told Lilly.

'Why, is he going to grow up anytime soon?' She climbed the stairs. 'Just sit down and shut up until we make port. It won't be more than half an hour, anyway.'

Stan huffed and crossed his arms as Lilly vanished.

Ron snorted and smacked his lips in the next cell.

'Gimme a sweet!' Stan demanded.

Suddenly Lilly tumbled down the stairs head over backside and landed at the foot of their cells with a thud.

'Ow,' she growled, clutching the back of her head.

'What happened to you?' Stan asked in bewilderment.

'Um,' she said with a frown, standing up. 'I think I was just blown down the stairs by the *wind*.'

They frowned.

The ship lurched.

Winds and rain battered the *Red Sail* from all sides.

Lilly returned to the top deck and staggered. The ship swayed from side to side, its sails billowing back and forth wildly.

A wave hammered into them from the starboard side.

Lilly yelled out and grabbed the nearest mast.

127

The *Red Sail* tilted to one side.

The entire crew sprinted starboard and leaned against the rail rising upward into a slant.

The ship just about righted itself.

'How much farther to the port?' Lilly yelled at Orl.

'Fifty yards at most!' he shouted. 'I don't think we'll make it!'

'The hell we won't! Steer for the beach to the left! That way we won't cause much damage!'

Orl took the helm and spun it.

The ship lurched unsteadily to the left and zigzagged towards the beach south of Portmyr.

~

Meanwhile, two men ran across the beach.

Lyseria raced through the thundering winds ahead of them.

'Which one is that, anyway?' one shouted. 'I don't recognise her!'

'Who cares? If that thing knocks over those rocks, we'll be in for—'

The wind knocked Lyseria off course. She swerved into the rocks around the beach, sending them rolling down the sandy plain into the waves below.

~

Orl had just about wrestled control of the ship when a bang sounded.

The *Red Sail* jolted around until it faced the opposite direction.

'What happened?' bellowed Lilly.

Orl ran to the hull and she followed, watching him peer overboard.

'A boulder knocked us around!'

Lilly jerked her gaze back to the beach, her face screwed against the rain.

Several rocks bounced out to sea from the shore – and were heading straight at them.

Lilly let out a low moan.

~

The Ambassador cracked his whip.

Lyseria cowered, her tail between her legs.

'She should be in Serpus right now,' he said to the two keepers. 'What is the Creys' dragon doing here unattended? Have you seen anyone Truphorian in the area this evening?'

'What I want to know is why we're getting a full-blown storm on the frigging equator,' one of the keepers said grumpily. 'We've never had so much as a breeze in these parts, and as soon as Lilly-Anna Crey arrives, the weather decides to kill anyone coming into the docks.'

'Assuming she isn't delayed by the weather, who's to say she hasn't plummeted from this dragon and is lying dead somewhere on this beach?'

'That ship, presumably,' the grumpy employee said. 'I think that's her colours.'

The Ambassador followed the man's finger.

A ship bearing the emerald flag of the Creys approached at a slow, wobbly pace, made slower by the large boulders knocking into it from all sides.

'They aren't planning to stop on the beach with all those rocks in the way?'

A wave threw a particularly large rock at the nose of the ship, crumbling the front mast to a splintery pulp.

The *Red Sail* carried on, regardless.

'I suppose they are,' one of his men replied.

~

Orl wrestled with the helm as loud singing emerged from the deck.

'Why are they singing?' Lilly asked over the uproar. 'This is hardly the time for a musical!'

'I assume it's to avoid doing anything to help,' Orl said bitterly. 'They've been hiding ever since the storm began. Only the original crew of the *Red Sail* are doing anything to help.'

Lilly frowned. 'But I brought the others from Sot's original crew. They're *pirates*. How can they be frightened of a bloody—'

A crash interrupted her from overboard.

'A boulder's just made shit of the front,' Lilly said with a groan. 'The bottom decks will be flooding soon, we need to get off—'

'How? We can't use the rowboats, we'll be killed in this madness! We'll just have to hang on, I think we can just about make it!'

Lilly stared out at the beach thirty yards away and for the first time noticed a dragon on the shore. She didn't need to squint through the maelstrom to see whose dragon it was.

'Who's nicked my dragon?'

'Not important,' Orl said. 'There's another boulder coming.'

~

'This is madness,' the Ambassador snarled, fastening a rein around Lyseria's neck.

'You're not going after that ship, are you?' his man said in horror. 'Look at the poor creature! She's miserable in this storm!'

Lyseria sat with her back hunched against the rain, her wings plastered to her sides.

The Ambassador threw her a piteous glance. He released her reins to signal the two men.

'Bring the cart around,' he ordered. 'If Lilly-Anna and my son really are on that ship, they'll need a lift home, as well as Lyseria.'

They nodded curtly and jogged up the beach.

The Ambassador watched the ship intently. Boulders had ravaged the front, leaving the waves to flood the bowels of the ship. Still the *Red Sail* slowly made its tortured ascent to the shore. The good news was that the last of the boulders had finally drifted behind them, leaving them with just enough boat to make port.

The bad news was that the thunder was starting.

~

'I think that's the last rock,' Lilly said, scanning the sea.

The water was getting higher, she noticed. No – the boat was sinking, she realised with dread.

'Can you hold on?'

'Just about,' Orl said, wrestling with the helm. 'We might need to swim the last few yards, mind.'

Lilly gulped. Anti-perk of living in a landlocked city: she'd never learned how to swim.

Well, that's me finished, she thoughts dourly. *And Stan, actually. And R—*

She froze.

And bolted below decks.

'Where are you going?' Orl shrieked.

She opened her mouth to reply and was interrupted by an enormous rumble.

The air rippled.

They turned their gaze to the sky worriedly.

'I need to get Stan and Ron out of the brig,' she said, tearing her gaze from the clouds. 'They'll drown if we don't—'

A flash blinded her, followed a second later by more thunder. They stared up in horror at the mast.

Which had exploded into flames.

Lilly ran without a further word.

She hurried through the bowels of the ship, insofar as she could through five feet of water. The waves lapped over Lilly's neck and shoulders. She swiped a ring of keys from a hook by the door.

'Help!' a voice called.

Lilly waded to the cells and forced the key in the lock.

Stan and Ron stood up to their necks, terrified. Remnants of wood and debris floated on the surface of the water, the apparent remains of the dividing wall that had separated their cells.

Another wave swept over them, slapping them full in the face.

Spluttering and coughing, Lilly threw the door open, grasped Stan and Ron in each arm and dragged them to the stairs—

—and discovered a battle of the elements above decks.

The flaming mast fought the wind and water pummelling it from all sides.

'I can't steer, Lilly!' Orl shouted from somewhere in the chaos. 'The fire's eaten the back sail, I can't steer her anywhere!'

Lilly swung around and back, frantic. 'Where the hell are the escape boats?'

The escape boats had been washed away completely, except for one.

Stan and Ron crouched in the centre of the boat as the crew flooded towards it.

'What are you doing? Don't growl at them!' Ron said hysterically.

A crew-mate landed on the boat from above.

Stan shoved him overboard.

'The siren says to keep them off!' Stan bellowed, his eyes feverish. 'If they get on, we'll die!'

'Has it occurred to you that the siren's advice might be a bit, I dunno… dodgy?' Ron shrieked in his face. 'Let them on, we can fit at least ten—'

'No! There's only room for us!' Stan snarled, and he bit a hand reaching to them from the water.

Lilly raced down from the ship and hopped on board.

'This thing had better hold,' she said, searching for an oar. 'Stan, will you pass me the—'

Stan locked his teeth around Lilly's outstretched hand.

It was the bandaged one.

Lilly punched him with her good hand, sending him sprawling across the edge of the boat.

'Don't bite me!' she snarled. 'I don't care *how crazy you are*!'

She yanked the oar out from under him and knocked him unconscious with it. Finding a second oar, Ron helped her steer them around the wrecked ship.

The tide was coming in, thankfully carrying them in a rough route to the beach. Lilly and Ron tackled the turbulence between them. Once the boat was stable, Lilly turned her head back to the *Red Sail*.

The fire was putting itself out, but the waves were also engulfing the ship, half of which was already gone from view. Lilly saw Orl leap from the remains of the forecastle and land in the waves below.

'Can he swim?' Ron asked worriedly.

He didn't need to.

Lyseria soared over the boat and dived into the waves. She emerged a moment later with Orl in her claws. Lilly was relieved to see him flailing wildly. At least he was alive.

She pulled her attention back to her own predicament and just about managed to manoeuvre their boat along the tide.

The *Red Sail* crumbled, masts and burning sails imploding into the grey maelstrom.

At least the Devourer is safe, she said to herself in relief as the Red Sail vanished. *It's safe, miles and miles away if Si has anything to do with it.*

The boat drifted atop the waves now. The beach came into closer range, the view obstructed every so often by large bits of debris carrying members of the *Red Sail's* crew.

About three yards from the shore, the boat lurched dangerously. Before they could act, it upturned them into the water with a splash.

Stan jolted into consciousness with a scream and swallowed a mouthful of water.

Lilly felt mud sliding under her knees. The three slid onto the beach, the wave landing heavily over their heads.

The Ambassador waded into the ankle-deep water. Orl, having been deposited onto the beach a moment earlier, made to follow and toppled into the sand instead.

Lilly accepted a hand from the Ambassador and pulled Stan up with her, Ron clinging to his sleeve in turn. She cast a gaze at her husband-to-be, for the first time.

He shared the delicate frame of his son and a great deal of his facial structure, all beneath a full head of silver hair peppered with white. On the Ambassador, however, the lines at the corners of each facial feature stood out most to Lilly, the years between them wreathing his good looks like a shroud.

The Ambassador lifted her knuckles to his lips in greeting. His fingers were *pruny*, she spotted with distaste, eyeing the protruding knuckles in particular, covered with loose rings of skin.

Her stomach tensed in renewed reluctance. *Oh, hell no.* She shivered. There was no way in hell she was lying in bed with this man. Seth had another thing *coming.*

'An unorthodox way to make port, my lady?'

'I'm a princess, not a sea dog,' she growled, scowling.

She flicked her hand out of his. Rain and seawater dribbled coolly down her neck, making her shiver.

'Nice of you to help, by the way,' she added in a sour grumble.

'You had it covered,' he said with a wink. 'I was preparing Lyseria for rescue if you needed it, but it turns out my son required it more than you.'

Orl lifted his face from the sand to glower at him.

'Don't underestimate him,' Lilly said sharply, earning a look of slight alarm. 'If he hadn't taken the helm, we would have died long before you'd seen us.'

Orl sat up with a grateful smile.

The Ambassador offered her an arm, looking faintly impressed.

'Karnak, at your service, my lady. Allow me to escort you and your companions to a carriage. We have a long journey to the mansion and we could do with somewhere dry to sit.'

Lilly smiled thinly. She pointedly ignored the proffered elbow.

Orl rose to his feet. She threw him a fond glance. Despite the miserable weather, it made her a little better seeing his sour expression fold into something grateful.

~

One mile from the coastline and counting, the *Devourer* floated serenely in no particular direction.

Si guided it lazily around the settling storm.

'Thank Christ she's gone,' Tully said, leaning on the rail.

Sot pivoted to face a handful of crew-mates lingering on the main deck.

'The coast is clear!' he called down to them. 'Princess Pirate Wench has officially buggered off!'

Sot's heavy sigh of relief was echoed by tenfold.

'Looks like I've got my ship back,' Sot said, arms folded in satisfaction.

'You've got a short memory,' Si said.

He barked orders at the deck and jerked the wheel to the right.

The *Devourer* curved gracefully towards the shore.

'I'm the full package, remember?' Si said with a smile. 'Surgeon, chef, lady-killer... and extremely dashing pirate captain.'

'Which is just as well,' Tully piped up, 'because if she had any more of her father in her, she would have killed you outright.'

'Don't pretend I'm just your insurance package,' Sot scolded. 'If it weren't for me, this ship would fall apart.'

'Yeah, yeah,' Si said flippantly. 'Tully's still first mate, though.'

'Eh?' Sot shrieked, incensed.

'Well, we can't hide away the most handsome Beult brother and let Captain Dashing here have all the fun, can we?' Tully said with a grin.

'Oi,' Si barked. 'Who said you was the most handsome?'

'You know it more than anyone,' he said. 'You married my sister, didn't you?'

Sot froze and licked his lips. 'Did you just say he married his own sister?'

Si rolled his eyes.

'I was adopted,' he said. 'When he was small. Anna came along while I went off with King Theo in me teens.'

'Oh, so not only have you shacked up with your adopted sister, you've also went and desecrated a little girl?'

'This is why I broke his arm when I joined the crew,' Tully said.

'I didn't know who she was, alright?' Si exclaimed, releasing the helm to throw his arms in the air. 'I went off with King Theo in the war, to mind his little nephew, right? Few years later I come home and this pretty girl answers the door. What else am I supposed to do?'

'Keep your trousers up until she gives you her full name, generally,' Tully retorted.

'I was a young man in them days, I had a lot of pent-up tension,' Si argued.

'You were thirty-two.'

'That's a young man!'

'And she was sixteen, you filthy son of a—'

'Alright, pack it in!' Sot barked, stepping between them before a fight could break out.

'Funny, that,' Tully went on regardless, hopping from the rail. 'I was living with her at the time, age twenty-three. Never felt the need to bang her, myself.'

'You watched her grow up, dint you? I didn't, I don't see a little sister like you do, I just see a beautiful woman—'

'Who looks just like me,' Tully finished.

'Oi, don't you dare, she looks nuffing like you!'

'Naw, mate, she just has the same mannerisms and general facial features,' Tully said, 'that's nuffin, is it?'

'She is nuffin—'

'Don't matter anyway to you, does it?' Tully snarled, stepping forward. 'As long as she has tits and a bunghole—'

Si threw himself at him.

'Alright, that's enough!' Sot slammed himself between the two, shoving them away from each other. 'We have things to do, remember? And none of it involves killing each other over your tart of a sister.'

'Oi!' Si and Tully said in unison.

'Never mind "oi!",' Sot snapped. 'We've waited fifteen weeks to get rid of her, we ain't wasting any more time.'

Si growled and shoved himself away from the helm. 'He's right.'

Shoving Tully out of the way and getting a shove in return, Si leaned on the edge of the rail.

The horizon was nice and clear now, he observed. The storm seemed to have dropped out completely.

Almost as though by magic…

'Come on, then,' Si called to the crewmen on deck as the ship headed for Portmyr. 'We have real work to do.'

PART THREE: RAINING BODIES

eth's bloodshot eyes bored into the baby shower cake in horror.

It was shaped like a swollen belly, complete with breasts and a phantom hand protruding slightly out of the top. It did not look appetising.

Neither did Cienne, who sat beside him in a similarly swollen fashion. She cradled a platter of sardines like she would cradle the child that would probably never be born.

Hands and scattered conversation made their rounds over the table of finger food, shying away from the cake in equal earnest.

Jimmy clapped his hands together. 'Right then, now that the two-month delay is behind us, let's finally celebrate the new arrival to the royal family—'

'Who is a month late,' Cienne drawled. 'And counting. Can we open the presents and leave, please?'

Jimmy tentatively eyed Cienne's savage glare.

'Er, yes, let's bring the… presents over,' he said in a small voice.

Seth yawned widely.

'Are you sure he's late?' Eleanor asked. 'You're still getting bigger—'

'The baby's still getting bigger, the baby!' Jimmy hissed.

'The baby, I mean, yes,' she corrected.

'Maybe it's twins,' Seth said with another yawn.

Silence fell on the drawing room.

'Never,' Cienne snarled, 'ever… say the "T" word. Ever.'

The silence resumed.

'Alright,' Seth said timidly.

The pause ensued.

'Oh look, a little basket!' Queen Eleanor trilled, for want of a better remark.

Jimmy fetched the basket.

Seth's face stretched open again.

Cienne grasped his chin and slammed his mouth shut, making his teeth clatter.

'Isn't that sweet, Cienne?' Eleanor asked desperately. 'All the little… blankets and things.'

Jimmy plonked the basket on Cienne's lap.

'And the... handle...' Jimmy said lamely.

Cienne ignored them both and glared at Seth through narrowed eyes.

Tendons protruded from Seth's neck as he suppressed the urge to yawn.

'Well, let's cut the cake, shall we?' Jimmy said.

'Let's not, it's hideous. What did *you* get for me, Seth?'

Seth hesitated.

Cienne gave him a sweet little smile. It practically radiated venom in anticipation of his reply.

Seth licked his lips.

'The uh, buh, baby.'

He pointed at the rotund swell beneath her flowing gown.

'Anything else?' she asked frostily.

'I can give you a hug if you like,' Seth added.

Cienne's lip curled hatefully.

'I'll just... put this over here,' Jimmy said slowly.

He took the basket to the other end of the room in an attempt to diffuse the tension.

Eleanor sighed heavily and made a beeline for the wine.

Seth yawned uncontrollably, turning away from Cienne for reasons of safety.

'So,' said Cienne's lady-in-waiting. 'Did Erik suggest any possible ways of, you know... bringing the birth?'

'He suggested one way,' Cienne said in a monotone. 'It traditionally requires the presence of a man, however.'

Seth froze with a grimace.

'No other way, then?' Jimmy said quickly. 'Walk of the grounds, some light aerobics maybe—'

'None at all,' she said over him, her eyes boring into the back of Seth's head.

Eleanor returned with two cups of wine.

Seth snatched one of them in both hands.

There was a terse silence in which the guests ate and Seth drank.

Jimmy glanced out the window at the sundial below. It was approximately four o'clock.

He turned to the guests and listened idly to conversation.

Just as a white bonnet lifted to reveal a white mask. It winked at him.

Jimmy grinned.

Eleanor cleared her throat and gestured at the presents. 'What do you think of the gifts?'

'Hmph. I think I'd like some time alone to rest,' said Cienne. 'Would you mind taking the guests for a tour around the castle?'

'A tour?'

'Yes, a tour. Or three.'

'I will join you,' said Seth, rising.

'Surely,' Cienne said icily, 'having lived in the castle your entire life, you would already know where everything is?'

'Actually, you'd be very surprised,' Seth said, trying to escape.

Cienne punched his crotch.

Seth gave a strangled shout and collapsed beside her again.

'You can do that later. We'll spend some time together, just you and me.'

'And me,' Jimmy said in earnest. 'And...'

The white bonnet had vanished.

'Oh,' he said, dejected.

The guests filed out behind the queen dowager.

Cienne waited for Jimmy to leave.

'Anyone fancy a board game?' he asked brightly.

'Piss off, Jimmy.'

'Yes, my lady.'

'I'll walk you out,' Seth said, bolting to Jimmy's side.

'It's three yards!' she snapped.

They jogged across the room and halted by the hallway door, out of earshot of Cienne.

Jimmy held out a hand.

Seth shook it.

Then they embraced.

'I want you to know you've always been my best friend,' Seth said with feeling.

'There's still time for the feeling to be mutual, sir,' Jimmy said.

'I don't think there is,' he whispered in despair.

'Seth!'

They broke apart. Jimmy gave him an encouraging nod.

Seth put on a brave face and, as slowly as possible, shut the door.

Jimmy ran downstairs before the ground had time to shake.

Seth's mother slouched in the queen's throne as he arrived downstairs.

'So much for the tour,' he commented.

'They all went home,' she said, rolling her eyes. 'As if I'd offered to cut their heads off as opposed to show them around a castle.'

'It's the tension that does that. You could cut it with a knife in there.'

'*Stop yawning!*' shrieked the speaker by the fireplace.

'That doesn't sound good,' Jimmy said with a wince.

'*I told you, I'm not in the mood!*' Seth's voice resonated from the brass sound horn in the wall.

'*You're always in the mood!*'

A girl with a basket of clean sheets froze at the foot of the stairs.

'I'm tired! OI! Stop it!' Seth shrieked. 'You'll pull it clean off, look, get off me, alright, fine, do what you want—'

A shudder ran through Jimmy's core. He knew Seth's refusal wouldn't last long.

He snatched the clean sheets from the girl and, sprinting across the room to the fireplace, shoved them, basket and all, into the speaker.

After some frantic kicking, the royal couple's voices faded out and the quiet resumed.

'Never,' he emphasised to the girl, panting, 'take those out of there. *Ever.*'

'But what if she—' began Eleanor.

'Ever.'

~

With a slight breeze in his hair and the sand clinging to his fine blue clothes like gold dust, Royston Joyce felt glorious.

He stood on a small hill just south of Minu, the primary mining spot for Far Isle immigrants. Immigrants planted their roots everywhere, Royston noticed. He was going to change that, make no mistake – or at the very least stop them from thieving his life partners.

Royston diverted his attention from his troubled love life and brought an eight-pointed star from his cloak. Aiming one of the points north towards Minu, Royston sang three notes in a soft tenor and listened for the landscape to change.

You didn't see Copers first under any circumstances. The rumble of the earth always came first, as if to herald the coming of danger.

Which is precisely what Royston was thinking for a split second before the city came – and what he should have been thinking a good deal harder beforehand, he realised as he suddenly flew through the sky for a few hundred leagues and landed face first into a glass ceiling.

Royston Joyce died that day. He wasn't entirely surprised. A shard of conservatory through the left temple tends to have some nasty side-effects.

What was surprising was the way, once the doors to the city appeared, a giant invisible finger flicked him halfway across the country. A finger from a hand rather like that of a god…

~

Lilly opened her eyes at sunset to find herself at an angle.

A steep hill met her gaze as she stuck her head out of the window, and at the summit of it stretched a vast animal enclosure.

Fire was coming out of it.

'Your mansion's in there?' Stan asked in horror, his head outside the window opposite.

'No, no,' Lord Karnak said, his accent a lilting edition of the Truphorian inflection. 'This is merely the dragon sanctuary, where we breed creatures like that of Lyseria. She refused to come with us in the cart, doubtless she will have flown here after the storm to await your arrival.'

'How do you know she'll know the way?' Lilly asked.

'I know dragons.'

A screech erupted from within the enclosure.

Lilly squinted into the netting.

'Please don't tell me those two are making love,' she grimaced.

A collection of grey scales writhed and rolled in mid-air in a flurry of disembodied wings and legs. It was just as well the pens were huge, Lilly thoughts. Each dragon had plenty of room to move around, and it looked like they needed it.

Karnak followed her gaze.

'Alas, no,' he said. 'They're just fighting. We've been trying to get them to mate for weeks. Their mating ritual is not much different, but—ah, now they're mating!' he said in triumph.

'They remind me of my brother and his wife,' Lilly said, making a face.

Karnak grinned. 'I have heard your sister-in-law is... spirited.'

'I call it violent,' Stan said with a wince.

Lilly grinned, recalling the shovel incident.

'I call it green-fingered,' Ron said with a grin.

They frowned at him in varying levels of disgust.

'You know? The shovel?'

'Ah,' they said in realisation.

'Yes, that was a tad uncalled for,' Karnak said.

'Oh, he didn't mean it like that,' Lilly said hurriedly, 'he really did just mean the shovel—'

'Yes, as did I, yes,' he corrected.

'Yeah,' Stan said. 'Don't forget you're marrying a Crey, though. The Fleurelles are supposed to be the nice family.'

Lilly stuck her tongue out at that.

The coach rolled uphill and sure enough, Lyseria soared up to meet them.

Lilly leapt out of the carriage and hugged her around the head.

Karnak watched in interest. 'You like dragons?'

'Just my one,' she replied, the side of her head pressed to Lyseria's ear.

Karnak smiled thoughtfully.

Orl approached Lyseria and tentatively stretched out an arm.

Lyseria bowed her head and tolerated a pat.

'I'd have thought you'd be at home with dragons,' Lilly said.

'Only the ones in books,' he replied, stroking Lyseria's neck.

Lilly gave him a half-smile. 'Do they talk about my lot over here often?'

'In undertones of malice. My father requested this alliance ten or twelve years ago and King Theo declined on personal grounds. The country's been a thrall of Adem's supplies since. People reckon this entire arrangement has a catch somehow.'

Lilly nodded. 'Understandable, I s'pose. No offence or anything, but my dad kind of had a point. The age difference aside, our children would be inheriting a wasteland and draining Adem's resources without the obligation to pay for any of it. I don't think my brother knew what he was buying.'

'He was buying an army,' Karnak piped up.

He came up behind them, his hands in his pockets.

'I'm sure it hasn't escaped your attention that the Emmetts have finally broken into the realm of land owners.'

'I thought they owned Mellier?'

'Their ancestors did,' Karnak replied to Lilly's question. 'They then married into the owners of Portabella, the Leyons, combining the regions into what is now called the continent of Portamellier. The Fleurelles usurped this crown some decades later.

'My point is that now they have clinched Stoneguard, they will have their eye on bigger fare: and the nearest country is in dubious hands at present.'

'What do you mean, dubious?'

'The Emmetts are receiving a mystery tax from King Seth,' he said. 'A payment some people may perceive as a bribe.' He shrugged. 'None of my business, of course. I only wish for my trade and my bride.'

Lilly's blue eyes narrowed. 'If it's none of your business, then you won't mind refraining from insinuating that my brother committed murder.'

His eyes widened slightly.

'He wouldn't hurt a fly,' she went on, icily. 'I won't accept any slander stating otherwise.'

As Karnak opened his mouth to protest, a man sprinted out from within the sanctuary.

A dove perched on his shoulder. Karnak looked at the bird with a grave expression.

'Good news?' Stan asked, eyeing the bird.

Karnak accepted a message from the man and read it.

'No,' he said, pocketing the paper. 'Quite the opposite.'

Lilly held her breath.

Orl turned to her. 'A messenger with a dove heralds a death.'

'And this death occurred beneath my roof,' Karnak said. 'Or what's left of it. Will Lyseria safely carry passengers?'

'If one of them is me,' Lilly said.

He nodded.

'We'll need to send you home as soon as possible,' he said. 'One of your men has been murdered.'

~

142

His flesh had mouldered away years ago, leaving a dark spot where his innards had been spilled. Skull upturned, jaw dropped, the skeleton yawned into the vacant sky.

Despina eyed the late traveller nauseously.

'D'you always have to take us down the route full of dead people?' Elliot accused Marbrand.

The desert surrounded them in all directions, the exception being their wake. The district of Wandyr had proven to be a dismal diversion to the quest when the mayor had begged to come with them, making their arrival into the amber waste more welcome than anticipated. They continued west alongside a comforting view of the sea as their three camels trudged dutifully behind them to the mining town of Minu.

Putting the skeleton out of mind, Despina turned her attention to the map in Marbrand's hands.

Zeyl was their next destination approximately twenty leagues north of Minu – and it was the first of the eight Dead Cities. It was rumoured to have been deserted due to a flash flood caused by a poltergeist, which made Despina feel a lot better... not.

She tried to focus on the sound of her steed's monotonous chewing as flies whizzed in figure-of-eights around their heads.

'Russ?' Elliot asked suddenly. 'Still got that letter?'

'The one from the priest, back from the day the king died?'

'That's the one.'

Marbrand clicked his fingers. 'Forgot all about that!' He patted a trouser pocket. 'Must give that to young Ronald after we've sorted his mother out. King's orders.'

'What does it say?' Despina asked curiously.

Marbrand tapped his nose in Despina's direction.

'It's not crucial information... yet,' he said with a wink. 'Once we find Aaliyaa and Ron, I'll tell you... and everyone else. It's a surprise.'

'A good one?' Elliot asked hopefully.

'Oh yes.' He grinned. 'A very good one.'

Despina frowned, annoyed. She despised secrets. 'What kind of surprise?'

He winked at her again. 'Let's just say King Sam didn't quite leave this world without a sound.'

He stashed Father Toffer's letter back into his pocket and said no more about it, despite Despina's adamant glaring.

Elliot's expression told he had more to say on this matter. 'You don't reckon Queen Aaliyaa knows about this mysterious letter?'

Marbrand's smug expression faltered. 'She might do.'

'I take it it's not a very good surprise for her, then?' Despina said.

'Not so much, no.'

She opened her mouth to ask more when he ushered her to be silent, pointing ahead.

A figure walked across the sands in a laboured waddle. Despina found it hard to tell if he was approaching them or continuing ahead.

Marbrand squinted at him. 'Any weapons?'

Elliot followed his gaze. 'None that I can see.'

They approached the stranger warily as he stumbled across the sand and wrestled with his headscarf.

'Good evening!' Marbrand called. 'Having some headgear trouble, are we?'

The man threw his head forward and hauled the thing off, throwing it into the sand and eyeballing it.

Despina rolled her eyes.

'I'm just about getting sick of you,' she snarled. 'What do you want now?'

'Come to warn you away from the Dead Cities,' the Bastard said irritably, rubbing sand from his already sandy-coloured hair. 'No need to be so unfriendly.'

'Oh yes, we've heard,' said Marbrand conversationally. 'We won't be staying long, just passing through.'

'What are you talking about?' Despina asked Marbrand.

'I've just warned him about the witches' coven in the city,' the Bastard said idly.

'No you didn't, you didn't say a word about witches' covens!'

'I didn't to you. The queen's in an old bell tower in Minu, so that halves the walking distance for you.'

'Why are you telling me where the queen is—'

'Ah, that sounds like her,' Elliot said darkly.

'What sounds like her?' she demanded angrily.

'Aaliyaa,' the Bastard said irritably, rolling his eyes. 'You know, the woman you're looking for? I've just informed them I've seen her screeching bloody murder at the miners.'

'No you haven't! You haven't said any of these things!' she exclaimed.

The Bastard sighed and rubbed his eyes.

'We're having two conversations at once,' he said. 'Keep up! I knew you'd be rude once you saw me, so to save time and explanation, I split the air a little so that you could have your rude conversation on one half and I could calmly explain the situation to your friends on the other. I'm just about to tell a rather amusing joke about—d'you want to hear it?' he asked suddenly in excitement. 'I'm really proud of it, listen to this, listen...'

Despina stared at him in bemusement.

'What's the difference between the Queen of Stoneguard and the Queen of Adem?'

Despina paused and hesitantly lifted a shoulder.

'The Queen of Stoneguard is anaemic!' he said triumphantly. 'D'you get it? She has an iron deficiency! And the Queen of Adem doesn't, because she has a shovel made of iron, and... it's a good joke, isn't it?'

He grinned idiotically.

Despina simply frowned.

He heaved a sigh. 'You have no sense of humour.'

'... because her shovel's made of iron!' Marbrand and Elliot said in unison, and the two started laughing.

'See? They liked it!'

The Bastard grinned like a moron, pointing.

'I guess you had to be there,' Despina said drily. 'Are you going now?'

'How ungrateful!' he exclaimed in disbelief. 'I cross the blistering desert to help you with your quest, *and* tell a brilliant joke, and you're nothing but rude to me all day! No pleasing some people.'

He grumbled, walking past her in disgruntlement.

'See you again!' Elliot called brightly. 'What a nice bloke.'

'Yeah, he's hilarious,' Despina muttered. 'We're headed to Minu, then?'

'Yep. That makes things a lot easier,' Marbrand said happily. 'Just goes to show, you never know how much help a complete stranger will give you.'

Despina gave a derisive snort.

~

Halle ran forward, and quickly ran back again.

'Chicken,' sneered the suspiciously loquacious dove.

Halle glared at it. 'For a species so fragile they flee from a change in air temperature, you're hardly one to talk.'

'Ever been caught and shoved into a pie on Winter's Eve? No, I didn't think so.'

Halle glared at the creature again before uneasily turning back to his next obstacle. According to the talkative avian, the next riddle proclaimed thus:

Labyrinths lead to a severe embrace.

Annoyingly, the bird failed to divulge the meaning of this second line of nonsense, leaving Halle to pursue his only idea and attempt to hug the labyrinth's resident Minotaur.

Hiding behind a dusty sandstone wall, he quickly revised his options and massaged a dislocated shoulder as the dove delved into a pessimistic monologue.

'... waiting in darkness with a pack of strangers, who all happen to be territorial males, mark you, waiting, just waiting for the knife to come down from any direction before you either get to escape into the path of a pack of archers or simply be chopped in half before the light of day hits you—'

'How sad I am for your plight.'

'Oh, ha, ha, very wry,' the bird said. 'So what are you going to hug this time? A dragon?'

'Now who's being wry? No, I thought I'd ignore the riddle and try starving to death instead.'

145

'No need to be nasty,' it said mildly.

Halle had a misogynistic instinct that it might be female.

'I'm just wondering when you were going to turn around and do it right.'

Halle pivoted. 'This isn't enlightening me.'

'You have to travel through the maze, you tit,' it said, its voice echoing in his head, where it had come from since the thing had made itself apparent. 'That's what it's there for.'

'But what about the embrace bit?'

'That's for later. You have to get to the end first or you won't be embraced.'

'But I'll get lost.'

'The term "lost" is relative,' it said knowingly. 'Just tell yourself you know the way and walk.'

'Anything else "relative"?' he said sourly, trudging forward.

'Everything is relative.'

'Of course it is.'

He turned left, rounded a corner, turned right and stopped.

'Are you sure I'm not lost?' he asked dubiously.

Two huge arms snatched him roughly, jarring his injured shoulder.

The labyrinth swirled as he was pulled backwards into a wall and deposited into a pond.

Several streams led from it.

The grubby water lapping around the middle of his torso, Halle waded to the bank and tried to push himself up, only for the bank to swallow his hands.

He yanked them back and stuck them under his armpits.

'Is the term "stuck" relative?'

'Nope, stuck's stuck,' he said apologetically.

~

Elliot collapsed into a sand dune and peeled his shirt away from his back for the fifth time that day.

'I need that balm,' he said with a moan. 'My back is on fire.'

Despina rifled through a rucksack from on top of her camel. Marbrand leapt from his own steed as Elliot caught the jar of balm on the head with a yelp.

Dusk was starting to fall on their makeshift camp, marking the end of their second week in the waste. Despina dismounted to set up their tent as Elliot smeared a glob of cream across his shoulder-blades.

'Oi,' Marbrand said softly, interrupting them in their tasks. 'Who's that coming?'

Despina sighed heavily and turned, expecting the Bastard with another of his fabulous jokes.

Instead, she found a small group of around six people, each brandishing a small bundle.

Marbrand rose, pulling his sword free.

'Lower your blade, sir,' a heavy Far Isles accent said, in a deep voice that rumbled like an avalanche. 'Please. We mean you no harm.'

Marbrand kept his fingers around the hilt, but he pointed the blade to the ground.

As the group approached, they got a better look at the six men. The man who spoke led the group, a man of middling years who bore a vague resemblance to Marbrand except for his prominent cheekbones – a Cientra feature.

Marbrand suddenly recognised him.

Sergeant Ankovich, a presumably former member of the Hornes' night watch, approached, wiping dust from his eyes.

'Sergeant,' he greeted cautiously. 'What brings you to the desert?'

Ankovich looked at him with a start, halting a handful of yards away from the trio.

'Marbrand,' he said in surprise. 'I thought I recognised your blade.'

He placed a wrapped bundle of indeterminate content on the ground.

'I was laid off by Emmett when he took Stoneguard,' he said sourly. 'Framed me as a threat to the palace because I shared a nationality with Queen Aaliyaa. Which brings me to your question.'

He gestured towards the five men around him. Three were of an age with himself, but bore a particularly more distinct look – their grey hair was knotted into thick locks right up to their scalp and their beige skin covered with swirling white ink. They held similarly embellished swords on their hips, these instead swirling with intricate carvings.

They're not from here either, Despina surmised.

She turned her gaze to the last two. They were much older, bearing the same look as the three warriors.

'My companions come from the far end of the Dead Lands,' Ankovich explained. 'We have come to put the queen into custody. It's fortunate we ran into you: we may need your help.'

'What are you arresting her for?' Marbrand asked.

'Never mind that,' Elliot said, gazing at the group with a dubious frown. 'You're not here to... eat us, are you?'

Ankovich started laughing.

Marbrand glared at Elliot.

'What?' he said, his hands out. 'You've heard the rumours. They come from Cientra, team up with blokes who don't know better, take everyone prisoner, cook 'em over a spit.'

'You'll find that's the Rhillit, actually,' Ankovich said with a grin. 'Our lot are just known for sleeping with our siblings. Putting aside the racial stereotypes: may we sit?'

Marbrand flourished a hand to their camp.

'So,' Marbrand said. 'What do you need Aaliyaa Horne for?'

147

'She's up to something, and it isn't good,' Ankovich replied, sitting cross-legged beside one of the older men with the others settling down behind them. 'I was just accompanying this fellow, Kzar,' he gestured to the old man at his side, 'to the desert. He thinks he might be able to find out exactly what she's plotting.'

'Greetings, Kzar,' Marbrand said politely.

Kzar was unresponsive.

'He's a mute,' Ankovich explained. 'He can't hear you, and he can't speak our language. But he can communicate with the dead and tell us their advice in an old tongue, which this fellow,' he pointed at a second tribesman, 'can translate.'

'And how is that going to help us find out what she's up to?'

'He's summoning something,' Despina said.

She lifted one end of the cloth covering the bundle belonging to Ankovich.

Some kind of green plant had been harvested.

'What the hell is that?' Marbrand demanded, rising to his knees.

'It's a herb we use for the process,' Ankovich said hurriedly, placing a reassuring hand on Marbrand's shoulder. 'Kzar needs to speak with a Cientra spirit group, and to communicate with these spirits he needs to be—'

'High as a kite,' Elliot finished.

'Basically,' Ankovich said.

'That's an utter disgrace!' Marbrand shrieked.

'Don't be like that, it isn't as bad as most narcotics out there,' Ankovich soothed. 'I've had it a few times after training my sons in the yard. Takes a lot of the aches away, helps with sleep. It's fabulous—'

Marbrand barked a laugh. 'I'll bloody bet it is!'

'Look, what are you getting uppity about it for? God knows we need these kinds of remedies at our age! You can't tell me you haven't been finding it hard to train or climb stairs the last few years?'

Marbrand spluttered and fell silent. He had a point.

'It's medicinal. And if it helps Kzar's work, then what harm?'

'And you need to do this here in front of the child?' Marbrand said angrily, pointing a finger at Despina.

'We need to do this here in the desert. The child's presence is not required.'

Marbrand turned his gaze to Despina.

'Go out a few yards into the desert,' he instructed. 'Elliot will go with you.'

Despina nodded and rose, Elliot following suit.

'Surprised you'd want to be near that filth, Russ,' Elliot said with a smirk.

Marbrand glowered at him in silence. He didn't feel like explaining to a young man that the medicinal properties did in fact appeal to him somewhat.

Elliot wasn't like to understand in any case, being as strong as an ox. *Bastard*, Marbrand thought with reproach.

Once Marbrand was satisfied with the distance between Despina and the camp, he turned back to Ankovich. 'What do you need to do?'

'Help me unwrap the rest of these bundles,' Ankovich said, 'and set up a brazier beside Kzar. Then we'll need to burn it.'

'All of it?' Marbrand asked incredulously. 'There's enough here to knock out a horse.'

'The more of it he inhales, the deeper into their realm he goes,' Ankovich said. 'And he'll need to cross a lot of protection to get to these particular spirits.'

'What's so special about them?' Marbrand asked.

'They've been guiding Aaliyaa through the Dead Cities. That's what Kzar reckons, anyway.'

Marbrand personally reckoned Kzar had his eye on the free ton of weed, but he kept his opinions to himself and helped them unwrap the 'herb'.

A few yards away, Elliot had wisely decided to move the camels away from the group and were getting them settled. Despina sat on one of their rucksacks with her chin in her palm, eavesdropping.

Spirits, she thought to herself, wondering if any of these spirits bore a resemblance to the Creys. She decided to find out for herself. Glancing back at Elliot, she curled into a foetal position using the rucksack as a pillow and closed her eyes.

If there were spirits involved, that meant Sal'plae was involved.

Despina relaxed her body and quickly fell asleep.

'Hello,' a voice said in the darkness. 'You're new to this, aren't you? I can tell. My name is Geldemar, Despina. You can open your eyes.'

Despina's eyelids bolted open – then she quickly realised she didn't have any eyelids to open.

Everything was in shades of purple, just as she had read in the books. However, the side-effects described were missing. She felt no heaviness in the air, no shortness of breath, no air of disembodiment –

'That's because you're not here, my dear,' Geldemar said.

– all of which was replaced by a silver-haired man in a black jerkin.

Despina tried to talk before finding that she had nothing to speak with. Instead, she thought as clearly as she could, 'What do you mean?'

'You're not experiencing any of the symptoms because you're not fully here,' he explained. 'You're just looking in. But I'm butting in, do excuse me. Just thought I'd welcome you to the fold. Not many make it this far without going insane. My name is Geldemar, by the way, did I mention that? I expect you've heard of me.'

'Nope,' Despina replied shortly.

Geldemar's face fell. 'Oh, really? Oh dear. It appears you have more homework to do. Never mind. Best be off, I'm due a visitor in a moment. It was a pleasure to meet you, Despina.'

149

He walked towards the group and vanished.

Despina frowned in his wake. Are all spirits this odd? She was beginning to think they were.

She turned back to the task at hand and watched.

Another moment was spent lighting a brazier. Once a small fire was flaring, Ankovich started slowly piling leaves onto the brazier, smothering the flames momentarily.

Thick smoke fluttered out from beneath the pile of leaves. The shrivelled little man known as Kzar crossed his legs beneath himself and craned his neck back, letting his eyes glaze over.

After a moment of silence, Despina jolted at the sound of a voice.

'Testing,' it said in the silence. 'Test. Test. Testing.'

Kzar and the others were unmoved, although Marbrand did look very relaxed all of a sudden.

'Testing.' Geldemar's voice floated around Despina's head. 'Nothing? He needs more of the herb, evidently. Oh, hurry up then, you know you want it more than he needs it,' he scoffed.

Ankovich held a hand poised over the brazier, the leaves dangling an inch over the flames in waiting.

Kzar lifted a hand into the air.

Ankovich spread his fingers.

The leaves drifted onto the brazier. Once the flames grasped hold of them, they crackled loudly and another gust of smoke emerged into the air.

Despina saw Marbrand breathe in deeply, contrary to his earlier feelings on the substance.

'Hello?' Geldemar said.

Kzar's face didn't register any contact from Geldemar.

'Blast,' Geldemar said angrily.

'What are you trying to do?' Despina wondered in his direction.

'Get him to hear me,' Geldemar said.

A few faint clouds of black appeared behind Kzar and swirled together to form Geldemar's appearance.

He waved a hand over Kzar's face.

'Come on, aren't you zonked enough yet?'

Kzar rocked slightly on the spot, his eyes half open.

'Any sign of the spirits yet?' Ankovich said in a whisper.

Kzar gave a faint shake of his head and blithely lifted a hand again.

Ankovich paused. 'More?'

Kzar grunted yes.

Marbrand, impatient, snatched a large handful of leaves from the pile and threw it onto the brazier.

The flames ate them up greedily.

'Can you hear me now?' Geldemar asked pleasantly.

Kzar's eyes snapped open, alert.

'Aha, now we have business,' Geldemar said in delight, rubbing his hands together. 'Friend, I am he whose knowledge you seek. Can you understand me clearly?'

Kzar grunted ambiguously. Then he waved his hand up again.

'Don't be a greedy sod now, I know you can hear me,' Geldemar said, his arms crossed in disapproval.

An oblivious Ankovich hoisted more leaves onto the flames, filling the camp with dark grey smog.

Kzar inhaled deeply, satisfied.

'Marbrand was right, he's nothing but a lush,' Geldemar muttered with a growl.

He grasped Kzar by the shoulder and gave him a harsh shake until the old man toppled onto his side.

Kzar coughed and looked around himself with a start.

Marbrand and the rest of Ankovich's party watched him, expressionless. His physical body hadn't moved an inch, apparently.

'As I imagine you've read,' Geldemar lectured grandly, presumably to Despina, 'ordinary people haven't got the power to shed their bodies like clothes and enter another Aspect of the universe, but they can temporarily leave their bodies by other means. Wannabe magicians have tried for hundreds of years to transcend from their humdrum lives and enter Sal'plae to join humankind's most powerful individuals.'

'Bet none of them thought of silly smoke,' Despina joked.

'Actually, that was the first thing they tried,' Geldemar said with a smile. 'They just haven't been trying the right ones. This fellow's tribe are revolutionaries in their field, in that they are the only people who bothered splashing out on the good stuff. Oh, don't mind me, friend,' he said to Kzar, who watched him with bemusement. 'My young friend is merely shadowing our discussion for her studies. She's quite the powerful sorceress, though you wouldn't believe it by the way she dresses.'

Despina flicked him the bird, or at least an imaginary equivalent.

'Now, back to business,' Geldemar said, looking professional. 'I hear you're looking for Aaliyaa Horne.'

Kzar gathered his bearings before snarling, 'And what kind of beast have I been encumbered with this time?'

Despina frowned. 'I thought he couldn't speak?'

'I can't,' Kzar snapped at the sky. He evidently wasn't aware that this was the same girl curled up a short distance from where he was sitting. 'My tongue was taken from me by a creature of this realm, much like the one standing before me. That doesn't mean I can't think, though.'

Geldemar flung his head back, his eyes rolling to the heavens.

'He's exaggerating. I didn't take his tongue. I just gave him a mild speech impediment.'

'Speech impediment??' Kzar exploded. 'I can't speak any tongue but that of an ancient civilization from before the time of man! That is not a "speech impediment", that is a crippling of my mind!' Something suddenly occurred to him. 'Wait! You're the blasted one who did this to me?' He squinted at Geldemar. 'You've changed your face since the last five decades. Why?'

'For fun,' Geldemar shrugged. 'I do it every so often, when the whim takes me. But anyway, back to Aaliyaa Horne.'

Meanwhile, back at the camp, Marbrand shut his eyes, hard. The smoke was getting into his head, turning the twilit sand dunes into a hazy mess of brown and black. He glanced over at Elliot and Despina's makeshift camp.

Despina was fast asleep with her head against their rucksack, but Elliot sat up beside her, looking zoned out. *A testament to the strength of the weed*, Marbrand thought cynically.

Ankovich blinked rapidly, trying to keep his mind clear enough to keep an eye on Kzar.

'Are you sure this isn't some sort of con—' Marbrand began.

Kzar's eyes snapped open and his mouth opened in a hideous growl.

One of his men snapped to attention, an open book in hand, ready for translation.

A stream of what seemed to Marbrand to be nonsensical gibberish poured from Kzar's mouth, rousing the entire camp from their stupor, except for Despina.

The man flicked through the tome in his hands speedily.

'Well?' Ankovich asked impatiently.

'She's searching for the Antichrist,' the man said, still flicking.

'You mean some sort of religious figure?' Marbrand said.

Kzar fell silent for a moment before spluttering a single syllable.

'Prophecy,' the man said.

Another syllable fell from the old man's lips.

'Knight,' said the translator.

More single words burst out from Kzar, each punctuated by a pause for their translations.

'Dragon.'

'Daughter.'

'Phoenix.'

'Child.'

'Mother.'

Kzar keeled over shortly after uttering the last word, lost in a deep sleep.

'What a steaming pile of horseshit,' Marbrand said derisively. 'As I suspected.'

The translator scribbled down each word in the back of his book.

'No.' Ankovich took the book from the translator and examined the words carefully. 'This is to do with the prophecy.'

'Everyone and their bloody grandmother are to do with the prophecy,' Marbrand said. 'We know Aaliyaa Horne is a religious zealot, anyone could make up this rubbish based on that. What's so important about the rest of this gibberish?'

'The Knight of Thorns is a role in the prophecy,' Ankovich explained. 'Someone has to fill that role in order for the prophecy to be fulfilled. Whether it ends in the world being destroyed or not depends on who fills that role – rumour is, the prophet who saw this vision saw in fact two visions, of two possible outcomes. Everyone is already speculating on the identity of the Antichrist; they've been at it since day one. What everyone is forgetting is who the rest of the players are.'

'So these players, the Child, Mother, whatever, each have a contributing factor on the outcome of this prophecy?'

'It names them specifically,' Ankovich agreed.

'He could have been properly specific and named them outright,' Marbrand grumbled. 'You know, bit of consideration and all that.'

'Kzar isn't the prophet,' Ankovich informed him. 'Neither is his source, by my reckoning. The prophet is most likely an outsider who simply doesn't know their names.'

'So the Creys are out the window,' Marbrand said.

'Not necessarily. The current scions of the Crey line don't exactly cross the general public as the most noble of individuals.'

'They're yobs, you mean.'

'Basically, yes,' Ankovich said with a shrug. 'Aaliyaa Horne is trying to piece together the prophecy, so in order to track her down, we'll have to do the same.'

'Any idea what this prophecy's all about, then?' Marbrand asked, putting out the brazier with a handful of sand. 'I gathered the bit about Howard Rosethorn and the king, but there can't be that much fuss for a cocked-up rescue mission.'

'Not a notion,' Ankovich said. 'We're not even sure if Howard Rosethorn is in fact this Knight. That whole episode with him searching for King Samuel Horne could have been completely separate – Samuel Horne was a usurper, remember. What seems logical is that the one he was supposed to keep alive was Theo Crey, and if the Knight was supposed to save him, we can assume it was from the Antichrist – but I can't see Aaliyaa Horne hunting down the killer of King Theo Crey, somehow.'

Seth Crey's figure carrying off a blood-coated chopping axe lingered in the forefront of Marbrand's mind for a moment. He had to agree – he didn't think Aaliyaa would risk getting rid of a possible ally, and there was no way she could know that Seth was the one who did it.

'I'm thinking we get onto the priests in Stoneguard,' Ankovich said. 'I'm told that's where the Prophet is rumoured to be hiding. Perhaps they're suggesting a version to the queen that we can follow and find her.'

'Bit of a problem with that,' Marbrand said with a wince. 'Seems the place was burnt down shortly after Prince Vladimir's send-off.'

'What?' Ankovich exploded, rubbing his eyes between his thumb and forefinger. 'Bloody hell. Were they all killed?'

'I don't know about killed, but I saw the ruins myself,' Marbrand said. 'Wasn't a lot of room for a priesthood to hide.'

'Bloody hell,' Ankovich repeated.

He heaved a sigh and rose to his feet.

'I'd better get Kzar back to the village,' he said by way of goodbye. 'He's going to be out cold for the next hour, at least according to his men. At any rate, Aaliyaa Horne's input towards saving the world will not be welcome. She'll no doubt make out it's all about her – you know what she's like. If you find her, you know what to do with her.'

'I thought you wanted to claim her?'

'Alive or dead, I'm not fussed which,' Ankovich said bluntly. 'Preferably dead, if it comes to it. By the time she gets to Stoneguard, Emmett will have expired her without much difficulty anyway.' He gave Marbrand a parting salute. 'Mind yourself.'

Marbrand gave him a nod as he and his companions hoisted Kzar upright.

As the group packed their belongings, Marbrand's glance passed momentarily on a forgotten package of plant. Furtively, he slipped it into his rucksack.

Despina watched Geldemar wave off the dissipating Kzar.

'Why didn't you just tell him she was hunting Lilly-Anna Crey?' she asked him.

Geldemar tilted his head to one side.

'Now how did you know that?'

'Overheard you pondering how to tell him without telling him outright,' Despina said. 'What's the idea with that, then?'

'I like watching them squabble over who the Antichrist is,' he said with a grin. 'There's no point setting up a chess game by putting the king in check.'

'Why play games with them? Why not let them find her?'

'Just for fun, that's all,' he said with a glint in his eye that told Despina he had other intentions.

She sighed. Secrets, secrets, secrets. She decided she didn't care. Load of old bollocks anyway, she thought to herself, thinking that if anyone could really see into the future, an account of it would be written somewhere.

'Fine,' she said, rolling her eyes. 'Be that way.'

~

II

Seth was just nodding off at the kitchen table when a man, loudly, cleared his throat.

He flinched awake with a grunt. 'What?'

'I've come to make a precognitive business proposal,' the stranger announced. 'My name's Jon.'

Seth blinked and stretched with a wince. In between his wife's present temperament and recent nights spent in his throne as opposed to his bed, Seth had a feeling his spine would spell 'Crey' before this child had a chance to be christened it.

'What's precognitive mean?'

'Seeing into the future.'

The man's eyes widened as though he had let something slip.

'It's a metaphor,' he added hurriedly.

'That answers my next question,' Seth said. 'What time is it?'

'About four in the afternoon.'

Seth froze.

Jon waited with a patient smile.

'You haven't seen—'

'A man in a white hat and black boots on my way in?' he finished. 'Nope. Can't say I have.'

Seth relaxed and regarded the salesman in front of him.

Jon was short and skinny with a heart-shaped head that seemed slightly too big for him. He smiled amiably at Seth through black, badly-trimmed facial hair. 'Chipmunk' was the first word to come to mind, possibly on account of his nasally-sounding voice. Seth didn't particularly like chipmunks, but since he wasn't wearing a large white hat Seth decided to give him the benefit of the doubt.

'So what are you selling?'

'Eggs,' Jon said promptly.

'We don't need eggs, we have those things that make them, you know...'

Seth waved a hand in the air vaguely, with a yawn.

Jon lifted his eyebrows. 'Chickens?'

Seth expelled an audible 'awl', blinking repeatedly.

'That's it, those.'

Jon's friendly smile withered, as friendly smiles generally did midway through an exchange with Seth Crey. 'You see, that's why I call it a precognitive business proposal.'

'Why?'

'Because very shortly, you won't be having any chickens at all.'

Jon smiled enigmatically.

Seth frowned, nonplussed.

Jimmy threw open the courtyard doors with a bang.

'She's eaten all of the chickens!' he fumed. 'The front pen's empty!'

Seth eyed Jon.

Jon smiled again.

'How much a carton?' Seth asked, with reluctance.

Jimmy blinked. 'A carton of what?'

'Eggs,' Jon said cheerfully.

The butler's eyes narrowed. 'What kind of eggs?'

'The out of a bird's arse kind of eggs,' he responded.

Jimmy's mouth opened in the beginnings of a sarcastic comment. He froze. 'What time is it?'

'Minute past four,' said Jon. 'He's late.'

'Is he?'

Eleanor poked her head into the hall from the stairs. 'Sweetheart, Cienne's asking for you.'

'Tell her I'm entering into negotiations,' Seth said immediately.

'For what?'

'Eggs.'

'We have hens for that.'

'We have what for that?'

Jimmy stared incredulously at Seth.

'Hens are chickens,' he said in disbelief.

Seth's nose wrinkled. 'Are they?'

'Yeah!' he said emphatically.

'Oh,' Seth said in interest.

Jimmy was speechless for a moment.

'Anyway, we've run out,' he said to Eleanor, deciding that the bounds of Seth's stupidity were too vast for him to comprehend at that moment.

'Run out? How?'

A burp sounded from the courtyard.

A flame entered the room from the door, flanked by several blackened feathers.

'Oh, the dragon's back, then,' Eleanor said in dry realisation.

The jade-coloured carpet running down the centre of the room lit up at the end with a *whoof*.

Jimmy hurriedly grabbed Seth's water goblet and put the fire out. 'You should probably see her, your majesty.'

'No, why should I?' Seth asked sulkily.

'You see how easily disaster was averted by me putting out that fire?' said Jimmy. 'The destruction that will ensue if you don't see her highness isn't going to be so easy to resolve. Besides, it's in fact the law.'

'I am the law,' Seth said haughtily. 'The king doesn't take orders from a pregnant psychopath.'

'Actually, there's a law that states the king has to take all orders from his queen – provided she was a virgin when they married,' Jon piped up.

Seth laughed loudly. 'What a load of bull! I never saw my father take any orders from…'

He turned slowly towards his mother.

'Mum?' he said in horror.

Eleanor looked sheepish.

'You weren't a virgin?'

'Not as such,' she said, 'no.'

She looked at the floor.

'Did my father know?'

'Oh yes, he got a discount and everything for it,' she said bitterly.

'It's said that the day they met for the first time, he shook her by the hand, looked her square in the eye and turned to her father to say, "Man, you've overcharged me. That is not a virgin",' Jimmy supplied.

'You can see why I fell for him, can't you?' Eleanor said, deadpan.

'I heard he could mind read,' said Jon. 'I wish he was my old man. He was really cool.'

'That's one word for him,' Eleanor said with a shudder.

Seth tried to put all memory of his father's coldness, in life and death, aside.

'So who was the other man?'

Eleanor made a face. 'Can't recall.'

'Mother,' Seth said darkly.

'Seth,' she pleaded. 'You really don't want to—'

'Don't make me ask Uncle Richard.'

Eleanor flinched. So, for some reason, did Jon.

She heaved a sigh. 'Alright, it's the Ambassador of the Dead Lands.'

Seth's eyes bulged.

'You mean,' Jimmy said in horror, 'the bloke your only daughter's just been married off to?'

'Ooh, that's awkward,' Jon piped up with a wince.

'Mum, why?' Seth wailed.

'Because he wasn't your father,' she said grimly.

'Just how old were the two of you when this happened?' Jimmy asked, curious.

'… fifteen.'

'Both of you?'

Eleanor winced. '… he was… quite a bit older.'

Seth stared into space.

'Lilly,' he said mournfully. 'I've married my baby sister to a pervert.'

'At least you'll have a lot in common,' Jimmy said, ever the optimist. 'I'll just go make some tea.'

'Got a cup for me?' Jon asked.

Jimmy hesitated.

'S'pose,' he said with a shrug, exiting.

'Why did you let me send her to him?' Seth demanded. 'Why didn't you say anything? He could have been our father if...'

Terror swept across his face.

'Oh, don't look at me like that! Theo waited a year before... doing anything anyway, to make sure I wasn't already with child,' she snapped. 'Besides, he would have known immediately anyway. I swear he almost *could* mindread.'

'*Ah yes, Adrienne,*' Theo's voice whispered in his ear.

Seth silently agreed.

There was silence for a moment.

'You gonna buy any eggs then, or what?'

Seth glared at Jon.

'No. We'll get more hens, and in the meantime we'll make do with...'

He huffed and glanced at his mother for help.

'Blue things, big tails, you know. Eyes in them...'

Eleanor narrowed her eyes. 'Peacocks?'

'Yes, peacock eggs!' he finished grandly.

'See, here's the thing,' Jon said.

Another burp roared into the door, accompanied by some longer feathers.

'She's getting a bath later,' Seth said viciously.

'Just so long as I'm paid before you attempt it,' Jon said brightly.

A bald man in a white cap that was much too small for him trudged dejectedly from the kitchen.

'The pantry's empty and the kitchen order still hasn't come in from the farms yet. Would his majesty like to try something from the vegan menu this evening?'

Seth pulled a hideous face.

Jon produced a carton of eggs from the recesses of his jacket pocket.

The cook caught it from mid-air hurriedly and peered inside. 'How'd you manage not to crack any of them?'

'Magic. Any sign of my tea?'

'Tea? Dunno, Jimmy's not in here.'

The cook shrugged, turning back to the kitchen.

They waited in silence as a cleaner came in to sweep up the burnt feathers.

A miscellaneous servant produced an omelette for Seth. Seth accepted it eagerly, rising to do so.

What he did receive was the undercooked equivalent across his forehead as a white cloak billowed past Jon.

Jon squinted at a vein pulsing across Seth's newly-slimed forehead.

'Making less effort with his aim these days,' he commented.

Seth bared his teeth and screamed piercingly.

158

'This isn't good,' Eleanor said, stepping back.

Seth launched himself into the Phantom Egg Flinger and jumped onto his back, bringing him to the ground.

'Who are you?!' he shrilled, shaking him by the throat. 'Answer me!'

'I can't believe he managed to catch him,' Eleanor said in awe, as though watching an archery tournament as opposed to her son having a minor breakdown. 'Sleep deprivation aside, he is not a fit man.'

'I can't believe he tried to be the Phantom Egg Flinger without any training,' Jon added.

'Training? What do you—'

'Get off!' the Phantom Egg Flinger shrieked, wriggling. 'It's me, I was just pretending! I'm not the real one, gerroff!'

Seth frowned, loosening his grip on the masked man to roll him over. He pulled his mask off and his eyes widened. 'You.'

Jimmy squirmed underneath Seth.

'What the hell are you playing at?' Seth shouted.

'I kept missing it!' Jimmy exclaimed. 'I wanted to see you humiliated! It was a once-off, I swear, it'll never happen again—'

'No it will not, because I'm going to wring your skinny neck!' Seth snarled, throttling him again.

'Hang on, I haven't had my cup of tea yet,' Jon objected.

'Seth!' Eleanor scolded.

Seth relinquished him with a scowl. 'Put him in the Tower.'

'No, not the Tower!'

Eleanor dragged Seth to his feet by one ear.

'You're having a child, remember? Who's going to clean up its dirty bum? You're going to do it yourself, are you?'

Seth made a face. 'Ew, no.'

'I'm not doing it!' Jimmy squealed. 'My reputation's sketchy enough as it is!'

'Shitty nappy or hanged by the neck until dead,' Jon said. 'Difficult choice, that.'

'I see your point and ignore it,' Jimmy said, adamant.

Seth glared down at him. 'Get out of my sight. And stay away from my eggs!'

Jimmy scrambled to his feet and fled to the kitchens.

Seth tried to control his breathing and turned back to his abandoned omelette. Jon watched him roll it into a tube and stab it with a knife.

'How are the eggs?' he asked brightly.

'Not bad,' Seth said with half an omelette in his mouth.

'Yeah, considering all the weird things ravens eat.'

Seth choked.

'Ravens?' Eleanor asked in horror. 'Are they even edible? They eat eyeballs and poisonous insects!'

Seth threw up.

'Evidently not,' Jon observed. 'I never tried them.'

Seth shuddered and gagged.

'I take it you didn't like my experiment?'

'No!' he croaked.

'You'll want normal poultry eggs, then?'

'NO! I want chicken eggs!' Seth said loudly.

'That's what poultry are, dear,' Eleanor said patiently.

'Why have they got so many names?' he asked crossly, wiping his tongue out with the edge of his sleeve.

'I'll take that as a yes, then,' Jon said easily. 'You're very lucky, actually, because only half an hour ago I bought some very nice speckled—oh bloody shagging shit,' he swore.

Seth jerked his head up. 'What?'

A burp answered his question and singed his eyebrows.

Seth's upper lip twitched. 'She's definitely getting a bath later.'

~

'She was here yesterday!'

'I know, I saw them lock her away myself yesterday,' Orl said. 'Only…'

The pen's steel netting had been ripped apart on one side, the hole facing a chicken farm a short distance away. Several silhouettes scrambled through the farm, which was smoking.

'She does like chickens,' Lilly confessed.

'I like madeira cake, but I don't rip whole rooms apart for it.'

'But it's not a room to her, it's a prison,' she pointed out. 'She doesn't take well to captivity.'

'So how do we get home now?' Stan asked angrily. 'And if you utter the word "boat", there's going to be a fire.'

'Correct me if I'm wrong,' Lilly said, gesturing around them, 'but there are about fifty thousand more where she came from.'

'Yes, but she was the tame one,' Orl said flatly.

They strolled back down a makeshift corridor of sorts, flanked on all sides by enclosures filled with dragons. Many were trying to attempt Lyseria's trick, to no avail, which didn't impress Lilly. Clearly they were not very good quality.

'I suppose this is a good opportunity for you to choose your new dragon,' Ron said cheerfully as they met him outside the farm. Because of the terrifying nature of the work, a lot of strong liquor had thoughtfully been left in random areas of the farm for the employees. Naturally, Ron wasn't allowed in there.

'If we want to go home, yeah,' Lilly said grumpily. 'Since my selfish pet decided to bog off home. I assume that's what she's gone and done. She always loved Seth best.'

~

Meanwhile, in Adem:

'Bathy time!' Seth announced, shoving a kitchen porter forward.

The boy stumbled a little and halted, sponge in hand, to stare in terror into Lyseria's massive jaws.

Which snapped shut as a clawed foot connected sharply with the boy's torso and sent him skyward over the keep.

With another wide yawn, Lyseria stretched against the back wall of the keep.

Seth jerked his gaze away from the flying porter to meet a look of acute animal hatred.

'Maybe not bath time, then,' he said stiffly, backing away slowly.

~

'As long as you're sure she's at home this time,' Ron said. 'And that she won't go neurotic when you return with a friend.'

'I'll pick a boy. She'll like that. Then when they spawn that'll be birthday presents for Seth's kid sorted for the foreseeable future,' she said brightly. 'We all win.'

'Except for the dragon bather,' Stan said in an extraordinary display of foresight. 'Why can't you just get a dog like a normal person?'

'I'm a princess,' she said. 'I shall have a dragon *and* a dog.'

As if on cue, the Bastard tottered over, panting heavily.

'Speak and thou shalt receive,' Lilly said happily, kneeling to catch the terrier as his legs gave way. 'Aw, look at him, he must have been wandering around for hours. The poor bugger's knackered.'

'"Knackered" isn't even the word,' the Bastard grumbled in between pants. 'Eight hundred leagues of desert I pottered across to see you, and what do you talk about? Birthday presents for the *legitimate one*. Knackered,' he scoffed sourly.

'You know what I'm gonna call him? Albert,' Lilly said. 'He looks like an Albert.'

'What?' the Bastard said in a low tone.

They headed for the demi-mansion the Ambassador inhabited when he travelled the four hundred leagues from his home to visit his dragons.

'He's cute, innee?' Lilly trilled.

She rubbed the Bastard's head aggressively, almost hard enough to take off fur.

'I'll make him a little collar when we get there, with his name on it.'

'What, frigging Albert?' the Bastard seethed.

Oblivious to the dog's mutterings, Lilly kissed his head, making him grimace.

161

They made for the mansion conservatory to view the scene of the crime.

Karnak stood over the body impassively, his hands behind his back as one of his men examined the corpse. Shattered glass crunched underfoot as the four approached to flank him from both sides.

The body in question lay flat on his face, limbs splayed.

'Any news?' Lilly asked, halting beside him.

'We think Lyseria may have kicked him here on her way out of the premises,' the Ambassador said with a frown. 'Except dragons don't usually kick people when they have flame at their disposal.'

He glanced at the Jack Russell terrier in Lilly's arms.

'A sanctuary of dragons not enough for you?'

Lilly favoured him with a sheepish smile.

He turned his gaze back to the man lying in front of them. 'At any rate, judging by the bruising on his chest and the broken ribs, it looks as though he was, I don't know, slapped in the chest by something massive and propelled to the conservatory ceiling. Just after I'd had it fixed from the last Truphorian accident.'

'What do you mean by propelled?' Stan asked uneasily.

'Well, that's just it. We're not entirely sure. It's as though God himself lowered a giant finger and flicked the poor man away.'

The Bastard grinned, his tongue lolling from the side of his mouth.

'Ominous,' Lilly said. 'But how do you know he's one of ours? I've never seen him before.'

'Nobody in this country stays this pasty-faced for long,' he said. 'He arrived very recently.'

'By dragon?'

'If so, not one of mine. I wonder who else has dragons around here?'

'Someone with lots of money and patience,' Lilly said wryly. 'Could be Emmett, you know, if he hadn't puked when he first saw Lyseria.'

She examined the body intently, taking in the shoulder-length blond hair and frosted green eyes.

'He looks well-off, but I don't recognise him.'

'Portabellan?' Ron asked.

'Too dressed down,' she said. 'You've seen Cienne.'

Karnak stared down at the man. 'I may have a theory.'

They glanced at him.

'There have been rumours,' he said, 'I don't know if they're true… I've heard there is a secret organisation of anti-totalitarian noblemen making themselves known around the continents.'

'Doing what?' Lilly asked.

'Negotiating for now,' he replied. 'They've sent representatives around the kingdoms to offer governing services to the countries – taking over leadership in the king's stead, that is. They've been at it for some years, I gather, but have only made headway recently after being rejected and eaten for the past twenty—'

'Eaten?' squeaked Stan.

'Oh yeah, people are a delicacy in some countries, convicts and so on,' Ron piped up. 'Particularly in my mother's country, apparently.'

'Indeed,' Karnak said solemnly. 'At any rate, it isn't inconceivable that they might have asked someone who was in a particularly bad mood.'

'Mmm,' Lilly agreed, thinking. 'You don't reckon he might have been trying to steal my dragon to Adem? I've seen her kick people plenty of times.'

'Does she?' Orl asked in interest. 'It's not a typical reaction for her kind.'

'Maybe she was being merciful?' Stan said.

'Another unusual reaction for her kind,' Karnak said. 'She's a unique creature indeed if she's shown mercy before.'

The crunch of glass from above startled them.

They leaped out of the way and sprinted for the wall.

Another corpse dropped from the sky.

Lilly scanned outside of the gaping hole in the ceiling. 'No dragon.'

Another crash made her swing around to face another corpse –

– and then the entire ceiling collapsed.

Bodies fell from the clouds like rainfall, two, three, four, five. The group quickly bolted to the walls, their arms over their heads.

Two giant carcasses marked the end of the chaos, one on either side of the group huddling against the wall.

With a cursory glance to ensure the sky above was clear, Karnak examined one of the dead giants.

'This one isn't mine.'

Orl nudged him. 'This one was.'

He pointed to the second dead dragon. Its black scales glimmered as an oily trail of blood trickled from between them.

'It's the one Lilly chose to take home.'

~

III

'Oh, look, a castle,' Marbrand said brightly. 'Looks like we're sleeping in luxury tonight. Just as well that stranger stopped us before Ankovich came along.'

Despina rolled her eyes. 'That's right, encourage the bastard.'

'What's that, love?'

'I said, let's have a look-see,' she said hurriedly, leading the way.

It wasn't a castle as far as Adem's kind went. Despina regarded it more as a decorative bell tower as they left their steeds tied outside and entered the cracked door to ascend the sturdy concrete spiral staircase.

Night was setting in, giving everything a navy tinge. Elliot lit a torch and hung it beside the door of their temporary lodgings.

'It's very bare for a castle,' Despina said.

'Well, I suppose some monk was probably staying here,' Marbrand replied. 'That and they scarpered as soon as Queenie stuck her nose round the door.'

They unpacked their things in comfortable silence. Marbrand gave the contents of the fireplace a poke. Apart from the fireplace and their belongings, the room was bare. Despina wondered what kind of monks carried furniture with them to flee from a foreign queen as Marbrand fumbled with their bags.

'You got any tinder left?'

'Used the last of it in the desert,' Elliot said in reply.

'Damn that blasted weed,' Marbrand snarled under his breath.

'Is there anything we can use instead?' Despina asked.

'Apart from our clothes and the map?' Marbrand asked. 'Or we can use your dolly. You'll be very warm then.'

'Ha, ha,' Despina sneered.

'I'll check the rest of the tower,' Marbrand said, rising to leave the room.

They made themselves comfortable as Marbrand's footsteps faded upward. Despina pulled her doll from her bag and gazed at her likeness, thinking of that night with the purple light. Was there a reason they had bumped into the Bastard? He seemed adamant that they follow her when they entered Portmyr and found the doll. Was she ruling Marbrand's decisions with the dolls she still had? And if so, why be so careless with Despina's?

And how the hell did the Bastard fit into this? He was an enigma. Despina would have found it attractive were it not for the fact he was a bloody nuisance.

She jerked her attention away from the nuisances of the world as Marbrand emerged from upstairs.

'Nothing for the fire?' Elliot asked.

'We're not staying,' he said, beginning to repack.

'What? Why?' Despina demanded.

He held out a hand.

Two dolls of indeterminate description lay inside his palm.

'Aaliyaa's been here.'

'So why are we leaving?'

'I've figured out what she's up to. She's been altering our plans to send us to these Dead Cities and distract us from who she's really after.'

He produced a roll of parchment from his belt and gave it to her.

Despina unrolled it.

'The Knight of Raining Thorns,' she read. 'This is something to do with the prophecy. She's worked out who the Antichrist is.'

The knights glanced at her in alarm.

'You know of the prophecy?' Elliot asked, incredulous.

Despina hesitated a moment.

'Well… yeah,' she said, with a snort. 'It's a knight on a horse chasing a man with a dragon. All prophecies are like that. There's a new flavour every week.' She quickly decided to change the subject. 'So who's she after?'

'The clergy in Stoneguard figure the Antichrist to be the new arrival to the royal family, but then, they say that after every royal birth announcement.'

'You mean she's heading to Truphoria?' Elliot asked in dread. 'So all this has been for nothing.'

'Pretty much. We need a dragon, and not just for travel.'

'Who's the new arrival?' Despina asked. 'There are two. Which is it?'

Marbrand hoisted his belongings onto his back. 'The Crey one.'

~

Lilly strapped the saddle onto the beast, who wriggled and snorted hatefully.

'Is this necessary? He hates it.'

'Absolutely,' Karnak said firmly.

He snatched the straps and tightened them for her, to her immense disgust.

'If that many people are falling from the sky, we have to keep you as safe as possible. There's a chance something powerful might be killing the beasts to assassinate you.'

'Yes, let's solve it by strapping her to a doomed dragon,' Orl muttered.

Karnak shot him a look, yanking the strap tighter.

Dusk began to settle over the sanctuary. Lilly climbed up on another massive dragon, her second choice. She gave Stan a hand up behind her and turned to Orl.

'You gonna be alright on your own? I can ride with you if you prefer.'

'No, I'd better not. I get into trouble whenever I think of riding with you.'

Lilly frowned at him, her head tilted at an angle.

Orl winced. 'Sorry. Wrong choice of wording.'

'While you're up there,' Karnak suggested, 'you might scan across the desert for half an hour or so and see if you can find anything.'

'Why, what are we looking for?'

'I have a suspicion that this organisation of Mr Halle's might have some sort of base in there,' Karnak said. 'If we can find it, it may answer our question of how our friend ended up through my ceiling.'

Stan glanced at the two dragons he and his friends were using. 'Shouldn't we take some supplies in case we get caught in a sand storm or something?'

'The weather's fine today. You'll only be paying a flying visit.'

Lilly's dragon snorted again and squirmed. Karnak and four other men held him fast via six strong leather bonds, but he still moved far too easily for Stan's liking.

'I'm off!' he exclaimed, leaping from the dragon's back and landing clumsily on the dust. 'I'll go with the other one, this one's calmer.'

Lilly eyed Albie, who scratched his paws on the dragon's hind ankle.

The Ambassador picked him up under the ribs. 'He's coming too?'

Lilly nodded, and the Ambassador handed him over.

The Bastard curled himself into a ball against Lilly's stomach, unperturbed by the dragon's discomfort.

'Shall we head off, then?' Orl asked finally.

'Try not to annoy anyone,' Karnak told Lilly.

'I'll make no promises.'

Orl and Stan left the ground first, their silver-scaled dragon launching herself skyward. Lilly's dragon followed, massive black wings belting down the heavy wind as the group moved west.

The desert rolled past beneath them. Lilly's steed surged forward every now and then to nip his friend's tail, only for the silver to bolt away hurriedly. After an hour of this, the female got fed up and sped on ahead, carrying Orl and Stan into the depths of the desert.

'I've decided I quite like this dragon,' Stan said happily.

His knuckles whitened on the scales of her back regardless.

'This one likes me,' Orl said, giving her a fond pat on the back. 'She's well behaved. Most of the time. How's Lilly doing?'

Stan turned his head back and frowned.

'They're not there.'

Orl's eyes widened and he swung the silver around. She pivoted in mid-air to face the others.

Who hurtled towards the ground at an alarming speed.

~

Wind pounded into Lilly's face, as though slapping her repeatedly with a cold towel.

Her knuckles whitened around the rim of the saddle. She felt her hair work loose of her usual bedraggled knot. It flapped against Ron's face as he clung to her jerkin.

The dragon's head lolled back against the wind.

Lilly glimpsed a flash of silver and felt a rush of hope – until they hit the ground.

The impact threw Lilly's face hard into the dragon's scales. They toppled onto the desert floor.

Orl leapt off two feet before touching down and stumbled into the sand. 'Lilly!'

Lilly rose slowly with a wince, a hand to her nose. It came away bloody.

Ron stirred, nursing his ribs with a grunt, and Albie lay curled into a frightened ball, shivering.

'That wasn't very nice!' the dog wailed at the world in general. 'I nearly died again, I was terrified! What d'you do that for?'

Lilly eyed the howling dog piteously before turning to the horizon, rising for a better look. Apart from the shadowy recesses of sand dunes ahead, the landscape lay a bare amber as far as the eye could see.

'Lilly, are you alright?' Orl skidded to a halt in front of her, touching her face. 'Your nose is slightly sideways.'

'We have more problems than a sideways nose.'

She pointed at what she had mistaken for a sand dune.

A corpse lay broken ahead.

Orl squinted at it. 'Another one?'

'Another dead dragon too,' Ron pointed out, poking Lilly's former pet.

The silver took one look at the scene and turned to high-tail it.

Stan snatched her reins, Orl and Lilly following suit.

'Oh no you don't!' Stan snapped, holding her fast.

The silver's head drooped in resigned disappointment.

'There are more up ahead,' Ron said. 'Loads more.'

Orl followed his gaze. Sure enough, dark shadows marked the sand ahead in all directions.

'We need a bird's eye view,' he said, gazing at the silver dragon. 'Lilly, are you alright to come?'

She lifted an eyebrow at the fallen dragon. 'Assuming my next steed doesn't have congenital heart disease.'

Stan and Ron eyed the horizon with varying degrees of apprehension as the dragon took off.

'Trails of dead bodies seem to be my lot in life,' Ron said glumly.

'As long as it isn't trails of body excrement for me to clean up, I'll grin and bear it,' Stan added with a grimace.

Fifty feet above them and counting, Lilly peered over the dragon's shoulder at the trail of cadavers below. Suddenly her brow furrowed. 'It's a message.'

Back on the ground, Ron listened to another of Stan's Crook-side histories with a frown of concentration.

'... all over the floor, going straight from the dining room right up the stairs to the top of the house, and guess who has to clean it up?'

Ron shivered with him in empathy.

Stan sighed. 'That's why I avoid attractive women, they make too much bloody mess.'

Ron grimaced. 'Never had much truck with all that "making love" business.'

'No, me neither,' Stan said. 'I mean, marriage seems nice – like what you and Qattren have—'

'I'm more like a lodger than a husband,' Ron pointed out.

'—but, you know... I don't feel comfortable doing anything more as a couple than holding hands,' Stan said, dejected. 'D'you think that's weird?'

The silver descended a few yards above them.

Lilly and Orl dismounted behind the two.

The silver glanced herself over with a sigh of relief.

'Not weird as some things. You know, me and Qat had an interesting discussion the first time we found a trail of corpses,' Ron said cheerfully. 'See, we'd found a bloke hung from a tree, and he'd had his knackers chewed off by some sort of wild animal—'

He was cut off by a thump and an enormous dust cloud.

'Christ, Lilly, what d'you do now?' Stan exclaimed.

'Nothing, I only patted her on the head!'

The silver had flaked out in a now familiar fashion, a glistening stream of blood splitting a trail in the sand.

'That's three dragons you've killed now,' Ron announced.

Lilly gazed at her mournfully. 'I need to hug my dog.'

'Spin on it, death-bringer!' the Bastard barked, retreating.

Ron sighed. 'Looks like this trail is our only hope.'

'It's not a trail,' Orl said. 'That's what we came back to tell you.'

'It's a message,' Lilly explained. 'Spelled out in dead bodies.'

'Wonderful,' Stan said nauseously.

'What does it say?' Ron asked.

Lilly pictured the macabre text, written in blood and flesh and cursive writing.

'"Your days are numbered",' she quoted.

Stan bit his lip. 'Who's counting?'

'Someone incredibly specific, evidently,' Orl said, a touch cynically.

'Why, what else does it say?'

'"It's six, by the way".'

~

Retribution Halle looked down at his expensive attire in mourning. No amount of sorcery-like readjustment could fix this mess. The suit was finally past it.

He turned his attention to the more pressing matter at hand. He was in the centre of a pond that branched out in seven directions. There was no judging north from south. It seemed to be a perpetual midday.

Establishing that general navigation – even if he had any in the first place – and common logic – notably the unbiased-in-his-favour kind, which he had yet to master – would make the task easier to accomplish by zero per cent, Halle went out on a limb and waded straight ahead.

Meandering gently and trying not to touch the slick mud, Halle made it to the end of the stream to suddenly find himself staring down into a boardroom.

The eight primary leaders of the First Democratic Republic sat around a circular table. Halle himself sat at the head of it.

168

The real Halle watched his past self from somewhere in the ceiling as the figure handed around some maps in a familiar fashion.

'One for you,' he said cheerfully, handing one to Erstan, 'one for me, one for you,' he handed Roy a map of the Far Isles, 'and one for me, one for you—'

'I don't like this method of assigning world leaders,' Roy said with a frown. 'Surely we should put more consideration in deciding who owns—'

'Oh, you won't be owning it,' he said brightly. 'I'm the leader, I own *everything*. You just get to look at it. One for me...'

'I'm sure I didn't word it quite like that,' present-day Halle objected.

'This city has been throwing riddles at you for the past week. It can translate bullshit faster than you can spew it.'

Halle threw the dove an irritable glance. 'Speaking of riddles, why are we looking at this?'

'Because it's a secret.'

'Well, you'd better divulge this secret right now, before I start preparing you for a pie,' he growled.

'No, I mean that past event is a secret, that's why you're looking at it,' the bird said, affronted. 'This pod is the city's archives. It holds every secret in the world.'

'This is starting to seem like a very elaborate hallucination.'

'It is, but that doesn't mean it's unimportant,' the bird said. 'Turn back the way you came and try another stream. At random.'

Retribution sighed and obeyed as commanded.

What he saw in the next pod of secrets shook him to the core. It wasn't an easy task shaking a selfish man, but this had shaken him. Badly.

'That was a child,' he said in horror.

'Infant,' the dove corrected. 'Or would have been, if his parents had a choice in the matter. Now he's a small dog, part-time.'

Halle made a face. 'He's a part-time dog?'

'Yes.'

'What is he supposed to be the rest of the time?'

A suspenseful silence ensued for a minute or two.

'A demi-god.'

Halle stared into space. 'God.'

'A demi one.'

'With that kind of trauma... can he remember it all?'

'He remembers everything.'

He made a face. 'Even his own conception?'

'Everything.'

'Adem's really in for it, then. I can't imagine being in a healthy state of existence allowing one to recall one's own conception from the *inside*.'

The dove didn't reply. 'The stream continues.'

Halle looked out on to the meandering river as the misty rendering of the Bastard's death dissipated. He trudged forward tentatively.

Had he entertained his brief idea of returning to his past self and ripping up his map of Truphoria, he mightn't have stumbled on the next secret of the world. In fact, had the dove not been present, he might have had the good fortune to die in blissful ignorance or, if he was really lucky, leave Copers in blissful ignorance and start a less stressful career, like catering.

As it was, he sat through the next two hours' worth of events and left through the exit when the revelations were done.

The dove came with him with no regrets. It hadn't had this much fun since sending Aaliyaa Horne off to her son's funeral, and it wasn't going to let another good show go to waste.

~

Ron picked a bag of coins up between his thumb and forefinger.

'This is immoral,' he said uneasily. 'Even Qat never stole from the dead.'

'Qat isn't in the desert with no supplies,' Lilly snapped.

She rose, pocketing a knife and moving on to the next victim without batting an eyelid.

'But Qat is supposed to be an unhinged sociopath,' he said. 'What does that make us?'

Before anyone could answer, a scream erupted from the west.

A man sprinted in figures of eight. He wore a red suit with gold trim, like many of the men surrounding them – except that the man inside was still alive and covered in a thick layer of mud.

'The Antichrist,' he gasped, sprinting past, clutching his shoulder, 'dragon... a plot, it's all a plot... thieves, thieves *everywhere*! It's all a plot...'

Lilly watched him pace in circles, shaking his head.

'Sir?' she ventured.

'Thieves!' he shouted, making Lilly jump. 'Lies, all lies! Bloody Phantom Egg Flinger! Thieves *everywhere*!'

They stared at him in bemusement.

'What's wrong with him?' Ron asked.

'Got mugged by the sound of it,' Stan guessed.

Halle spun in circles for a moment and froze, his eyes fixed forward.

The Bastard sat in front of him, licking his parts.

'He's dressed like the rest of these men,' Orl said, gesturing.

'Must mean he's about to die,' Lilly said. 'Could be one of those outfits that dictates your fate, like a priest's robes on a sex offender.'

Halle shivered for a moment and bolted forward.

Albie raised his head and gave a little whine.

'We should ask if he knows anything about this secret organisation,' Lilly said, turning to face the man.

Just in time to see Albie sailing into the distance.

Halle lowered his foot, glaring after him distrustfully.

'Did you just kick my dog?' Lilly shrilled.

Halle babbled unintelligibly and ran into the east, tripping and falling onto his face along the way.

'Nutter!' Lilly exclaimed, one hand over her brow against the approaching sunset. 'He kicked him bloody far, didn't he? I can't even see him!'

~

A quarter of a mile northwest:

Despina stood idly outside the pens as Marbrand pestered the dragon breeder.

'And you're sure he won't, let's say, go on a murderous rampage and kill everyone?'

'We've neutered all our animals,' the man said patiently. 'He won't be rampaging in any way whatsoever.'

'Are you sure? Because I do hate to blunt my sword on good money, you know.'

Despina heaved a sigh and gazed at an approaching bird.

She suddenly discovered it wasn't a bird when Albie landed sideways into her face.

She landed into the ground with an 'oof'.

'What the hell is that?' Elliot asked with a laugh as he picked at a cooked chicken.

She picked up the dog by the scruff of the neck and glared at him.

'Hello,' he said timidly.

Despina recognised the Bastard's voice immediately. She rose to her feet.

Marbrand threw her a quick glance and turned to the nearest dragon. 'We'll borrow that one.'

Stalking furtively away so the two wouldn't notice, Despina carried the dog to the front gate and lifted her right leg backwards.

'No,' Albie said in alarm, wriggling, 'no, not again, my bum's bruised enough as it is! NO!'

She released his fur and kicked him as hard as she could. He didn't quite reach a quarter of a mile this time, but it was an admirable effort.

~

Lilly gave up searching for Albie and turned back to Orl. 'You think this bloke's worth following?'

'He's worth questioning,' he said. 'But we can't chase a mad man around the desert without any supplies. We'll die if we don't get help fast.'

He was right. Lilly could feel the heat eating into the back of her neck already.

171

'Oh, we won't die,' Ron said confidently.

Lilly glared at him. 'Unless you have a whistle to summon your missus, I think we probably will.'

Ron reached into his pocket. 'I don't have a whistle, but I have one of these.'

Stan peered at it. 'A copper coin,' he said dully.

'Not just any copper coin. A copper coin that can take us to that man.'

Lilly threw her hands into the air.

'What is it about people owning magical vehicles of instant travel and not telling me about it?'

'Well, see, it's not as straightforward as that,' Ron said with a wince. 'It doesn't take you just anywhere... it takes you to the Seven Devils. Who are friends of ours,' he reassured them hurriedly. 'They're just not very... easy to work with.'

'It's a coin that takes us to the gates of hell,' Stan said flatly.

'Or heaven,' he added brightly. 'Depends on your perspective. Lilly would love it.'

'Thanks,' she said wryly.

'Dare I ask,' Orl said cautiously, 'but how does this help us find that man?'

'They know where everyone is,' he said. 'They can find him and send us to him... for a price,' he added.

'Is it worth it?' Stan asked fretfully.

'Gotta be better than standing around and sweating,' Lilly said. 'How do you use it?'

'Drop it heads up,' he said, 'and it takes everyone in a two-foot radius to hell. Not something you want to drop in a crowded street.'

'Drop it tails up?'

'It takes you up in chains,' he said, looking sheepish. 'But we're friends, like I say, so...'

'Right,' Stan said tiredly.

'Best drop it heads up, then,' Lilly said firmly, gesturing at everyone to gather around.

Ron rubbed the coin between his hands. The other three surrounded him closely.

'Should we cross our fingers for luck?' Orl asked.

'Don't jinx it,' Ron warned.

He flicked the coin into the air.

They followed it into the air and into Ron's hand. He slammed it into the back of his other hand, the others bowing their heads together.

King Theo's head stared into the south, and winked.

A cloud of dust marked the group's departure.

~

IV

Cienne inhaled through clenched teeth.

It was happening again. Where the bloody hell was Seth?

She sat up in bed and fiddled around on top of the bedside table until she found a bell.

Jimmy arrived directly.

'It's probably a false alarm,' he said with a yawn, helping her to her feet.

'It still bloody hurts!' she snarled. 'Where's Seth? Where's my mother?'

'Mother-in-law,' he corrected.

She made to give him a look indicating the equivalent fury of the seven armies of hell before doubling over with a whine. She dragged herself to the small tube in the wall that was her end of the sound tunnel leading to the throne room.

'Seth!' she wailed into it.

No reply.

Jimmy grimaced. A memory of himself kicking a basket of washing into the horn reoccurred with a start.

'Um...' he trailed off.

Her knees buckled again and Cienne's eyes widened.

'Uh-oh.'

She started rifling under her skirt.

Jimmy began to respectfully cover his eyes when her hand re-emerged, blood glistening on her fingers.

'Oh my God,' he said in a low voice.

Cienne met his gaze in horror, threw herself against the speaker and howled.

'SETH!'

The sound bounced down the speaker, increasing from loud howling to very loud to excruciatingly cacophonic before being sharply cut off by a large basket of bed sheets.

Lying across his throne just a few feet away, a large pillow softening the solid arm beneath his head, Seth snored gently, his face half-buried in the white fabric.

As Cienne screamed obliviously three floors above him, he dreamed happily of sitting on a sunny hill with a small boy beside him, smiling at him...

~

Lilly traced a crack in the double doors before knocking. A hatchet, if she wasn't mistaken. She wondered if they would let her borrow it sometime.

The mahogany opened a crack and a golden eye peered out.

'State your allegiance,' Geldemar intoned. 'And beware! I'll not accept false flattery.'

'I worship Salator Crey,' Lilly said confidently.

Geldemar swung the doors open. 'Blasphemy!'

'You'd know, you made it up,' Ron said playfully.

Geldemar grinned, stepping aside.

The full regalia that the legends decreed was plain to see. Intricately decorated weapons and expertly painted portraits littered the room – although they were a little more energetic than the histories told and were throwing themselves in the visitors' direction with extreme enthusiasm.

Lilly and Orl ducked in opposite directions with a wail.

The broadsword bounced off the door behind them.

'Can you... tie those up or something?' Lilly asked in alarm. 'Attacking your worshippers isn't doing much for your religion.'

Geldemar gave a huff.

'Oh, alright, spoilsport,' he grumbled, clapping his hands.

The broadswords dropped to the floor.

'Should have worshipped us if you didn't want a large blade thrown at your face,' he said. 'We turn them away from the souls of the pure.'

Lilly glared at him in annoyance.

Geldemar grinned, a silver tooth shining to match his short silver hair.

'Did you copy Vladdy's tooth?' Ron asked curiously.

'Yes, it's an imitation,' he said with a smile. 'I didn't have the heart to rip the authentic article from his mouth. I copied his outfit as well. I find he has a certain style to him that I find rather fetching.' He patted his black tunic down fondly.

Lilly withdrew in boredom and gravitated to an odd scenario in the centre of the room.

Six individuals – two of them conjoined twins and one of them a topless male Lilly somehow found familiar – stood around a spiral staircase leading from below the floor to above the ceiling.

Or so it seemed until a man scrambled up them from beneath the floor on all fours and glanced around.

'What?!' he barked. 'What the hell's going on? You told me there'd be wine on the top floor! What am I doing back here?'

'You haven't gotten to the top yet,' Geldemar called from the door. 'Keep going! You're nearly there, love!'

The man bared his teeth at him and rose to his feet.

Geldemar leaned in behind Lilly's shoulder.

'Never-ending staircase,' he murmured. 'Don't tell him, we have a bet going on how long he tries to get that wine.'

'That's trippy,' she commented.

'That's the afterlife,' Geldemar said with a wink. 'If I take a fancy to you, that is.'

She watched the poor man ascend.

'Why does he bother?' she wondered.

'Ah, but this is special wine that gives him an ascension to demi-god-dom with a single sip,' Geldemar said. 'Or so it says in the legal document we left lying around for him to find.'

Geldemar swung around to Ron, who jumped.

'I suppose you've caught Qattren at it, then?' he said in disdain. 'Go on, what do you want us to do to her?'

'What?' he asked, nonplussed. 'No, I haven't caught her at anything – why, what's she done?'

'Oh, nothing serious,' he said idly.

He waved in the vague direction of the staircase.

It collapsed on top of its screaming victim.

'Oi! I was about to win!' the topless man protested.

'Tough, I'm bored with it now. Make yourselves at home, lady and gentlemen, the table should reassemble itself shortly.'

The prisoner materialised against the wall to their right, shackled to the bricks. He looked up, apparently noticing them for the first time.

'Ronald?' he said in surprise.

'Now, here we are,' Geldemar said cheerfully, gesturing to the circular table rising out of the rubble.

'Ron!' he called.

Ron appeared not to notice.

'Ronald! Help me, unchain me before the water font comes back! I'll give you anything, gold, riches… the kingdom! I'll give you my claim, just please let me out!'

'Hey, Vladdy,' Ron said absently, strolling past without a second glance.

His eyes widened and he shuffled backward until their eyes were level.

'You…' Ron said, pointing at his nose, '… you're supposed to be dead.'

Vladimir hung dejectedly, his hair sticking up on end and his eyes ringed with dark circles.

'Oh, didn't you know?' Geldemar cut in, sidling up to him. 'We took him as payment for the small army we loaned her last year. I didn't have the heart to let him go to waste, so I claimed him for myself. He's very well behaved for a temperamental megalomaniac, aren't you, Vladdy, dear?'

He caressed Vladimir's cheek and patted it, to Vladimir's potent disgust.

Ron looked lost. 'I… don't know how to feel about this.'

'Didn't Qattren tell you?' Geldemar asked before his face cleared. 'Ah, that'll be because I never mentioned it. My bad. Usually, he's up in my private quarters, you see. He's my butler,' he said proudly. 'He's coming along, you know. Menial labour suits him.'

'He's being tortured, though,' Orl said in discomfort.

'Oh, we were just bored. It'll be business as usual tomorrow, don't worry. And besides, he deserves it.'

'He *died*, though,' Lilly said, incredulous. 'Isn't that enough?'

'Oh, darling, no,' Geldemar said with a chortle. 'This is penance, for giving his mother free reign over the land instead of chaining her to a wall where she belongs. No, no, he belongs here now. Anyone careless enough to get blown to kingdom come at his age ought to at least stay a while and learn his lesson.'

A water font rose in front of Vladdy, turning slowly clockwise.

Vladdy stared at it in horror.

Ron trembled on the spot.

'And Ron?' Stan demanded. 'What about him? He's just supposed to grieve like that for no good reason, is it?'

'Ah, Ron,' Geldemar said with a sigh. 'A needless casualty.'

He wrapped a hand around the back of Ron's neck, to Ron's discomfort.

'But you have to understand, your brother is dead,' Geldemar said gently. 'He won't be coming back. This is all that's left, this little essence. It may have been beneficial in the long run for you to let him go in your own time, but alas, carelessness on my part has ruined that.'

Ron pinched his lips together. 'Why can't he come back?'

'The rules that keep him here do not exist at home,' Geldemar said softly. 'He would cease to exist. You can come to visit whenever you like, of course.'

Ron clenched his teeth.

'Do you have any idea,' he gritted, 'the amount of help he could be if my mother knew he was here? She's doing this out of grief, do you know how easily we could stop her if we just told her—'

'That the Seven have embraced him into their household?' Geldemar replied wryly. 'She already knows this. Of course he would be here, it's only natural for her best boy to live in the realm of the gods. He's prayed hard and long, since he was a child. He's a good boy.

'But Ronald, now… that Ronald's always been a troublemaker. Of course he'd be jealous of his big brother serving the gods, he was always jealous of poor Vladdy. And now he's telling her that her beloved, benevolent gods are *tricksters* out to punish Vladimir for claiming his rightful queen! The atrocity! Why, it appears her youngest child is in fact the devil's plaything after all.'

Ron breathed heavily, his fists clenched at his sides.

'You see, things are never as easy as they appear at first sight,' Geldemar went on. 'Letting your mother – indeed, letting *you* know even – that Vladimir still existed in a way would *not* be a clever idea. Don't worry, there are plenty of ways of stopping your mother without bringing my butler into it.'

Ron met Vladimir's gaze.

His older brother looked imploringly at him, more vulnerable than Ron had ever seen him before.

'Looks like I can't help you,' Ron said quietly.

176

Pain settled into Vladimir's face.

'At least visit me,' he croaked through a lump in his throat. 'Please at least do that much.'

Ron tensed and walked away from him without a word.

Vladimir flung his gaze to the floor, shaking.

'Qattren has a lot to answer for,' Lilly said under her breath.

Orl nodded. 'She appears to have questionable taste in friends.'

Ron halted in front of the table, dragging his knuckles through his scalp.

Stan followed him, placing a hand on his shoulder.

'Please tell me this is some sort of dream,' Ron said.

Stan squeezed his shoulder. 'Just try to process it for a minute, alright?'

'How?' Ron exclaimed in a whisper. 'My dead brother is standing over there! How am I supposed to process that? I'm only just managing to wrap my head around his death, never mind this… this…'

He threaded his fingers through his hair and tugged, wincing.

Stan grabbed his shoulders.

'The facts,' he said. 'Just process the facts. He's dead. And he's here now. The how, why, and how you feel about it can come later. Preferably away from any psychotic deities.' His gaze bored into Ron's. '*Breathe.* He's here now. Just breathe and remember that. Save the rest for later.'

Ron inhaled, eyes fluttering shut. He nodded.

'So what brings you here?'

Lilly reluctantly tore her gaze away from Ron.

'We could do with some help. You know, when you've finished tormenting my friends' relatives?'

Geldemar at least had the good grace to look sheepish. 'What can I do to help?'

'We've found this pile of dead bodies not long ago and some friend of theirs went loopy and ran away before we could ask him any questions about it. Any idea how to find him?'

'Ah, Retribution Halle,' Geldemar said immediately.

He walked to the fountain in front of Vladimir and ran a hand through the water.

'Here we are,' he said, peering at the rippling water with Vladimir craning his neck behind him to see. 'He's sprinting at high speed for the asylum just outside Serpus. He's about an hour away from his destination, by my reckoning.'

'He's an hour away from Serpus?' Lilly said incredulously. 'We saw him in the desert a minute ago!'

'He has a dragon keep smack-bang in the middle of the desert, right where no one would think of looking for one.'

'Can you take us to him?'

'Why, of course,' he said with a smile.

'Why, of course,' Vladimir mimicked with a shiver.

'… BUT: you must play for it.'

'Oh, sod that for a lark,' Ron submitted immediately. 'I've heard all about your games. One of them is chained up over there, for a start.'

'Oh, please, at least hear out my proposal,' said Geldemar with a grin. 'If you win our game, we drop you off outside the front door of the asylum, just in time to intercept our mutual friend. If we win, we drop you off anywhere in Truphoria that we desire.'

'Excluding the internals of a man-eating monster?' Stan asked hopefully.

'Well… alright, if you wish,' he said with reluctance. 'Now: what shall we play?'

His companions piped up eagerly behind Lilly.

'Snooker?'

'Golf's fun. We haven't done that for a while, and the Creys' windows have been a bit too pristine lately.'

'Cards is traditional,' one of the conjoined twins piped up haughtily.

'Why doesn't one of us choose, since it's our lives on the line?' Lilly suggested wryly.

'Snakes and ladders.'

They turned to Ron in alarm.

'That's a stupid game!' Lilly exclaimed.

'I like snakes and ladders,' Ron said meekly.

'It's a game of chance and probability,' Stan said. 'They *control* chance and probability.'

'Sounds good to me,' Geldemar said cheerfully.

He clapped a hand across the water again.

Vladimir winced with a pained groan as the image in the water changed back.

'Ronald can play yours truly, the rest of you can make yourselves at home. It might well be that, one day.'

Having decided that loss was imminent, Lilly decided to acclimatise as everyone else crowded around the two contenders. She wandered to the mysterious water fountain for a nose.

Vladimir was grimacing hard into its depths, unable to take his eyes away.

Lilly peered in, Stan at her heels.

'Ew, are they going at it?' She grimaced, tilting her head to one side. 'He isn't very good, is he? Who are they?'

Vladimir's upper lip twitched.

Stan frowned. 'I think that's your brother.'

They lurched backwards. 'Urgh!'

'This truly is hell,' Lilly said in horror.

'It's my lot now,' Vladimir said miserably. 'Just this scene, over and over. He plays it on a projector every second day, the bastard.'

'Why this one?' Lilly turned her head away, holding a hand up to block the sight. 'I get his range is limited, but he's surely done better work.'

'It's not the means we celebrate, it's the result,' Geldemar said cheerfully, coming up behind her. 'This is the conception of his children.'

'Ew,' Lilly exclaimed before pausing. 'Child*ren*?'

'A boy and a girl,' he said proudly.

'Oh great, twice as many presents to buy,' Lilly said, rolling her eyes. 'Nice one, Seth.'

'Her doing, actually – it's generally the mother that causes twins, biologically. And also the one who suffers for it, which she'll be finding out right about... now-ish. Anyway, your turn, Ronald, dear,' he said quickly, before Lilly could register the remark.

Ron frowned at the six-sided dice in his hand.

'I'm sure these dice are changing,' he said suspiciously. 'There was never a side with an eleven before.'

'We're screwed, then,' Stan said.

'Only if we end up where he is,' Lilly said, jerking a thumb at Vladimir.

Ron threw the dice half-heartedly.

'Ooh!' he said suddenly.

One said two, the other said six. There were eight spaces between Ron's pebble and the final square.

Ron's hand moved over the board with quick precision.

'I—lose?' he finished, uncertain.

A snake lifted itself from the board and ate the piece.

'But it landed...' Lilly trailed off.

She reached for the snake.

'Ah! That's cheating!' Geldemar scolded, slapping her hand away.

'So's enchanting the board!' Lilly accused hotly.

'Not in this world.'

'Now you're a liar too!'

'Be wary of who you call a liar, Lady Crey,' Geldemar said softly. 'Half your family are liars. And you never did figure out what happened to your father, the most illustrious liar of the lot.'

Lilly's eyes thinned. 'Be very careful.'

'My apologies, I forgot how hard it hit you,' he said, somewhat smugly. 'Heard you were in tears, poor thing. Not so butch after all. It appears your brother isn't the wimpy sibling after all.'

Lilly was silent

Within seconds, a dagger had landed in the centre of Geldemar's chest. Vladimir hissed from behind them.

'That's a bad habit to have around here,' he informed them in a whisper.

It burst into flames and fizzled out, without leaving so much as a stain on the front of Geldemar's shirt.

'Enjoy your journey, my friends,' Geldemar said softly.

The four exploded into dust with a purple flash.

Geldemar pivoted sharply to face Vladimir.

'Make a note to remind Qattren,' he said in a low voice, 'to *never* let me allow hoi-polloi into my fortress ever again.'

'Yes, sir,' he said, a picture of obedience.

Vladimir glared after him as he wandered off with the others and swallowed a mouthful of spit too ready to hit Geldemar right between the eyes.

~

Moments later, Lilly found herself in a very familiar foyer.

Stan and Ron stood in the doorway of the main room with their mouths hanging ajar.

'Well, that's another dagger wasted,' she grumbled.

Orl gawked into the doorway and swallowed repeatedly, with apparent difficulty.

Lilly made a face. 'What are you all looking at in there?'

Not a word was spoken.

Stan, Ron and Orl were trapped in the thralls of disbelief, irate fury and unwilling arousal respectively.

Lilly shoved past them and her eyes widened.

'Oh.' She gave her shirt a cursory glance as Qattren danced, *naked*, on the stage. 'I feel so... inadequate.'

~

Si and Tully sat opposite each other on either side of a small table in the captain's cabin. It was nearing midnight – the two strained their eyes to make out the pieces in the dull light of the oil lamp hanging above their heads.

Si scooped a queen from the chessboard and replaced it with his knight in one fluid motion.

'Gotcha!'

Tully scowled.

'That,' he seethed, 'was a *fucking* cheat!'

'Ah-ah!' Si tutted. 'Language!'

He placed the queen to one side, giving the tiny wooden head a pat.

'Besides, there's no cheating about it. You stuck her in my path fair and square.'

'You can't hop over other pieces like that, that's a fucking cheat!'

'Language, I said. No need to be a sore loser-to-be. Knights can jump over whatever they want, it's the others that can't jump over pieces.'

'You're just making it up as you go along!'

'I am not—'

'Lies!'

'You just can't stand that I'm more intelligent than you—'

'Lies and buggery!'

'Shut up and do your go, you big baby—'

180

They shouted over each other for ten minutes, the words 'lies' and 'buggery' factoring a lot in between prolific bouts of swearing from both parties.

Despite the raised voices, a slight sound floated into their ears and stopped them in their tracks.

'…*boys*…'

'What was that?' Si said.

Tully kicked Si's horses over one after the other with his king, the intricate procedures of chess forgotten.

'Oh, cut that out, you're ruining it!' Si said, batting his hands away.

Tully flicked all the pieces onto the floor, hands splaying, childlike.

'Can't play anything with you, can I,' Si said crossly, 'you always have to throw a wobbly—'

Faint singing cut across him again, a high soprano.

'Who's doing that?' Si said irately, craning over his hammock to peer out of the porthole.

The shimmer of scales passed across the glass – a sea serpent, Si guessed.

He exited the room at speed, Tully at his heels.

Groups of crew members gathered at the rail, peering down. Si elbowed past and followed their gaze.

The serpent emerged, sank, and re-emerged from the water, very close to the hull.

'What the hell is that? Tully, you've better eyes than me, can you see…'

He turned to his brother.

Tully stood in the middle of the deck, staring into space with a vacant expression.

'Hello!' Si trilled, waving with both hands.

Tully's mouth hung open, his eyes rolling upwards.

'Don't mind if I do,' he said after a moment.

He hurled his shirt over his head, untied his trousers and let them drop to the floor.

'What are you… what… put your clothes back on!' Si shrieked, completely at a loss.

Tully stomped on the edges of his boots, desperately trying to toe them off. His trousers tangled around his ankles, obstructing his path.

'Can you hear me, shit-head?' Si shouted at him. 'I said—'

Finally freed of his clothes, Tully bolted forward.

Everyone – including Si – recoiled away from their naked crewmate with a chorus of 'Ugh!'

He ran for the rail and vaulted it, vanishing into the night.

'What's the matter with him?' Si said, his face screwed up in bemusement.

Sot swallowed repeatedly, wringing his hands on the rail.

'The pirate witch,' he hissed.

Si rolled his eyes. 'Oh, piss off—'

'I've just realised what she's actually supposed to be,' Sot said, his eyes bulging. 'The legend isn't about a witch. It's about...'

The soprano trilling restarted, floating up from the ripples left by Tully's splash.

'... a siren.'

Si heaved a sigh. 'Drop a line.'

'There's no point now, she'll have eaten him by this stage—'

'I'll be the judge of that,' Si said.

He stripped off his jerkin and vaulted the rail after him.

'Oi!' was the last thing he heard before the water consumed him with a crash.

Emerging from the waters to gather his bearings, Si took deep breaths, tried to forget about the icy water and sank into the depths again.

He could see a sparkle far beneath him and dove for it, limbs sweeping through the waves with ease.

A dark shadow revealed itself to be Tully.

Si surged forward and grasped an arm, pulling him upward.

The siren didn't resist. She simply followed them. Si assumed the siren was a she, anyway. He wasn't willing to stop and ask.

The two burst to the surface, Si gasping for breath, Tully unconscious.

'Throw me a line!' he screamed up at the rubbernecks above. 'I'm touching his bollocks and I don't like it!'

The siren whispered to him. *'Come to me...'*

The men at the rail dispersed, feet trampling on the deck.

Si blew air through pursed lips, teeth chattering. He was growing heavier by the minute, it seemed.

Abruptly, he was pulled downwards.

The scaled creature clung to his left ankle.

Si thrashed wildly.

Tully drifted out of his grasp, floating off on the surface of the water.

Si plummeted into darkness, water filling his throat. His chest grew increasingly tight.

The darkness softened around the edges. He felt himself drift out of his own body. Voices and sounds washed in and out of hearing, familiar sounds.

It was the Beult household. He was surprised he could still conjure an image: it had been so drab and uninteresting it barely warranted commitment to memory. A plain brown square in a back alley of Serpus marked the entrance he had called home nearly three decades before.

Ah, bollocks, Si thought to himself. *I'm dead, aren't I? This is me life flashing before my eyes.* He geared himself up for disappointment.

The bustle and commotion of feverish cleaning occurred inside: lots of cleaning. A king was coming.

Si's inner visual skipped the rest of that morning – he quickly went from playing quietly on the curb outside to standing in the centre of the main room, hands clasped behind his back. He knew what he had been brought here to revisit.

An enormous King Theo – substantially larger here than he would be on Si's subsequent meetings with him, possibly on account of Si being a skinny eight-year-old – crouched before him, a hand braced against his own knee.

'Silas?' he boomed.

Si stood to attention, as one only can at age eight and a half.

Theo placed a hand under his chin and, gently, turned his face from side to side.

'Remarkable,' he muttered.

He then released him to offer Si his hand.

'Delighted to meet you, my boy,' he boomed pleasantly. 'I can tell we're going to be firm friends, isn't that so?'

Si nodded eagerly, shaking the big man's hand.

And fell into darkness again.

'*I can give you what you want,*' said the voice in the deep. The one who had sung to him for the past week, only he had been so busy daydreaming about the woman in question, he hadn't noticed the music wasn't in fact situated inside his head after all.

'Merri?'

He glanced around for her mane of red hair, but couldn't find her, of course, on account of having plummeted into darkness.

'*I can give you anything,*' her voice whispered, her accent too distinct to be coincidental.

'Not this,' he whispered, releasing air bubbles. 'He's dead...'

'What about this?'

The image altered itself.

Si found himself straddling a man's thin chest. His knuckles whitened around the throat of a blue-faced Seth Crey.

A white-hot streak of hatred passed through Si's lungs, made pleasant by a layer of potent satisfaction.

Seth croaked something.

Si felt Seth's throat working between his hands and remembered with a start that he wasn't breathing either.

The vision clapped out of being.

Si thrashed in the water again, limbs flailing.

A smooth hand slid up one side of his neck, then another.

Serenity washed over him again.

Another face floated up from the deep, not dissimilar to the last but softer, feminine. Lilly.

An image of their first meeting in the Forest alternated between visions of them both on the ship together, two scenes flicking back and forth.

'Sorry,' he said hastily, tucking himself away.

Lilly pulled the end of her jerkin to glare at the pungent piss stain marring the left side.

'Didn't see you there,' Si said. He held out a hand.

Lilly recoiled from it.

And recoiled from it again – only this time she was fifteen years younger, a little girl in a floral dress that was more dirt than linen.

'Don't be shy,' Theo said kindly from behind her.

'I'm not shy,' Lilly said defiantly, her voice a note or two higher. 'He just smells bad.'

Si, on one knee before her, gave his armpit a sniff. Fish. That'd do it.

'Ugh, you're right in all,' he said, his nose wrinkling.

He wafted at his armpit in exaggerated agony.

Lilly smiled at him in faint amusement.

Splintered visions of pulling her for a dance, her pouring him a drink, him fighting at her side all merged and danced across Si's vision before slowing to a halt at a scene that made Si's heart crack in half for a second time.

Lilly sat cross-legged on the ground, turned to face one corner of her cabin, in tears.

In this version, Si managed to sum up the courage to approach. Drumming his fingertips on the crown of her head, he sat beside her, an arm draped over her shoulders.

Lilly's head tucked itself onto his shoulder.

'I can give you your family,' said Merri.

Si believed her.

The sound of Merri's voice brought forth another vision, this one slightly more heated.

'Merri—'

Two interspliced events once again, one a familiar memory, the other new to him. A scene he had played out in exact detail only in his imagination, with her, in different places at various different angles—

Si's eyes bolted open.

'You ain't Merri.'

The soft hands on his face grew claws.

Si lashed out, fists and knees.

The creature lashed back, swinging a spiked tail and sending waves of agony down his ribs.

As they struggled, the visions continued stubbornly, Merri's face floating into view, so close to his own...

Si tried desperately to ignore it.

An audible thud sounded, inches from his face.

The point of a blade emerged from the siren's nose. It screamed piercingly, the sound wrenching Si's brain even through the water.

Sot shoved her out of the way. Hooking an elbow under each of Si's arms, Sot kicked upward.

The world went black for a moment until his back thudded onto the deck.

Si's chest reared up. He rolled to one side and threw up – right into Tully's face.

Tully, in a deliberate motion, wiped the warm sea water from his brow.

'I am never,' Si groused, 'playing chess with you again.'

Tully grinned at him, lying flat on the deck to Si's left.

Si looked him up and down. 'Put your clothes back on, you hussy.'

Tully laughed shortly. 'In a bit. I like the feel of the moonlight.'

Si flopped onto his back, staring at the stars. A warm dribble from his upper lip alerted him to a sizable slit on the right-hand side. He, gingerly, prodded it.

'How long was I down there?'

'Not even thirty seconds,' Sot said from behind Si's head.

Si craned his neck, the top of his head rolling on the polished wood.

Sot stood – rather pretentiously, Si thought sourly – with a foot planted on the dead siren. Si eyed the pile of flaccid tentacles and returned his gaze skyward, his thoughts on the visions. The images concerning Merri once more buried themselves in the depths where they came from, but the other two stood out, stark and vivid against the stars.

He glared into the dark.

'Change of plan.'

He thrust himself into a sitting position.

Tully and Sot watched him attentively.

'We're ditching the dead cities and heading for the church. Turn us starboard and circle back to Portmyr.'

'But what about—'

'Bollocks to 'em.' Si met Tully's glance, quirking an eyebrow. 'Let's go see a wedding.'

～

V

Seth's neck popped.

He bolted upright in his throne and smacked a hand against the back of his neck.

He *hated* when that happened.

He glanced out at the early morning sun, shining through the stained-glass window in various shades of pink. Yawning, he rose to his feet.

It was beginning to look like a beautiful morning. Spring had finally reached the palace, throwing its heat into the room within the pink haze. He gazed up at it in well rested serenity, albeit with three fingers digging into the knot in the side of his neck.

It had been a good idea to sleep downstairs – he hadn't heard a peep out of Cienne all night long. Nor had he heard her for the last few days, he realised: it was only when he visited her or drew breath outside the bedroom door that he heard any noise from her at all.

Out of sight, out of mind, he surmised with a shrug.

He turned to the sound horn behind his throne and was about to stick his head inside to call her when he spotted an obstruction.

He reached inside and dislodged the blockage.

A misshapen basket tumbled out of the speaker with several bedsheets sliding out in its wake.

Seth blinked uncomprehendingly.

A scrap of parchment fluttered onto the pile of laundry. Seth picked it up and straightened the wrinkles.

I need you. I'm scared!

The bloody handprint beside his wife's wobbly handwriting was all he needed to see.

Seth bolted for the stairs.

He stumbled for the top floor, two at a time until he tripped and nearly broke his nose on the wall in front of him. He kicked the door open on each floor until he reached his destination and sprinted down the hall until, heart throbbing in his throat and his arteries freezing, he shoved the heavy door of his quarters open and made a beeline for the bedroom.

The door hung wide open.

Seth pressed himself against the doorframe, feeling as though he might be about to throw up.

A bloody streak tarnished the cream-coloured sheets on the bed that, until very recently, they both shared. Cienne sat dejected and exhausted beneath them, her head tucked into Eleanor's shoulder.

Jimmy sat a small distance away on the bedside table, traumatised.

'Why didn't you come down and wake me up?' Seth asked in a shrill whisper.

'There was no time, it was happening too quickly,' said Eleanor, stroking Cienne's hair. 'We needed to figure out what to do.'

Seth clenched the door frame. His gaze was locked onto the baby basket, left next to their bed just in case.

'I need to sit down,' he mumbled, turning to the drawing room.

'Aren't you going to hold him?'

Seth went cold. 'I don't want to do that.'

'Why not?'

'Because he's dead, why would I want to touch a dead baby?' he snapped, the words rolling out more steadily than he felt they should.

Cienne frowned and lifted her head to stare at him. 'He isn't dead.'

Seth blinked. 'What?'

'He's not dead, who told you that?'

186

He gestured to the bed in exasperation.

'The blood is a pretty good indication! And Jimmy! His face says it all!'

'Jimmy's face is saying nothing. Jimmy's face does not feel well,' Jimmy groused, grimacing into space.

Seth frowned and strode to the basket, peering.

A red-faced boy with a tuft of fair hair turned his head slightly with a grunt, two tiny hands pressed against his ears as though their conversation was in screams instead of whispers. He had been washed and swaddled some time ago – his hair was soft and dry, catching the morning light.

'See? He's fine!' Eleanor said in reassurance, reaching over to squeeze Seth's elbow. 'Honestly, we don't even know where all that blood came from. Apart from a bit of a fright, it all went swimmingly.'

'"Swimmingly" is a nice word for it,' Cienne growled under her breath.

Seth couldn't take his eyes off the basket.

His son – his *actual son* – lay wrapped in a white blanket, squinting up at him with dubious blue eyes, safe and sound.

'Can I pick him up?'

'Of course you can,' Eleanor said with a grin.

Seth bent double and scooped him up around the ribs, hoisting him up to eye level.

'Hello, little man,' he said in amazement.

The child gawked at him in alarm. 'AAH!'

'AAH!' Seth echoed despairingly.

He swung him over to Cienne's lap and deposited him there.

'Here you go.'

He wrung his hands nervously, making a face.

The child roared inconsolably, sobbing loud and fast.

'He doesn't like me, does he?'

'He doesn't *like* having his head bobbing here, there and everywhere,' Eleanor scolded, not unkindly. 'You're supposed to support the back of his head, not grab him around the ribs like a cat. Try picking up the little girl this time.'

Seth blinked, nonplussed. 'What little girl?'

'Your little girl? Don't tell me you didn't see her?'

He followed her finger to the wall, where a washing basket assumed the role of his daughter's cot.

'Oh,' he said faintly. 'It *was* twins.'

Cienne pushed on his arm. 'She's been looking at you since you came in. She wants to meet you.'

Seth squinted at the baby.

The baby squinted back. Malevolently, he thought.

Eleanor shook her head in disdain and, planting both hands on his back, pushed him across the room.

He sidled around the bundle of blankets and leaned over.

187

She stared unblinkingly at him.

Seth sent his mother an imploring glance.

Eleanor edged past and lifted the child into Seth's arms.

The small bundle lay delicate and motionless in the crook of his elbows. The child's eyes widened, locked to his face.

He met her gaze and counted slowly to five. She seemed content.

'Her name's Virginia,' Eleanor said gently.

His nose wrinkled. So did the child's, apparently in imitation.

'Ginny,' he decided. 'Ginny for short.'

'I told you he'd do that,' Cienne grumbled. She reclined on the pillows with the boy in her lap, flinching and wincing. 'What are you naming the boy then, since my names are so inadequate?'

Seth wasn't listening.

Ginny wriggled a bit and resumed their staring competition. *Was that a smile just there?* He bit the inside of his lip and smiled back. She was smiling at him!

A tiny vibration erupted from the depths of her blanket.

The smile fell away from her face, followed by a long, contented blink.

Seth grimaced slightly. *Oh. Maybe not, then.*

'Well?' Cienne pestered.

Seth tore his eyes away from Ginny's.

'I dunno, I can't think of anything.'

He looked back at Ginny and kissed her firmly between the eyes.

She frowned a bit, but was otherwise un-irked.

Cienne softened at this. 'We made that.'

He gave her a helpless grin. 'We did. Both of them.'

He adjusted Ginny's blanket.

'We're going for a walk, I think,' he announced.

He caught sight of Jimmy, staring into space with a disturbed expression. 'You alright?'

Jimmy was catatonic.

'I'll… sort you out later,' Seth decided.

Exiting his quarters, he halted by the stairs, checked he had proper support on her neck and back and made sure once more that she was not in fact about to bawl her head off.

She stared up at him with eyes that matched his own.

In colour, anyway.

Seth smiled fondly at her and descended to show Ginny her new home.

~

Lilly stood dumbfounded at the door of the main hall.

The Crook was her second home. Watching Qattren frolicking on stage in the altogether was like the idea of introducing Orl to her parents only for him to get drunk, climb on the chandelier and throw bonbons at them. Assuming King Theo wouldn't have killed him on sight for tongue-tangling with his only daughter.

The act itself was chaste by Crook standards. A large sheet of red silk billowed around Qattren, hiding the important parts while revealing enough for the imagination to play with. It was certainly keeping Lilly and her acquaintances gripped – even Stan and Ron. Although admittedly Stan did seem more incredulous than aroused, and Ron's dribbling was more out of blind fury than anything else.

'What the hell is this?' Ron hissed in horror.

'This,' said Keith Large, 'is our special weekly act.'

Stan's uncle, and the proprietor of Stanley Carrot's much loved family home, stood proudly at their left, a yellowing silk suit stretched over a beer belly in absolute denial.

'Lovely, isn't she?' he went on, beaming.

Lilly pivoted slowly.

'Your special weekly act?' she said, deliberating on each syllable. 'You've hired the most formidable ruler of Truphoria and beyond as a weekly burlesque dancer?'

'She's multi-talented,' he said in defence.

'Does my brother know about this?'

Keith laughed in defiance. 'You really think that pervert would be cooped up with the missus if he knew about this?'

'Probably not,' she mused. 'I actually reckon he'd pay her double the rate to dance on our dining table. Ew.' She grimaced at a mental image of Seth's reaction to the show. 'I won't tell him if you won't.'

'Why didn't I know about this?' Ron demanded. 'She's my wife!'

'Yes, but we all know who wears the trousers in that household,' said Keith. 'Or removes them, as the case may be.'

'How long has she been doing this?' Stan asked.

'Since she auditioned nearly a year ago,' he replied proudly. 'You missed a good show that day. That was her on top form.'

'QATTREN!' Ron roared.

Qattren jumped and caught Ron's eye in terror. 'Ronald!'

The silk sheet fluttered to the floor.

The crowd cheered.

She snatched up the sheet and wrapped it around her breasts, fleeing from the stage.

'Oi, you've got another half an hour yet!' Keith protested.

She swept past, the group at her heels.

'Is this your new hobby?' Ron demanded shrilly. 'Taking off clothes in front of everyone?'

'I thought we had agreed against exclusive rights to each other,' Qattren said mildly.

She waggled her fingers at a passing regular.

'We agreed on a marriage based on the traditional weekly game of snakes and ladders,' Ron said angrily. 'One year of Tuesday evenings you owe me. One. *Year.*'

Qattren wisely decided to resume the conversation with the calmer members of the entourage.

'I take it Geldemar sent you here?'

'You need to invest yourself in some less-volatile friends,' Lilly advised.

'Perhaps. What brings you here? I thought you were getting married?'

'We were, until a dead body fell through his glass ceiling. It's been postponed until such time as the weirdo from the desert can be questioned – or killed, whichever happens first.'

'And why is it that the Princess of Adem is investigating this as opposed to shopping for wedding gowns?'

'Because…' Lilly grimaced. 'I don't want to, alright? He's old, like, *ancient.* I'd be *his* mum,' she jerked a thumb at Orl. 'I don't want to be a mum, much less one to this lug.'

'No, step-mothers don't generally snog their husband's kids,' Stan said.

'Shut your face,' she said, reddening slightly.

'So why has Geldemar sent you here?' Qattren asked. 'Apart from to try to embarrass me, that is.'

'To find the bloke trying to buy out the monarchies,' Stan supplied.

'Ah, Mr Halle,' Qattren said tiredly. 'What's he done now?'

'His associates are lying all around the Ambassador's premises, stone dead,' Ron said. 'And Lilly's killing all his dragons.'

'I'm not killing them!' Lilly exclaimed. 'They just happen to be dropping dead while in my vicinity. It's a complete coincidence.'

Qattren's eyes thinned. 'Not quite a coincidence.' She faced Ron. 'Any word from your mother?'

He blinked. 'No, why should there be?'

'There's an obvious connection. Politicians whose plot was to take over the kingdoms: dead. Dragons, a species famously related to the end of the world: dead. A queen whose kingdom is in jeopardy, with an obsession towards the seven gods and their prophecies: missing. It doesn't take a genius.'

'Yes, but maybe this person knows where she is,' Lilly pointed out. 'Last we saw of him, he had popped out of nowhere, kicked my dog to who-knows-where and ran away very fast for the nearest dragon. If anyone can drive someone as mad as that, it's Ron's mum.'

'Kicked your dog? For what, piddling on him?'

'Just looking at him, by the looks of it.'

'I wasn't aware you had a dog. What kind of animal are we talking here?'

'Small, shrill, white thing, with a brown spot on his back. Like this one.'

She pointed at a nearby dog and froze. 'Hang on, this *is* him!'

Lilly lifted Albie into the air and he licked her chin.

Qattren stared at him with a frown.

'Was he with us this whole time?' Ron asked, baffled.

'No, Halle kicked him halfway to the horizon,' Orl said, giving the dog a worried glance. 'How did he get here so fast?'

'Someone must have kicked him back just as we were leaving,' Ron said with a shrug. 'Although that makes me wonder why Geldemar didn't mention him. Speaking of lunatics, we came to find the asylum in the city. I presume you've visited the place often?' he asked Qattren spitefully.

He frowned and waved a hand in front of her face.

She blinked and tore her gaze from the puppy in Lilly's hands.

'It's on the far east of the city,' she said distractedly. 'There's an alley running east from the execution square on Arthur Stibbons' Street. It leads to the main thoroughfare travelling through the city, the asylum is on the end of it. If you walk you won't arrive until dark, but I can take you, if you like.'

'Thanks.' Ron paused. 'Is something the matter?'

Qattren glared at the Bastard in silence.

He glared back. 'What?' he barked.

Qattren's eyes widened at the sound of Seth Crey's voice.

She leaned forward, looking him straight in the eyes.

The Bastard leaned back, slightly frightened.

Lilly blinked.

'Is there something wrong with my dog?' she demanded, glancing down at him.

'He isn't a real dog.'

The four blinked.

The Bastard gulped.

'Of course he's a real dog,' Lilly said in disbelief. 'What else could he be?'

'Nothing,' the Bastard squeaked.

'He's a ghost.' For a moment Qattren looked like she was about to cry.

'Qat?' Ron said gently, touching her shoulder.

As soon as his fingers touched her skin, she exploded.

The group coughed hysterically, Qattren's dust clinging to the inside of their mouths.

'I don't touch her often,' Ron said darkly, 'but when I do, that *always* happens.'

'What's everyone got against my dog?' Lilly wondered, stroking his head and ears.

'He's a ghost,' Stan said morbidly.

'Oh, come off it,' she scoffed. 'And here I was thinking *she* was a sane, intelligent woman.'

'Tell me about it,' Ron said glumly.

'She knows where the asylum is,' Stan pointed out. 'Sod me if I know *any* sane person who knows where their local mental hospital is.'

~

A robed man stood outside the palace of the Creys and ushered five men inside.

'Do exactly as we have discussed,' he ordered. 'And keep your hoods up *at all costs!*'

They nodded beneath their cowls and hurried inside.

Three floors above them, a howl erupted from the tiny wicker basket inside the royal bedroom.

Seth let out a combination of a groan and a whine.

'Put it back in, the novelty's worn off.'

Cienne made a disgusted noise.

'Where's that stupid bell?' she snapped, rifling on the nightstand to her left. 'So much for childcare: of course the nanny disappears on the children's first few hours of life.' Cienne elbowed the small of Seth's back. 'Get up and settle him.'

'No, you… squirted him out, you settle him.'

'You squirted him in! Do it!'

'No!'

They paused for barely a millisecond.

'JIMMY!'

Jimmy's voice floated in from the manservant's room to the east.

'If you give him to me, I'll sell him.'

Seth bolted into a sitting position. 'You are a cold, cold man!'

The boy coughed and spluttered, the sobs coming too quickly for him to manage.

Seth growled obscenities under his breath and flung the blanket from himself. Bending his knees at the foot of the basket, he slid his hands beneath the boy's head and back as his mother instructed and held him aloft like that, as though holding a bag of flour.

Ginny looked on from her makeshift bed of laundry, enraptured. Clearly loud noises in the night were fine by her book, as long as her brother was unhappy. *She's going to grow up to be a miniature Lilly,* Seth thought.

He shifted the boy up and down in a vague attempt at comforting him.

He screamed on.

'Now what?' Seth said to the world at large.

'Take him to the servants floor or something,' Cienne grumbled, rolling away from him.

Seth glowered at her, an eyebrow arching.

Twenty years you've been pestering me for one of these, he thought, though he dare not say it aloud.

He carefully manoeuvred the boy into his elbows and left his quarters, mumbling.

'What do you want from me?' he said in a pained whisper. 'This isn't my job! I'm supposed to visit you once a month and stuff you with cake, not nurse you! The wet nurse is supposed to sort this bollocks out. Where do the servants even go at night?'

The boy offered no helpful suggestions. He just kept screaming.

Seth scanned the corridor, hoping that the sound would wake someone with more experience. No one appeared to hear him: his mother slept like a brick, but she had about a billion ladies-in-waiting. Where the hell were they when you needed them?

Debating on the idea of barging into random quarters and hastily deciding against it, Seth heaved a sigh and took the boy downstairs, hoping to find some type of night staff in the kitchens to take over.

~

Outside, two armoured night guards stood in front of the entrance as the three hooded strangers approached. The guards' spears fell into a defensive 'X' shape.

'What business have you here at this time of night?'

The central figure raised a crucifix from the depths of his robe.

'We have come to take confessions,' he said mildly.

'All the way from Stoneguard?' the second guard snorted. 'You'll be a long time at it taking confessions from this pervert.'

'Not to mention the maniac he sleeps with,' added the first with a short laugh.

'Well, in that case, why don't I show you a list of common depravities and you can just tick next to the relevant atrocities?'

The door opened just as the guard began another quip. Knives flashed.

The two guards clanged onto the gravel, helms off and necks slit from ear to ear.

~

Seth flinched at a clatter from outside and decided to ignore it.

He had paced the perimeter of the throne room before the child had quietened. Still no servants had emerged. Seth had searched the entire kitchens and each antechamber with no avail. *Where the hell are they?*

The boy grizzled, wriggling too often for Seth's comfort.

The front doors rattled in the entrance hall. *Bloody guards.*

Seth moved to the east antechamber for some peace and quiet.

Gingerly placing the boy onto one shoulder, Seth turned to close the door behind them when a voice made him freeze.

'Watch the staircases and doors. More servants could emerge at any second.'

Seth peered out, holding the door open a crack.

193

Five hooded men stood at various parts of the throne room. Two of them barred the entrances to the hall, each with a knife glinting in the candlelight.

Seth swallowed firmly.

A single drop of blood lay whole and undisturbed in the centre of the room.

He stared at it in horror before turning his gaze to the tiny body on his shoulder.

~

The dragon touched down hard, throwing up a dust storm.

Marbrand leaped down and lifted Despina to the ground.

Elliot followed. 'I feel awful.' He burped.

'Stay with the dragon, then,' Marbrand said impatiently. 'I've got a bad feeling in my gut. We might be too late.'

The entire forecourt was deserted – totally unlike what it should be for a castle manned by a guard that was seventy per cent nocturnal. A person lingered solitary by the front portcullis.

'The cowl doesn't look like a good sign,' Marbrand muttered.

He walked forward nonchalantly, Despina at his heels.

After a moment, Elliot gave a huff and followed, holding his stomach.

Marbrand came up behind the silhouette and reached out a gloved hand.

'Excuse me,' he said lightly, tapping a shoulder.

The man jumped theatrically, his limbs and robes flapping.

'The hell do you want?' he snapped.

Marbrand blinked, the voice familiar.

'Sir Marbrand of the palace night guard,' he introduced himself, trying to recall who this man reminded him of. 'May I ask what brings you here on such a chilly night?'

Despina eyed Elliot with unease.

He squeezed his eyes shut and made a face.

'I am just waiting on some acquaintances,' the stranger said haughtily.

Elliot paled.

'And, may I ask, what is the palace night guard doing frolicking with a dragon twenty yards away from their post?' he said scathingly.

'We're off duty,' Marbrand said immediately. 'Got a bit of holiday pay, so I thought I'd get myself a pet dragon. They're all the rage these days, you know.'

Despina stepped away from Elliot in the interests of self-preservation.

The stranger looked Marbrand up and down. 'Haven't you got some swording to do?'

Elliot pitched forward and threw up on the stranger's robe.

'Bloody hell!' Marbrand snapped, rubbing his eyes.

'I told you I felt awful!' said Elliot in a voice like gravel.

The stranger stripped off his robe in disgust, throwing it to the ground to reveal plain white breeches and a shirt.

'Sir, I'm terribly sorry about...' Marbrand trailed off.

The man's distinctive salt-and-pepper goatee became evident in the torchlight.

'What the hell are you doing here?' Marbrand snapped.

Father Toffer wrung his hands.

'Erm...'

He bolted past them and sprinted downhill.

Marbrand was about to follow when they heard a scream from inside the keep.

~

Seth found an ornamental box of official-looking documents and spilled the contents onto the table, padding the box with a table cloth.

He lifted his nameless son inside, making sure the silk was comfortable.

'You alright, little man?' he whispered, stroking his head.

He stared up at him in silence, exactly as Ginny had done earlier.

That's it, let's bond as we're about to die, he thought cynically before shaking that off. Sod them. He wasn't dying today. He had a child now – two of them. Things were going to be different.

Seth hid the box behind a curtain on the windowsill, leaving the lid open and making sure his son couldn't be noticed from the doorway.

Outside, the strangers waited.

One of them had his back to the antechamber door, concealing the knife behind his back. Seth could hear it on the other side, drumming against the doorframe, tap, tap, tap.

Seth swung it open.

The man skipped away.

Seth gave the intruders a good eyeballing.

'What do you want?'

A man – their leader, Seth assumed – swung around and bowed.

'We have come from the city to give a blessing to your new arrival,' he said indulgently, his hands pressed together in front of him.

'Which city?'

He paused. 'A friendly one. Quite like Serpus.'

Except without a name and sort of near the region of Stoneguard, Seth thought wryly.

Aloud he said, 'Well, the christening isn't for six weeks. You can bless him then.'

'But it's customary to bless the child shortly after birth.'

'In the middle of the night?'

195

'During night feeds,' he corrected. 'Lessen the chance of us interrupting his afternoon nap.'

Seth squinted. 'With knives?'

Cloth shifted around them as knives were hastily disguised.

Seth glared at each of them and turned back to the main one.

'He's asleep, actually,' he said, irritable. 'That would be your cue to bugger off.'

The monk winced. 'No, I'm afraid it is not.'

He raised a hand.

Two men rushed at Seth and grabbed his arms, dragging him away from the open doorway.

Seth wrenched himself away desperately, with no avail.

'Now,' the man said amiably.

The men forced Seth's arms behind his back and pushed him onto his knees.

'We can do this the friendly way or the decidedly more hostile way. As a man of the gods, you can understand my own personal preference.'

'You're not from here, then,' Seth spat. ''Cause there's only one god in this country, and his descendent says you can *piss off!*'

The man clicked his tongue off the roof of his mouth.

'The hostile way it is.'

He produced a small knotted whip from the confines of his robe and belted Seth across the face with it.

His head jerked to the left sharply. The right side of his face seared with agony.

'Where is the Antichrist?'

'What?' he squeaked, his face a throbbing mass of pain. 'I, I don't know!'

The whip cracked again, catching his ear this time.

Seth yelped and shuddered, his mouth hanging open.

'The infant!' the attacker snarled, raising the weapon. 'Where is the child?'

'That's none of your business.'

Seth cried out as the whip struck the side of his neck.

'If you don't divulge the location of the child, we'll have to be more severe.'

'Do what you bloody want, I won't tell you where my boy is,' Seth snarled.

The man tutted, putting away the whip. 'Take his right index finger.'

Seth jerked and twisted around.

One of them snatched his index finger. Cold steel pressed against it, unmistakable.

'Last chance,' the man taunted. 'The boy?'

Seth spat on the man's robe.

He drew a breath and gave a short signal.

And Seth screamed.

Blood oozed down his wrist. Seth writhed in the men's arms, shaking and sobbing wildly. The howl reverberated across the hall. Abruptly, Seth was silent.

Fresh screams erupted from the east antechamber.

Infant screams.

Seth shook violently. 'Don't touch him.'

The stranger moved towards the door.

'Please,' Seth begged, his eyes streaming.

He reached the door and peered inside.

'I SAID DON'T TOUCH HIM!!'

Seth threw himself from the men's grasp.

An arm snatched him around the neck, choking him.

The man nodded to himself and faced Seth.

'That's all I wanted to know,' he said mildly. 'Now where's the other one?'

Seth hesitated a mere second. 'There is no other one.'

A jerk of the man's blade sent Seth staggering onto his knees.

Seth's strangled cries came muffled by his own clenched teeth.

'The girl? Upstairs with her mother, perhaps?'

He flicked a signal. A cloaked man jogged for the stairs.

Terror swept down his spine for the second time that night, pulsing.

'No,' he whined, tears rolling down his face.

Another signal. Another man hurried into the antechamber.

Seth hung by his elbows, shivering uncontrollably.

A body tumbled down the staircase in a flurry of black robes.

Everyone frowned in bemusement.

The doors slammed open and Marbrand sprang in.

Seth ducked.

Marbrand's blade swept over his head, cutting a man's head open across the nose.

Seth face-planted onto the flagstones as his attackers fled.

Marbrand cut one down in quick succession. He drove the blade through the other's back and ended its path in Cienne's throne, waving his apologies at Seth in the process.

He released his grip on the sword and staggered back, chest heaving.

Seth pushed himself onto his knees, holding his blood-coated hand aloft.

Marbrand approached to examine it.

'Cut it off,' Seth gritted. He squeezed his eyes shut. 'It's agony, just cut the whole bloody finger off.'

Raw flesh glistened on Seth's middle finger, a remnant of skin dangling off the edge of the nail.

Marbrand sucked in a breath. 'The bastard flayed you.'

Elliot descended the stairs at a hop.

'Hello,' he said cheerfully.

Seth stared at him. 'How did you get in? They had guards by the doors—

'

197

'I sent him to the back, down to the boiler room,' Marbrand said. 'He climbed up the chimney shaft. Is the child alright?'

Seth shivered ceaselessly, eyes streaming.

'The queen got a fright, and the little princess is a bit upset, but apart from that, they're fine,' Elliot reassured them.

'What about the boy?'

Marbrand blinked. 'What boy?'

Seth pointed at the antechamber. 'My boy, the other twin. He was in there.' He sobbed. 'One of them went in after him...'

Marbrand took a dagger from his belt. 'Stay there—'

'No.'

Seth shoved himself upright and swiped Marbrand's dagger as he went.

They crossed the hall together. Seth pushed the door open.

A bloody face stared back at them, filled with terror. The robed man lay plastered across the council table, head twisted upward and sideways at an awkward angle.

Sitting in Seth's chair overlooking the fireplace – in which a door hung open – a girl in her teens held a very wriggly baby with blond hair.

She glanced at Seth pleadingly.

'Please take him before I drop him,' Despina said.

The dagger clattered to the floor.

Seth rushed around the table and scooped the boy from her arms.

Despina met his thankful gaze and froze.

'You,' she said in a hushed voice.

Seth's brow furrowed slightly. 'What about me?'

Despina's eyes scoured his face, up and down, mouth hung open, straining for words that wouldn't come. A realisation appeared to come to her then and her face cleared.

'Um... you're...'

She hesitated.

'Seth Crey,' she finished lamely.

He lifted his eyebrows. 'I know. Less impressive in person, aren't I?'

He smiled at her embarrassment and gave her a wink.

She offered a sheepish smile back.

Seth checked the infant over. The boy had settled as soon as his father held him and was now slowly drifting off to sleep.

'Sir.'

Marbrand looked at him expectantly.

'What's your given name?'

He hesitated.

Despina bit back a grin.

Seth met his gaze. 'Well?'

Marbrand licked his lips. 'You want the real one or the fake one?'

Something twitched in Seth's jaw.

198

'We'll start with the real one, shall we?' he said coldly.

Marbrand sighed and rubbed his eyes. 'Sadie.'

Seth stared at him.

Despina giggled treacherously.

'And,' Seth said, all suspicion obliterated, 'and your other name?'

'Russell.'

Seth nodded slowly. 'The new one... suits you better.'

'I like to think so.'

Seth looked at the unnamed twin.

'Mind if I borrow it?' he asked, meeting Marbrand's gaze.

Marbrand blinked. 'You want to name him after me?'

'He'll grow into it,' he said with a grin.

He was speechless for a moment. 'It would be an honour, sir.'

Seth grinned at each of them in turn. He gazed down at his son. Russell Crey. It was perfect.

Cienne was going to hate it almost as much as he hated the name Virginia.

~

Si gave the dock an impassive gaze.

Nightfall rendered the sandstone in shades of grey. Tiny spotlights illuminated buildings in fractured light, picking out disjointed edges and corners, amber against black shadows.

The *Devourer* eased into Portmyr at a leisurely pace, in silence bar the soft susurrus of water against the hull. Tully watched his brother from the rail beside him as the port enveloped them.

Si's gaze intensified. Things rarely boded well when it did that.

Tully followed it to see a small party gathered at the dock, official coats of armour gleaming in the torchlight. They watched the skies above, waiting.

Tully wondered what happened to Lilly. They had passed the remains of rowboats and splintered hull earlier in the day, floating listlessly on the waves. He hoped Lilly was alright.

He glanced at Si again, wondering if he felt the same. It was hard to tell what he felt these days.

The deckhand leapt onto the dock and caught a line, tying it off.

Si and Tully lingered a moment longer as the deck creaked to a halt below them, bobbing slightly.

'You never did tell me what we've been ordered to do exactly,' Tully said distantly.

Si hesitated.

'Hard to pinpoint it in exact terms,' he said.

Tully rubbed his face with both hands. 'We ain't getting ourselves in trouble, are we?'

Si paused again. The silence lingered a much longer time.

'We'll see,' he said finally.

Tully let his eyes slip out of focus. *I'll take that as a yes.*

He leaned his elbows on the rail and hung his head.

~

VI

Lilly grasped a steel bar in each hand and leaned against the asylum gate.

Insofar as the midnight sky allowed them to see, it didn't particularly look like an asylum. The thatched roof made it look like a country pub, only with a barbed gate and military walls around the front.

'I don't like this,' Stan said nauseously. 'I've heard people die horrific deaths in this place.'

'How?' Lilly said derisively. 'All they do is lock them in a room with their sleeves tied together and feed them soup so they can't choke.'

'Room? It used to be cages,' Ron said. 'At least it did in Stoneguard. My mum had me committed once when my dad was away.'

'Naw, Cienne passed a law against that cages malarkey the other month, after the old man went,' said Lilly. 'You know, in case she had another Episode and Seth had her committed.'

She turned to the gate and gave the bell beside her a shake.

'I'll stay out here, I think,' Stan declared.

'On your own? In the dark?' Lilly said wryly. 'That's brave for you.'

'Orl's staying with me.'

'Eh?' Orl said in disappointment, gazing at Lilly.

'I'm sure she can question the madman perfectly fine without you gazing lovingly upon her,' Stan sneered.

'That's slander!' Orl said hotly, his face burning.

'No, it isn't,' Lilly said in amusement. 'Anyway, you need to stay out here in case we get committed and need someone to fetch Jimmy.'

'Why Jimmy?' Ron asked. 'Your brother's the king.'

'Seth's probably the least intimidating king since King Seb was crowned age two,' said Lilly. 'A tall dark-haired stranger dressed in black with a royal permit to do whatever he likes to people? *That* is much more persuasive.'

The asylum door opened.

A woman in a purple knitted cardigan emerged.

'Come for a visit, have we?'

Lilly blinked. 'You run this place?'

She nodded brightly, her messily-drawn bun of silver hair bobbing back and forth.

She looked more like the proprietor of an orphanage than the head doctor of a psychiatric hospital, or so Lilly thought, but she wasn't being picky. Anyone without a rectal probe and a beginner's manual on lobotomy was good enough for her.

'You don't have visiting hours, then?'

'Oh yes, but everyone's always so busy at those times, so we just let people in whenever. The residents enjoy the break in routine.' She gazed fondly inside at her unseen treasures. 'Anyway, it's much nicer to have the residents' family in on their own time, isn't it?'

Lilly's eyes thinned. 'Hmm. Well, me and my brother Ron have come to visit our father, Mr Halle.'

'Oh yes, he's just arrived a few hours ago, he'll be pleased to see you! It'll help him settle in, I daresay. He never mentioned any family, though,' she said with a minute frown.

'He's been like that ever since I had that, erm, *illegitimate child*,' she said with emphasis, drawing on their established backstory.

'With me,' Ron improvised.

Lilly shot him a sidelong glance.

He linked their arms self-consciously.

'Oh, that'll explain it,' she said, her frown evaporating. 'We'd, er, better not remind him of that. Will your friends be joining us?'

'No, no, we'd better check ourselves into an inn,' Stan said brightly. 'You and Ron will want a room together then, Lilly?'

Lilly scowled at him.

'Come inside! My name is Liz,' the lady said brightly.

She opened the gate wide and beckoned them inside.

Lilly and Ron followed Liz into the thatched building with apprehension.

'I'm not sure about her,' Ron murmured to Lilly. 'She's too… fruity.'

'I suppose you have to be in a place that's technically sanity's graveyard,' said Lilly. 'What's getting me is how easy it was for us to get in here. It's shifty. You still have your knife, right?'

He patted his holster.

Liz strolled ahead across the largely empty foyer and circled the desk at the back.

'You haven't any weapons, have you?' Liz chirped. 'Our residents seldom have trouble finding them. We'll give them back before you leave.'

'Balls,' Lilly said.

Ron relinquished the knife and tinderbox.

Lilly showed Liz the empty holster where her own weapon had sat before she stabbed Geldemar with it.

'Lost it,' she explained shortly. It was hardly a lie.

They followed Liz through a door next to the desk and down a long, torch-lit corridor. Instead of locked doors like Lilly had anticipated, open arches greeted them, holding soft chairs and books – which didn't bode well when mixed with torches and any possible pyromaniacs in the building.

Lilly gazed into them distantly, the chairs in particular. It had been a while since she'd last sat in a soft chair, she thought wistfully.

They got to the end of the corridor and Liz extracted a ring of keys from her belt.

'I ask that once I open this door, you wait exactly ten seconds before entering,' she told them sweetly.

She rattled the key around in the lock and slowly pulled the door towards them.

A shrill screech erupted from inside. Ten seconds of fast-pounding footsteps was rudely interrupted by a slam.

Liz had apparently slammed the door on the face of what appeared to be a resident.

'Don't mind him, he doesn't mean any harm,' she said in amusement.

She opened the door to reveal the crumpled body of a young man, his arms strapped to his sides, twitching.

'He gets a bit overexcited when a door opens near him. Follow me, your father's in Room P.'

They stepped carefully around the brown-haired bundle of leather straps.

A variety of people surrounded them: thin people, pale people, people with wide bloodshot eyes, people with blindfolds around their eyes as they congregated in a corner, chatting as if nothing were amiss. It was a relief to Lilly's mind. She'd been expecting a lot of knife-throwing and excessive crossbow use – normality where the Creys were concerned.

'These are the low-risk residents,' Liz explained, as if reading Lilly's thoughts. 'We let them roam as they please – as long as they don't leave the door we entered. The high-risk each have their own room at the back of the house, which are right… here.'

She halted at a locked door identical to the last one and, bizarrely, handed Lilly and Ron a rain cloak from the rack beside them.

Lilly eyed it in bemusement.

'Put it on,' she chirped, sliding hers over her shoulders. 'It's just a precaution to stop the low-risk annoying the high-risk and vice versa.'

The two covered themselves hurriedly. Liz turned a knob beside the doorframe.

Water erupted from the ceiling, drenching everyone in a three-foot radius of the door.

Patients scattered like frightened hens.

'Why?' Ron wailed. 'Why would you have this in a facility designed to help people?'

'To make it easier for the staff to keep them inside,' Lilly answered for her.

'Right, here we are!'

They halted at a door marked with a 'P'. Liz extracted a ring of keys from inside her jumper and opened the door just wide enough for Lilly and Ron to squeeze through.

'Mr Halle!' she called behind them. 'It's your children here to see you, dear!'

'I have no children, who've you let in?' The figure unfolded himself from the corner of the room. 'I told you to kill anyone who came looking for me! Don't you ever listen?'

Lilly frowned. 'He's that bad, then?'

'Only without his pillows,' she said endearingly. 'We shouldn't be encouraging him really, but we'll be weaning him away from them in a few days. Yell when you're ready to leave!'

She shut the door behind her and latched it, to Lilly's discomfort.

'So,' Ron said, 'you like pillows, then?'

Cushions and plush toys covered the walls and floor, making it difficult for Lilly to keep her balance. They were glued on – badly, she thought, when a stuffed elephant peeled free from the ceiling and bounced off the top of her head.

Halle himself sat cross-legged on the carpet of plush, his arms wrapped around himself – voluntarily, that is, apart from a sling holding his left arm aloft. There was no bed in the room, Lilly noted. Not that he needed one.

What he really needed was a change of clothes. He wore the same leotard he had worn in the desert and it had seen better days, to say the least.

'What do you want?' he said, eyeballing them from the floor.

'To ask you some questions,' Lilly said.

'Forget it,' he said immediately. 'I'm not incriminating myself any further. You lot can sod off.'

Lilly, having spent far too many years getting her own way, decided to ignore this. 'What were you running from in the desert?'

Halle shook his head stiffly. 'Nope. Not telling. Not saying a *single* word.'

'Oh, it's secrets we're playing, oh, I love this game,' Lilly said dryly. She faced Ron. 'Right, let's get him out of here and take him to meet Jimmy. He's brilliant at this game once we give him a sharp knife.'

'No!' Halle said in alarm, crawling forward to grab her leg. 'Don't make me leave! This place is safe! It's the only safe place!'

'Where they tie people's sleeves together and install water features above the doorways?' Ron said. 'We can take you somewhere safer if you just tell us what's happened.'

'It's a secret,' he hissed, spittle flying from his mouth. 'Nowhere is safe.'

Lilly sighed and wrestled Halle's fingers from her boot. She knelt.

'Listen,' she said in a whisper. 'I'm a Crey. We don't like secrets. Particularly secrets that disrupt the marital arrangements of a princess.'

Even if she doesn't want to get married in the first place, she added internally.

'Now if you don't tell me precisely why your men have been falling from the sky stone dead at my feet all week, then yes. Nowhere will indeed be safe for you.'

Halle glared at her. 'If I tell you, I will *die*.'

She leaned forward.

'If you don't tell me, you will die *instantly*,' she emphasised. 'So you might as well tell me.'

Halle heaved a shaky sigh. He pressed a particularly large pillow to his chest with his good hand.

'It's the city,' he muttered. 'It's killing them.'

'What city?'

'Copers. The lost city.'

'It's killing them?' Ron asked with a frown. 'How? It's just buildings and rocks.'

'It was built by warlocks,' he said. 'Why do you think no one can find it? It moves around the desert, all the time, away from passing civilisation. Nobody but the warlocks knew how to summon it, and they died shortly after building it. Killed each other off apparently.

'Then one of our lot, Erstan, found Copers on his way to propose democracy to the Ambassador, and he discovered how to summon it.'

He pulled a star-shaped gold ornament from his robe and held it face down in the palm of his hand.

'There's a song, three notes,' he said. 'Once that song is sung by someone in the desert with the star, the city will come. As long as the topmost point is pointing north.'

'How do you know which point is the top one?' Ron asked.

He didn't deign to respond.

'What's the song, then?' Lilly asked after a moment.

He didn't respond.

Lilly waved a hand in front of his face.

He slapped it away.

'Why is the city killing them?' she pressed. 'What did they do?'

'We came to conquer it,' he murmured, almost in tears. 'Show everyone we didn't need a king to make a place work. The city didn't like that. It didn't like that at all.'

Ron's eyes narrowed. 'Are you sure it's the city that's killing them? 'Cause that sounds a lot more like my mother—'

'No!' he snapped. 'She's not even a player here. She's just a blip. She didn't want to change the city, we wanted to. And now we're going to pay, the whole stinking lot of us. Not that it matters.'

Lilly frowned. 'How can it not matter? They're your friends.'

'It doesn't matter,' he went on. 'It's your lot you need to be worried about. All of you.'

'All of who?'

'All of you, the Creys.'

His eyes turned up to meet hers.

'All thanks to your brother,' he seethed.

Lilly rolled her eyes. 'What's he done now?'

A dagger materialised into Lilly's sheath.

She didn't notice.

'Well?' she asked again, irate. 'What has my brother done?'

The dagger slipped from its sheath and landed point-first into Halle's thigh.

Halle stared at it and screamed.

Lilly went cold.

'*Shit!* Sorry, sorry, sorry, shush, shush, look, it's fine,' she hissed desperately, patting his arms. 'Don't scream, look, we can help, it was an accident! I'll fix it, look, it's not that bad, I've had worse, look, see?'

She held her bandaged hand up in demonstration.

His right hand curled around the handle.

'No, don't pull it out!'

He pulled the blade from his leg.

Blood pooled around him, staining the pillows.

Halle gawked at the blade, glassy-eyed, as he turned it on his face.

Lilly stared in horror. 'What are you doing?'

'I'm not doing anything!' he howled. 'This was your fault!'

He pushed the dagger into his throat as Liz opened the cell door.

'What's happened in here?' she demanded, as if to a naughty child.

Halle's hand slipped from the handle. He flopped to one side, totally limp.

'Madam,' Ron began, trembling, 'there's been a horrible accident—'

Lilly leapt in. 'We couldn't stop him—'

Liz spoke in a calm, quiet tone. 'I see you've come to the right place. I have two rooms that would be perfect for you!'

Her voice became jolly very fast.

'Oh no,' Lilly said with a gulp.

She cleared her throat.

'Right, I'll be level with you, we lied,' she said in an explosive exhale. 'We aren't related to him. My real name's Lilly Crey, the King of Adem's sister, and this is—'

'Not her lover,' Ron said abruptly.

'Ronald Horne of Stoneguard, I believe,' she said with a bright grin. 'That's why I let you in, dear. We've been waiting for you two for some time.'

Lilly and Ron glanced at each other.

'Balls,' Ron said shortly.

~

Twilight had settled over the Creys Keep as Corporal Moat glared down at the two late-night visitors.

'What do you want?' he snapped from the gate house.

'We've come to speak with Jimmy,' Stan called up. 'It concerns Lilly-Anna Crey.'

'Lilly-Anna Crey is in the Desertlands,' Moat snarled. 'Now piss off. I've already had a bollocking from the king himself for leaving someone in uninvited.'

'Lilly is supposed to be there, yes,' Orl barked up from the closed grid, 'marrying my father. Or she would be if she wasn't currently locked in an asylum some miles away. Should the king hear that his soon-to-be nephew-in-law was refused, I imagine he would be very displeased indeed. Bring me this Jimmy immediately!'

Moat sighed. 'I've already let in one murderer this week! If I let in any more, I'll be sacked!'

'Being sacked will be the least of your problems once the Ambassador of the Desertlands learns his bride was left locked in an asylum at your command!'

Moat sighed again.

'Oh, alright!' he exclaimed, snatching the portcullis crank with both hands. 'But I'm expecting a ten-year contract from your blessed Ambassador at *least* if King Death sacks me!'

Stan and Orl jogged inside, Albie at their heels.

~

'I hate the bloody day shift,' Marbrand growled.

They stood outside the front door of the keep, Marbrand leaning heavily on the double doors with his hands in his pockets.

The late morning sun shone heavily on the trio. Ten guards surrounded them in full ceremonial regalia: steel armour patterned in enamelled scales and a snake-head helm topped with a silly green plume for good measure. The light ricocheted from one man to another, a white ray bouncing from breastplate to pauldron to helmet, concluding its journey in the spot right between Marbrand's already smarting eyes.

Jimmy opened the doors.

Marbrand staggered backwards into the throne room, fighting to keep his balance.

'Thought you two were night watch?' Jimmy asked with a frown.

'We were, until Marbrand had the bright idea of bagging us a promotion,' Elliot grumbled.

'Ooh, don't you just hate it when people do their jobs properly,' Marbrand sneered, regaining posture.

'At least the job description is fixed,' Jimmy said. 'You know, not changed around to suit every unusual happening that occurs, such as the king's sister being thrown in the nut house.'

'Lilly-Anna's miles away,' Marbrand said.

'She is,' Jimmy agreed. 'Just not as many miles away as we thought she was. Got a key for the armoury?'

'I'll just file my next question under "ask Lilly",' Marbrand said with a half-smile.

He took a key from inside his sleeve and threw it into his hands.

A whistling breeze heralded Lyseria's arrival.

Marbrand gawped up at her large silhouette. It soared overhead in a beeline to the grounds behind the palace. He was suddenly reminded of his near-death experience in Portmyr and shivered.

Males don't flame, he thought in embarrassed hindsight.

Jimmy ducked to the left in the nick of time.

The pulpy remains of a cow landed between them.

'While I have you here,' Marbrand said as Jimmy was regathering his bearings, 'you wouldn't know anything about Lyseria's breed, would you?'

'I know *everything* about her breed,' Jimmy said. He tugged a handkerchief from his sleeve and dabbed a blood spatter from his trouser leg, his nose wrinkling. 'You tend to make a point of reading up on a thing that kills half your staff.'

'What have you learned about her time of the month?'

Jimmy raised an index finger.

'That's just it: I only know what Qattren Cream Cake told everyone. Nobody else has this backed up: I've turned the Crey library upside down and sent letters to everyone I can think of, no one knows anything about it. As far as anyone's aware, all of them flame via stomach acids. No one's ever heard of exploding eggs.'

'So why does she do it?'

'Wish I knew,' Jimmy said glumly. 'You'd have thought she'd let one off often, but it only seems to happen when it's convenient. I've even asked that Orl kid about it. He laughed in my face.'

Marbrand scrutinised the mound of charred and half-gnawed flesh, pondering this information with bemusement.

Despina's gaze wandered around the castle grounds as Jimmy wandered off.

The merchant carts were just leaving upon dropping off the palace supplies, but one carriage stayed put as several woman disembarked to enter the palace. Despina's eye caught one woman in particular and her blood ran cold.

'What the hell is *she* doing here?'

'Who?' Marbrand asked.

She threw him a startled glance and grabbed a helm from one of the guards' heads.

'Oi!' he protested.

They watched her bemusedly as she rammed the helm on her head and tied it hastily, turning her gaze to the coach every so often.

'Mother. *Abusive* mother,' she quickly explained.

'Ah,' Marbrand said, relaxing.

He stared into space.

Then he froze.

'Shit,' he hissed, snatching another man's helmet and following suit.

'What, your mother here in all?' Elliot asked with a laugh.

'Not her,' Marbrand said, pointedly turning his back on the coach. 'The missus.'

'Oh dear,' Elliot said with a grin. 'The pregnant one?'

'Stop grinning, you'll draw their attention on us!' he snapped.

The group of women giggled at Marbrand and Despina, shuffling past them into the widening double doors.

Elliot peered after them.

'Which one?' he asked.

Slowly, Marbrand lifted off his helm.

'The shortest one.'

'She doesn't look pregnant anymore,' he commented.

'No,' Marbrand murmured, examining her avidly through the gently closing doors. 'She's aged well.'

'Looks a bit young for you, now you mention it,' Elliot said, watching the woman in question, a brunette bringing up the rear who could only be late forties at most.

Despina eyed them uncomfortably.

'Excuse me?' she said blithely. 'You're supposed to be guarding the door?'

The guards rattled to attention. They had been ogling her in all, she realised with disgust.

'Yes,' Marbrand said abruptly, shutting the doors on his wife's back. 'That's enough bird watching, let's get back to standing at the door and watching nobody come in. Yes.'

Despina grinned and rolled her eyes, all thoughts of the ramifications of Miriam Marbrand's arrival temporarily forgotten.

~

Karnak sighed heavily and eyed the afternoon sun with hostility.

They should have been back by now – they had *dragons*, for Christs' sake. He briefly entertained the notion that his son had eloped with her. There was no mistaking the looks of adoration he bestowed on her in her presence.

Nah, he thought with a snort. *He doesn't have it in him.*

A knock to the door interrupted his ponderings.

'Some men to see you,' the messenger said in broken Truphorian.

'Send them in.'

A torrent of footsteps marked the entrance of more men than the Ambassador had anticipated.

He pivoted.

A dozen men stood before him, with at least another dozen in the hall behind them. All wore worn garments of rough spun linen and leather, and all looked weather-beaten and ruddy-cheeked. Sailors, by the look of it.

'What do you lot want?'

The head of the group smiled, a blond man with sunken, yet striking, blue eyes.

'We've come for the wedding,' he said brightly, leaning back and forth on his heels, his hands in his pockets.

'And you are…'

'Friends of Princess Lilly-Anna, sir,' another said from the man's left, mousy-haired with a dark beard. 'We man her ship.'

Karnak's expression blanked.

'Ship?' he said politely.

'Her pirate ship,' Si piped up.

He and Tully each favoured him a boyish smile, dimples and all.

Karnak met each man's gaze with mild interest.

'We'll start from the beginning, shall we?'

~

Liz opened the door.

'I've come to pick up Lilly-Anna Crey,' Jimmy said amiably.

'She's been sectioned, I'm afraid,' Liz said sweetly. 'We'll return her once she's cured.'

'You'll have a long way to go before you can call her cured, her last name is a synonym for lunatic,' said Jimmy. 'Moreover, the king has sent me.'

He produced a warrant, with a wax seal in place of a signature because Seth couldn't be arsed to sign it.

Liz took it in her hands and read it thoroughly. Then she tore it in half.

Jimmy watched the two halves flutter to the ground impassively. 'I see how it is.'

He turned to his companion.

Who handed him a loaded crossbow.

Liz swallowed audibly.

'Ah,' she said softly.

Jimmy raised an eyebrow, tilting the weapon down to her abdomen.

'I'm told liver failure is the slowest, most *painful* way to die,' he said with emphasis.

'I'll… just fetch her, shall I?' she said hurriedly. 'I'm sure we can release— er, discharge her early… and perhaps Ronald Horne as well,' she said as an afterthought. 'Yes, Ronald Horne as well.'

'Lovely,' Jimmy said brightly. 'We'll just wait here while one of your staff goes to get them, shall we?'

The crossbow didn't move an inch until Lilly was close enough to whisper, 'I love you, Jim.'

'Don't say things like that,' Jimmy grimaced as they proceeded to the coach. 'They've been looking to lobotomise you for years. You can't afford for Seth to behead me just yet.'

He glanced at Ron. 'What's with him?'

A mustard-coloured Ron sashayed out of the door in figures of eight before collapsing face first into the cobbles.

'Exposure therapy,' Lilly said, rolling her eyes.

~

VII

Virginia Crey, in her three days of life, reckoned she finally had post-womb existence sussed out.

There were some main categories of life-form that had taken some time to distinguish.

There were Ladies, which flapped their arms a lot and made high-pitched noises that made her ears hurt. One of these provided nourishment and was given to be known as Mummy.

Another type were Men, which were scoffed at by the Ladies and avoided eye-contact with Ginny, which she thought was nice. One of those was special, with yellow hair, who spoke to her softly and stroked her hair. He was called Daddy. She quickly decided to like him.

There was a small one that, like her, was always wrapped in a blanket. His name was Russell. She despised him instantly.

Ginny also knew by proxy that she lived in a castle and was the cutest little princess the whole world had ever seen. She figured that was all she needed to know about life.

Until Aunty Lilly arrived.

Daddy glowered at the anomaly before them as Ginny lay cradled in his arms. Ginny's head flopped to one side in observation. The person confused her. They weren't a Man and they weren't entirely a Lady either – more like a mish-mash of the two. They looked like a Lady in stature and facial features, but they dressed and held themself like a Man, which made no sense because Ladies always wore Pretty Dresses. Didn't they?

As Ginny struggled with the intricacies of gender issues, Seth glared horribly at his little sister, who at least had the decency to cower. He was preoccupied with the rather more alarming element to Lilly's attire, which included a copious amount of blood splashed down one side of her jerkin.

'What have you done now?'

'Nuffing much,' Lilly said. 'The fact that I ended up in the nut house is merely due to a series of accidents and coincidences.'

Seth pressed his eyebrows together. 'You *stabbed* one of the inmates!'

Jimmy produced a letter from his pocket and flicked it open with a flourish.

'According to the official asylum records, "a knife jumped out of Lilly's scabbard and landed in his leg, whereupon he suffered a spasm resulting in him pulling the knife from his leg and accidentally ripping his own throat out".'

'You wrote that, I imagine?'

'Well, I assisted with the final draft,' he said, folding the page in satisfaction.

'Lilly!' Seth scolded.

'It was an accident!' Lilly said loudly. 'I didn't kill anyone!'

'Except the dragons,' Stan said from behind her.

'I didn't kill them either, *Stanley*,' Lilly snapped. 'They just… dropped dead whenever I looked at them.'

Seth eyed her dubiously. 'How many?'

'Three,' Lilly said sheepishly. 'Or four.'

'Four!' Seth stared at her in utter astonishment. 'What did you do, fart on them?'

'No! I didn't do anything, they just dropped dead!'

'So how did you get here?' he demanded, irate. 'If they drop dead whenever you touch them? How did you get back? Did you even *leave at all?*'

'Of course we left! We got to his place and then some bloke fell through the ceiling and we went investigating who he was and how it happened and…' She sighed. 'Nah, you wouldn't believe me.'

Seth leaned forward in his throne and said menacingly, 'Try me.'

Lilly huffed.

'Ron took us to hell with his magic coin and one of the Devils sent us here so we could ask the lunatic about the trail of dead bodies in the desert.' She glowered at his expression. 'Can I hold the baby?'

'No, don't *touch* the baby!' he snapped, recoiling with the child.

'Seth,' Lilly began.

'You don't want to be a normal person like everyone else, do you?' he snapped, sitting back in the throne. 'You just want to stay here for the rest of your life, acting the maggot to *annoy me.*'

'No, I didn't come back to—'

Seth spoke over her. 'I have better things to do now than babysit you—'

'I'm not lying!' she roared.

Seth wasn't listening. '… you've only come back here to—'

'Listen—'

'PISS ME OFF!!' he yelled over her, making her recoil.

Ginny started to wail.

'No, not you, pigeon,' Seth murmured, pecking her hand and rubbing her arm until she quietened.

Lilly was silent. If Seth didn't know better, he'd have thought she was about to cry. Although she had been doing a lot of that lately.

Seth sighed heavily and scowled at the offended and gossip-mongering expressions of Stan and Jimmy respectively.

212

'Can I have a minute alone with my sister, please?'

Stan waited for Lilly to nod before Jimmy escorted him to the next room.

Seth watched Lilly carefully. She looked miserable and angry and hurt – all emotions she caused in others rather than expressed herself.

He exhaled and stood up. 'Take this, my arm's gone dead.'

Lilly held her arms out as he deposited the infant into them with care.

Ginny stared at her with eyes like saucers, her feet peddling slowly.

'What are you looking at?' Lilly asked softly.

A delicate crease appeared on her brow, her tiny nose wrinkling.

'She says you smell funny,' Seth said with a smile.

Lilly didn't smile back. She commenced a staring competition with Ginny instead, pretending Seth wasn't there.

Seth turned his eyes to the ceiling.

'What are you thinking?' he asked gently.

She frowned, trying to figure it out herself. 'I don't want to marry him.'

'Lilly, I know, but—'

'I want to marry his son instead.'

Seth blinked. 'The cry baby?'

Lilly glowered at him.

Seth shook his head in disbelief. 'Why? His head. It's shaped like a—'

'I like him!' she protested.

'He doesn't own anything, though,' said Seth. 'He's illegitimate.'

'So?'

'So, marrying his father means we inherit an enterprise,' he pointed out, 'whereas marrying a potato head is just growing more potato heads.'

'He doesn't have a—' Lilly began.

Seth raised an eyebrow.

Lilly exhaled. 'Alright, maybe he does,' she relented, 'but you're no oil painting, and Cienne erected a shrine for you at a time when you were literally erecting nothing at all for her—'

'Alright, say it a bit louder, the ceiling didn't quite carry it to the farthest edges of the castle,' Seth said, making a face.

'Sorry. But, you know… I want something like that.'

'Really?' Seth's nose wrinkled. 'Because Cienne was quite irate about the—'

'No, I don't mean that. I want…' She wagged her head from side to side. 'I want that kind of devotion. Not "I'll give you some money for her". I don't want to be like Mum and Dad.'

'No, he paid naff all for her,' he agreed.

Lilly scowled. 'Seriously. And I don't like being sent off like a present to someone and not a person getting married. None of you were even going to come to this wedding! You were just going to leave me, your little sister, get married to an old man while you sat here with my dowry and this!'

She lifted Ginny upwards slightly.

213

He looked at her incredulously.

She suddenly felt a pang of regret. 'Alright, that was unfair. But... you didn't need to spring this on me so quickly. I'm your sister, not a toy you can flog to the highest bidder.'

He watched her silently.

'I'm sorry,' he said, to her surprise. He splayed his arms helplessly. 'That's how I was married. It's just normal.'

'But it shouldn't be!' Lilly burst out. 'We can change it now.'

'We can't,' he said. He dropped his gaze. 'We need the money.'

Her face dropped.

'I see,' she said flatly.

They stood in silence, admiring the baby.

'I was going to send Mum, you know,' he said.

'Mum,' she scoffed.

'Until I learned what she'd been up to with your husband forty years ago...'

He trailed off with a grimace.

'What?'

'You don't want to know,' he said adamantly.

She held his gaze intently.

He stuck his hands in his pockets. 'Don't look at me like that.'

'Like what?'

'Like you're about to get your way.' He rolled one side of his jaw. 'He doesn't want you to marry his son, he mightn't pay as much for you to...'

The tears began.

'Oh no, don't do that...' he moaned, throwing his head back to stare at the ceiling.

'Dad didn't want this,' she said.

Seth rolled his eyes.

'Don't start!' she snapped, a tear falling onto Ginny's eyebrow, making her blink. 'I know you and him didn't see eye to eye, but you didn't need to step over his dead body like that! He didn't want me to marry that fossil, you should have respected that!'

'It doesn't matter what he wanted, does it? If he'd picked out the perfect man for you, you still wouldn't like it! You just don't want to be told what to do, ever!'

Lilly wept silently, her face distorted.

Seth closed his eyes tiredly. He licked his sleeve to scrub her forehead with.

'Listen.'

He planted a kiss on her newly cleaned forehead.

'It's not my decision to treat you like cattle. He'll have my arse if I don't make you do this, you know, that... Duke of Osney, whoever he is...'

'Uncle Richard, he's Dad's younger brother,' she croaked.

Seth blinked. 'Is he? Didn't know that. The old man used to just call him Osney.'

Lilly snorted in remembrance.

'Anyway. What if you went back—'

'Seth, nooo,' she wept.

'Listen,' he prompted. 'What if I came with you?'

She glanced at him. 'You mean to walk me down the aisle?'

'Or chain you to the priest and let you get on with it, but alright, if you want,' he replied with a small smile. 'And we have to bring Mum.'

Lilly grimaced. 'She'll make me wear a dress.'

'It's your wedding, it's going to look off if you show up in bloodied leather,' Seth grinned. 'Anyway, it might put him off you. He likes you better in trousers.'

Lilly arched an eyebrow in distaste.

He eyed her silently and nodded to the stairs.

'Come with me. We'll see if the old ball and chain will let me out.'

Lilly gazed down at Ginny. 'She's beautiful, by the way.'

Seth smiled down at her. 'She came out of my willy.'

Lilly retched ever so slightly.

She levered Ginny into her hands and held her out. 'You can have her back now, thanks.'

Seth scooped the baby up, grinning from ear to ear. 'Wait until you see her brother.'

'Oh yeah, I heard she milked you dry,' Lilly said, earning a loud laugh.

The front doors opened and an attractive young man entered, bowed and said something in tongues.

Seth frowned at him. 'Pardon?'

A small boy with a pointed nose peered out from behind the visitor.

'Presenting his royal highness, the half-prince of Portabella.'

'Oh, the mother country,' Seth said in realisation. 'Here you go, then.'

He strolled over and casually plonked Ginny into his arms.

The half-prince looked alarmed. Lilly assumed he was supposed to be handsome with his curly acorn-coloured hair and feminine facial features. Fat lot of use if he was afraid of children, even immobile ones.

He mumbled something in a shrill voice.

'He says, "What is this?",' the translator added helpfully.

'It's your half-niece,' Seth said, and waited for their exchange.

'"I don't want it!", he says,' the boy translated.

'Neither did I at first,' Seth replied flippantly. 'Funny thing about children, they grow on you. Follow me, she's upstairs.'

Seth and Lilly led the way to the spiral staircase in the corner.

The half-prince followed, holding Ginny at an arm's length in front of him.

'*Half*-prince? I don't get it,' said Lilly with a frown.

215

'Children born to a second consummated wife over there don't count,' Seth said as they ascended together. 'Cienne is her mother's only child, so she's the country's sole heir. Well, I say her, but I mean me,' he said brightly. 'Or Russell now, because he's her first boy. This bloke's just their backup plan in case we all get killed.'

He suddenly halted and turned to scoop Ginny from his half-brother-in-law's hands.

'Do *not* get any ideas.'

The man stared at him uncomprehendingly.

They reached the door to Seth's quarters. Seth handed Ginny back to Lilly to open the door.

'You wait here, private family function,' he said to the half-prince, pushing Lilly inside and slamming the door in the man's face.

'Lilly!' Cienne said in surprise.

She sat at the writing desk in the drawing room and cradled a sleeping baby in her arms. Lilly decided the look suited her.

'I wasn't expecting you back for a few weeks yet.'

'Neither was I,' she admitted.

'Is everything alright?' she asked in concern.

The woman could smell tears a mile off, Lilly thought cynically.

Seth entered his bedroom, closely followed by their mother.

'Yeah, I'm just... bottling it a bit,' Lilly trailed off.

Cienne nodded understandingly. 'I know how you feel. Look at the mess of a human being I ended up with.'

Lilly laughed, albeit falsely. The joke would have been funny if Cienne didn't worship him to death.

'Oh Mum no, it's hideous!' Seth exclaimed from the next room.

'What's going on in there?' Cienne said.

'He's packing, I assume,' said Lilly. 'He's going to come with me to the wedding, with Mum. Assuming he doesn't kill her with her own embroidery, that is.'

'But you'll look so handsome in it!' Eleanor protested from next door.

'Mother, I love you dearly,' he drawled, 'but the hideousness of your embroidery is parallel to that of a maggot-filled corpse left out in the sun. I'm picking out my own clothes, thank you very much.'

Seth carried some plain looking clothes to the desk.

Eleanor stood dejectedly at the door with what was undisputedly the worst example of intricate embroidery to exist in Adem. Lilly eyeballed it and decided Seth's comment was unjust to the corpse.

Cienne watched Seth root around for some belongings. 'You're leaving now?'

He glanced at her. 'Will you be alright? I can stay if you like—'

'No, you should go, it's Lilly,' she said hurriedly. 'I just hoped everyone would be around for a bit first.'

216

Seth stroked her hair. 'It won't take long. I'll bring her back afterwards before he can deface her.' He grimaced.

'Anyway, your brother's only outside the door,' Lilly added.

Cienne made a face. 'Alain? I barely know the boy, except to gather that he fancies Seth almost as much as I do.'

Lilly snorted derisively. She doubted if all Fleurelles had as bad taste as Cienne.

'And take Jimmy with you, alright?' she added. 'He could do with some time away. Every time he looks at Ginny he breaks out in a cold sweat.'

Seth half-smiled and let a handful of Cienne's hair slide from his grasp.

He strolled to the bookcase, which had formerly been a weaponry display area in King Theo's reign.

'I've put your boyfriend in your rooms, Lilly,' he said, turning to give her a stern glance.

'I'll kick him out directly, sir,' Lilly said obediently.

'Very well, then,' he said, satisfied. 'Take some of these, he wanted to borrow them, and I can't make out their funny spelling anyway. Ooh, this might interest you.'

He thrust *Ye Olde Book of Dragons* in her direction.

'Might teach you how to stop killing them by accident. Call it an early wedding present.'

Lilly stuck her tongue out at him. 'It's big and heavy, I imagine I can make some use of it.'

Seth winked.

'You'll be away for quite a while, then,' Cienne said.

'We'll bring him back in one piece,' Lilly said in amusement, placing a dozing Ginny into her basket to accept her book from Seth.

Cienne smiled thinly and eyed her husband. 'Any chance of a kiss goodbye, then?'

He arched an eyebrow. 'Promise you won't bite me this time?'

'I'll make no promises on that account.'

Lilly watched her brother lean across the desk to lock lips with his wife for five minutes or so. It depressed her to think that in a few weeks, her own much older husband would be doing the same to her.

~

Ron eyed the jar uneasily.

His own liver bobbed up and down in the yellowing vinegar, rotating slightly. Unlike the healthy brown specimen Qattren had made certain to show to him before inserting into his body, his own was covered in bulbous stains, mustard-coloured to match his jaundiced skin.

He put a hand on his abdomen and stared at the vaulted ceiling.

Erik snored from the desk at the far wall. He had exhausted himself in his hysterics regarding the sudden recovery of what he considered to be a dead man walking: Qattren thankfully came to the rescue with some kind of earth magic and gave Ron a hasty liver transplant just as Erik was measuring him for his casket. That just left Ron lying in bed awake, and alone.

His eyes flicked to the cabinet under Erik's desk.

Spirits would no doubt be in attendance.

Oh dear.

The old itch began to niggle, tingling from the base of his spine down to the tips of his fingers.

Ron twitched and slapped his arms to dismiss it. No. *No.* No.

No.

He hesitated.

And threw himself at the cabinet.

Nausea overtook him momentarily, making him pause. A dull ache spread through his insides. Qattren's procedure left no scars or openings to stitch, but the flesh remained tender to movement. He knelt at Erik's feet, breathing deeply to the sound of the medic's soft snoring. His knees became cold and stiff on the icy flagstones, and his palms resting on either side of him soon followed suit.

A well of despair opened up in him.

What was the point?

He visualised what would happen next: the spirits sliding hot into his stomach, his freshly healed body aching with the undulations of his frantic gulping, the itch momentarily sated. But what then? Once the distraction of the sensation was over, there were only two further options: drink some more, or deal with the intrusive thoughts.

He sat back on his haunches, stomach twisting. His gaze turned to the yellow blob in the jar. No.

Not worth it, he decided.

He crawled back into his bed, his belly throbbing. Squirming into the sheets, he buried his head into the pillow. The itch morphed into the regular depression the lack of satiation caused in him: the pain of being unwanted, unneeded, unloved. Worse, hated: his brother had hated him, his mother hated him, his uncle had looked down on him as if he was a piece of dogshit smeared into the ground. At least his father had loved him. But when he wasn't abroad or busy with political matters, he was lost in an alcoholic stupor of his own. Probably for the same reasons. And now he was dead.

Ron swallowed down a lump in his throat.

She was all that was left now. The Hornes were almost gone – he was the last one. For all he was worth.

Self-loathing simmered in him.

Just as the itch drove his thoughts to the cabinet again, the turret door clicked open.

Lilly sidled in, peered at Ron and made a beeline to the cabinet, kneeling to fasten it shut with a belt and a padlock.

Ron glowered at her over the folds of his blanket before turning his head away in silence.

Dusting her knees off, Lilly rose. Casting a glance at his thin, threadbare blanket, she rifled in a nearby wooden chest for a thicker one and, delicately, laid it over Ron's stationary form.

Ron's sulky expression softened.

Silently, Lilly crept back out, pulling the door gently behind her.

She cared about him, he realised blankly. So did Stan, actually. Even Qattren, in her own twisted, slightly traumatising way. They were his friends. Most of them.

Something rolled against his nose. He lifted his face to see a wrapped sweet sitting in a groove in the fabric.

The self-loathing faded out, as did the ever present itch. He held the sweet under his chin. He had friends now. The thought warmed him, much like the alcohol did, only better.

Ron held it under his chin adjacent to the sweet and drifted into peaceful sleep.

~

The Phantom Egg Flinger stood inside the throne room entrance, wearing a faint smile.

Dragging a massive rucksack behind him, Jimmy wheezed his way down the stairs and froze, turning to check the sundial outside the staircase window.

'You're precisely four hours early,' he observed. 'And also about a week and a half late. Seth hasn't been tortured in ages.'

'I figure the new members of the family can pick up the slack on that front,' he said heartily in a nasally voice. 'I'm packing it in now. I've come to hand myself in.'

Jimmy blinked. 'You're confessing?'

'Adhering to my punishment.'

'Throwing in the towel?'

'Throwing myself at the king's mercy. I'm told he has much in abundance.'

Jimmy snorted.

'Who told you that, then?' he said cynically, nodding towards his own burden.

Seth barged past Jimmy on his way down the stairs, kicking his baggage down the last couple of steps on the way as his sister and her entourage followed in his wake.

'… if we head off now in the coach, they'll just be ready for us and we can head off immediately and be back in time for the twins' christening. Hello,' Seth greeted the Phantom Egg Flinger casually as he walked past.

'Howdy,' he said cheerfully.

Seth froze and spun on one heel.

'*You*,' he hissed at the hat in particular. 'What do you want?'

'He's come to throw himself at your mercy, sir,' Jimmy said.

Marbrand poked his head in the door.

'Sir, the coach is here. We'll have to head off now or the damn captain will leave without us.'

'Hang on a minute,' Seth said, holding up a finger.

'Seth, come on, we've been held up as it is,' Lilly said, dragging him by one arm.

'But… but he's handed himself in!' he protested shrilly, pointing with the hand Lilly didn't currently have a grip on. 'I want to punish him! I want—I want to see him get egged!'

'It'll hold, now come on!'

'I want him egged! I WANT COMEUPPANCE!!'

He shrieked as Lilly and Marbrand dragged him out of the door by an elbow each, his heels scoring the ground.

Jimmy turned to the Phantom Egg Flinger.

'Would you be so kind as to return in a few weeks, when the king returns?'

'I'll see if I'm free,' he replied cordially.

~

In the depths of the Desertlands, Copers yawned.

The city scanned its confines sleepily. There was only one resident left.

It scanned the waters surrounding the country lazily from its highest point, calculating the length of time it would take the *Royal Cantankerer* to arrive at Portmyr. Just enough time, Copers reckoned.

It slithered east and shuddered to a halt two miles from the Ambassador's mansion. That should make things easier.

Now there was only the hard part left.

Copers began to make its Monument.

PART FOUR: THE WEDDING

I

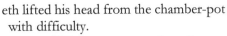

eth lifted his head from the chamber-pot with difficulty.

'This was not what I was expecting,' he strained in a gravelly voice.

'What were you expecting for your first visit to the open sea in all thirty four years of your life?' Lilly asked in amusement.

He groaned from deep within his stomach and dropped his head onto the rim of the pot with a dull *dong*.

'Don't worry, sir,' Jimmy said reassuringly from a safe distance behind him. 'I've spoken to the captain, he says the rest of the journey shouldn't take much more than three weeks.'

Lilly blinked and turned to face him. 'Three weeks? Are you sure?'

'That's what he said,' Jimmy said with a shrug. 'I didn't think it was much either, but he seemed adamant.'

Lilly narrowed her eyes. 'Huh.'

Jimmy peered out of the window. 'We don't seem to be moving much, do we?'

'Is that a bad thing?' Seth gritted through clenched teeth.

'I'm gonna double check,' Lilly said, rising from her kneeling position beside the chamber-pot. 'Will you be alright?'

Seth threw up.

'He'll be fine,' Jimmy assured her, patting the top of Seth's head.

Lilly boarded the top deck, squinting at the bright afternoon sunlight, a sharp contrast to Seth's gloomy quarters. The captain, a curly-red-haired creature who was the apparent namesake of the ship, stared contentedly into the depths of the sea.

She strolled over and tapped a broad shoulder.

'So,' she said casually. 'Three weeks, eh?'

'Aye, weather permitting,' he said cheerfully.

'Hmm. How stupid do you think I am?'

The captain gave her a bemused glance.

'We've only been on this ship for two weeks,' she said. 'It takes *fifteen* weeks to get from Maketon to Portmyr without stopping. How the hell to you manage, on a normal ship, with shit all wind, to get us there from Breaker's Hold in a third of that time?'

He gulped. 'The weather's fabulous for sailing, you know.'

'After two weeks, we should still be in the middle of winter in Adem's fishing territory,' she pointed out. 'This is nicked, isn't it?'

'It isn't nicked! What do you take me for, a pirate?'

Lilly narrowed her eyes, but said nothing.

'The Queen of the Forest came to me one day. She upgraded it for me, so Prince Ronald would get there and back safely.'

'It's a cross-realmer, it has to be built as a cross-realmer, not "upgraded" out of mundane matter,' Lilly said, drawing from Sam Sot's frequent lectures. 'By upgrade, you mean she nicked it for you, don't you?'

'Not nicked! Confiscated!' he corrected. 'And re-issued to me, a respected, cooperating member of society. It was nicked by pirates first, anyway. She just salvaged it for me and plonked a sorcerer on board.'

'Pirates?'

She glanced around incredulously with new eyes.

'I knew it looked familiar! The bitch stole my ship!'

'*Your* ship?' He looked frightened. 'Shit.'

'No, ship. And a bloody nice one, too.'

With a nice crew, she thought sadly, wherever they are.

She worried about Si in particular. She had a bit of a soft spot for him, despite the knife-throwing incident. She hoped that was all there was to that. It was bad enough fancying her future step-son without a knife-throwing Seth Crey lookalike to go with him.

She rubbed her wounded hand again in remembrance.

'So you've been travelling through Magicland while we were preoccupied with King Seasickness?'

'Aye,' he said. 'Only a few miles at a time, so you wouldn't be that suspicious. We didn't think you would notice.'

'Seth despises sorcery, you know.'

'I know, the queen told me. Something to do with a bad experience last year,' he said. 'You won't tell him, will you?'

Lilly regarded him, lifting an eyebrow.

'I won't tell him,' she said after a moment.

He breathed a sigh of relief.

'On condition that you land us in Portmyr by tomorrow morning.'

'What?' he asked, terrified. 'And how am I supposed to explain that to his highness?'

'You'll think of something,' she said with a smile, returning to the cabin.

'Wait, are you going to dob me in to your husband instead?'

'Might not have to if I get my ship back,' she said slyly.

'Tough, it's my ship now,' he said in a stroppy tone, sticking his chest out. 'The *Royal Cantankerer* was named for its captain, not a skinny pirate princess.'

'Firstly,' Lilly said, pivoting, 'that has to be the worst name for a ship ever, not to mention inaccurate considering you aren't even royalty.'

'I have roots,' he objected.

'And secondly,' she continued, ignoring him, 'a pirate does not lose her ship unless the crew votes otherwise or the pirate dies. And I don't think even Queen Qattren could fell that lot, inept as they may be, meaning you've just about pissed off a lot of pirates, skinny princess ones or otherwise.' Her eyes narrowed. 'And it's the skinny ones you need to worry about.'

'I've got Queen Qattren on side,' he said.

'And I've got Queen Qattren's *husband.*'

He sighed reluctantly.

'Fine,' he relented. 'But I want a dragon for my trouble.'

'Better ask Seth for that, they belong to him now. And bring him a bucket while you're at it,' she added as an afterthought. 'A big one.'

~

Night fell on the vacant horizon as Orl descended to the lower decks to bed. His path was blocked by Jimmy, who gave an apologetic wave.

'That expression doesn't bode well.'

'The king isn't very well and he's chucked up all over his bed,' Jimmy explained briefly. 'Would you mind lending him your room for the night? I'll have his cleaned up for you as soon as I can.'

Orl heaved a sigh. 'Is this going to be a regular occurrence when my father marries Lilly?'

'Depends if the queen gets pregnant again and he has to avoid her,' he said bluntly. 'I hope you've left the chamber-pot empty, the local sea life has suffered enough ordeals for one night.'

'It's serviceable,' Orl said, deflating. So much for an early night.

He entered briefly to swipe some books from his cabin before retreating to Ron's cabin to wait for his new room to be cleaned.

Lilly rolled over again to the sound of retching. She sat up in frustration, throwing the sheet from herself.

The crew had been instructed to furnish four compartments with small featherbeds and dedicate the entire captain's cabin to Seth. Strangely enough, Lilly preferred the hammock and couldn't sleep a wink.

She glanced out of the porthole to see a stream of something indescribable fall past into the sea.

Course, Seth could be to blame for that, Lilly thought.

She grimaced and bolted upright.

The full moon shone enough light into the bowels of the ship for Lilly's eyes to adjust. Orl's cabin door was not far ahead of her, hanging ajar in an inviting manner.

She paused. Seth would kill her if he caught her doing that. And as for Orl's father…

But how would they know? she asked herself. They know my hobbies, they're hardly expecting me to still be a virgin? If they were, they were going to be very disappointed.

Besides, Seth was too busy with his head overboard making the ocean a little fuller to catch Lilly doing anything untoward.

And it had been an awfully long time since she'd last…

She jogged to the door.

Alas, the cabin was empty.

Lilly deflated and wondered where a bibliophile went in the middle of the night. His borrowed books from Seth were missing, she noticed. It was no wonder he had a squint, trying to read in the moonlight. Or perhaps Jimmy had nabbed him and left him to babysit Seth for a while. That sounded plausible.

She climbed into the covers to wait. She wasn't about to leave a walk go to waste. She rifled under the pillow in annoyance and pulled out a book without a title, the corner of which had been making a home in the back of Lilly's head. That was an annoying habit.

She tugged the blanket over herself, burying her head in the pillow. The bed smelled of sweat and ink and biscuit crumbs. It smelled of Orl. She wondered idly when the crew were going to enter Qattren's second realm and jump to Portmyr.

Her question was shortly answered by a looseness in the air and a purple tinge.

Outside, Seth trudged through the bowels of the ship to his new cabin, repeatedly rubbing his eyes. He really was ill. He was seeing everything in shades of purple.

He made it to the doorframe and leaned on it, struggling to catch his breath. Thankfully the nausea had subsided, at least. Perhaps he was getting used to the water after all. He didn't even feel like they were moving anymore.

He pushed the door open a bit and frowned into the contents, squinting.

Was that Lilly trying to look attractive in his bed?

Seth made a face. He didn't recognise this method of marriage-evasion, but he was putting a stop to it.

Seth's gaze flickered from his sister to the deck to Lilly again and an evil thought entered his head.

He let out a long moan.

Lilly's eyes bolted open.

'That's it, nearly there,' Seth moaned, stepping forward heavily. 'Let me just lie on this bed and remove my clothes—'

'NO!'

Lilly struggled out of the sheets and fell off the bed.

Seth burst out laughing.

Lilly bolted upright, glaring at him from the floor.

226

'Scared you, didn't I?' Seth said with a giggle. 'What are you doing in my bed, anyway? I'm spoken for, you know.'

'Ew, don't be horrible,' Lilly grimaced, climbing back onto the bed. 'I thought your cabin was the other way?'

'It was, me and your lover swapped,' he said, sitting next to her with a grin. 'So what's all this?'

She didn't meet his gaze. 'Thought he'd be in here.'

Seth dropped himself against the pillow, his arms over his head. 'You like him this much?'

She nodded sullenly, fiddling with a fold in the blanket.

'His old man might die soon,' he said with a shrug. 'He's pretty old.'

'He doesn't seem as old as he is,' she said. 'He'll outlive us all out of spite.'

'We said that about our old man, remember?'

She glared at him.

He regretted the retort immediately after it had left his mouth.

'You'll be alright,' he told her, patting her forearm. 'You could do worse, even the old man had to admit that.'

She nodded sagely.

He held out an arm.

Lilly dropped onto his shoulder.

'You could always come home,' he said. 'In fact, you're more than welcome, because you're young enough to be passed off as a widow and remarried a few more times.'

He rubbed his hands together.

Lilly giggled. 'Until a dozen armies storm the Serpent's Knot, wondering where their butch Crey wife has gone.'

'With a letter saying she ran away with the chambermaid.'

'Apple don't fall far from the tree, eh?'

'Oi, I did not,' he shoved Lilly's elbow away from his stomach, 'I did not run away with, stop elbowing me—'

'Another red-head, I heard,' Lilly began.

'Hey! I didn't do anything with the chambermaid, the thing with the chambermaid, shut up,' he cut across himself as Lilly sniggered, 'the thing with Anna, I was *pretending* to have relations with her to make the real mistress jealous. And they weren't red-haired, they were auburn.'

'That's just a red-head trying to be a brunette,' she said, making Seth laugh.

'You're just jealous because they had bigger tits than you.'

'Seth, women are not defined by the size of their breasts,' she said patiently. 'And mine are quite ample, I'll thank you.'

'Nobody loves you for them.'

'Naw, they're too busy admiring yours.'

'Yes, I was the proud owner of three pairs once upon a time, complete with accessories,' he said with a smug smirk. 'Never mind, you're lovable on the inside.'

'Luckily, so are you,' she said, patting his face.

'Are you saying I'm not attractive?'

'Well, old ladies like you.'

Seth laughed twice loudly. 'I can't get rid of you, I'll need someone to bat off the old ladies.'

'I already do, they get it into their dear little heads that we're already a couple.'

She suddenly caught a whiff of Seth's armpit.

'Dear God, you stink!'

Seth frowned into the ceiling of the cabin. '"Dear God, you stink.".'

'You do, you reek!' she said, covering her nose and mouth.

'Now you'll have to die.' He pressed her face against his armpit.

'AH! Stop it! This isn't regal at all!' she yelled in a muffled voice.

'Shush!' he ordered between laughs. 'Retract your argument!'

'Get off my tit, you sick freak!'

'Sorry?'

They burst into deafening guffaws.

Jimmy watched on, slightly fearful.

'Is this what comes after sibling rivalry?'

'We've digressed into a romantic relationship,' Seth said almost seriously.

He rolled on top of Lilly, who exclaimed in disgust.

'She looks so much like me that I can hardly... oh my God,' he shuddered, the pretence failing.

'I'm not entirely sure where the joke ends and the true act begins,' Jimmy said in discomfort.

'Not today, my friend,' Seth grimaced, sliding to the floor. 'I need a piss. Has he taken the pot with him?' he demanded, rifling under the bed. 'What a swine.'

'Over here, by the door,' Jimmy said helpfully.

Seth rose to his feet.

He watched Seth turn his back before leaning towards Lilly to mouth, 'Orl's in your cabin.'

Jimmy winked.

Lilly lifted both eyebrows in intrigue.

'Oh, someone's left me a note,' Seth said from the chamber-pot.

'Did you put that there?' Lilly asked the butler. '"Please don't crap the bed today.".'

Jimmy arched an eyebrow. 'That's never stopped him.'

Lilly giggled at the thought.

Seth tilted his head back, squinting at the small roll of parchment.

'"Just for stealing my room",' he read aloud, '"I'm shagging your sister".'
He frowned at Lilly.

'He's probably joking,' she said evenly. She licked her lips. 'I'm off to bed.'

'Stay where you are!' he barked, pointing at the bed.

'Sir, I believe you're spoken for,' Jimmy scolded.

Seth ignored him. 'You may not be a virgin, my dear, but I am not suffering at the hands of another pregnant woman for at least three years, and certainly not on my holiday. Now lie down on *one half* of the bed and go to sleep.'

Jimmy exited to the sound of the afterthought, 'And no touching yourself, either!'

~

Dawn cracked through the window of Orl's stolen room and seagulls told Lilly that they were making port. She turned her head towards her brother, who had one arm around his face and the other snaking up the wall behind his head in an eternal stretch. Carefully, she slid from the bed in silence and jogged onto the top deck.

Orl stood outside the captain's cabin, leaning on the rail to squint into the sun.

'Oi!' Lilly called, jogging to catch up. 'Sorry about my brother stealing your room. It's just when he throws up, he really...'

'I noticed,' he said, with a smile. 'I could see it outside the window. I also noticed you didn't go to your room – in passing,' he added. 'Where did you end up sleeping?'

'With Seth.' She noted an expression of horror threatening to surface. 'He sort of confined me there after someone left him a letter threatening to have relations with me.'

Orl winced. 'That was a joke. I wouldn't really try to, you know...'

Lilly lifted an eyebrow. 'Shame.'

He blushed and licked his lips.

There was a moment of silence broken only by the crying of seagulls.

'I've... got a book in my cabin,' Lilly said slowly. 'Would you like to see it?'

Orl inhaled deeply. 'Yes.'

They jogged below decks.

~

Seth stretched his back into an arch.

Jimmy carefully laid a set of clothes on the bed next to him, right in the space Lilly had previously filled.

'Where's Lilly?' Seth wondered.

229

Jimmy shrugged, picking up Seth's chamber pot. 'No idea.'

He peered at the congealed vomit within, his nose wrinkling, and threw the entire thing out of the porthole.

Seth frowned at this.

'Spoke to the captain a moment ago, by the way. We've arrived.'

Seth blinked. 'In Portmyr? How?'

'Apparently a dense hoard of seagulls collided with us overnight and carried us across the ocean, miraculously without disturbing anyone's sleep,' Jimmy said wryly. 'I think this is Queen Qattren's doing, sir.'

'You mean,' he said, in horror, 'she did that... exploding thing...'

'To the ship and its passengers,' he finished.

'... to me?'

'You appear to have travelled with us, sir, so I presume so.'

Seth grimaced down at himself and rubbed his torso, recalling the last time Qattren had pulled him into Sal'plae.

'I need to find Lilly,' he said hurriedly, shaking the memory off. 'I feel fragile.'

'You *are* fragile, sir,' Jimmy reminded him, shaking out a shirt.

~

'I'm quite nervous, actually. Reading it in a book doesn't quite prepare you for the prospect of the real thing.'

Lilly closed the door behind them.

'We could actually look at that book, if you're that nervous.'

He shook his head. 'Once you and my father consecrate the marriage, I'll barely stomach looking at you.'

'Nice.'

He paused for a moment, considering what he said. 'I'm sorry.'

Lilly watched him piteously. 'Do you want to do this?'

Orl nodded helplessly.

'Cool. Look, just... stand there and do as I say. Alright?'

Orl simply stood there helplessly.

Lilly grasped the sides of his neck in both hands, tilted her head slightly to the left and his to the right, and gently pressed their lips together.

The door opened.

'We're here! Lilly, do you know anything about Qattren doing something to the...'

Seth froze.

The two broke apart.

'Seth!' Lilly exclaimed with a manic grin.

He simply stood there, one hand on the open door and his mouth slightly ajar.

'Good morning, your highness,' Orl said weakly.

230

He gave him a little wave.

'That's my sister,' Seth said, deadpan.

He gulped. 'Uh-huh.'

'*My* sister,' he emphasised, licking his lips.

He flung his fist back and punched Orl in the jaw.

He sprawled over to the bed, holding the right side of his face.

'Oi!' Lilly snapped.

She punched Seth back, sending him flying on top of Orl.

'Try that again and I'll cut you!'

The two of them lay stock still, shocked.

'Ow,' Seth squeaked.

II

Marbrand rapped on the door thrice.

The Ambassador opened it.

'Ah, the accidental dragon slayer,' he said amiably.

'Presenting to you his royal majesty, Seth Crey, the king of Adem,' Marbrand replied.

He stepped aside to reveal a heavily bruised Seth Crey with a flourish.

'Who's named his first son after me,' Marbrand added happily. 'I'm the namesake of the next *king*. Of *Adem*.'

'You smell like a forest fire,' Karnak told him in interest.

Seth threw Marbrand a sharp glance.

He hastily hid a pipe and a half-empty packet of crushed plant in his trouser pocket. 'I do not.'

Karnak raised an eyebrow with a mild expression.

He turned his gaze to Seth and blinked, eyeing his blackened eyelid in interest.

'Taken a knock en-route, your majesty?'

'Something like that,' Seth muttered.

He pushed Marbrand out of the way to enter the Ambassador's mansion.

The great hall of the mansion opened out before them, the shining wooden floors and high windows giving the place a gentle coolness to contrast the crippling heaviness of the air outside. A massive carpeted staircase formed the focal point of the hall.

Seth faced his soon-to-be-brother-in-law in the centre of the hall, flanked on either side by a pungent Marbrand and, as ever, Jimmy. A long line of guards and retainers stood behind Seth, at Marbrand's insistence – even the guards who had hidden in the corner of the ship whilst Lilly had blackened Seth's eye.

'I hope you have enough rooms made up,' Seth continued, dragging his gaze from the high ceiling. 'My mother's come with us.'

'Ah, Eleanor?' He smiled fondly. 'Yes, I remember your mother.'

'So I gather,' Seth said with a shiver.

Karnak peered out of the door in anticipation. 'So, where are the lovely ladies?'

'A lovely few hundred miles away, I imagine,' Seth drawled. 'My mother took too long to get off the bloody boat, so we left without them. They'll be here in as long as it took Mother to finally get dressed.'

'In as long as it takes a woman to make herself beautiful,' he mused, enraptured with the thought of her. 'That needn't take long what with your mother's... assets.'

'Oh God,' Seth mouthed in disgust.

'Speaking of beautiful women, how is your lovely wife?'

'Unavailable,' Seth said sharply.

'A boy and a girl, I hear it told,' he continued as though he hadn't heard. 'All three are well, I trust?'

'Cienne's undercarriage hasn't been the same, but apart from that, yes,' he said coldly. 'Where's my room?'

'On the third floor, first door on the right of the stairs,' the Ambassador said. 'The same altitude as your quarters in Adem, you should feel right at home. My family butler will escort you.'

Jimmy eyed the butler as a striking pink ruffled shirt became apparent beneath the blond man's overcoat.

'Who dressed you this morning, then?' he asked in amusement.

~

In a coach travelling steeply uphill, Lilly eyed her mother before glancing down at her muddied-and-bloodied attire.

'Should I feel ashamed?' she said. 'That you've tarted yourself up for the wedding more than I have?'

Eleanor frowned at her, affronted. Her gold-embroidered silver dress shimmered.

'It is not *tarty*, Lilly-Anna. I think you'll find my make-up is very natural, thank you.'

'You've painted your face with masking plaster made of a cow's intestinal tract. I suppose it's natural in *that* sense.'

Eleanor scowled at her and readjusted her hair.

'And why have you bleached your hair? It looks like a banana peel tied in a knot. And besides, you were born ginger, weren't you?'

'It's to identify me as a Crey,' Eleanor snapped, 'and will you stop criticising me? I'm only making myself look acceptable for my little girl's wedding, whether she likes being a little girl or not. And I was not *ginger* in my youth,' she said haughtily. 'I was golden brown, just like you.'

'Mine isn't golden anything, it's just mouse shit colour.'

She observed her as a whole, banana knot to gold-trimmed shoes.

'You've never dyed your hair before! Why the—'

'Well, I should have! I looked terrible! I was as grey as a mule, and no one thought to tell me!'

'We have a mirror in each bedroom, Mother,' Lilly said. 'We're not in the dark ages.'

'We've arrived, your highnesses,' Elliot said from outside.

Lilly and her mother piled out of the coach, under the shadow of a massive white building. The smaller edition inside the grounds of the sanctuary was nicer, Lilly thought. She wondered if she could talk him into residing here instead. Without him.

The Ambassador met them at the front door, accompanied by Seth, as Lilly regrouped with Stan, Ron and Orl to lead the way. Queen Eleanor followed closely behind.

'Greetings once again, Princess Lilly-Anna,' the Ambassador said with a bow. 'And greetings, Queen Mother.'

He sidled past Lilly to take her mother's hand and kiss it.

'You have not aged an hour since we last met, my lady.'

Eleanor twittered happily. 'Thank you, my lord.'

Seth made a disgusted noise and rolled his eyes, nodding at Lilly to follow him inside.

'If I get like that with women at that age, I want you to kill me horribly.'

'You're already like that with women, they just don't flirt back,' Lilly said with a grin, earning a thump on the arm.

'You'll be pleased to know I've made all the arrangements for the wedding ahead of time,' the Ambassador informed them. 'Except for the wedding gown, of course.'

'Don't worry, I've brought one,' Eleanor said brightly.

Seth smirked.

'You haven't embroidered it, have you?' Lilly said darkly.

The Ambassador clapped his hands before Eleanor could retort.

'So… the guests are all present, the arrangements are ready to go. When shall we have the wedding?'

'Tomorrow,' Seth said. 'Before she legs it again.'

Lilly shot him her most hideous scowl.

'So it shall be,' the Ambassador said brightly, rubbing his hands together.

He held an elbow out to Eleanor, who took it, smitten.

Lilly stepped in front of Seth as he made to follow the two upstairs, presumably to provide adult supervision.

'I need a word,' she said sharply.

Seth frowned slightly. 'About?'

She pointed at their mother and her new pet.

He followed her gaze and his eyes widened in alarm.

'Oh, Lilly,' he soothed, taking one of her shoulders in each hand. 'Don't worry, he's old-fashioned. They did things one woman at a time back then.'

Stan, Ron and Orl were standing a step behind them during this exchange.

Stan whined a quiet 'ew'.

She looked up at him in childlike terror.

'I hadn't thought of that,' she whimpered, her mouth ajar in abject horror.

'Not to interfere in royal matters,' Stan piped up, 'but if that ain't grounds to break it off, I dunno what is.'

Lilly shrugged out of Seth's grasp.

'Naw, Stan, it's different when your brother's sanctuary of dragons is at stake,' she snarled.

She shoved her way past Seth to ascend the stairs.

Seth watched her stomp upstairs and touched his bruised nose gingerly.

'I'll add a clause!' he called up as she vanished to the left. 'I'll barricade the woman if I have to!'

Angry muttering could be heard from the upper distance.

Stan watched Seth stare in her wake.

'He wouldn't suggest that, would he?' Stan asked, to be sure.

'No,' Seth said with conviction. 'He knows her by now. She'd set him on fire and cook his penis off the flames.' He gazed up at the landing above them. 'I don't think it's that she's angry about.'

'Maybe not, but I'm sure I heard her mutter the word "castrate" earlier,' Ron said.

'Woman problems,' Stan said knowingly.

'No, her woman problems send her into a "castrate first, discuss it later" theology,' Seth said. 'She's in love. That was *not...*'

He held an index finger up in Orl's face.

'... an invitation,' he growled at him.

~

They gathered on a selection of soft chairs in a library in the Ambassador's quarters, awkwardly. Seth sat on the arm of Lilly's chair as her fiancé claimed ownership of the settee, flanked by his son and his biggest fan, Eleanor Crey.

Stan and Jimmy stood at the door in the standard Staff position, and Ron was moving the wheeled ladder to each bookcase and climbing up and down it, just for fun.

'So,' the Ambassador said amiably. 'How was the journey?'

Nobody answered.

Orl had his face inserted into a massive tome with cracked leather.

Seth leaned on the back of the chair behind Lilly and *glared* at Orl over the rug, as if he was avidly ogling Lilly as opposed to reading quietly.

Eleanor fiddled shyly with her dress.

'It was fine,' Lilly said dully.

A brief pause ensued.

'The weather was lovely,' Eleanor muttered timidly.

'Rather stifling under all that makeup, I imagine?' Seth said, each word laced with venom.

She shot him a sharp glance.

'I quite agree,' the Ambassador intercepted. 'She doesn't need it at all.'

Eleanor gave him a much softer glance. 'Oh.'

Seth glowered at him and twirled a section of Lilly's ponytail around one finger.

Silence.

'I got an interesting call the other week from a group of strangers,' the Ambassador said in interest. 'They claimed to be friends of Lilly-Anna. Apparently, they wanted to come to the wedding!'

'Shit,' Lilly whispered.

Seth frowned down at her, perplexed.

'Who were they? Were they friends of the family?' Eleanor asked.

'They'd sailed with her, or so they said,' he replied, his gaze locked to Lilly. 'I dismissed them, of course.'

'Why?' Lilly demanded.

'They could have been anyone,' he answered, his eyes twinkling. 'Burglars, murderers, usurpers... even pirates.'

Seth frowned at him.

'Hundreds of miles from the ocean?' he asked sceptically.

'It's happened before. At least one of them have ended up in these very walls at some point.'

Lilly swallowed carefully.

Seth lifted his eyebrows, unconcerned.

Ron's foot slipped on the twelfth rung and he righted himself on the ladder with a little squeal.

'So why are you called the Ambassador if you own the country?' Seth asked.

The Ambassador smiled, finally feeling he was making progress.

'The short of it is that I arrived as the Truphorian Ambassador to find the president of the country running for his life from—'

Seth yawned. Audibly.

'Seth,' Eleanor said tiredly. 'How old are you?'

He started counting on his fingers.

'Thirty-one, two, three... four!' he exclaimed with a toothy grin. 'Almost as old as the Ambassador was when I was born!'

'A couple of years younger than that, actually,' he said quietly.

Jimmy frowned and mouthed his own calculations to himself.

Seth bared his teeth. 'How old *are* you exactly?!'

'We're *all* old enough to dispense of the childish behaviour you're displaying,' Eleanor scolded. 'You should take a leaf out of his book in that regard.'

Seth hissed through his teeth. 'And deflower a girl decades younger than me before she's even married?'

'He's already done that,' Lilly said.

'Lilly!' Seth snapped through his teeth.

'Oh, *sorry*, was that a secret?' she sneered.

'Enough!' Eleanor snapped, reddening.

'We're here for a wedding, not a scrap,' the Ambassador said. 'We should be celebrating!'

Lilly burst out laughing.

'Marriage has never, nor will it ever be, a cause for celebration. "Nuptials" is synonymous to "bartering" – and my brother didn't barter me to you so that you could bugger our mother! So get your hand off her thigh, wipe that smug smile off your face and stop acting like this arrangement is anything other than disgusting!'

Orl looked up from his book in surprise.

The Ambassador slowly lifted his palm from the queen mother's thigh.

'I believe I am needed elsewhere.'

He rose to leave.

'Father,' Orl began.

'I sincerely hope your opinion of me changes, Lilly,' he said softly.

She stared up at him, eyes wide.

'In the meantime, I will of course respect you first and foremost in this marriage. There was never any intention to the contrary.'

Her gaze shifted to the rug underfoot.

He folded his lips together and gave her a nod before turning to leave.

Another pause ensued.

Seth and Lilly simultaneously avoided their mother's eyes.

'Ooh, a pop-up book!' Ron exclaimed, oblivious.

Seth turned to give him an odd glance.

~

Night fell over the Dead Lands. The mansion of the Ambassador didn't have chamber pots, Seth realised with dread – they had a different invention altogether for that business, something called a *toilet*.

Seth approached the thing with apprehension. It gleamed a shiny white, with a lidded bowl above the seat beside a wooden pulley hanging from the ceiling. He did not like the look of it at all.

236

A voice from the corridor startled him. He closed the door to examine the thing further.

Slowly, Seth laid a hand on the pulley and gave it a tug.

Water began to swirl inside the bowl with a loud rushing noise.

Seth leaped out of the way with a frightened expression.

'I don't like that one *fuck*,' he announced to the bathroom at large.

He exited quickly.

His mother stood in the hall, with a man.

Seth backed around a corner and narrowed his eyes at her.

She laid a hand on the Ambassador's arm.

'I've missed you, you know,' Eleanor said softly.

So that's why you dyed your hair, Seth thought sourly.

'I have missed you even more,' he said.

They locked eyes for a moment before simultaneously rushing into an embrace and staggering through the nearest door.

Seth rounded the corner to glare at the space they'd been standing in, aghast.

'Dirty old bastard!' he exclaimed shrilly.

Lilly's door opened and she peered out at him irritably. 'What?'

'Nothing,' he said hurriedly. He had to think of her mental health, after all.

She regarded him sourly and closed the door.

Seth heaved a sigh. He thought about Lilly's outburst and the hurt in the Ambassador's face. Clearly he'd gotten over it quick enough, he mused with a shiver. Would this make him cancel it like Lilly wanted all along? Seth hoped so. He just wanted his little sister back.

And a chamber pot wouldn't go amiss, he added mentally. He was bursting for a piss – just not enough to go near that thing again.

He stood in the middle of the corridor, shifting from foot to foot. He finally came to a decision, picked a door and knocked on it.

Fifteen minutes later he descended to the kitchens and pissed in his stew pot, just to make a point.

~

III

Bells rang from the Church of Fiery Repent. Sunrise baked the mansion grounds, bustling with preparations.

'My liege, really, I don't need a reward,' Marbrand protested.

Jimmy tried vainly to put a jacket on Seth, standing a foot behind him with the garment outstretched as he strode across the drawing room.

'No, you save a kid's life, you get a reward, that's how it works,' Seth insisted, bounding from one valuable knick-knack to another. 'What about a couple of these? They'll look lovely on the mantelpiece.'

'I don't have a mantelpiece, sir,' Marbrand said.

He watched Seth return the crystal paperweight to the other end of the room.

Jimmy dropped the jacket against his knees with a groan.

'Anyway, don't they belong to the Ambassador?' Marbrand added.

'Probably.'

Seth swung around, nearly slamming into Jimmy in the process.

'You don't have a mantelpiece? Do you *own* a house?'

'No sir, I sleep in the barracks—'

'For Christs' sake!' Jimmy exclaimed.

Seth frowned at him.

'If you wanted a house, all you had to do was ask,' he said mildly.

'No, not that!'

Jimmy shoved the jacket in Seth's face.

'I've been trying to put this on you all morning! Whenever I try to dress you, you race around like a rabid lunatic, and the rest of the day you sit on your ass doing nothing! It's pissing me off!'

'Is this how you speak to your superiors?'

Jimmy's eyes rolled up into their sockets.

'No, Lady Gertrude,' he grumbled apologetically.

'Mmm,' she grunted, a five-foot ball of indignant fury. 'You could have dressed him in something a little more extravagant! And why aren't you wearing your uniform?'

'Uniform?'

Seth pointed to an outfit with a sheepish wince.

Jimmy clapped eyes on it, his jaw hanging open.

'Oh,' he said dully.

'I'll be outside the door, your highness,' Marbrand said with a bow, exiting quickly. He'd finally found a woman more frightening than his wife. Sticking around went against his self-preservation.

Down the corridor from them, Lilly woke to the sound of knocking.

She opened the door to her quarters, her hair sticking up on end.

'You're not getting married looking like that, are you?' Si said with a grin.

'Si? What do you want?' she asked with a yawn.

'I never received an invitation to your piss-up,' he said. 'That and Sam might have accidentally got our ship nicked on our way in.'

'Lucky I got it back then, eh?' Lilly retorted, giving his sternum a playful shove.

'So when's the ceremony? I gotta get me a suit,' he said, gesturing down at his patchy leather attire.

'This afternoon. You can follow the twinkly train, if you like.'

'Anything to see you in petticoats,' he said with a smirk. 'There anything interesting in those hundred-year-old shirts?'

'Nothing *you* should be interested in,' she sniped, 'since you shouldn't even *be* here…'

She paused.

'How *did* you get in?'

He licked his lips guiltily.

'Apparently I have an uncanny resemblance to his highness the King of Adem,' he said. 'Which came in handy when the footman—'

'Guards! An imposter has entered the building!'

Si bolted down the corridor as a number of guards sprinted after him.

Lilly roared with laughter.

'A little help would be nice!' he called behind his shoulder.

Seth reached the top of the stairs, gawking after them.

'A friend of yours?' he asked Lilly.

Si skidded to a halt in front of the nearest window – i.e., hole in the wall where a window would go if the mansion happened to reside in a land where wind was something to be avoided, not welcomed – and, simply, leapt.

Head first.

Three floors up from the ground.

Towards a yard with no greenery.

Seth laughed loudly.

The guards craned their necks out.

'He's gone!'

'He is now, he's just dropped head-first at an altitude of about fifty feet,' Seth said, grinning broadly in trademark Crey sadism.

'Everyone in the first and second floors have a washing line hanging outside their balcony,' Lilly said, shaking her head. 'You can't expect a self-respecting pirate to enter a fortress and miss a glaring security detail like that on the way in.'

Everyone nodded in sudden understanding.

Then Seth and the guards frowned.

'Pirate?' they said in unison.

$$\sim$$

Noon. The ever-relentless sun cooked the air to a stale dryness.

Nevertheless, the train trudged uphill to the silver embroidered Church of Fiery Repent, erected to honour the namesake of the Creys' dragon, Lyseria. It seemed apt for the Ambassador to join the clan here, or so he thought pleasantly from inside the front coach.

Outside, fanfare hitting the train from all sides, two multi-coloured jesters somersaulted on either side of the road, striped attire jingling in time with the excited cheering of the small-folk.

One of them got a bit overexcited and leaped onto the side of one of the litters, sticking his head inside to blow a wet raspberry.

He was promptly grabbed by the face and sent flying into the crowd of onlookers.

'I'm up *far* too early for your shit!' Seth roared at him, slamming the door shut.

The crowd took little notice.

Dragons, baby ones, each measuring at about a foot long, zipped overhead in every colour under the sun, puffing smoke clouds into the air to herald the arrival of the second-to-main attraction – a massive midnight blue animal, six yards long from nose to tail, wingspan the same and a half, scales glinting cobalt and royal blue and turquoise and dull green as it burped white and yellow flame vertically into the heavens.

Everyone jumped and gasped at the sound of the sheer power produced – except for the dragon tamer, who cowered between the steed's flexing shoulder-blades shrieking 'Why, mother, why could I have not had my apprenticeship on a pony farm?! THERE'S NOTHING WRONG WITH HORSESHIT!'

Nobody heard him, not that it could have hurt the spirit of the affair. If the dragon had flicked him off and eaten him before going on a flesh-fuelled rampage, it wouldn't have dampened the mood. The poorest country in the world hadn't been so happy in centuries; they had to make the most of it, while they had the chance.

The train drove on, past the crowds and into new crowds, the dragons making a crescendo above as the tamer sweated up a stink and nearly fainted from the heat.

At last, the obelisk of Arianna Lyseria's final resting place obstructed their path and the train split into two, circling the obelisk, one coach left, one coach right, left, right, until they formed a row before the immense entrance to the substantially more immense Church.

Si stood at the foot of the obelisk, his face reddening – though not from the sun.

'GET,' he screeched, 'YOUR NUISANCE ARSE DOWN FROM THERE AND *GET IN THE CHURCH!*'

'In a bit!' Tully called down, his voice strained. 'I'm *nearly* there!'

Si throttled the air.

Many, many feet into the rippling hot air above them, Tully tilted back from the blocks, stretching his elbows flat. He huffed a breath through pursed lips, his cheeks ballooning, and tugged himself flat against the bricks once more, stepping up onto another foothold.

Seth hopped from his litter first and watched them in interest for a minute.

'GET OFF!!' Si shrieked, eyes bulging. 'We have *shit* to go through before we go in! You're holding up the *entire show, you bastard*!'

240

'One more leg up!' Tully called out, elated with himself. 'Just one slap of that big bell-end at the top and I'll be down!'

Tully's arm yawned skyward, fingers twitching in anticipation.

'Sod ya then! You can bloody get on with it!!' Si howled with rage.

He plucked a piece of dirt from underfoot and hurled it at him.

The clump of sand burst far too many yards below to have caused Tully physical injury, but he flinched at the sound and snatched hold of the pillar's tip with an animal wail, one foot dangling.

Seth squinted at Tully's tiny silhouette, baring his teeth.

'Whatever,' Jimmy said in a tired monotone.

Seth, shrugging in agreement, bounded ahead of everyone into and down the long, long aisle of flame-patterned carpet to his seat at the front row.

Jimmy trotted in his wake, trying to look inconspicuous.

The Ambassador entered next and watched in amusement as Seth frowned at a couple of acolytes in his seat.

The two women's heads were completely shaven, to Seth's bemusement: their pates gleamed in the sun.

Jimmy tapped one of the nuns on the shoulder.

'Go on, hop it,' he snapped, jerking a thumb over his shoulder.

The nuns rose, affronted, and shuffled off with their hoods up.

Seth gestured for Jimmy to slide into the pew before him.

The Church slowly began to fill as the throngs poured into the drafty edifice. Churches seemed to be drafty wherever they were, but this one had a convenient location to sell drafts for extra income.

Qattren blessed this convenience as she materialised in the centre of the aisle in her peacock-feather dress, amidst the usual ripple of screams and bodies moving swiftly away.

Ron sat and stared at the back of Seth's head nauseously.

'I have a bad feeling, you know,' he said in a low voice.

Stan dropped himself on Ron's left and followed his gaze.

'You're right, his hair *is* getting a bit thin. And he's got dandruff.'

'No, not that,' said Ron.

Seth glanced back at them, running a dubious hand through his hair.

Ron twitched in his seat. 'I feel like something bad's going to happen.'

'Ah, that'll be because Lady Gertrude is here,' Stan said.

He pointed to the right hand side of Seth's pew, where his grandmother squirmed her way to the other side of a miserable-looking Jimmy.

Ron didn't think that was it either, but before he could say as such, a soft voice breathed in his ear.

'Have I missed anything?'

'Nope, the bride's outside, faffing with her dress,' Ron sighed. 'I thought you were giving it a miss?'

'Not at all, I love a good wedding,' Qattren said in anticipation.

She crossed her legs, adjusting her silk skirt and its numerous feathers.

'And I'm a friend of the family. I'm expected to attend.'

'Friend, is it?' Seth said with a snort.

Qattren turned to the back of Seth's head in surprise.

'I think you'd find me quite lovely if you gave me a chance,' she said airily. 'Oh, you have a bit of dandruff, just...'

She flicked a strand of hair sticking out of the crown of his head.

'... there.'

Seth scowled at the altar, his jaw set forward.

The throngs began to settle and a harpist began to play...

... and Lilly entered the room.

People turned to gaze at her as she strolled casually down the aisle, one hand lifting the hem of her skirt impatiently, the lilac linen fluttering slightly behind her.

It wasn't very extravagant for a wedding dress, the accusing eyes of Lady Gertrude communicated to Jimmy in particular for some reason, but Lilly ignored opinions like that religiously anyway.

She halted beside Seth with a deep breath and held her hand out, healing-palm facing upward.

Seth's bandaged fingers slid into hers, cupping them in his.

Then to everyone's bemusement, she elbowed him over and sat beside him, with Orl crossing the aisle to perch at her left.

Seth frowned at her palm, the bandage adorned with purple linen to match the dress.

'What happened to your hand?'

'Got stabbed by a pirate. What happened to yours?'

'Priest flayed it.'

Lilly winced. 'Ow.'

Ron leaned forward and tapped Lilly's shoulder.

'Oi! I thought you were getting married?'

'Oh, didn't I tell you?' Seth said, turning with a smile. 'She's not getting married until next week, to this one.'

He pointed at Orl, who grinned sheepishly.

'This is my mother's second wedding.'

Stan lifted his eyebrows. 'So that means you get two dowries, then?'

Seth simply rubbed his hands together with a grin.

Lilly elbowed him. 'You still owe me my bribe for wearing the dress, remember?'

That was when she noticed Jimmy hiding between Seth and Lady Gertrude.

'Who dressed you this morning, then?'

Jimmy scowled and folded his arms over a mass of bright pink ruffles.

'This is so embarrassing,' he grumbled.

Seth giggled treacherously, earning a hideous scowl.

The guests nattered in a dull roar to the smothered sounds of the harpists, laughing at unknown jokes and exchanging tales.

'So,' Seth said casually, turning to face Lilly. 'You have a pirate ship now?'

She gulped.

He eyed her dubiously. 'Where's *my* pirate ship?'

'I didn't know you wanted one. We would have saved you the one we burned Qattren on a while back.'

'You mean *my* ship? With *my* money on? Which you *stole*?'

'Speaking of pirates,' Lilly said hurriedly, glancing around, 'd'you see where the crew got to? I thought they were following us?'

Seth shrugged, uninterested. 'My doppelganger was screeching bloody murder at some prick at the top of the obelisk, last I saw. So anyway. Do you have a pirate name then, or what?'

Lilly frowned. 'Like what? No-Beard?'

'I don't know, don't they make one up for you when you join or something? Did you consider Lilly-Willy?'

'Lilly-Willy?' Orl asked, laughing.

'We used to call her Lilly-Willy when she was little,' Seth said with a grin, 'because we were convinced she would grow a—'

'—willy out of sheer willpower,' Lilly finished with a sheepish smile.

'Lilly Willy and her Willy-powered Willy,' Seth recited with a moronic lilt.

Qattren watched them with a faint smile as they laughed. That was when she spotted Si skulking on the side lines, directing members of the crew towards specific positions among the throng. He met her gaze briefly and gave a small nod.

Qattren simply watched him impassively.

Lilly glanced back at the entrance worriedly.

'She's taking ages,' she said to Seth. 'Think I should check on her?'

'She's a big girl, she can look after herself,' he said. He shifted up in his seat. 'D'you think I've got time for a piddle? I'm about to spring a leak in a minute.'

'Just don't go on the graves again, eh?' Jimmy said with distaste.

'It's good for the roses. Actually, that's a number two, but now I mention it...'

He earned groans of disgust as he rose to squeeze out of the pews.

He halted his gaze on the entrance and rolled his eyes.

'Typical,' he grumbled, sliding back in beside Orl.

Everyone turned to see the queen dowager enter, her silver-gold gown flowing behind her and shining in the sunlight. Five minutes later, they watched the end of the dress finally enter after her as she made her slow ascent to the altar, where the Ambassador waited patiently, his hands folded behind his back.

Lilly pushed Orl forward slightly to poke her brother.

'Lucky escape,' she whispered, nodding at the long trail with relief.

Eleanor reached the top of the church and took the Ambassador's right hand, laying her own right hand on Seth's shoulder in passing.

'Thank you,' she said quietly.

Seth smiled and gave her a wink.

The couple faced each other and the priest commenced his joyful drone.

Seth fidgeted quietly and sighed heavily, pulling Orl's coat tails over his lap.

'You might experience some splash back,' Seth leaned towards Orl to mutter.

Orl's eyes widened and he removed the coat altogether, covering Seth's lap more efficiently.

Seth leaned back on the pew and sighed contentedly to the faint sound of flowing water.

'Dirty bastard!' Lilly exclaimed in a whisper, gawking incredulously.

'It's not that, it's urine,' he informed her. 'She's my *mother*, you freak.'

Lilly snickered uncontrollably.

Seth finished what he was doing and folded Orl's coat up between them. Orl shoved it to the floor, touching it as little as possible.

Eleanor and the Ambassador joined hands as the next stage of the ceremony ensued.

Qattren spotted Si give a signal.

A wet *thunk* marked the arrival of a scimitar in the Ambassador's throat.

~

IV

Orl gasped, a hand on his own throat.

Lilly and Seth bolted upright, whey-faced.

The Ambassador gurgled, the blood rushing from his face, leaving his usually healthy complexion a light grey. Blood poured over the immaculately aimed blade and pooled at their feet, soaking into and travelling through Eleanor's wedding trail.

He and Eleanor exchanged one last horror-stricken glance.

His thin body folded.

Eleanor screamed.

A man bolted upright from the far edge of the pews. Tully vaulted the barrier in front of them and sprinted at Eleanor. After a few loud rips, they abandoned the gown's long trail and fled down the aisle.

Everyone else stared at the Ambassador's body in shock, until Orl cried out.

'Wait!' Lilly called to him, reaching out to him.

He swatted her hand away and shoved past Seth to approach his father.

The strangled coughs had subsided, leaving his mouth hanging ajar. His eyes stared at the vaulted ceiling, vacant and glassy.

Orl stared at the corpse in miscomprehension, his fists pressed to his mouth.

The crew of the *Devourer* rose impassively.

Screams erupted and blades were drawn. The church burst into uproar.

Lilly watched in horror, unable to move.

Orl stared obliviously at his father's eyes.

Sam Sot strode up behind him, holding a short sword.

Lilly howled.

Sam thrust the sword between Orl's ribs, causing his punctured back to arch.

Orl's eyes bulged at one of the stained-glass windows.

Sot retracted the blade and moved to the throng, leaving Orl to crumple to the ground.

Lilly simply stared, her body seized in an icy grip.

Seth watched the chaos unfold, eyes wide and mouth slightly ajar.

Then he snapped out of it and grabbed Lilly's elbow.

'Run!'

He pulled them both from the pew and into the swiftly exiting throngs.

Qattren grabbed Ron, who grabbed Stan just as the crowd faded and purple coated the air.

Qattren tried to step home as their surroundings slowed and they abruptly slammed to a halt at the gaping entrance to the church.

Qattren slammed her hands on an invisible barrier.

Seth Crey's image stood behind the barrier, blocking their path with a smirk. The only indication that this wasn't Seth – apart from the fact that Seth was frozen mid-sprint a few yards behind them – was a slight alteration of the eyes and a scar down the left side of his nose.

'Sorry, Qat,' he said, flashing her a half-grin. 'You won't find any help here.'

With that he *repelled* them.

They felt their bodies *slide* back together and soar backwards into the crowd as motion returned with a vengeance.

They landed heavily on the ground and quickly pulled themselves upright before the crowd could trample them into the carpet.

'We're trapped here,' Qattren said, her voice strained as they held on to each other. 'If we want to leave we need to run.'

Stan wheezed, slammed over and over by fleeing nobility.

'But the crowds—'

'Just go. Hang on to us.'

The three of them surged along with the crowd, arms locked tight.

The pirates were everywhere, few in number but unseen, distinguishable only by the calm, determined stride in place of the procession's frenzied sprint, slaughtering selectively but broadly. Qattren scanned the crowd for Seth and glimpsed him ahead, dragging Lilly to the exit. She pulled Stan and Ron in the same direction, sprinting for the choked entrance.

Breathing heavily, Seth ran fast, shoving through the throng with his left shoulder and keeping a firm grip on Lilly's left elbow. Her fingers pinched his forearm as they ran, until a sudden surge from the crowd caused their grip on each other to slip.

'Lilly!'

He snatched her left wrist roughly and yanked her towards him, nearly pulling her arm off.

Her face was white and horror-stricken.

'Come on, quickly, you'll be alright, come on!'

He kissed her knuckles and ran once more, Lilly stumbling in his wake.

To his horror, he could feel his grip slipping again.

Her hand vanished.

He pivoted and sprinted back.

Lilly was being dragged to the altar by a man with greasy blond hair and piercing blue eyes that were both beautiful and terrifying.

'Lilly, love, you need to understand, I never wanted any of this,' Si hissed in her ear.

He hooked one arm around her neck and planted one hand across her mouth.

'I never wanted to hurt you, under any circumstances,' he went on. 'It's just my job, you see, my boss insisted and, well, you wouldn't want to annoy him…'

Her eyes widened. *Emmett.*

'… he gave me a fancy-ass ship to run and you made a fool out of all of us with your little ambush on your boyfriend's ride home. Emmett doesn't like a good lesson to go to waste—'

'LILLY!' Seth bellowed.

Two guards from the Creys' retinue snatched Seth under the armpits and made to carry him to safety.

'GET OFF! LILLY!'

Si released Lilly's mouth to grab her waist and lift her onto the altar.

'SETH!' she hollered.

Si snatched her bandaged hand and twisted it.

An explosion of pain quietened her to a faint whimper.

'BE QUIET! D'you want more trouble, is it?'

Tears poured down her cheeks.

'Sorry about your boyfriend, by the way,' he said, stepping over Orl's body as they passed.

Lilly turned her face away from him, weeping freely.

'… thought you were good for each other. *Really.* I told Sot not to kill anyone important. Casualty of war, I suppose.'

246

Lilly's cheeks were warm with fresh tears. Her bandage was warm too: Si had reopened the wound. Blood coated her hand and dripped down her forearm as she clutched his elbow, imploring his grip to loosen.

The guards dragged Seth away from them, his heels scraping on the carpet.

'LILLY!' he screamed again helplessly.

'I KNOW HER NAME, THANK YOU!' Si screeched at him. 'WHY DON'T YOU SCREAM GOODBYE BEFORE YOU LOSE YOUR VOICE?!'

Seth paled and struggled against them. The guards out-weighed him by twice over each and simply lifted him away.

'Let me tell you what's going to happen,' Si shouted at Lilly over the roar of the throngs.

He pulled Lilly through a door to the back quarters of the church.

'Since Prince Ronald is AWOL, we're gonna have to go to Plan B. That, little sister, means giving you to Aaliyaa Horne before she cops we're working for the wrong side. We won't let her kill you, don't worry. I fully intend to be friends after this, which will be difficult if you don't stop BLOODY KICKING ME!'

He flung her against a wall, pinning her there.

'What do you mean,' Lilly said hoarsely, 'little sister?'

'Oh, don't you know?'

Si grinned, twirling a knife in his hand.

'I'm your big brother. Bastard brother, that is. I'll be sure to give Seth our love when I come to strangle him in his sleep tomorrow. See you later, sis.'

Lilly had time to wonder where he was going before he flung her to the door.

A robed woman, her head shaved, clutched her shoulders and pulled her... somewhere. With a start, Lilly realised her body was dissipating into dust.

Her surroundings faded in a purple haze.

~

Seth wriggled as his entourage deposited him into the coach. He landed a fist into the mouth of the biggest one and bolted for the church as the guard stumbled backward.

Tully snatched him around the ribs with one arm and thrust him back.

'You need to stay outside,' he told him firmly.

'Who the *hell* are you?' Seth shrieked in his face.

'I'm a friend of Lilly's—'

Seth bellowed with laughter that was mirthless and slightly maniacal.

'Like *your* little friend is? Get out of my way.'

'Sir, he just saved your mother's life!' Marbrand snapped at him from behind.

247

He circled Seth to help Tully restrain him.

'Get in the coach, there's a good man,' Marbrand said sarcastically.

'No! My sister's in there!'

'I'll get Lilly, just get in the coach and leave!'

'No, I'm going—'

'You couldn't protect your family from those priests on your own, what makes you think you can take *them* on?' Marbrand demanded bluntly. 'Go to the coach. *Now*. Me and the lads will bring her back.'

Seth eyed him doubtfully, trembling.

Marbrand gave him a brisk nod.

Seth sucked a breath through his teeth and dragged himself to the coach, sitting opposite his mother with his head in his hands. Eleanor watched him in silence, shaking.

To Tully and Marbrand's immense bemusement, Lady Gertrude emerged from the church with Jimmy cradled in her arms. She made a beeline for Seth's coach and deposited him beside Seth.

Jimmy cowered under Seth and Eleanor's perplexed stares.

'I don't want to talk about it,' he said in a small voice.

Since they lacked the capacity at the moment to laugh at the situation, they unanimously decided to ignore it.

Eleanor jumped upright and craned her neck out of the coach door. 'Sir!'

Tully lifted his head to attention.

'Will you join us?' she asked, her voice hoarse. 'I would thank you for your deed today.'

Tully hesitated and nodded, striding to the coach.

Marbrand tore his gaze away with difficulty and tore off into the church.

Stan intercepted him halfway. 'Who are you looking for?'

'Lilly-Anna—'

That was enough.

Stan raced into the door ahead of him.

Ron made to follow when Qattren snatched his hand, interrupting his protestations in a cloud of dust.

The front entrance of the church was swollen with escapees. Stan squirmed his way into the maelstrom. The pirates had retreated, leaving panic and desperation behind. Stan made a beeline for the altar, vaulting guiltily over scores of the dead in his path. He turned and scanned the fleeing throng by the door. He didn't see any of the crew anywhere.

He examined his surroundings and found a door by the back of the altar. It was open a crack.

Marbrand skidded to a halt behind him and followed his gaze. 'Unwise.'

Stan glanced at him. 'I can go in and talk to them. I was part of their crew—'

'Most unwise,' he cut across him.

Stan heaved a sigh. 'It's worth a try.'

Marbrand exhaled reluctantly.

'Five minutes,' he told him. 'Then I'm going in with Pointy.'

Stan nodded. 'Fine.'

He jogged to the door and vanished inside.

Marbrand's body clock was remarkably accurate. Nevertheless, he waited an extra minute and a half before unsheathing Pointy and running in after Stan.

The back door hung open, letting the sunshine from the graveyard spill in.

The room was completely empty. Stan, Lilly and the pirates were gone.

~

The coach rolled to a halt outside the mansion.

Seth slid from the coach, his mother and butler at his heels, and made for the open doors.

Tully followed a short distance behind, trying to seem inconspicuous.

'Good afternoon, your highness,' the doorman greeted him.

Seth walked past without acknowledgement.

The man peered outside curiously. 'Where's the Ambassador? And the other guests?'

'Dead,' Seth grunted.

The man blinked in alarm. 'How?'

No one bothered replying. The blood staining the hem of Eleanor's dress gave sufficient explanation.

Seth made for the stairs and ascended to the drawing room in his quarters.

He sat on a settee to the right wall and the others joined him, Eleanor on the left, Jimmy on the right.

Tully hovered by the door, unsure of the social etiquette.

There was half an hour of silence before Eleanor spoke up.

'You don't think Lilly ordered this, do you?'

Jimmy looked at her incredulously.

'No,' Tully said, belligerent.

'They took her, Mother,' Seth said quietly, in a monotone. 'She didn't organise anything: they wouldn't have killed Orl otherwise. In fact, they wouldn't have killed anyone, because Lilly wouldn't kill people over a *boy*.'

There was another pause.

'What if it was all a trick?' she whispered again. 'What if she was leading the boy on? Toying with us to make us rearrange to evade suspicion—'

'My lady,' Tully said.

They looked at him as one.

'I was part of the crew,' he said quietly. 'Lilly had nothing to do with this. I wouldn't have hurried you out if I thought she had anything to do with this.

This is all Silas Beult's doing.' A look of pain crossed his features. 'He's... he... it was nothing to do with Lilly. I swear that's the truth.'

Eleanor gaped at him, her mouth open.

'Silas Beult?' she said in a whisper. 'Is he—'

'Is he the one with the blond hair?' Seth cut across her. 'The one who pretended to be me?'

Tully nodded. 'I didn't think he'd do this, I swear to God. We were Lilly's friends. Or I was,' he added under his breath.

'Has he...'

Eleanor swallowed repeatedly.

'Has he been manipulating her?' she asked strongly. 'Has he been telling her anything about—'

'She had *nothing*,' Seth said loudly, 'to *do with this*. Their friend just *told* you this.'

Seth glared at his mother.

'You didn't see her *face* earlier,' he hissed. 'The girl went *grey*.'

Another pause.

'I'll get some booze,' Jimmy decided.

~

Marbrand jogged out to Elliot. 'How many coaches have left?'

'Just the Creys',' he said. 'Everyone else has gone back inside for their dead.'

Marbrand nodded slowly.

The pirates had left roughly two hours ago, and the nobility had judged it safe to re-enter. Some currently took turns to carry the dead outside; many were in there simply to pray. Marbrand didn't see the attraction with either activity.

'Any idea where they might have taken the princess?' Elliot asked.

Marbrand shrugged helplessly. 'To the ship, I would assume. Wherever that is.'

Elliot frowned, puzzled. 'I thought they called her the captain now?'

'Yes, but she made the mistake of leaving the old captain alive,' he reminded him. 'Whichever one he is. Although I recognised the one that killed Orl, you know.'

'Really?'

'Yeah, I recall him calling up to old King Sam a couple years ago, looking for money on behalf of Captain Hopkins. Sam Something, I'm sure. I remember because the king liked him, for having the same...'

He drifted off blankly.

Elliot blinked. 'Name?'

Realisation crossed his features.

'Yes. And King Sam gave him the money in return for sending supplies back and forth from the Shades to Breaker's Hold. In fact, he hired them on a permanent contract, until the Creys' dragon attacked their ship shortly after King Sam went missing last year. They're in the employ of the Hornes, only it's not the Hornes anymore, it's—'

'The Emmetts,' Elliot said. 'But what do they want with Lilly-Anna? I thought they would target Ron and Aaliyaa first and seal their regency of Stoneguard?'

'I don't know,' said Marbrand, toying with the hilt of his sword. 'I'm going to need to do some investigating. Don't let anyone leave without them speaking to me first.'

Elliot nodded and made for the nearest group of mourners.

'Oh,' Marbrand said, halting him. 'The bloke that brought Queen Eleanor to the coach. Have you seen him around anywhere?'

'Oh, he went in the coach with them,' Elliot said. 'I saw the queen ask him to join them, say thanks for helping her out.'

Marbrand waved a finger back and forth in the air. 'Interesting. I'm going after him, question as many witnesses as you can find and let me know if anyone comes up with anything interesting.'

~

Lilly opened her eyes. It seemed to be a mostly pointless exercise.

A lengthy bout of motion sickness followed her return to the physical world. Her current surroundings were pitch black, but she knew it was a dungeon immediately after discovering her knee in a puddle of someone else's excrement and banging her head on all three walls and the ceiling in quick succession.

She found it difficult to concentrate. Her thoughts had returned garbled: as if the roiling of her stomach had translated to the inside of her skull. The last thing she remembered was Seth surreptitiously piddling under the pew during their mother's second wedding.

Orl was between them, looking mournfully at the corner of his best jacket sitting in Seth's line of fire.

Lilly whined, her windpipe tightening.

Orl was dead.

Her head slumped forward of its own accord and landed against a brick wall.

'Lilly?'

Her head shot up and swivelled to the right.

'Stan? Where are you?'

'In the cell across from yours,' he said, his voice wavering. 'Are you alright?'

A sob escaped her throat. 'No.'

251

Stan shuffled forward and stretched his arm out from behind the bars.

The corridor between them was so narrow he was able to slip his hand around Lilly's shoulder with little strain.

'Lilly, I'm sorry about Orl.'

She sniffed and grasped his wrist. 'I'm fine.'

'You will be,' he agreed. 'Don't get sad, get mad. That should be easy for a Crey, right?'

Lilly released a hollow laugh. It was an empty noise.

A door unlocked some distance to their right.

A plate slid down the corridor towards them and the door slammed shut again.

They ignored the loaf and flask and stared soberly into the darkness.

'I can't believe they'd turn on their own kind.'

Lilly turned her head to hear him better. 'What?'

'The pirates. I mean, I know we weren't really their kind,' he added, 'but they knew we were only there for a laugh, right? And the free ride to the Ambassador's, obviously—'

'They weren't pirates,' she said monotonously. 'Pirates never turn on their own kind. And I could have killed Sam if I really wanted to, they knew that. They weren't pirates. They were just pretending, same as us.'

'So they were after Ron, then.'

'Probably. Did he get away?'

'I think so. Qattren was with him.'

'Good.'

There was silence for a moment. Half of her days were taken by solemn silences these days, Lilly reflected.

'What do you think they'll do to us?' Stan whispered.

Lilly decided not to reply. She grasped the flask of what she assumed was water and took a long gulp.

She coughed loudly. Her throat was on fire.

'You alright?'

Lilly raised the flask to her nose with a frown. 'This ain't water.'

Stan gulped. 'What is it, then?'

'Whiskey.'

Stan blinked in bemusement and stuck a hand outside the cell to scrabble around for the loaf of bread. He pulled it apart experimentally but alas, there was no key.

'Must have just mixed up the water flask with...' he said, his voice fading as though he was walking away.

'Say that again louder? I can't hear you.'

There was silence.

'Stan?'

No answer.

Lilly reached her arm out as far from her cell as she could and groped between the bars of his cell for Stan. Her hand fell on half of the loaf instead and her surroundings began to brighten.

'Stan, you there?' she called again before the cell walls melted away and she landed cross-legged with a jolt in a small courtyard.

She squinted in the hot sunlight and glanced at the bread in her hand.

'Magic bread? How did you get this in there?'

Qattren proffered a faint smile. 'I have my ways.'

Ron offered her a hand up.

Lilly took it, pulling herself up and giving a shaky Stan a stricken nod.

'Where are we? Where *were* we? How d'you know where to find us?'

'I sussed out where Aaliyaa was,' Qattren said simply.

'We figured they were with her since they're trying to trap her,' Ron added. 'They work for Mister Emmett, he hired them to kill her.'

Lilly gaped at him, affronted. 'How long have you known this?'

'Oh, since they caught Qat on the ship,' he said idly. 'She told me they were using me to lure her to her death. Why?'

'It would have been nice to know this earlier!' Stan exclaimed.

'Qat told me to tell you, but then Si threatened me so I had to wait until we got to shore.'

He caught Lilly's irate expression.

'And then I forgot,' he said with a shrug. 'Sorry.'

Lilly rolled her eyes, officially giving up on Ronald Horne.

'So where are we?'

'Copers,' the Monument replied.

~

Seth glowered up at Marbrand. 'You haven't got her, have you?'

'We've been questioning the guests about the pirates, trying to trace them down.'

'That's a very long way of saying "no",' he said dully.

Tully lifted a hand from the back of the settee. 'Can I help?'

Marbrand spotted a note of reluctance in his voice.

'Please. I would ask you a few questions as well, your majesty, if you're up for it.'

Seth glared at him through his eyebrows. 'Do I have to get up?'

'No, but may I sit? My blisters are getting blisters from all this walking.'

Seth nudged Jimmy off and patted the settee next to him.

'What have you found out so far?'

'Only the description of the man who stabbed Orl,' he replied.

He sat and lifted one boot onto his knee to rub his sole with a wince.

'Which is basically what we knew already. He's the only one anyone got a good look at.'

'What about the blond one?'

'Which?'

'The one who took Lilly,' he said. 'Anyone see him?'

Marbrand shook his head. 'Not that I could find out, anyway. Can you give me a more thorough description?'

Seth shrugged vaguely.

'Blond hair, darker than mine, greasy looking. A head shorter than me. Blue eyes, only they were weird, they look at you like he wanted to stab you. Probably because he wanted to stab me.'

'He looks like you, then,' Jimmy said.

'I don't look at people like I want to stab them,' he said hotly.

'No, you just look at them like they're a piece of shit,' Tully said bluntly. Seth turned around to snarl at him.

'That's because that's what they *are*,' he said.

Tully bit his tongue. Marbrand thought he could sense the phrase 'saved your mother' trying to push its way through him.

Seth turned his attention back to Marbrand.

'You would have seen him around here this morning, before we left. He came into the mansion, told the footman he was me and went upstairs to talk to Lilly. She said he was a "friend" of hers.'

Marbrand nodded slowly, staring at the carpet. 'Did he say anything? What did his voice sound like?'

'A dying cat,' he said immediately.

Tully snorted quietly.

'That's what he sounded like, I distinctly remember thinking it at the time.' Seth blinked in realisation. 'I'm pretty sure the name "Emmett" was uttered.'

Marbrand's head bolted upright then. 'Are you sure?'

Seth nodded, then frowned. 'I think so.'

'He did,' Tully said, breaking his silence.

Marbrand turned to face him. 'Can you fill in the blanks?'

Tully nodded. 'It wasn't her we were after, it was Ronald Horne,' he said quietly.

'Why does he want Ronald Horne?'

'Because Aaliyaa Horne does. I don't know any more than that.'

He frowned at Seth's grimace of disgust.

'What?' he barked, breaking his respectful façade. 'He keeps secrets from people, that's how Silas has ever been. Any time you ask the man a straightforward question, it's "wait and see". I only know what I was supposed to know. Nuffing more.'

Seth heaved a sigh. 'Where is Ronald Horne?'

'With his wife. He could be bloody anywhere,' Marbrand grumbled.

Something occurred to him then.

'If Aaliyaa Horne has something to do with them, that might mean they're headed to Minu. That's where I last saw evidence of her presence.'

'Think you can track her from there?' Seth asked.

'Worth a shot.'

He extracted a purse and threw it at Marbrand. 'Go for it.'

~

V

The Monument yawned widely and audibly without moving a muscle – if you could call what he had muscle, being constructed of gold-coloured marble. Lilly was surprised she hadn't noticed it earlier. It was a man, one of the watery-eyed intelligent types, a thick leather-bound tome lying on top of a set of splayed fingers while the right hand was poised in mid-air, brandishing a quill pensively. It was also speaking quite fluently without moving its mouth.

'I like to think I'm the most famous city,' he was saying proudly, 'being the one so notoriously known for being unfindable. The trouble is, people often only search a certain location once and they wonder why I'm not there – mistake this city for something along the lines of the other seven, you know. Stationary. Awfully boring, if you ask me, just sitting there doing nothing, it's no small wonder they've been deserted for so long, they don't even want to look for any inhabitants, I mean, talk about unsociable—'

Qattren cleared her throat politely.

The Monument also cleared his throat, sheepishly.

'Sorry, I'm digressing slightly, aren't I? Unrestrained stream of consciousness. Tends to happen a lot when you get into the habit of talking to yourself. You learn a lot about the internal mindscape, mind you—'

'Sorry to interrupt,' Lilly cut in, 'but... what are you exactly?'

'Ah,' the Monument hesitated, clearing his throat again. 'I am Copers.'

'I thought Copers was a city?'

'It is,' he replied. 'You are presently within Copers – the courtyard of the basilica, to be exact. You are within me, along with my Monument, which is a shadow of me, if you understand. I am within myself, if you will…'

'A warlock tried to enchant the city so he could hide it beneath the ground and move it at will to any location on the country, using this,' Qattren said over him as he waffled on.

She held up the star Halle had given Ron.

'He ended up personifying the city – and he's been sliding around the desert muttering to himself ever since.'

'Contemplating,' the Monument corrected haughtily.

'Why can't people find you?' Stan asked curiously.

'Ah, well, that's because they spend all bloody year running around looking for me that I can't catch up with them,' he said in annoyance. 'That and they have entirely the wrong attitude to live in this city altogether.'

'What do you mean by that?' Qattren asked in interest.

'Take Retribution Halle, for instance,' the statue said. 'Came flying in here one day with his group of reprobates and decided to take over the city. Use it as an example to the monarchies of the world that a group of publicly elected men could do the job of an anointed king. I wasn't having that – they'd have the place razed in a fortnight, the way they were speaking to those families. I got shot of them sharpish.'

'You threw them out of your city?' Lilly asked. Something occurred to her then. 'That message written in dead bodies – that was them, wasn't it?'

'Trust us to land in a homicidal city,' Stan said glumly.

'That was an accident,' the statue protested. 'My barriers are stronger than I gave them credit for. The message was intended for their group to stumble upon the next time another cretin flies in on one of their stolen dragons. I didn't mean anything by it, it was to frighten them away from what they insist on trying to understand.'

'Why not explain to them yourself?' Qattren asked. 'Show a man a riddle and chances are he won't be able to solve it, but show them a weapon and explain what you'll do with it and they'll reconsider their options.'

'Or attempt to steal the weapon for themselves,' he explained breezily. 'Humans hear what they want to hear, and the rest is learned with violence. Copers was built for warlocks to understand, not mortals. It's the same as your Sal'plae. No one knows where to find it, and the people who do don't know how to use it – apart from you, my dear. You have quite a knack for it.'

She gave a small curtsey – only a small one, mind you.

'Is that how Qattren found you?' Lilly asked him. 'Through Sal.. whatever you call it?'

'Well, no, the banshee broke the bloody door open,' the Monument grumbled. 'So to speak, that is. Usually, I have a barrier up around my walls so that when a visitor enters Copers, they have to prove their worth before being allowed to roam the streets – like our late friend Mr Halle experienced. Now it's like a room with a wall missing. My last resort was the message you stumbled upon earlier.'

'You killed visitors before they can enter the walls,' Lilly said dully, 'and you go on about the other cities being unsociable.'

'Yes, well,' he went on, 'as soon as Aaliyaa Horne entered, the whole system broke down! Couldn't get rid of her! Got so caught up trying to fix the riddles I left the city above ground, and I still haven't fixed them yet. Anyone could walk in here now – that's why I moved myself here by the Ambassador's mansion, where thankfully you arrived just in time to flush her out for me.'

'She can't be powerful enough to overcome a warlock barrier,' Qattren said. 'Was someone with her?'

'There was only her and a little dog when the barrier crashed,' the Monument said. 'God knows who's gone through after that.'

'Did this dog have a brown spot on his back?'

'Albie?' Lilly asked in bewilderment.

'Possibly,' the Monument said uncertainly. 'He was a little white terrier, if that helps.'

'When was the last time you saw that dog?' Qattren demanded, turning to Lilly.

'Um, I'm sure he was on the ship with... wait,' she trailed off, confused. 'He was definitely at home when we... he...' She turned to Stan questioningly. 'Wasn't he?'

Qattren rolled her eyes. 'I told you he wasn't a dog.'

'Well, he doesn't look like a cat, does he?' Stan snapped.

'It couldn't be *him*... could it?' the Monument asked.

Qattren simply looked up at him worriedly.

Lilly glared at the two of them.

'When you're quite finished with your telepathic conversation, would you mind telling us how we get out of here?'

'The pirates are patrolling the entrances,' Qattren informed her. 'But I can get past them without much hassle. It's Aaliyaa finding you after we get out is the problem.'

'What does she want me for?' Lilly asked.

'She thinks you're the Antichrist.'

Lilly blinked. 'And am I?'

'No, your nephew is,' Qattren replied.

'The dead one,' the Monument clarified.

~

Witch Burning: an Intensive Instruction Guide was placed aside as a knock sounded on his bedroom door. Si got up in disgruntlement and opened it.

'What did I tell you about—'

There was no one there.

He frowned and glanced up and down the corridor before firmly shutting the door and turning to his bed.

Qattren stood between him and the bed with a faint smile. 'Hello.'

Si blinked. 'What do you want, witch?'

She licked her lips and smiled again in explanation.

'Oh.' He shrugged. 'Alright then.'

He pushed her backwards onto his bed and flung his shirt over his head.

He was just relieving himself of his trousers when Qattren extended a hand out to him. She pressed the flat of her palm on his stomach.

'Close your eyes,' she said softly.

257

He felt a faint tingling sensation in his lower bowel, but considered this normal under the circumstances.

'How shall we start, then?' he asked pleasantly, his eyes still closed.

'How indeed.'

His eyes bolted open.

Gomez Emmett glared at him over a table covered with maps.

Tent walls billowed around him where sandstone walls had once stood tall and true. A draft blew over his nether regions, reminding him that he had left his clothes behind.

'*What* are you doing?' Emmett hissed.

Si gaped at him before returning his gaze to his lower torso. He smacked two hands over his delicate parts.

To his horror, Felicity stood beside her brother, cradling a baby boy known unfortunately by the name of Azrael.

'Do you want to borrow my cloak?' she asked worriedly.

He simply stared at her despairingly.

'Please take my cloak,' she begged. 'It's only there, on the table… you'll get flu, looking like that—'

Si hobbled over and, shifting his grip on himself, released one hand to snatch the cloak gratefully.

Gomez Emmett turned white with fury.

Si wound the cloak around his waist.

'Leave,' Emmett said softly.

'Okay,' Si said in a shrill squeak, backing away.

'I'll speak with you later.'

Si gulped on his way out of the tent. 'Can't wait.'

~

Qattren entered the courtyard of the recently evacuated building, dusting her hands off.

'The coast is clear now.'

'Admirable,' the Monument said in awe. 'The way you adapted your approach according to the tastes of your—'

'Thank you,' Lilly said with a grimace. 'What did you do with Si? I trust he met an unpleasant end.'

'Not yet,' Qattren said with a slight smile. 'He's currently in the grounds of the Emmetts' castle-to-be, in hasty search of some attire.'

Lilly smiled faintly. 'Sounds good enough for me. Any sign of Aaliyaa?'

Qattren shook her head.

'She hasn't got anything to do with your crew,' she informed her. 'They're planning on capturing her too, along with you and Ron. You were bait, to bring her and Ron to them.'

'And here was me thinking I was loved,' Lilly said with a sigh.

'I admire you a great deal, if that's any consolation,' the Monument said helpfully. 'If my barriers were working, you would be among the only people worthy enough to gain entry into my city.'

'How do you judge people to be worthy enough to stand in your streets?' Ron asked coldly.

'By examining their intentions,' he replied mildly. 'You would all be worthy, because of your simple wish to purge me of miscreants. You're welcomed in the way the cleaner would be welcomed into your home.'

'You mean we're the Jimmys of your city?' Lilly asked.

'Jimmy's the butler,' Ron said.

'That's just the head cleaner,' Stan said.

'Well, I regard you as more of a *respected* employee,' the Monument corrected.

'Which Jimmy isn't,' Lilly agreed.

'So my mum trying to kill the Antichrist doesn't count, then?' Ron asked.

'I'm not the Antichrist, Ron,' Lilly told him irritably.

'Plenty of people would beg to differ,' Stan pointed out.

'Yeah, they can't be far off,' Ron commented.

'Shut up, Horne. I guess that means she wants to kill me, then,' Lilly said grumpily.

'Probably. We'll have to find out,' Qattren said.

'Why does everything have to be a big showdown with you?' Ron asked sourly. 'Is there something wrong with leaving my last remaining family member alive and just running away instead?'

'Yes,' she said shortly. 'She can run faster than us.'

~

'Since when?' Marbrand demanded.

'Since you gutted the first one we sent you and bloody lost the last one,' the dragon owner said crossly, rubbing his steed's scaled head. 'Where is he, anyway?'

'Well, I don't know! I had people to rescue at the time! Elliot, what happened to the last dragon?'

'We left him outside the Creys' place while we arrested that priest,' he said. 'I chained him next to Lyseria, so I imagine he'll be fed and everything.'

Marbrand smacked a hand over his eyes.

'She'll have killed him, then,' the owner said mournfully. 'He's only a miniature, you know. She's twice his size, she'll rip him apart.'

'Sorry about that,' Marbrand muttered, still covering his eyes, 'but it was a royal emergency—'

'I don't care, that's two dragons you've killed now!' he snapped. 'That's not a royal emergency, that's animal cruelty!'

'Oh, come on, they'll make more!' Marbrand protested, gesturing at the thing.

'You think just because you wear metal clothes, that gives you God's right to slaughter perfectly innocent dragons!' the man said hysterically, throwing his hands in the air.

'Well, yeah, it kind of does!'

Elliot nudged him.

'Got a plan,' he said surreptitiously.

Louder he said, 'Looks like we'll have to slum it with a horse, then.'

Marbrand sighed heavily and they turned to leave.

Just as the owner returned to his dragon, the two of them ran up behind him and pulled his legs from under him.

'Oldest trick in the book,' Marbrand commented as the dust cloud settled.

Elliot's face fell.

'Someone already thought of it?' he asked, disappointed. 'I thought I was really clever there until you said that.'

~

Aaliyaa Horne strode down the centre of the slaughterhouse, the Bastard resting comfortably in the crook of her elbow.

'I really appreciate this, you know,' the Bastard said contentedly. 'It's not every day you find a nice lady willing to help you out without having to give you a silly name. I mean, Albie. Seriously?'

'Ridiculous name,' Aaliyaa said, shaking her head.

'Yeah,' he exclaimed, his tail wagging in understood affection. 'Still, at least she'll have the opportunity to apologise before she kicks the bucket. You know, for naming me Albert, nearly killing me, *losing* me half a dozen times – if I weren't the way I was, I would have died long ago, you know. And I've been there, dying. It's not particularly nice.'

'I know, dear, I know,' she soothed, reaching a table by the wall and depositing the Bastard on top of it. 'Maybe the next time will be better, now you have the gods by your side.'

'I'm in no hurry to find out, lady,' the Bastard said with a shiver.

Something occurred to him then. He frowned up at her from his haunches.

'What d'you mean, the next time?'

Aaliyaa revealed a large knife from within her cloak.

'Uh oh,' gulped the Bastard.

'Don't worry about a thing,' she said lightly, running a whetstone down the blade. 'The gods smile upon you, little dog. This is only a technicality, a shedding of your physical bonds in order to Ascend.'

260

'Love, I don't need to Ascend, trust me on this,' he said quickly, scuttling away on toenails that needed clipping.

'Once you sacrifice yourself for the final time, death will no longer be a problem,' she coaxed, bringing the blade closer.

'I don't want to be sacrificed again – let me alone!'

'You've been a good servant, you deserve a reward—'

'A biscuit would suffice!'

A slam sounded of wood on wood.

'Hello, Mother.'

'Oh, thank God,' the Bastard groaned, sinking onto his belly.

Ron approached his mother warily, his lips pressed tightly together.

His eyes widened. He halted a few yards away, his hand over his mouth in horror.

She looked like a rotting corpse.

She had once been quite a good looking woman of forty-eight years, but now...

Her hair was burnt in several places and there was scarcely any of it left, either – charred bald patches shone wetly on her scalp through the sparse strands that were left. Her face and neck matched it, part red, part black and crusty.

Standing in front of an exploding church will do that to you, thought the Bastard wryly – she got off lightly, all things considered.

'What do *you* want?' Aaliyaa asked, her voice hoarse.

'I could ask you the same question,' he said, his hand over his nose. She still smelled of burnt flesh – the smell travelled for *yards*. 'Explain about the dragons, Mother.'

Aaliyaa froze. 'So you *were* with her.'

'You knew this,' he reminded her.

'I didn't want to believe it,' she seethed, stepping forward, knife still in hand. 'That my son would socialise with the likes of the Antichrist.'

'Lilly might not be as *lovely* as you are,' Ron drawled, 'but she's not as bad as all that.'

'I should have known since you were born,' Aaliyaa snarled. 'You're nothing but a heathen that relished in causing your brother grief.'

'Oh, are we name-calling now?' he asked with a mad grin. 'I've got a word for you, if that's what we're doing.' He leaned forward on his toes. '*Incest.*'

Aaliyaa froze.

Ron lifted a letter into the air, bearing King Samuel's seal, which was broken.

'Now, I'm no expert,' he said casually, 'but when the crown prince of the realm has a mummy and daddy who are half-brother and -sister, I gather that goes against some of the laws around here. Nature.'

Aaliyaa inhaled shakily in silent fury.

261

'… marriage… the *gods*. You know, the laws that can kill you if you break them. Still, you did your wifely duty in the end, as is clearly evident.'

He gestured down at himself.

'Which is a relief for me.'

Aaliyaa pursed her lips and rolled them from side to side.

'Now that we have our parentage cleared up,' Ron said lightly, tucking the letter safely into his jacket, 'I have a little job for you. Declare Vladimir and his son illegitimate so that the true heir can claim the throne.' He smiled. 'That's me!'

'Why would I want to do that?' she asked coldly.

'Because there's a crew working for Mister Emmett that are looking for you,' he said without missing a beat. 'And they're not looking to ask you over for tea.'

Her eyes narrowed. 'Why should I believe you?'

'Because I have brought you Lilly-Anna Crey.'

She chortled wryly. It sounded like gravel shifting underfoot. 'I thought she was your friend?'

'I can make new ones. I'm charismatic, you know. Get that from my father.'

'I still don't believe you.'

'You should,' a voice said from the doorway. 'He's telling the truth.'

Ron turned amiably to Marbrand as he strolled casually to the middle of the slaughterhouse.

'You turned to the Creys, why on earth would I possibly believe you want rid of her?'

'I turned to Creys to keep an eye on what King Samuel was doing,' he explained. 'When he died, I thought it was the opportune moment to get the wheels in motion. What the Hornes didn't realise after the Battle in the Orchard was that ghostly territory is still, above all, *territory*. Territory someone should have claimed a long time ago.'

'When you declare me the sole rightful heir, I shall finish what my grandfather started,' Ron said grandly. 'I'm going to take over Truphoria. And Antichrist or not, we can't have Lilly getting in the way. I already have the Forest – my marriage to Queen Qattren has made certain of that. Now I just need one more ally – and who better to lay my trust on than my own mother?'

Aaliyaa glared at him scornfully.

'Greed is the sin that led to your brother's death,' she told him soberly. 'I will not participate in such games.'

Ron blinked. 'You what?'

'My issue with the Crey girl is solely of spiritual concern,' she continued. 'She is the Antichrist, come to the Dead Lands to claim her accomplice, the Dragon. I have done away with all candidates for that position. All that is left is the Antichrist herself.'

Ron hesitated, his bluff fading.

262

'No way of changing your mind, then?'

Aaliyaa half-smiled. 'I knew you were lying to me.'

She raised her knife.

Marbrand raised Pointy.

Her gaze flickered from Marbrand to Ron.

'I can kill your friend Sadie right here, you know,' she said conversationally. 'Or you can give me the Crey girl and leave with your sole remaining father figure intact.'

Ron held eye contact with his mother for a moment.

'Bring her in,' he told Marbrand without breaking eye contact.

Marbrand bowed his head and sidled to the door, lowering his blade behind him slowly.

They waited a moment as Lilly was dragged in by one elbow, her hair askew.

Marbrand pulled her between the Hornes and threw her to her knees.

'Have you any last words?' Aaliyaa snarled, stepping forward to lay her blade at Lilly's throat.

'Yeah,' Lilly replied softly, holding eye contact. 'How did you know it was me?'

Aaliyaa snorted.

'You think you were being discreet?' she sneered. 'Whoring yourself out to the Ambassador and his son, to search their sanctuary for your accomplice? It was obvious.' She licked her lips with a smile. 'But there was just one problem with your plan. You didn't realise that the Knight of Thorns was at your throat the entire time.'

Ron blinked. 'Who, me?'

'Hardly,' Aaliyaa spat. 'You're nothing but the Devil's string puppet, as you ever have been. I speak of another, one true of soul and kind of heart.'

'What, the dog?' Lilly said belligerently.

'The dog is a reincarnation of Seth Crey's bastard child,' Marbrand sneered. 'Are you aware of that? Qattren of the forest kingdom informed us. I'm surprised it's eluded your attention that you've been going around the countryside with the undead nephew of the Antichrist.'

Aaliyaa turned to give the dog a foul glance.

The Bastard cowered, his tail between his legs.

'I'll deal with *that* in a moment,' she hissed through her teeth. 'But to answer your question, no, I don't speak of the *dog*. I speak of the man you call Stanley Carrot – the Saviour, the fourth Christ, and my intended lover.'

The door swung open fully and a wide-eyed Stan stared in.

'Eh?' he exclaimed.

'Yes!' she exclaimed back, smiling radiantly at him. 'The gods have decreed us a match. Together we will create the child of the world, the combined incarnation of the Seven Gods.'

'But you're *old!*' Stan howled.

'They're pulling your leg, Mum,' Ron said incredulously.

'The Seven Gods have decreed it, it must be true!' she snapped.

'I've met them, they're not nice people,' Ron said.

'Blasphemy!'

'Oh, everything's blasphemy to you!' Ron snapped in annoyance.

'Enough.'

She swept forward, past Lilly and Ron and Marbrand to where Stan was shuffling hastily backwards.

She lunged forward and clutched his hands in her own. They squelched as one of her blisters popped, emitting a foul odour.

'Come,' she hastened, pulling him into the room.

'No,' Stan strained against her grasp, 'you need medical attention on *many* levels—'

She pressed the handle of the knife into his right hand.

'Expel the hell-bringer and join me in the marital hall of the gods.'

Stan shook his head slowly.

Aaliyaa glared at him. 'Why not?'

'As to the obvious reasons about our union, I'll leave those unspoken,' Stan said wisely. 'But killing Lilly… no, I can't do it. Not with my bare hands like that. It's not right.'

She gazed at him. 'I agree.' She took back the knife.

Ron breathed a sigh of relief.

So did Stan, assuming she had a change of heart regarding the union.

Aaliyaa took a small knitted doll from her cloak and handed it to him instead.

His face fell.

'Break her neck using this,' she whispered. 'Spilling blood is a sin unto the Seven, I see now that you are right. *This* is how it should be done.'

Lilly stared at it in horror.

'What have you been using that for?' she asked fearfully. 'Have you been making that persistent itch in my—'

'Silence!' Aaliyaa barked, to everyone's relief.

She pressed the doll in Stan's hands.

He looked from it to Aaliyaa's knife to the doll to Lilly helplessly.

'I don't want to kill *full stop*,' he elaborated.

Aaliyaa tutted and leaned a hand on her hip.

'If you don't, I'll have to find a new Knight of Thorns who will,' she said harshly. 'Which means you'll have to die. Kill or be killed. Your choice.'

Stan trembled.

Lilly stared at him pleadingly.

Bizarrely, Stan noticed Lilly's dog nodding at him.

'Do it,' Albie told him. 'It'll be fine, I promise. Go for it.'

Stan gazed at him in bemusement. When did he start talking Truphorian?

He gazed at Lilly again apologetically and decided to trust the dog.

264

Lilly squeezed her eyes shut in dread.

He pinched the doll's head in his right fist and the shoulders in the left and twisted sharply.

Ron flinched.

Aaliyaa gasped.

Lilly opened her eyes.

Aaliyaa's head was facing the wrong way.

Ron watched in horror as his mother froze for a moment before flopping to the ground.

Stan dropped the doll to the floor. 'Ron, I'm so sorry!'

The Bastard leapt from the table, tottered over Aaliyaa's corpse and licked Lilly's hand on his way out.

'You're welcome, Aunty,' he said behind him.

They watched him leave.

'This whole hour has been extremely odd in every sense,' Marbrand said distantly.

'You're telling me,' said Lilly. 'It... makes sense poetically that Seth begot an actual dog after running around like a bitch on heat last year, but... it's still slightly weird.'

'Just a bit,' Marbrand agreed.

Stan stared at Aaliyaa's lifeless body.

She stared unseeing into the ceiling.

'I've made you an orphan,' he squeaked.

Ron watched him piteously.

'Wasn't your fault,' he told him softly. 'She handed you the wrong doll by mistake. You weren't to know.'

'But I was intending to kill Lilly!' he exclaimed. 'Because the dog... told me to.'

He eyed Lilly.

'No hard feelings,' Lilly assured him.

They decided to slip out quietly then.

All except for Marbrand, who hung back to search Aaliyaa's corpse for any more dolls.

He didn't find a single doll of Lilly anywhere.

~

VI

'What do you mean, we're leaving?' Seth yelled.

'I mean, the captain says we have to leave for home, sir,' Elliot stammered.

The Creys had been duly chucked out of the Ambassador's mansion as soon as his body had re-entered it. Eleanor had been dragged weeping away from him as he lay open-mouthed on a sheet in the main hall, his son lying alongside him.

Shame, Seth thought. He'd liked Orl.

They now stood on a pier of Portmyr's docks, waiting alongside the *Devourer* for Marbrand to show up. Seth rubbed under his armpits, wiping pools of sweat away with a grimace.

'We're not going anywhere until he brings my sister back!'

'He'll find his own way back with her, he's good like that. Please get on the ship, sir, you're causing a scene—'

'I don't care!' he shrieked, throwing his arms wide.

A passing deckhand ducked out of the way.

'What would you do if I was making you leave your baby sister to be killed in a strange country?'

'I don't have a baby sister, sir, I wouldn't know,' Elliot admitted.

'But what if you did?'

'She wouldn't be a looker,' he said, pointing at his own face.

Seth pulled his hair with a mad grimace.

'You have... no empathy whatsoever! It's like your brain is broken! Did your mother give you any wits at all?'

'Naw, got my dad's brains, unfortunately,' he said ruefully, shaking his head. 'Right thicky, actually, my dad. Had the same name as your little boy, did you know that?'

'Oh yeah, that's encouraging,' Seth muttered.

'Seth!' a thin voice screeched.

Lilly threw herself bodily into his arms, her elbows wrapped around his neck.

Seth nearly toppled into the water.

'Lilly!' he exclaimed, regaining balance.

'Mission accomplished,' Marbrand said tiredly, strolling past to board the ship. 'Time for a beer.'

Seth snatched Lilly's head by both sides and turned it this way and that.

'Are you alright? What did they do?'

'Nothing, I'm fine,' she said, her eyes streaming.

'They didn't rape you or—' Seth pressed urgently.

'No.'

'Why are you crying, then?' he asked gently, wiping her eyes.

'I thought you might have died in there,' she choked, 'I didn't know if you were okay, I didn't want to think of you being pulled out of there on a, on a—'

'Alright, alright, Lilly, it's alright,' he soothed.

She pressed her face into his collar and sobbed noisily.

He squeezed her ribs and planted a kiss on her cheek, without even cleaning it first.

Elliot watched them with a smile. 'Aw. 's like that play they show in Arthur Stibbons Street, you know, the one where they die in each other's arms?'

Seth scowled at him and mouthed an alternative to 'go away'.

Elliot boarded the ship, affronted.

Seth deposited Lilly onto her feet and stroked her hair back.

'Come on,' he said quietly. 'Let's go home.'

He led her onto the ship ahead of him.

Stan and Ron followed closely behind them, both looking morose. Ron eyed Stan and clapped a hand on his shoulder.

Seth draped an arm around Lilly's neck and steered her to her cabin, and she felt a little better.

~

Aaliyaa didn't feel well.

The chapel she suddenly found herself in was awfully familiar. Its walls were bronzed with stained oak and adorned with portraits of the Seven.

'Aaliyaa,' Geldemar said in interest. 'What went wrong, my dear?'

She eyed the other Six sitting silently around the ellipse-shaped table behind him.

'The girl,' she said dejectedly. 'Despina... her doll didn't work. I could not gain control... I couldn't bend her will, it belonged to another...'

'The dog?' he asked gently.

Aaliyaa frowned in thought.

'But,' she began, 'but the dog was pushing her. Yes. He was pushing her to my cause. He directed the monks to the Creys, and her friends to follow them, so none of them could stop me. Yes, that was it. That's why I left their dolls behind.'

'But what went wrong with Lilly-Anna, Aaliyaa?' he asked again.

She paused. 'I killed myself. I handed Stanley my doll instead of hers. I made my own doll, you see, to protect myself from the sorceress, and...'

Her face fell.

'I never made a Lilly-Anna doll, did I?'

'Nope.'

'Oh dear.'

'You handed a perfect stranger your life,' Geldemar said.

'Her path was already laid out! It showed Stanley as the Knight of Thorns! My visions from you decreed it!'

'They decreed that he murdered Lilly, which to your knowledge he did... until you *died*. You couldn't have known to the contrary...' He grinned. 'Which was exactly the point.'

She frowned for a moment. 'Does this mean I get an Ascension?'

He gazed at her and slowly shook his head.

Geldemar and the other Six faded from view then, and their surroundings melted away, leaving nothing but a black room, dimly lit.

To her horror, King Theo grinned at her, a scarred doppelgänger of Seth Crey at his side.

'Can I do her in?' the Bastard asked excitedly. 'Go on, let me do her in!'

'... ALRIGHT, GO FOR IT,' Theo decided.

Seth's marred copy pointed a finger at Aaliyaa and said, 'Pew!'

A bolt of lightning struck her between the eyes. She was obliterated before she knew what was happening.

'I LIKE THE LIGHTNING, THAT WAS A NICE TOUCH,' King Theo said in approval.

~

'I've been deceived again, haven't I?'

Qattren looked nonplussed. 'I haven't the slightest idea what you mean.'

Seth watched his country slide along beside him and waved as a few fishermen cheered at him.

'We left yesterday,' he gritted through a wide, fake grin.

Qattren blinked. 'So?'

'I don't like being exploded!' he exclaimed.

'You didn't bat an eyelid at the time.'

'I was *asleep*! You *violated* me!'

'I didn't *violate* you, I made the journey home a little faster. I thought you might want to come home to see your children, before you die of old age and suchlike.'

'I *told you*,' Seth snarled through his teeth, still grinning at his subjects, 'I didn't want anything to do with your silly fairyland! This is violation of my... dust,' he trailed off angrily.

Lilly ascended to the top deck blearily. 'I take it by your shouting that we've arrived early, then.'

'Nearly,' Seth said. 'How are you feeling?'

'Like shit.'

He smiled thinly at her and turned his gaze to the approaching port.

A small crowd had gathered on the pier to watch them make port. This was unusual by Seth and Lilly's standards: the only crowds that ever gathered to greet them in Serpus stopped for a snack first while the execution got going. The small-folk clearly tended to appreciate unarmed celebrities more in the countryside.

Unfortunately, the head of the crowd was the Half-Prince of Portabella, who waved cheerfully at Queen Eleanor and quickly commenced a fit of babbling.

'Queen Cienne has sent me to receive your arrival, your highnesses,' the translator said over him, 'and to send our condolences on the untimely deaths of—'

'I don't know what you're saying!' Queen Eleanor snapped at the two of them furiously. 'Get out of my way!'

She stormed to the imperial coach ahead, the crowd parting wisely to let her pass.

Seth gazed at his brother-in-law, the beginnings of an idea blossoming. He stored it away for later and ushered him out of the way, gently leading Lilly in front of him.

Qattren followed behind, proceeding to ignore the civilians as usual.

A familiar face popped out of the throng.

Seth's face smiled at her faintly, a scar running down the left side.

Qattren stopped in her tracks.

The real Seth Crey glanced back at her impatiently. 'What's wrong with you?'

Her gaze flitted from the real Seth to the scarred double and back again.

'Nothing,' she said faintly.

Seth rolled his eyes and jogged to catch up with Lilly.

The Bastard on the other hand tugged on his forelock in respect. He leaned forward in the crowd until he and Qattren were a foot away from each other.

'Shall we meet at your place, say, first Thursday of summer?'

Qattren blinked and reached out to grab him.

Her hand instead found the wrist of a middle-aged man, who eyed Qattren fearfully.

She blinked a few more times and released her iron grip.

'Sorry, I… thought you were someone else.'

A minute passed before she sheepishly released his arm entirely.

The man bowed in thanks.

When she got on the coach after Seth, she examined him thoroughly before scanning the crowd again. The double was, of course, gone.

PART FIVE: THE CHRISTENING

I

ome weeks passed as the spring turned to summer. The lords of Deight and Ryene happily lent them lodgings throughout the journey, more hesitantly in Qattren's case, which she nevertheless declined. She never liked staying indoors overnight and besides, unbeknownst to her companions, she had an appointment.

'Can't we go and visit the twins?' Ron asked her eagerly on the last week of spring. 'I love babies.'

'You have a nephew of your own,' Seth said dubiously. 'Go love your own babies.'

Qattren gave him a sharp look and turned to Ron.

'I have an appointment at home, on Thursday week. You're free to stay with Lilly, if you wish.' She paused. 'In fact, it would probably be a better idea for me to be there alone. The meeting might prove to be quite… delicate.'

Seth gave her a funny glance, partly because of her 'appointment' but mostly to reciprocate for the funny looks she had been giving him since they left the ship.

A couple of days passed, with Lilly looking desolate despite Seth's best attempts at amateur comedy. Stan and Ron made her laugh for an hour or so with a hastily-prepared sock puppet adaptation of 'Knighty-Knight Salamander' until the main character died and reminded her that she was supposed to be grieving.

Spirits raised considerably at the gates of Serpus. The coach made a beeline north, and a day later they met Cienne at the doors of the keep.

Seth drained a goblet of wine and, feeling a little tipsy, lifted his wife into the air in a bear hug.

She giggled uncontrollably and yelped, 'Ow!' as her head hit the top of the doorframe.

'You're back early,' she said as Seth lowered her back onto ground level.

'That was Qattren's fault. I'll tell you after I've eaten something. Where are my children?' he bellowed into the throne room, vanishing inside.

Cienne watched him in amusement and turned to her mother-in-law. 'How much has he had to drink?'

'No more than me. I wish it would make me that cheerful,' she said glumly.

Cienne embraced her. 'I'm so sorry. To both of you.'

Lilly tried to slip past unnoticed.

''s alright,' she muttered.

She ignored Cienne's offer of a hug and made a beeline to the kitchen.

Despina was inside, relinquishing a small child to Seth.

'Hello, Ginny!' he trilled. 'Look how big you've got! Look at you! Look at her!'

He shoved the child in Lilly's face.

'It's like she's a different child!'

'That *is* a different child,' Despina said with the relief of someone who had finally got a word in edgeways. '*That's* Russell.'

Seth's face went blank and he squinted at his son again.

'Oh. They... look very alike.'

He handed him back in embarrassment and proceeded to attack the lunch tray.

Lilly sat opposite her nephew and rubbed his head.

'Can I have a cuddle?' she asked suddenly.

Despina sat the twelve-week-old baby on Lilly's lap.

He turned his head upwards to squint at her intently. There was something of Seth in that squint, she noticed with a half-smile.

'He's just been fed,' Despina warned, 'so he might throw up on you.'

Seth turned with his mouth full and frowned down at Despina's notable lack of lactating cleavage.

'*You* fed him?'

He waved a sceptical hand at her bosom.

'We bottle feed them now,' she said in disgust, folding her arms. 'The farm has bottles for feeding orphaned lambs with. We clean them first,' she said to Seth's horrified expression.

'They're not farm animals. Why isn't *she* feeding them?'

'She burst into tears last time and claimed they were milking her to death. You were here that day, remember?'

'Yes, but I was trying *not* to be.'

Russell looked Lilly up and down as best he could from her lap and tugged on her shirt, just in case.

Lilly buried her nose in what sparse amount of hair he had.

'I'm probably never going to have one of these,' she said.

'You have more of a chance than I do,' Despina told her.

'Why's that?' Seth asked curiously, scratching his son's head where a patch of cradle cap was developing.

'I just have... problems.'

Marbrand poked his head in the door and nodded Despina over.

She made her apologies and jogged out, leaving the three Creys alone together.

'It'll get better, Lilly,' Seth told her, patting her head.

'I don't think I'm made for marriage,' she said. 'No one else gets half a wedding procession slaughtered before the event was even planned.'

Russell tried vainly to pull Lilly's shirt strings open, gave up and decided to chew them instead.

Seth paused. 'Do you want to stay with him for a bit while I find Ginny?'

'Okay,' she murmured. 'I need some time on my own, anyway.'

Seth nodded and left them to it.

$\sim$

Some yards below the surface of the Forest, Qattren sat imperiously in her throne, a dark green gown embracing her slim form and pooling onto the ground. She waited.

All the servitude had deserted the hall, leaving Qattren alone with nothing but a mural of a phoenix for company. Looking for something to do, Qattren shed herself and entered Sal'plae.

'You took your time,' he said with a smile.

He was his father's son all right. Seth Crey stared back at her with Adrienne's eyes, his fair hair cropped to the same length and his clothes matching his father's funeral attire. He even had the scars to prove it: one long mark cascading down his left temple down to the side of his nose, and countless other minor cuts down the side of his neck. All he needed was a name, but Qattren could feel one pushing into her consciousness without provocation. The Bastard.

Qattren did not smile back.

'How are you?' she asked simply.

He shrugged as simply as she had asked.

'Green suits you,' he commented.

'I wish you wouldn't change the subject. I hate when people do that.' She observed him carefully. No son could be his father's exact copy. It had to be an illusion. 'How did you come to be here with us, after what happened to you? It can't have been easy, surviving oblivion.'

'It wasn't nice, at any rate,' he agreed.

They paused.

'How are you doing?'

She blinked. 'Why should you care enough to ask?'

'You did.'

Her heart sank. 'Not enough to help you a year ago.'

'It wasn't your job to.'

She licked her lips. 'What was it like? That day...'

273

He shrugged. 'Hard to describe it, really. It was black, but it was warm, and I knew she was there and everything was alright.' He paused, stroking his scar. 'Then there was pain and everything went white, and then everything went *dark* again and it hurt a lot *more* and then I became this.' He shrugged nonchalantly. 'Means to an end, I suppose.'

She regarded him. 'You want revenge.'

He shook his head, meeting her gaze. 'I only want an apology.'

'But words won't do.'

He licked his lips, confirming Qattren's statement.

'It was terrifying,' he informed her. '*Utterly* terrifying. Total, absolute oblivion, separation from all of reality. Even after it's happened, it scares you, because you're never sure it won't happen again, more permanently this time.' He tore his gaze to the ground. 'You probably know all this already.'

'I never died before.' She watched the quizzical look on his face. 'I'm not one of you.'

He blinked. 'I thought you were.'

She shrugged. 'I'm different.'

He scowled. 'Lucky you.'

Qattren watched him piteously. 'Does your father know you're alive?'

She'd said the wrong thing. The Bastard's face twisted in fury.

'Alive?' he echoed. 'You call this being alive?'

He started unfastening his jacket before pointing at the scar over his nose. 'You think this is the only scar I was left with since the day of my birth?'

Qattren watched uneasily as he pulled up his undershirt.

His torso was criss-crossed with scars. It was as though every tree and animal collected by the Hole had collided with him, slicing and scratching him over and over. It was a terrifying thought.

'He doesn't believe in leaving things to metaphor,' he sneered.

He jerked his shirt over the scars once more, leaving his jacket hanging open.

'People who are alive have homes to go to at the end of the day,' he snarled. 'People who are alive have possessions, and favourite foods, and people who love them. Parents. *Mothers,*' he added in a hiss.

'Not necessarily,' Qattren said, gesturing to herself.

He snorted. 'You're different. And I'm nothing.'

Qattren paused for a moment before rising to her feet. 'You aren't nothing. You're just a child.'

His eyes narrowed, much like the way Seth's did when, well, whenever he caught sight of Qattren, really.

'Who brought you back?' she asked gently.

His eyes became like chips of ice. 'I'm not at liberty to tell you that,' he said coldly.

Qattren held his gaze, her own face warm and sympathetic.

'If you need someone to love you,' she said, 'I'll be that person. We're the same, me and you – apart from the fact that you died and I did not. If your mother didn't want you…'

She took his hand in hers.

'… then I'll have you.'

He slid his hand from hers. 'I'll do things you won't like.'

'Have you met Geldemar?' she asked wryly. 'We're quite close friends. He's not called a devil for nothing. You should know.'

He shook his head.

She frowned. 'They didn't resurrect you?'

'Nope.' He turned to leave.

'Wait!' she called as he faded from view. 'You're His, aren't you? Tell me what He's done to you!'

He didn't reply. He faded away entirely, leaving Qattren alone once more.

A frown tarnished her youthful features.

'Geldemar!' she roared.

~

'I've had an idea,' Seth began. 'Don't say no straight away.'

Lilly glared at him through her eyelashes.

They were sitting in the council chamber in the east antechamber, just Seth and Lilly. It was very suspicious, she thought with her eyes narrowed.

'You're marrying me off again, aren't you?'

Seth breathed in. 'Yes.'

Lilly rolled her eyes and punched the table they were sitting at.

Seth felt it rattle against his elbow. He removed it with trepidation.

'Let me guess,' she snarled. 'He was born at the turn of the millennium and his only child is a bastard son. Does he have a sanctuary of dragons or is the one quite enough for you?'

'No. This is different,' Seth said, timidly. He noted she had slightly *dented* the table top and refrained from correcting her on the situation regarding the dragons. 'Please listen.'

Lilly sighed. It sounded like a growl.

'You remember we met Cienne's brother at the docks?'

'The girly-looking one?' She recalled that he was almost as pretty as his half-sister. 'Yeah, why? Isn't he worth naff all because he's from the second wife or something?'

'Yes. That's why I'm marrying him to you.'

Lilly frowned and shook her head. 'Why?'

'I'll tell you,' Seth said with an eager smile, leaning his elbows on the table to gesticulate as he talked. 'He prefers the company of men.'

'Ha, ha, marry him to the butch—'

275

'No, no, that's not why,' he interrupted. 'He prefers the company of men, because women *repulse* him. I've spoken to Cienne about this. Apparently, they've been throwing women at him for years, trying to get him to turn, and he won't touch them. He's not interested. They've given up. But they still need to marry him to someone.'

Lilly listened.

'They need to marry him to someone, but there isn't a woman in all of the five continents who'll have him if he won't touch them. It's insulting, isn't it? Being married to someone who finds you disgusting. Unless,' he said, with another smile, 'you happen to need a marriage to get the council off your back, but not to make an heir. And here we are.'

Lilly raised an eyebrow. 'You want me to marry Cienne's girly little brother?'

'And stay here with us,' he finished brightly. 'He can bugger off to the mother country with an extra knot in the alliance with Adem and do whatever he's doing now, and you can do the same. Only you'll be staying at home. With us.' He lifted his eyebrows. 'What do you think?'

Lilly glared at him. 'I think there's a catch.'

'There isn't!' he said excitedly. 'That's the *beauty* of it! He doesn't need an heir! He's void. His mother's void. All of his siblings are void, except for Cienne. Our children are the only ones they can pass on their country to, and I have that covered times two! At least! Neither of you have to do anything! And if something does happen,' he added, nodding at Lilly's abdomen, 'you know, out in the gutter or wherever it is you do it, then we can say he did it during a visit or something! We'll lie to everyone, who's going to care?'

'Don't I have to… you know,' she said uncomfortably. 'At least once?'

'Did Qattren and Ronald Horne do it at least once?' he asked, sceptical.

'Good point,' she conceded. 'But his family will want proof.'

'His family have no choice,' he said gleefully. 'He's not going to produce a child anyway, what does it matter? What else are they going to do with him?'

A smile crept across Lilly's face. He was starting to convince her.

'And you think Cienne's brother will agree to this?'

'He's got his eye on the translator, by the look of it,' Seth said in a gossipier tone. 'I think he'll be over the moon.'

Lilly smiled openly at this. Then her face turned serious.

'I want half the dowry, though.'

'What? What d'you want that for, you get to stay here, you don't have to remarry—'

'He's not interested in women, you said so yourself,' she said with a wink. 'I need something to entertain myself with.'

Seth made a face. 'The Crook, I presume?'

Lilly nodded in earnest.

Seth grimaced and, eventually, nodded.

'Just… don't catch anything, alright?' he added. 'That includes babies – you're more of the "mad aunty" type anyway. Babies is *my* department now. You leave the babies to me.'

Lilly snorted with laughter.

~

Outside, Sir Marbrand was looking worried.

'What's wrong?' Despina asked him as they loitered outside the main portcullis.

Miriam came over.

'Oh,' she said darkly. 'That's what's wrong.'

'You have some explaining to do,' Miriam growled.

'I do, don't I?' Marbrand said with a gulp. 'Well, Miriam—'

'Not you, Sadie,' she said scathingly. '*Her.*'

He blinked.

'Despina?' he asked, nonplussed. 'Don't you want to know why I buggered off while you were expecting our child?'

'I couldn't care less, if I'm perfectly honest,' she snarled. 'I want to know what the hell *she's* been doing here with her magic.'

Marbrand looked confused. 'Magic?'

'You were *supposed* to tell *nobody*!' Despina hissed.

'And *you* were supposed to stay put! I spent a year looking for you! You've been gone for over a year and you never thought to—where are you going?'

Despina barged past her angrily and stalked off.

'Despina!' Miriam shouted, making to follow.

'Oi!' Marbrand grabbed her elbow. 'Who's Despina to you?'

'Don't you recognise her? I suppose not, you never clapped eyes on her before now, did you?' she snarled. 'She's your daughter!'

His eyes widened. 'My… *our* daughter? But you were pregnant over twenty years ago! Our kid must be nearly twenty-one, Despina only looks thirteen!'

'That comes from your side of the family,' Miriam seethed. '*My* family never had any involvement with witchcraft!'

'I dunno, your sister Beth always struck me as—*are you telling me she's been a sorceress the entire time and nobody had the bloody gall to tell me*??' he shrieked.

'You weren't bloody there! And you know what, now that you're so concerned with her, you can deal with it!'

She thrust a small sack of belongings into his arms.

'She's living with you, I'm not having sorcery in my house, its unholy. She's your problem now.'

Marbrand watched his wife stride away haughtily, and turned his gaze to the bag in his hand. He hoisted it onto one shoulder and jogged after Despina.

He found her five minutes later in the same spot he first discovered her before their journey, sitting against the wall with her knees tucked under her chin.

'She was going to have me exorcised by a priest,' she mumbled.

'I take it you don't mean the jogging kind?'

'Alas, no.' She scowled at the ground. 'Her and Aunt Beth, they had it out for me, thought I was ill or summink. That's why I ran away.'

'I figured.'

She fell silent as he set her bag of belongings on the ground next to her.

'You know,' he said gently, 'you could have let me know it was my daughter I was saving from those rapists.'

'Sorry,' she said in a small voice. 'Should have also told you I had magical powers during all that with Aaliyaa and the monks—'

'Would have made things easier,' he cut in.

She hid her face between her knees.

'I thought you'd shun me. I never liked doing it anyway, I could never make it do what I wanted... except for slight manipulation.'

She glanced up at him. 'Sorry.'

He shook his head.

'None of that. I don't trust sorcery, but you're no Aaliyaa Horne. Your grandmother gave you that, I reckon. I'm sure she used to use sorcery to do the dishes.'

She smiled slightly and looked up at him.

To his slight alarm, she got up and hugged him around the ribs, hard.

He wrapped an arm around her shoulders and rubbed her head with his free hand.

'Looks like I'll be needing a new house from the king after all.'

She smiled into his leathers.

'As long as you abide by my rules and make the tea, that is. *Without* cheating.'

She laughed shortly. 'You're sure you want a witch living in your house?'

'Anything's better than working for Aaliyaa Horne. She used to sacrifice Ronald's pet dogs, the bloody savage. But she must have had difficulty with other sorceresses,' he said in sudden realisation. 'Which suddenly explains why she threw away your doll. It obviously didn't work.'

'I don't think that's all of it.'

He tilted his head down. 'Why?'

She hesitated. 'I never said this earlier only because I thought you would get hurt.'

He tapped her on the head. 'About what?'

She lifted her face towards his. 'She couldn't get into my head because there was already someone in there. Someone not quite... human. Or technically alive.'

Marbrand frowned. 'A ghost, is it?'

278

'Maybe.'

'Do you know his name? Is he still in there?'

She shook her head. 'I haven't seen or heard from him since we left the Dead Lands. I don't think he has a name. He's just called the Bastard.'

Marbrand frowned into space. 'What did he want from you?'

'I don't really know... he just wanted you to stay away from the Emmetts. He threatened to hurt you and Mum if I let you...'

He regarded her in concern.

'If he comes back,' he told her, 'tell me immediately.'

'I will,' she promised, truthfully.

He gave her a nod and a faint smile.

Lilly lay back on the grass, staring into the sky.

The back gardens of the palace consisted of a dozen spiralling paths, an alternating pattern of concrete and grass and flowers with a circle of grass in the centre. Lilly lay in one such circle of grass, in a spiral just outside the front entrance of the chapel, her arms and legs splayed out around her. The tips of her fingers barely touched the gravel.

A silhouette poked his head over hers.

'Don't kill me straight away,' Tully said.

Lilly squinted at him, swinging an arm over her brow.

'I just want to apologise,' Tully said, wringing his hands. 'About the wedding.'

She sat upright, leaning her weight on her palms. Purple blotches marred her view of Tully's face. She'd been bathing morosely in her own grief for longer than she thought.

'I had no idea Si was planning that,' he said, crouching to meet her gaze. 'He must have plotted it while I was at the top of that bloody great dick-shaped pillar outside. I would have done something sooner if I knew.'

'I know,' she said softly. 'Thank you for looking after my mum.'

Tully smiled weakly. 'We still mates?'

'Of course we are.'

He deflated in relief.

Lilly met his gaze, unsmiling.

'I hope you're alright with Si dying at some point in the near future.'

The smile slid from his face.

'Seth has sent out a search warrant for him,' Lilly continued, keeping eye contact. 'He says he's going to bring him to the Tower and kill him for me. Seems to have forgotten I'm more than capable of carrying that out myself.'

Tully nodded slowly.

'Seth sounds like a good brother.' His expression hardened. 'Wish all of us were so lucky.'

Lilly turned her gaze back to the clouds.

They sat in silence for a moment, musing.

'He loved you,' Tully said.

Lilly closed her eyes. 'What d'you mean?'

'The way he was around you... he bloody loved you. I could tell. He treated you like a little sister. He never stopped talking about you. I would never have thought he'd do this to you.'

Lilly's mouth hardened into a thin line. 'Neither did I.'

She dropped her head to gaze at the flowers. 'Where are you staying?'

'Some inn in Castlefoot Market. Bloody expensive, but since Seth's paying for it to reward me...'

Lilly smiled at that. 'Make sure to run up a nice fat tab for him.'

'Obviously.'

They smiled at each other.

'Thinking of going off to Breaker's Hold,' he said after a moment.

'What's there?'

'Trade ships. Man can't live off the king's charity forever.'

'Be careful. All the trade from Portabella and Mellier come from there. Plenty of pirates around that area.'

'That's what I'm betting on,' Tully said with a wink.

Lilly grinned.

'You should come with,' he said, dropping cross-legged into the grass. 'Take over a pirate ship for real this time. Be a right laugh.'

'No thanks,' she said, her face falling. 'Bit put off after last time.'

Tully nodded.

'Shame, that,' he said. 'You were just getting good at it.'

Lilly beamed at him.

~

II

Seth followed Jimmy into the Tower, faced the white-clothed individual seated in the stool before them, and grinned.

'He came by a short while ago, but you were reacquainting yourself with the queen, so...' Jimmy trailed off, simply gesturing at him.

'Evening,' the Phantom Egg Flinger said amiably, his hands tied behind his back.

The bottom floor of the Tower was dimly lit via two bolt holes in the wall above the Egg Flinger's head, which was exactly the way Seth liked it. It showed scarce little in between the bare brick walls except for the three men and Seth's almost tangible glee.

'You're going to get the torturing of your life,' Seth said with relish.

'I notice you have no eggs upon your person,' the Egg Flinger said attentively. 'Thought that would be the first thing you'd have.'

'We ran out and that Jon bloke never came this week,' Jimmy explained.

'I think I can afford something a little more extravagant than that,' Seth said smugly, directing the Flinger's attention to the Iron Maiden in the corner of the dungeon. 'And we're not using that, by the way. We're going to be causing a lot more pain than that.'

'For chucking eggs at you?'

'Yes!' he spat.

He clicked his tongue off the roof of his mouth. 'Seems a bit harsh. It was only a joke.'

Seth raised an eyebrow.

'A joke?' he asked slowly. 'You went to the trouble of cracking raven eggs and whisking them into a paste to throw at me for a *joke*? Why go to so much trouble? Why be so calculated?'

'I have a lot of free time.'

'Yeah, but what point were you trying to make?' Jimmy asked. 'What did he do to you?'

''s not what he did,' he corrected. ''s what he's going to do to his children.'

Seth's expression turned icy.

'What are you insinuating?' he asked in a low tone.

'You're getting them christened, aren't you?'

'That's the usual idea with small children, yes.'

'That's why.'

'That's why what?' Seth snapped.

'Why I egged you.'

'You egged me because I'm getting my children christened?'

'Yup.'

'You're going to die,' Seth said lividly, raising a knife.

Jimmy halted him, pushing his arm down.

'What's that got to do with you?' Jimmy asked the masked man. 'If he wants to indoctrinate his children, that's his own business.'

'I just don't like it, that's all,' he said uncomfortably. 'You can't trust those robed bastards. They can get away with *anything*.'

Seth paused. 'That's true, but the grandmother insists on it.'

Jimmy rolled his eyes. 'You're not a king, sir, you're a wet wipe.'

Seth ignored him. 'Who do you think you are? To be telling me what to do with my children?'

'I'll be feeding them soon – eggs, anyway. That makes me half a parent, I reckon,' he said indignantly.

Seth's eyes widened in realisation. 'I see. I see *clearly*.'

He snatched the hat, then the mask from the Phantom Egg Flinger's face and threw them both to the side.

'The cow we take milk from doesn't try to parent our children,' he told Jon. 'Why should you?'

Jon shrugged. 'Maybe 'cause their father's a delinquent?'

The knife was pushed down again.

'I recognise you,' Seth said slowly.

Jon's smile took a hard edge.

'That'll be from the time you strung me upside down from the coach and fired arrows *at my head*,' he said, gritting the last three words through clenched teeth.

Jimmy threw Seth an accusing glance. 'What d'you do that for?'

'He was giving me a migraine,' Seth complained.

'I was just feeding my chickens!' Jon snapped. 'Thorough-bred, I might add, before you played golf with my best poultry and left me a dirty great scar on my eye.'

'I vote we string your majesty upside down from a coach and allow him to return the favour,' Jimmy suggested. 'It's only fair.'

'Whose side are you on, Jimmy?' Seth seethed at him. 'Do I need to remind you whose hearth you sleep at?'

'You mean *on*.' He jerked a thumb backwards at Seth's face. 'Treats me like a dog, this one.'

'Shame,' Jon said. 'You seem like a nice bloke.'

'Can we get back to the programme?' Seth said dryly.

Jimmy turned his attention back to Jon. 'What do you suppose we should do with you?'

'Let all this silly egg stuff pass under the bridge and hire me,' he said without hesitation. 'Oh, and kill the clergy.'

'Kill the clergy?' Seth said in disbelief. 'And provoke uproar throughout the entire country? Forget it.'

'Evict them, then,' he pressed in earnest. 'Give that big rainbow greenhouse at the back of the grounds to a tax-paying person that deserves it and leave them in the shit, where they belong.'

'Sounds like your dispute is with the church,' Jimmy said thoughtfully. 'Perhaps we should drop him off with the priest—'

'No, don't do that!' Jon's voice went shrill, like a small dog whose tail had been stepped on. 'I'll be good, I promise. Just hire me.'

'Hire you? You're clearly unhinged,' Jimmy scoffed.

'The dragon breathes fire, and you hired her,' Jon pointed out.

'The dragon's tame,' said Seth, then, 'Ish. Mostly. She's never thrown things at me, at any rate.'

'I know things, you have to hire me,' he told them.

'"Know things"?' Seth repeated. 'About what?'

'Stoneguard. The Emmett situation. You know, the bloke that's taxing you for his silence about blowing up that Horne bloke.'

A short silence ensued.

282

'It was an accident,' Seth said.

'Of course, the possibility that the man was bluffing could only have been extremely slim, couldn't it?' said Jimmy, rubbing his eyes.

'That's not all I know, either,' Jon said. 'But if you hire me, I'll keep it to meself and get you some info on him from a mate of mine who works for him. I don't go for that "assassin in the brickwork" bollocks, mind: that shit gets people killed.'

'We don't need information on them, we just need him to stop extorting us,' said Seth.

'By digging up something nasty to blackmail him in return,' Jon said. 'I know for a fact there's something hideous he did when he was a kid.'

'Brain his kid sister?' said Jimmy. 'Hardly takes a genius to figure that out, she's as thick as clotted shit.'

'Nope, complications during childbirth, kid was starved of air and nearly died,' Jon said in tones too bright for the subject matter. 'Everyone knows that.'

'I didn't,' said Jimmy, puzzled. 'I just thought it was the usual nobility incest thing.'

'At any rate,' Jon continued, 'should you decide to kill me, my friend will be waiting for a letter from me to arrive at his place in about... one week, and if it's not there, he's going to tell the whole world about what you did to Mister—'

'This is why you've handed yourself in?' Seth asked incredulously. 'To blackmail yourself into a job?'

'Pretty much.'

'Why do you want a job here so badly anyway?' Jimmy asked. 'I've worked here for nearly thirty years, it doesn't get any less shit.'

'I like the windows,' he said blithely. 'They're pretty.'

'Not when you're the one who has to clean them,' Jimmy said sourly.

Seth lifted an eyebrow and turned to Jimmy. 'What's the butler's butler called?'

'The footman, sir.'

'Is that an unpleasant job?'

'I can make it unpleasant,' said Jimmy happily.

'Right then, welcome aboard,' Seth said to Jon.

'I'm not going to get tortured, then?'

'Not all in one go, no,' Jimmy replied.

'Oh, that's alright, then. What about the church crap?'

'Still going ahead,' Seth said with malice.

'Particularly now we have someone to open and close the doors,' Jimmy added.

Jon's face morphed into an expression of profuse horror.

'*I'm* coming?'

'Oh, definitely,' Seth said with a smile. 'You can be our guest of honour.'

Jon eyed his new employer and tried not to look too wistfully at the Iron Maiden in the corner.

~

Gomez Emmett sent for Silas Beult and was relieved to encounter him fully clothed this time.

'Have you anything to say for that spectacle six weeks ago?'

Si shook his head meekly.

Emmett leaned his hands on the plan draft for the new keep and glared across the table at him, his elongated face blessed with acute irritation.

'Moments after you left my tent in the altogether, members of your crew began to make themselves apparent – also in the altogether. That would be thirty men popping into existence one after the other – in the *altogether*,' he added for emphasis, 'in front of my younger sister. Who was a rape victim.'

Si swallowed carefully.

'Aaliyaa Horne isn't quite as merciful, or indeed inventive, as that,' he went on. 'What happened?'

Si cleared his throat.

'We captured the bait for Aaliyaa, and her daughter-in-law showed up.' He licked his lips. 'She has a crude sense of humour, my lord.'

Emmett's eyes narrowed to slits, leaving the upper half of his face to consist of four black lines.

Si broke eye contact.

'What are you going to do with me?' Si mumbled.

Emmett folded his arms.

'You've proven yourself to be an incompetent captain,' he said, 'even with the comfort of being a secret one. Therefore, a place in the imperial navy is obviously out of the question.'

Si nodded miserably.

'However,' he said, 'due to the benefit your life plans prove to be to the future economy, I have no choice but to let you go free unscathed.'

Si blinked. 'Really?'

'I do not believe in the needless slaughter of future assets for mere reasons of indiscretion,' he said indifferently.

'Am I getting my ship back, then?'

'Oh God, no.'

Devastation swept across his face. 'Why not?'

'My little sister was very confused. It took two hours with a medic and several diagrams of the human anatomy to explain to her what—'

'Alright, I see your point,' Si said quickly. 'No ship. What am I supposed to do now?'

Emmett looked at him. Si could have sworn he saw a shadow of a smile cross his face, though no one would have believed him.

'That's up to you,' he said softly.

~

'Haven't you changed yet?' Eleanor snapped.

Seth moaned and rolled over onto his back. 'No, why?'

'It's your children's christening today!' Eleanor scolded. 'Go on, get dressed!'

'Tell them we're cancelling,' he said groggily, rolling back onto his face, the blanket cocooning him.

'No!'

A flurry of silk billowed onto his head.

'Put this on and go downstairs for breakfast,' the queen dowager said. 'Now!'

Seth groaned again and twisted around to scowl at the intricate embroidery of his apparent christening attire.

The queen had stemmed the flow of grief by throwing herself into the celebration arrangements. Heartbreak had sharpened her edges, Lilly observed, as the newly hired Jon got a scolding for his unkempt hair and a subsequent combing for his trouble.

'I've changed my mind, take me back to the Tower,' Jon gritted, the comb scoring lines into his scalp.

Lilly watched this in mild interest, her scrambled eggs untouched.

Seth jogged into the room in a hideous leotard of his mother's choosing. An infant hung from under each arm in identical frilly gowns.

'Cienne!' he said frantically. 'Which one's which?'

Cienne squinted from beside Lilly at the table.

'Ginny's under your right arm,' she replied.

He glanced down at his daughter, who giggled.

'Can someone take one of them? I've run out of arms.'

Cienne reached over the table and slid Ginny out from under his armpit.

'When is it?' Lilly asked.

'Noon,' Seth said, turning his son the right way up.

'I was thinking of going to the mausoleum. To visit Dad. Would that be alright?'

Seth gazed at her. 'Of course. Be back before two though, eh?'

Lilly nodded and rose to leave.

Seth handed a pungent Russell to the nanny with his nose wrinkled.

'Lilly.'

She turned, hoping the question 'Are you alright?' wouldn't be uttered again.

Seth gazed at her.

'Don't be late,' he told her. 'Stinky needs his godmother today.'

She smiled thinly and left.

285

'I'll tie the dragon around the front when I get home,' she said on her way out.

'Be a help. Thanks Lilly.'

The door closed.

Seth frowned into space. 'What have I forgotten?'

Jimmy shrugged, pouring him some juice. 'Is it important?'

'I think so, but for the life of me I can't think what it was.'

'What made you think of it?' Cienne asked, fiddling with Ginny's gown. 'Something Lilly said?'

'Something Lilly…' Seth's eyes bulged. 'Dragon. Dragon. Shit! Dragon! Shit!'

He bolted for the door.

'Oi! Where's Lilly?'

'Just buggered off on the dragon,' a voice called back faintly.

'Shit!' Seth exclaimed as Marbrand jogged in from the courtyard, Despina at his heels.

'What's happening?' Marbrand asked, halting at his side.

Seth turned to him, whey-faced.

'Lilly went to the mausoleum.'

Jimmy frowned at him. 'Unless the dead are rising up in rebellion, I doubt she has anything to worry about.'

'There's something there, we have to go bring her home before she finds it.'

'She's on a dragon, sir, she's probably long gone,' said Jimmy. 'Unless Queen Cumquat shows up, like she does—'

'We don't need her help to travel fast,' Marbrand said, turning to Despina.

Seth glanced at her.

'I, er… I'm studying sorcery,' she said timidly. 'I'm getting good at travelling in Sal'plae… kind of…'

Seth grimaced. 'The exploding thing.'

She nodded apologetically. 'Sorry.'

He sighed heavily. 'Let's get on with it, then.'

'But the christening!' Cienne wailed.

'We won't be long,' Marbrand said. 'What's this thing we can't let her find?'

'Her birthday present.'

Jimmy blinked. 'That's hardly an emergency. Her birthday isn't for ages.'

'Not next birthday, the last one. The one we missed.' Seth winced. 'It's not exactly a… safe present…'

~

286

III

Two figures walked down the Mausoleum.

'You're sure the christening is today?' the man with the sack asked.

'Positive,' the man with the newly mended crowbar replied. 'Got a parade going down Ablyminded Street and everything.'

They reached Seth Crey's crypt and the crowbar was wedged into the edge of the door.

'So we're thinking five tapestries,' the crowbar wielder was saying, swinging open the crypt door, 'two statues—'

'Uhm,' whined the sack man.

'What?'

'Can you see something glowing?' he whimpered, pointing. 'Over in that direction?'

The crowbar holder followed his finger. 'Oh dear.'

An orange flame was rolling towards them.

'Shut the door!' he howled.

They slammed the door and leaned their backs on it.

The fireball threw the door from its hinges, carrying the burglars with it.

The dragon screamed.

~

'Bollocks,' Despina said. 'I think we went the wrong way.'

Marbrand grabbed her shoulders and turned her around.

'Oh, never mind,' she said sheepishly.

Seth shook his elbow out of her grasp and ran forward.

Atop a great hill before them, the Mausoleum blotted the morning sun, the spire and surrounding crypts towering into the sky like an erect—

Seth skidded to a halt.

'Is it me or is the Mausoleum shaped like a massive—'

'Yes, it is,' said Marbrand, jogging past him. 'Couldn't you have moved us a little closer?'

'I told you, I still need practise,' she objected, following him uphill.

'Any sign of Lyseria?' he asked, craning his neck back, an arm over his brow.

Another smaller, more elegant silhouette passed over their heads.

'That's them!' Seth called.

They sprinted uphill in double time.

Lyseria touched down in front of the double doors and made herself comfortable.

Lilly slid off soberly.

Her walk to the doors was swiftly intercepted by Seth launching himself on top of her and knocking her face first into the path.

'Seth!' Lilly snapped, rolling over and wiping bits of gravel from her face. 'What the hell d'you think you're doing?'

'Get away from the door!' Seth shouted, getting to his feet and dragging Lilly up after him. 'There's a—'

A shriek interrupted him, rattling the double doors. One of them opened and two men dressed in black ran past as fast as their feet could carry them.

'You two again?' Seth barked.

They froze in alarm, but only for a moment before running off again.

'That was over the top,' one of them screeched at him on their way, sending his empty sack flying.

Lilly turned to Seth sharply.

'What was over the top?' she demanded.

Seth held his hands up in a reassuring manner.

'Long story short,' he said, 'I heard you saying ages ago that you wanted a dragon, so I bought you one for your birthday and hid it in there.'

'My birthday was ages ago!'

'I know, but you were away and then the kids were born and I forgot all about it—'

'How long ago did you hide that in there?'

He hesitated. 'Before the old man's funeral? A couple of weeks before?'

Another screech sounded.

They peered gingerly into the open door.

A long black neck protruded from the doorway to Seth's future crypt, wriggling and jerking. The head attached to it was looking very annoyed.

'It's stuck,' Lilly said angrily, glaring at Seth. 'How big was it when you put it in there?'

Seth gave her a timid shrug.

'About...'

He held his hands out, indicating about seven inches.

The dragon screamed again as if to let them know that it was, in fact, *not* a few inches long anymore.

'What on earth made you think that was a good idea?' Lilly shrieked at him.

'It was only a baby one!'

'It's not a baby anymore!' Marbrand shouted at him.

A crunch sounded from inside the Mausoleum.

'It's gotten free,' Marbrand said, pushing the two Creys back. 'Stay away from the—Despina!'

The young girl ran into the doors.

After ten minutes of idle rubbernecking, Lyseria finally rose to her feet and launched herself through the double doors, leaving splintered planks in her wake.

The three of them backed away and watched as Lyseria grasped Despina around the ribs with her back claws and slid her backwards along the floor, down the aisle towards the broken entrance.

Marbrand rushed in and scooped his daughter from the flagstones.

The two dragons collided and tumbled into the back wall with a crash and a back-to-back screech.

Seth flinched from outside.

'I think I just peed a bit,' he said weakly.

'Peeing isn't going to help anyone!' Lilly snapped. 'Why is she attacking it anyway? She never attacks other dragons!'

'Not male ones,' Marbrand called from just inside the door. 'This one's a girl.'

The other female snorted at Lyseria and wrapped her teeth around her neck.

Lyseria shrieked and tried to bat the younger animal away with one wing, to little avail.

'She'll lose,' Marbrand stated, watching them intently from a safe distance with his arm still firmly around Despina's shoulders. 'The other's younger than her. Stronger.'

'How?' Lilly barked. 'She's been trapped in a crypt for the past year with nothing to eat.'

'Between grave-robbing and priests tending to the general upkeep of the place, I imagine there's plenty of traffic coming in to placate the animal,' Marbrand said. 'I'd say goodbye to your pet, she's had it.'

Despina's eyes narrowed into the battle.

'She might be stronger, but she's also stupid,' she said. 'She's just blind attacking.'

He glanced at her questioningly.

She pulled Pointy from its scabbard and threw the blade at the black dragon's head.

The edge collided with one yellow eye and the animal shrieked, butting Lyseria away to turn on Despina.

'Now look what you've done!' Marbrand shrieked.

'Shush!' Despina barked.

She threw herself from her father's grip and launched herself at the dragon.

Then she vanished in a trail of dust.

The beast jerked her head from side to side, searching.

Marbrand hurriedly ducked out of the way as she roared lividly, throwing a ball of flame through the doorway in disgust.

Seth and Lilly hurled themselves to the ground, missing the flames by an inch.

'What made you change your mind?' Lilly asked.

Marbrand searched frantically for his daughter amidst the growing rubble.

Seth waved a flaming sleeve in the air frantically before patting it down with a sigh. 'About what?'

Marbrand screeched and ducked.

Lyseria bolted from the younger dragon's path, nearly killing him on the way out.

'Getting me a dragon,' Lilly said, her hair and clothes billowing in the wake of another fire ball above their heads. 'You always said no.'

Marbrand looked around furiously, craning his neck for a glimpse of his daughter, who was not there.

'Girl,' he howled over the din, 'you'd better appear this instant or you'll bloody regret it! I am your father! Apparently! As soon as you get a bedroom for me to confine you to, you will be confined the bloody hell to it! DESPINA!!'

'I didn't mean that,' said Seth, paying not one whit of attention to Marbrand's livid screaming. 'I was always going to get you one.'

Lilly stared at him with a frown and a squint, scraps of loose hair from her bun still blowing in the hot air. 'Really?'

Despina popped into existence against Marbrand's arm, wielding his sword.

He screamed.

She vanished again just as he'd gathered his bearings.

'OI!!'

'Of course I was,' Seth said, putting a hand on Lilly's shoulder and giving her a squeeze. 'You've only got one brother, who else is going to buy you these things?'

He glimpsed Lyseria approaching the entrance at high speed.

Seth pulled Lilly's head down, ducking his own beside hers.

Lyseria sailed over them, making a wide U-turn towards the spire of the Mausoleum.

'You're not my only brother, though,' Lilly shouted over the din.

Seth frowned up at their pet, wide-eyed. 'What?'

A BONG sounded as Lyseria collided with the bell on the way down.

Marbrand watched in awe, suddenly realising Despina's diversion in a flood of foresight.

'Si,' Lilly said, 'the one that snatched me.'

Despina materialised thirty feet below the black dragon, whose mouth opened in triumph and soared downwards.

'He's our bastard brother.'

Seth's jaw hung ajar.

Lyseria landed jaws first on the black dragon's skull and tore the top of her head off.

The howl of agony finally caught the Creys' attention. They gawked into the doors, breathing heavily.

The beast's skull was open to the elements, weeping profusely.

Lyseria sank her teeth into her opponent's wings and ripped them off as well, earning a hollow wail.

With blood and smoke peppering the air, the black mass of punctured scales turned limp, sailing to the ground.

'I'll get you a new one, Lilly,' Seth said distantly.

'You can keep it, mate.'

A massive thud marked the end of the chaos.

As the dust and debris settled, Despina brought Pointy down through the corpse's eyes, just in case.

Seth leaned back on his palms, deflating in relief.

His eyes widened with a jolt.

'Christening!' he yelped, pulling himself and Lilly to their feet.

Lyseria bolted out of the double doors, as if on cue.

Marbrand and Despina left the mausoleum, leaning heavily on each other's shoulder. Marbrand frowned at his employers as they sprinted after Lyseria, whistling and trying to wave her down.

'You're welcome!' he shouted irately. He dropped his forehead on Despina's hair. 'I need a raise.'

Despina simply panted.

He lifted his head to look down at her. 'You're grounded for that, by the way.'

Despina lifted her face upright with a disgusted expression.

'You what? Grounded to where, your barracks? I have nowhere to live!'

'I'll ground you somewhere, make no mistake,' he growled, grabbing the scruff of her neck and pulling her downhill. 'Ten feet beneath the surface of the earth, perhaps.'

~

IV

'Where have you been?!'

Seth flinched away from Cienne by force of habit and was shocked to discover it was Eleanor who had shrieked at him, not Cienne.

'We're late because of you!' Eleanor snapped.

'Only a little bit,' he said meekly.

'What happened to you, Mum?' Lilly asked in concern. 'You used to be so... mild.'

She ignored Lilly and swung her gaze on Seth's sleeve.

'WHAT HAVE YOU DONE WITH YOUR SLEEVE?!'

Seth flinched violently. 'It was an accident!'

'That's a lie! You did that on purpose! After all the effort I put into it!'

'I didn't!' Seth wailed.

Eleanor pinched her son's ear and dragged him to the stairs.

'Hurry up! We have to find something quick, we're already late!'

Seth winced grotesquely.

'It's only around the back of the castle! Let go of my ear! I can't walk upstairs backwards, can I?'

Cienne met Lilly's glance as Seth's shouting reverberated through the staircase. They gave each other a feeble shrug.

~

In the pantry, Jimmy was beginning to think his new employee might be insane.

Jon stood in front of the oven, staring over at the torch above it in disturbed fascination. He had the look of a possible pyromaniac, Jimmy thought.

Jimmy waved a hand in front of his face.

'Jon? Are you alright?' he asked tentatively.

'As happy as a rat in a pantry,' he said cheerfully. He then gave a hostile glare towards the hole in the corner of the pantry, eyes narrowed. '*That* rat, to be precise.'

'Oh, don't worry about him,' Jimmy said, pulling some bread from the oven. 'We have bigger rats to feed. Come on.'

'Let me just finish something off first.'

Jimmy backed away slowly as Jon lifted a torch from the wall and swung it from side to side, his gaze locked on the rat hole.

'He's definitely a pyromaniac,' he decided, walking swiftly away.

~

Outside, Ron was just waiting for Qattren to show up when his gaze met that of Gomez Emmett.

Making sure Marbrand was watching out for him, Ron approached.

'Prince Ronald,' Emmett greeted coolly, bowing slightly.

Ron waved him upright.

'I wasn't expecting to see you at a Crey celebration,' he said just as coolly. 'Rumour has it you had recently dispatched men to kill the king's sister.'

Emmett lifted an eyebrow. 'Is that so? Rumour is a curious thing.' He scrutinised Ron's facial features. 'What can I do for you this afternoon, your highness?'

Ron reached two fingers of his right hand into his left sleeve and pulled out the grubby letter he received from Marbrand. 'I believe you have something that belongs to me.'

He opened out the letter and handed it to Emmett.

Emmett took it with as few fingers as possible and read it thoroughly. 'Hmm.'

'Shall we meet inside the castle and make the necessary arrangements?' Ron said pleasantly. 'Felicity and the baby will want somewhere to live – I imagine we can make some kind of arrangement there. You'll want to accompany them?'

Emmett folded the letter neatly back into thirds.

And abruptly ripped it in half.

'Apologies,' he said to Ron.

He let the halves of parchment flutter to the floor, unfolding as they went.

'My hand seems to have slipped. The witnesses to the writing of that letter should back up your claim to your brother's illegitimacy – but oh, alas it appears they forgot to sign it. Must be a forgery, then.'

Ron stared at him in disbelief.

'Thanking you for your kindness, but our current arrangements will do just fine until the prince comes of age... oh,' Emmett said, pouring his goblet of wine over the torn letter. 'Apologies again. Most clumsy this afternoon – must be the wine. Farewell, your highness.'

He inclined his head and strode in the direction of a group of noblemen.

Ron was livid. 'Give me my castle, you miserable shi—'

Marbrand had to hurry over to stop Ron throwing himself at Emmett from behind.

~

Elsewhere, a small crowd of the female persuasion gathered outside the gazebo, from which a squirming Ginny was trying to escape.

Lilly tried vainly to restrain her.

'I'm worried about your mother,' Cienne said in concern, little Russell asleep against her shoulder. 'I think she's getting too anxious about this christening.'

'I'm worrying more about Seth dropping Ginny on her head in the middle of the chapel,' Lilly replied, holding the child out in front of her by the waist. 'The kid doesn't stop moving for a second.'

Cienne glanced offhandedly at Jon, who was handing drinks to some of the guests and pulling faces at the ones whose backs were turned.

'That's a good point,' she said with a worried expression.

Jon was quickly relieved of his tray by a greedy Lady Gertrude and, making sure that Jimmy wasn't looking, he strolled as casually as he could to the chapel across the gardens.

'Although, she seems to calm down when with him,' Cienne continued, talking about Seth. 'She falls asleep whenever he holds her. I'm surprised she hadn't forgotten him, after so long apart.'

'And vice versa,' Lilly said.

A white mask furtively connected with Jon's nose. He vanished into the doors.

'Hello!' a shrill voice trilled, its owner sprinting over. 'How's Ginny-Winny, then? Have you got a kiss for me? Have you? Have you?'

Seth planted a big soppy kiss on his daughter's nose before covering his face.

'Where's Ginny?' he said in a sing-song voice, to Lilly's tangible disgust.

Ginny giggled in anticipation.

'There she is!' he exclaimed, revealing himself. 'Where's Ginny, then? Where is she?'

He turned his covered face from side to side.

Lilly gave the scene a withering glance.

'There she is! Where's Ginny?'

'On her way to the moat in a bag,' Lilly said, rising.

'Hey!' Seth snapped, taking the child away.

'When's the priest coming over?' Cienne asked.

'Hopefully never,' Seth grunted. 'I hate priests.'

'Oh, I'm sorry to hear that, your majesty.'

Seth grimaced.

Lilly sniggered.

'Apologies, Father,' Cienne said meekly. 'You wanted to speak about the children's names?'

Father Giery scowled at the world in general, a thin comb-over shielding his head from the sun.

'I just need the names for the ceremony,' he said stiffly. 'And our records, of course.'

'What records?' Lilly asked.

'Our church records,' he replied mildly. 'We've recorded all of our parishioners for fifty years.'

'Uh-huh,' Lilly said quietly.

The priest cleared his throat. 'What is the prince's full name?'

'Pierre Alexander,' Cienne said immediately.

Seth scowled at her.

'His name is Russell. Like it or lump it.'

Cienne sighed.

'Fine, his first name's Russell,' she mumbled almost unintelligibly.

Seth glanced at Lilly and shook his head.

'Always has to have the last word,' he grumbled.

The priest murmured along as he wrote in a massive leather-bound tome with a stubby pencil.

'Have you considered including him as an altar boy at our church in later years?'

'God, no,' Seth said, horrified. 'I've heard stories about your—'

'Seth!' Cienne hissed.

294

'It would be most beneficial to include him in a... first hand education in the one true religion,' he said piously. 'Many fine men throughout history have benefitted from a deep knowledge of their faith.'

'We will consider it carefully,' Cienne said to placate him.

'Excellent. Now. What is the name of the princess?'

'Ginny-Winny,' Seth said fondly, patting the grinning baby's head.

'And her christened name?' the priest persisted.

The fond smile fell from Seth's face and he heaved a sigh.

'Virginia Emilia *Gertrude*.'

Cienne looked at her grandmother-in-law in horror.

Lady Gertrude smiled in approval.

'She threatened me with a sword, alright?' Seth protested.

The priest bowed his head and snapped the book shut, gathering his things to leave.

Lilly's eyes followed him distrustfully as he made a beeline for the chapel.

'Why did he want him to be altar boy so badly?'

'Plenty of kings were altar boys in their youth,' Cienne said. 'My father was one, if I remember him rightly. Many placed the priests they served on their councils in later life.'

'Well, I figure his motives are a little baser than that,' Lilly muttered.

Seth held Ginny closer, scowling in the man's wake.

'BAAAHH!'

It was at this point the family got an excellent vantage point to see Father Giery launching himself back out of the chapel, smoke trailing in his wake.

'This *criminal* has desecrated the holy chapel of the kings!'

He hoisted a man in a white mask out and thrust him onto the gravel.

'I did no such thing!' the masked man exclaimed, waving a blackened torch in the air. 'I was cleaning it!'

Seth plonked Ginny onto Lilly's lap and stormed over.

He pulled the mask from Jon's head.

'Why did you do that?' Seth hissed shrilly.

'I'm purging it,' Jon said haughtily. He jerked away from the priest with a shudder. 'Purging it with *fire*.'

Seth pulled Jon away towards the back of the castle by one ear.

'Alright. You had your chance,' said Seth firmly. 'You could have been a good little butler's butler, but you didn't want that, did you?'

'Hang on,' Jimmy called, jogging to catch up. 'Let's hear him out before we go throwing out any of the spud peelers, eh?'

'He blew his last chance the minute he put that mask back on his face,' Seth snapped at him. 'I'm peeling his nose off.'

'Oi!' Jon protested.

He stumbled with his head cocked to one side as Seth dragged him along.

'He asked you to make your son an altar boy, didn't he?'

Seth halted. 'What of it?'

Father Giery skidded to a halt beside Seth.

'Your majesty, perhaps we should deal with this miscreant ourselves,' he said quickly, 'whilst you rearrange your plans for—'

'Shut up,' Seth ordered.

He pulled Jon around until they were face to face.

'What of it?' he repeated with venom.

'He wanted you to be one of those,' Jon said shrilly, pointing at Seth. 'When you were little. But the king said no. He had a bit of common sense...'

Jon swung around and pointed a finger at the Duke of Osney.

'Unlike this shithead!'

Osney stared at him in bemusement.

'*My* dad was told it was a great honour, having his son in the church, being related to royalty and all,' Jon seethed. 'The priest thought it was a great honour, alright – having a victim that got washed regularly!'

The priest recoiled.

Seth's eyes narrowed. He glanced from Jon to the priest, back and forth. 'Who are you?'

The guests began to flock around them.

Eleanor muscled her way through the crowd and gaped at Jon.

'He's your cousin Mortimer. The Duke of Osney's boy.'

Seth pivoted in alarm to meet his mother's gaze.

'I'd recognise that curly hair anywhere,' Eleanor continued, her eyes locked on the hair in question.

Osney ran a hand through his own curly hair, which was now completely silver.

Seth glared at him. 'Where's he been all this time? What the hell happened? *Why is he working in my kitchen?*'

'We gave him to the church here, he ran away over twenty years ago.' Osney's eyes glazed over. 'I thought he was dead.'

'He is dead,' Jon corrected. 'Mortimer *did* die years ago. He died in the vestry age eight, with *this* bastard!'

He jabbed a finger at the priest.

Lilly's mouth dropped open.

'I knew it,' she hissed.

Eleanor glared at the priest. 'What did you do to him?'

'I think that's quite obvious,' Seth said levelly.

He released his grip on Jon's arm and beckoned the priest to him with one finger. 'Come with me.'

The priest backed away slightly. 'Why?'

'So I can peel *your* nose off.'

'Seth, no,' Cienne begged.

'Cienne—'

Seth paused to scowl at the nosy onlookers. 'As you were!'

They dissipated in disappointment.

'You heard the bastard!' he exclaimed, his voice hushed. 'He wouldn't shut up until he said you'd think about it! He wanted to violate our son!'

'But what if Jon's...'

'Look at him.'

The Duke of Osney reached out to comfort his son.

'Get off me,' Jon spat at him, recoiling. He jabbed a finger at Osney's face. 'If you *touch* me, I will do unto you with a *sword* what your little friend did to me with his—'

He stopped himself sharply, shivering at the memory.

Seth gestured at him.

'I have no recollection of him, and he's my first cousin,' he said. 'He should be a lord or something, and the *bastard* reduced him to Jimmy's lackey.'

He reached out and touched his son's head as he slept peacefully on Cienne's shoulder.

'I won't let him do the same to the twins. I *won't.*'

'You can't kill the man,' Cienne said softly. 'You'll cause a revolt.'

'No point killing him anyway,' Jimmy piped up, shooting Jon a worried glance. 'They'll just find some other pervert to replace him.'

His gaze locked to the grass beneath his feet, Jon breathed deep, shaking breaths.

Seth sighed and eyed Jon.

'Arrest the priest,' he ordered.

Elliot elbowed past the crowd and seized the priest by the elbows.

'Put him in the Tower,' he said.

Seth turned to the crowd as the robed man was hauled away.

'Come in and have a drink,' he announced. 'We will *not* be christening our children.'

The guests' eyes widened in shock as one.

'This will not do at all!' Lady Gertrude said harshly. 'I demand that we get another priest. As the lad's grandmother, I feel terrible for him, but that's no call at all for—'

'Give me my daughter,' Seth said tiredly.

He lifted Ginny from Lilly's arms and walked inside.

'Seth!' Gertrude scolded. 'You have no right to deprive these children of a religious—'

'Shut up,' he drawled.

He stormed for the keep before she could say another word.

~

V

Ron was waiting at the front gate for Qattren when Lilly found him.

'Mind if I join you?'

Ron turned his head to face her as she hoisted Ginny onto one shoulder.

'Thought the christening was about to start?'

'It was cancelled. Apparently the priest molested Cousin Mortimer when he was eight.'

'What's that mean?'

Lilly watched his confused, ignorant face wistfully. It was times like these she wished *she* was this clueless.

'Long story short, he went a bit mad and started a chicken farm. He calls himself Jon now.'

'So he's the Phantom Egg Flinger?' Ron asked in interest.

'So he is,' Lilly recalled. 'Guess that means he gets a formal pardon, then.'

Ron lifted his eyebrows. 'Good for him.' He eyed Ginny. 'What you doing with her?'

'Seth's questioning Jon some more. She was getting bored.' Lilly rubbed the infant's back fondly. 'No sign of Qattren?'

'No,' he said with a frown. 'She said she had an appointment, but that was weeks ago. '

They stood in silence as Lilly swung a giggling Ginny from side to side.

'I've decided to quit drinking for good,' Ron said.

'Really?' Lilly asked, impressed. 'Brilliant! How many days sober are you?'

'One, erm… hour,' he admitted. 'Talking to Mister Emmett will do that to you.'

'Understandable. The man's a prick, isn't he?'

'Yep,' Ron said through gritted teeth.

He took a breath, putting his encounter with the man aside.

'I mean it this time, though. No more alcohol for me.'

Lilly nudged him with her elbow. 'Good for you! I'm here if you need anything. Apart from booze, obviously.'

Ron smiled fondly at her.

Then Lilly caught sight of Albie.

'Who gave him the little jacket?' she wondered.

Ron gawked at him. 'No idea.'

The Bastard sat in the grass before them, licking his parts as a black leotard with gold trim gleamed in the sun.

'Ooh,' Ginny said shrilly, her mouth pulled into a little 'O'.

~

Marbrand halted in front of Seth and stood to attention.

'You asked to see me, your majesty?'

The sun shone down onto the chapel, the polished walls shining amber.

Seth stood outside the entrance, his arms behind his back. The fire damage was superficial to the curtains, Elliot had informed them, leaving much of the building still as good as new.

'I want to talk to you about your rewards,' Seth said.

'My liege, really,' Marbrand said, 'I really don't need a reward—'

'Three jobs, three rewards,' Seth insisted. 'Speak.'

Marbrand sighed.

'A new mattress is the only thing I can think of,' he said lamely.

'It shall be done,' Seth said with a grin. 'Two to go.'

He glanced up at the clouds in thought.

'My kid could do with a job,' he added. 'A well paid one.'

'I never liked that nanny my mother appointed for the twins,' Seth said thoughtfully. 'She shouts too much and smells like cabbage.'

'That'd do,' Marbrand said eagerly. 'And I would also like a house. A big one.' He paused momentarily. 'With stained glass windows, if possible.'

Seth tilted his head to one side.

'I always thought it looked impressive,' he explained sheepishly.

'Hmm.' Seth's gaze caught a glint on the chapel windows. 'Ah-*ha*.'

Inside the dining hall, Jon sat at the dining table next to Eleanor. She thoughtfully piled small cakes onto his plate, her aggressive dictatorship of the christening apparently forgotten.

'Are you alright, my dear? You're not eating.'

Jon was too busy glowering down at the intricate embroidery she had bullied him into wearing. It was putting him off his food, but he was far too polite to tell *her* that.

'I'm just not enjoying this nobility lark,' he said lamely.

'Why not? You only have to eat and wear nice clothes. I thought you would have preferred that to chasing rats out of the pantry.'

'I *liked* chasing rats out of the pantry,' Jon said dejectedly. 'And I miss my chickens.'

Eleanor patted his hand.

'We could always bring the chickens to live here,' she suggested.

Jon shook his head. 'Dragon.'

'Oh, of course,' she said, deflating.

A knock arrived on the back door.

'Jon—I mean, Lord Mortimer,' Jimmy corrected himself. 'You have to come out and see this. It's brilliant.'

Jon grimaced.

'I *hate*,' he seethed, '*hate* the name Mortimer. *Hate it.*'

He slid the chair backwards.

What he saw when he entered the rear gardens startled him. He was happy to see the monks of the Faith of Salator Crey sitting dejectedly on the gravel path, but it startled him nonetheless.

'Why do I get the feeling the next thing you say will be your death sentence?'

'I've evicted the clergy,' Seth announced. 'Just like you told me to.'

'That's why,' Jimmy said dryly.

'Why've you done that?' Jon asked in bewilderment.

'They haven't been paying their taxes,' Seth said triumphantly.

'The church doesn't pay tax!' a monk yelled.

'You do now,' Seth growled, 'and you owe me back-payment amounting to one chapel – which I have now seized, repurposed and bequeathed to one of my staff.'

'Take a look at this!' Marbrand exclaimed from inside, striding from one end of the chapel to the other in utter joy. 'We can put some walls here, and here, and a bedroom here for you, what d'you think?'

'Great,' Despina said uncertainly, standing at the front door and glancing in and out.

'I think *this* is the best wing for bedrooms, where the sun will hit it in the morning to wake you for work. Ooh, and we can put a big fireplace *here—*'

'The altar!' a monk wailed. 'The baptismal font!'

'Make a nice hand-washy sink,' Marbrand mused in agreement. 'We'll give it a lick of paint and stick it in the bathroom, I think…'

Seth grinned smugly.

Jon gazed at him in awe. 'Is this a joke?'

'The priest won't find it a funny joke when he's hanged tomorrow morning,' Jimmy said.

'That will learn him for sexually assaulting my baby cousin, won't it?' Seth said in satisfaction. 'I mean, really. It's a disgrace, what he did to poor Jon. We almost put him under *your* mercy, could you imagine?'

Jimmy nodded modestly.

'Ah, about that,' Jon said. 'Not keen on the aristocracy lark. I'd like to be Jimmy's butler again, please.'

Jimmy frowned. 'You mean the skivee?'

'Yep. And I want to be officially named Jon as well. Mortimer's a hideous name and it doesn't suit me.'

Jon frowned at Seth's expression of fury.

'What's that look for?'

'I've just evicted seventeen people in your honour!' Seth exclaimed, pointing at them.

'Yeah,' Jon said blankly.

'I could cause wars!'

'So,' Jon said.

'Millions of people could die from the repercussions of my actions!'

'But I'm bored of it now,' Jon said.

'The peasants will revolt to the point of—'

'But I'm *bored*,' Jon emphasised.

Seth gaped at him with his mouth open and turned to Jimmy for assistance.

'If he insists,' Jimmy said with a shrug.

Seth stared into space.

'Peasants,' he said in disbelief, walking inside. 'Honestly.'

~

Lilly was crying when Seth passed her quarters.

He peered in on her guiltily and decided to visit her once he'd gone to the privy.

Typically, he was intercepted by the new nanny as soon as he entered his chambers.

'Watch Ginny for a bit while I drop these to the boiler room,' Despina said hurriedly, holding a basket in front of her at an arm's length.

'But that's your job!' Seth protested. 'I'm not a servant, why should I--'

'I have to get rid of these before they stink out the joint. DON'T let her out of your sight or she'll crawl off the bed and break her neck!' she warned, hurrying out.

'But, but... *king?!*' he said, pointing at his own face.

She vanished.

He rolled his eyes and knelt next to the bed, where Ginny lay on her belly in the middle, looking at him.

'Are you going to be good and not move while Daddy has a pee?' Seth asked hopefully.

She snickered and hid her face in the blanket.

'That looks distinctly like a no,' he said gloomily.

He set his head on his arms to watch her practise her crawling, i.e., wiggle a bit until she moved a couple of millimetres and then look very pleased with herself for a few moments before trying again.

Seth observed this for a while and had an idea. Placing a finger by her elbow to mark her place, he moved his face closer to Ginny and said, 'Do you wanna race for me? Are you going to go as fast as you can so I can see how long I have to take a pee?'

Ginny grinned.

Seth grinned back and nodded in earnest.

'Yeah? Alright then. Three, two, one... go!'

He waved his arm in the air to beckon her on.

She gawked at him.

'Fast as you can, go on!' he encouraged her, counting to himself.

She squirmed along for a bit and promptly flopped onto one side.

'Good enough,' he said, pecking the top of her head. 'Be back in a minute. Don't move!'

He hurried over to the privy and slammed the door behind him.

301

A moment after, a small dog leapt onto the bed and perched next to her.

Ginny gawped at him and held a curious hand out, which he licked.

'Hello, little sister,' the Bastard murmured.

Ginny grabbed his nose.

The sound of running water ceased and Seth re-entered the bedchamber, adjusting his trousers.

His gaze caught that of the Bastard. Anger passed between them.

Jon placed rat traps around the third-floor corridor as a door opened and a white terrier flew out to hit the opposite wall.

'Aw, what did he do?' he asked, affronted.

'He was going to attack the baby,' Seth seethed, glancing back to check on Ginny. 'Dogs smother babies, it's a well-known fact.'

'That's cats,' Jon said.

'Don't care,' Seth snapped. 'Keep him out of my way.'

With that he slammed the door shut.

Jon looked at the dog piteously.

'Don't worry, I'm sure you can visit them when he gets bored of them. How's the end of the world coming along?'

~

Lilly wiped her eyes and was startled to see a baby smiling at her, out of nowhere.

'Don't tell me you can look at this bundle of joy and not stop crying,' Seth said playfully from behind Lilly.

Lilly gave a small giggle. To his credit, Seth was right.

She accepted Ginny and wrapped her arms around her.

'I miss our dad,' she explained as Seth dropped himself beside her. 'And Orl.'

'I know.'

She cuddled Ginny closer.

'You don't, do you?' Lilly asked after a moment. 'You hated Dad.'

Shame crept up his neck in a warm wave.

'Not going to lie,' he admitted. 'Orl was quite alright though, for someone with such a creep for a father.'

He shuddered, the thought of his mother and the Ambassador still fresh in his mind.

Lilly gazed at Ginny as she drifted off to sleep in her arms.

'I hate to prove myself wrong,' she said, 'but you're actually going to make an alright father.'

Seth snorted. 'You know I tried to race them earlier?'

Lilly started laughing.

'Ginny won, by lieu of prior training,' he said proudly. 'She's all tired out now.'

Lilly wiped a tear from her eye, this time one of mirth. 'She loves you.'

Seth gazed down at her fondly. 'I hope so.'

Ginny wriggled her head a bit against Lilly's shoulder and finally started snoring.

~

Jimmy was beginning to certify that Jon aka Mortimer Crey truly was insane. And the steak and kidney pie Jon had prepared especially for a stray dog didn't even convince him this time – or the fact that he was talking animatedly with said dog, either.

Jimmy figured it could have been the knife and fork beside the pie that convinced him in the end as Jon conversed with the canine reincarnation of Seth Crey's illegitimate son.

'He pisses me off too,' Jon said irritably to the dog, who seemed to nod in agreement. 'Leaves knives and forks lying around everywhere! But that's alright! The skivee can pick them up!'

'You could have been the one leaving them lying around if you hadn't insisted,' Jimmy said.

'Jimmy,' Jon scolded, 'we're having a private conversation here, mate.'

'Yes, but I wish you'd have them in your head like a normal lunatic,' Jimmy said with a sigh.

'And he leaves doors open all over the place!' he said to the dog. 'No wonder there are rats everywhere! The pantry's as good as empty because of him!'

Jimmy zoned out at this point and began to set up Seth's breakfast tray.

'Yep, he's a nuisance,' Jon replied to an apparent comment from Albie. 'First he kills King Theo, next he blows Vladimir Horne to kingdom come and now the pantry's empty!'

Cutlery toppled onto the tiled floor.

'What did you say?' Jimmy whispered.

'I said the pantry's empty!' Jon repeated, looking irate. 'Don't tell me nobody told you, we had to chuck everything to the dogs because the rats—'

'No, no, what d'you say before that?' Jimmy asked frantically.

'Knives and forks everywhere?'

Jimmy splayed his arms out and frowned at the ceiling.

'I mean about the king! "First he kills King Theo"? "Next he blows Vladimir Horne to kingdom come"—?'

'Oh, that,' Jon said idly, making Jimmy want to pull his own hair out. 'Everyone knows about that, that's not important. What's important is that the pantry is empty and we have nothing but flour and mouldy cheese left!'

'I didn't know about the king!' Jimmy exclaimed.

'Yes you did, I told you ages ago,' Jon said.

'When?' Jimmy said desperately.

'When I told you the pantry was empty.'

303

Jimmy throttled an imaginary equivalent of Jon in exasperation.

'Look, forget about the pantry for one second,' he said hurriedly. 'How do you know it was Seth that killed the king?'

'Saw him,' he said indifferently.

'And you didn't think about stepping in or anything?'

'Not my job to do that.'

'But he's the king!' Jimmy shrieked, flailing his arms about. 'Of the country we live in!'

Jon shrugged apathetically.

Jimmy watched him in disbelief.

'He's your uncle,' he said, holding a finger up. 'You're King Theo's nephew. He was your uncle, and you watched him die without doing a thing about it!'

'I wasn't there,' Jon said.

Jimmy spluttered.

'You just told me you saw the whole thing!' he said shrilly.

'I did,' Jon said. 'I can see into the future.'

The way he'd said it in the matter-of-fact tone of a chef explaining he can cook sent Jimmy so far over the edge, he decided to just give up and collapse onto the floor.

Jon peered down at him and tutted.

'Looks like *I'm* going to be the one feeding his majesty today,' he huffed.

He lifted the breakfast tray over Jimmy's lifeless body.

The Bastard pawed Jimmy's face gently and gave Jon his best attempt at a shrug.

~

VI

Dawn bruised the sky a dull pink.

Ron approached Despina. 'Are you free for a moment?'

The two queens, past and present, had thankfully taken the children to the gardens to enjoy the sun, leaving Despina to her own devices.

'I need to get home today,' Ron explained as they stood at the courtyard door. 'Qattren never showed up for the christening and I haven't seen her since. I need to see if she's alright.'

'I'll take you to Sal'plae, but it'll cost you,' she answered.

Ron sighed. 'Will ten pieces do you?'

~

Elsewhere, in the city of Serpus, Seth stood in the centre of Arthur Stibbons' Head, beside an empty noose. Seth caught his estranged cousin's eye and gave him a nod.

Jon nodded back.

~

Ron arrived in his home some moments later.

Qattren was sitting at the dining table, looking annoyed.

Anxiety crept up Ron's chest. 'What happened?'

Qattren rolled her eyes. 'He's rushed upstairs for a dramatic entrance. He'll be down in a minute.'

~

Seth watched the criminal climb the stairs and arrive on the gallows. Giery's face held the stiff, stony quality of determination. Not that determination would do him much good now, Seth thought with satisfaction.

The throng cheered.

Everyone loves a good execution in Serpus, Seth thought vaguely, reciting the idiom.

~

'Who are you talking about?' Ron asked curiously.

'You'll see in a minute,' Qattren said tiredly.

'What's all this about?'

~

The executioner pulled the rope over Father Giery's head and tightened it. His offense was intoned monotonously, but Seth wasn't listening.

A member of the clergy stared up at Seth from the crowd, a young man wearing a burgundy cowl and a neatly trimmed beard. Seth couldn't make out the stranger's expression, but it made him uneasy nevertheless.

~

Qattren leaned back in her seat. 'It's your brother.'

As the gallows' floor dropped in Arthur Stibbons' Street and Seth lost sight of the staring stranger, Ron heard footsteps on the stairs in the corner.

He turned in time to see black leather boots, a matching velvet outfit with gold trim and, to Ron's horror, a terrifyingly familiar face. His hair was now white, but that was unspectacular in the circumstances.

'Hello, Ronald,' Vladimir said pleasantly.

EPILOGUE

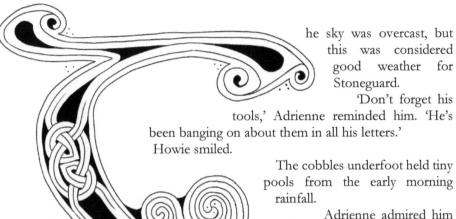

he sky was overcast, but this was considered good weather for Stoneguard.

'Don't forget his tools,' Adrienne reminded him. 'He's been banging on about them in all his letters.'

Howie smiled.

The cobbles underfoot held tiny pools from the early morning rainfall.

Adrienne admired him in the dim sunlight. They hadn't changed much since they left Adem over a year ago: his hair had grown a bit, hers a lot: and her acne scars had thankfully done a disappearing act.

If only the same could be said for some other scars.

Howie hoisted Archie's toolkit over one shoulder, holding his own bag in his free hand.

Adrienne adjusted his brown cloak and waistcoat and set a lingering kiss on his lips.

'Be back soon,' she murmured.

'I won't be long,' he promised.

'Say hello to Archie for me.'

'Will do.'

He knew better than to ask why she wouldn't go with him back to Adem.

Dropping his bag to place a hand around the back of her neck, he pecked her briefly and held the side of her head to his.

'I'll send you a letter once I'm there, yeah?'

'Love you,' she whispered.

'Love you more.'

She stood back against the door of their – formerly Archie's – semi-detached.

Howie waved and took the main road to the Shades.

She gazed at him for a moment longer before heading inside, closing the heavy oak door softly behind her.

The Bastard stared at the door in her wake, his grey eyes like iron and his eyelids heavy with thought.

'DON'T STAND THERE ALL DAY, WILL YOU?'

King Theo's ghost leaned his back against a fence behind him. 'WE HAVE A WORLD TO END, YOU KNOW.'

~

Dramatis Personae, for your reading convenience

The Faith of the Seven (who think Salator Crey is the devil):

Father George Toffer, head of the church of Stoneguard and its veritable assassination side-hustle

The Seven Gods… or Devils, depending on your point of view:

- Geldemar, God of Greed
- Gale, god of nature
- Theo, god of war
- Rubena, goddess of rebellion
- Fortune and Misfortune, conjoined twins of fate
- Liana, goddess of desire

The Faith of Salator Crey (who thinks the Seven are devils):

Father Giery, head of the chapel of Creys' Keep.

Salator Crey, the world's creator

The three Christs, his demi-godly children come down onto earth to get everyone drunk or something

Arianna Lyseria, Creator of Dragons

The Household of the Creys:

Prince Seth Crey, next in line to the throne of Adem

Princess Cienne Fleurelle, sole heir to the throne of Portabella and Seth's wife

King Theo Crey, Seth's father (deceased)

Queen Eleanor Crey, Seth's mother

Princess Lilly-Anna (Lilly) Crey, Seth's younger sister

Stanley Carrot, who Lilly owns now courtesy of his uncle, the local brothel proprietor

Lyseria, their dragon

James 'Jimmy' de Vil, the family butler

Lady Gertrude Tillet, King Theo's mother and Seth and Lilly's grandmother

Duke Richard Crey of Osney, King Theo's younger brother

Father Giery, the palace priest (aforementioned)

Cousin Mortimer, the Duke of Osney's son, missing and believed dead to all but King Theo

Captain Boris Necker, captain of the household guard

Corporal Moat, his nose-picking staff member

Sir ~~Sadie~~ Russell Marbrand, night guardsman and former captain of the Hornes' household guard

Elliot Maynard, night guardsman

The Household of the Hornes:

Prince Vladimir Horne, the prickly next in line to the throne of Stoneguard (deceased)

Prince Ronald Horne, his younger brother

Queen Qattren Meriangue of the Faerie Forest, married to Ron

King Samuel Horne, their father (deceased)

Queen Aaliyaa Horne, their mother and King Samuel's wife

Princess Felicity Horne (nee Emmett), Vladimir's wife

Lord Leroy Tetzel, Queen Aaliyaa's half-brother (deceased)

The Head Members of the First Democratic Republic of Truphoria:

Retribution Halle, head of operations

Erstan Gould, sub-head

Royston Joyce, a bit of a dickhead

The Household of the ~~Chronic Bowel Explosions~~ Buwol Uxpolisin family:

Karnak Buwol Uxpolisin, Ambassador of the Dead Lands

Orlando Buwol Uxpolisin, his eldest son

The Crew of the *Devourer...* or, well, the ones that count:

Sam Sot, the captain... apparently

Silas (Si/Two Finger Si) Beult, first mate, cook and surgeon

Tully Beult, quartermaster

The Emmett Family:

Gomez Emmett, Lord Protector of the country of Mellier

Gomez Emmett Jr, his son, current King Regent of Stoneguard

Felicity Horne nee Emmett, his daughter

Queen Persephone Fleurelle nee Emmett, Gomez Sr's sister and Cienne's mother, deceased

Historical Events of Note:

The Night of Raining Thorns

1345 YM (Year of Mortality) – twenty years prior to the events of *Rosethorn*

The night the Queen of the Forest's castle was exploded by a dragon, starting a series of detonations across the Forest to the outskirts of Serpus. The name derives from the residents of Serpus, who spotted a flash in the distance and a shower of rose thorns from the foliage of the Forest, which had been blown in their direction.

It was also the night Prince Seth Crey was attacked by an assassin during the festivities for his upcoming wedding to Princess Cienne Fleurelle. Around the same time as this attack, Queen Persephone Fleurelle, Cienne's mother, was found murdered in the woods surrounding the Creys' Keep.

These events sparked a brief conflict between the Queen of the Forest and King Theo Crey, the supposed instigator of her palace's destruction, wherein she employed demonic beasts to attack his men. The conflict ended suddenly but uneasily, with both parties avoiding each other's territory and ensuring their subjects do the same.

∼

The War for the Orchard

1315-1325 YM

A series of conflicts between King Seb Crey and Lord Janus Horne of Stoneguard for a series of provinces in Truphoria.

Truphoria once contained a series of provinces including Stoneguard and Adem, all ruled by the Creys – except for the forestry to the east, which had been conquered by the Queen of the Forest early in King Seb's reign. Lord Janus and a number of like-minded contemporaries decided to partition the rest of the continent into five independent countries – only for King Seb Crey to veto the decision in so flippant a fashion that it started a war – along with the then Prince Theo (aged 10) stealing an apple from King Janus's prized orchard.

One of these conflicts resulted in the involvement of the reclusive Queen of the Forest. In 1320 YM, she razed three of the six provinces in a fit of rage, consuming half of Truphoria in blue flames lasting several years afterwards. Everything from cities to countryside was completely destroyed in the blaze, including all wildlife, natural resources and people.

To hastily make amends for this catastrophe, King Seb reluctantly agreed to the partition, declaring Janus Horne King of Stoneguard, Truphoria's sole remaining province beside Adem and the Forest.

~

The Bloodthirsty Reign of King Rubeous Crey
1280-1295 YM

King Rubeous Crey came to the throne in 1280 upon the sudden disappearance of his father during Rubeous's coming of age ceremony. Following his coronation, he married thrice: to two women who lasted barely a year into the marriage before taking their own lives, and to his final wife Lilith, who bore him five children.

Only two of these lived past infancy. Using lack of dowry funds as an excuse for his actions, King Rubeous would murder and eat all children of his born female. Seb was the only child not subjected to this horror by lieu of being a viable heir.

When his younger sister was born, Lilith had a psychotic break shortly after labour. She dragged herself from the birthing bed seconds after bearing the child, hobbled to King Rubeous's chambers and bludgeoned King Rubeous to death before he had a chance to touch this newest victim.

His brother, the mild-mannered Gideon, was named King Regent until Seb, then two, came of age. He pardoned her immediately for the crime, given the tyranny of his brother's reign, and she would stand as King Seb's advisor during his reign in years to come.

Thanks for reading!

This book is self-published by Donna Shannon under the imprint DS Books. To help support the author, please leave a review on Goodreads, social media (@donnashandwich) or any online book retail outlet.

You can follow Donna Shannon on Wordpress, Goodreads, Facebook, Instagram, Threads and TikTok for all things books, art and general nonsense.

Many thanks for supporting an indie author in their journey!

Acknowledgements

My thanks go out to the usual suspects: namely everyone in my life currently, excluding that blasted Echo Dot Alexa thing.

It appears I need more than this one line, so to go into specifics:

Many thanks to the myriad colleagues, past and present, at the hospital and the college for their support in the release of *Rosethorn*, its subsequent re-release post-re-edit-of-Microsoft-Word-related-mishaps, and the upcoming release of this sequel. You will always have my gratitude for persuading me onto this path and keeping me on the cobbles despite the ever-present obstacle of self-doubt.

To everyone who provided reviews of *Rosethorn* so far, I love you. Seriously. I'm blessed to have come out of the publishing process with nothing but glowing reviews and I'm glad I received the opportunity to amuse you.

As ever, the Squid Squad (my first – and best – beta group) will always get a mention at the end of my books: Roy Leon, Jae Waller, Rochelle Jardine, Lilah Souza and Beau Jones. Thank you for being my writerly emotional support squishmallow, and for persuading me *out* of releasing *Finding Retribution* with a massive silhouette of the Wasteside Mausoleum on it.

Thank you also to those of you in the indie author community who have shared and liked my posts, cheered me on and given me opportunities such as author interviews and livestreams. I'm grateful for the opportunity to meet and connect with you all.

Lastly, my biggest thank you goes to my nan, who we sadly lost during the final edit of this book. I'm saddened that you didn't get to read it, but glad that I had your support regardless.

9 781739 433758